Love
Just Clicks

a Revelation Cove standalone novel

ELIZA GORDON

SGA
BOOKS

www.sgabooks.com
www.elizagordon.com | www.jennsommersby.com

E-book ISBN-13: 978-1-7771794-9-6
Kindle e-book ISBN: 978-1-9990516-7-9
Print ISBN-13: 978-1-9990516-8-6
Audiobook available from Dreamscape Media

First edition 2019 (as *F-Stop*)
Second edition 2020 (cover by Ashley Santoro) Alternate cover 2021 by SGA Books. Front cover image by Paff for Stocksy; back cover image by Eva Blanco for iStock by Getty Images. Cover updated 2024.

To Lila and Nat

JOIN THE RAFT!

Do you want to be the first to hear about new books, upcoming releases, exclusive sales, and/or life and publishing news? Then **join the raft**! I can also guarantee pictures of my very spoiled tuxedo cats and granddog, Pippin Took.

Sign up for Eliza's occasional, not-at-all-annoying newsletter.

In the wild, sea otters hold hands so they aren't separated in the tides. These groups of floating otters are called rafts.

Welcome aboard. So glad to have you. Can you pass the Dungeness crab, please?

ALSO BY ELIZA GORDON

Welcome to Planet Lara series:

Welcome to Planet Lara, Book One

Planet Lara: Tempest, Book Two

Planet Lara: Sanctuary, Book Three

The Revelation Cove series:

Must Love Otters, Book One

Hollie Porter Builds a Raft, Book Two

Hollie Porter's Hat Trick Christmas (A Christmas novella)

Open Me First (A Valentine's Day novella)

Standalone novels:

I Love You, Luke Piewalker

Dear Dwayne, With Love

ONE

SHERLOCK BONES IS WAITING outside the door for me. And he's brought me a present.

As per usual.

With Sherlock, you never know what the present will be (or if it's alive or dead). His heart's in the right place, and he knows that I keep the good cookies in the bottom drawer of my desk.

The bell on the photography studio's glass front door tinkles as I open it. "Sherlock," I say. He prances right in, his four-inch tail wagging proudly, his usually white front legs soiled with the evidence of his labor. I swear he's smiling. "What did you bring me?"

He drops my "present"—a mutilated tennis ball today—on the floor next to my desk and pushes himself onto his hind legs, as if posing for the ringmaster and his adoring audience.

"You shouldn't have," I say, patting his narrow, white-and-brown terrier head. "You got dirt in your ears, bud." He shakes his whole body like he's just jumped out of the bathtub. "Thanks. I just vacuumed."

I open the bottom desk drawer and pull out his favorite biscuits.

He poses for me again; I give him two. I'll wait to throw the tennis ball away after he leaves. I don't want to hurt his feelings.

He manages to get another few cookies out of me—because I'm a sucker for smart Jack Russells—and just as he's chewing the last of it, the studio door bursts open, allowing entry to one of the scariest women in all of Portland.

"Sherlock! You are the baddest dog in the entire world!" Mrs. Gianotti's Italian accent is as thick as her famous sauce, even though she's lived in Oregon for most of her life. Sherlock Bones responds to his mother's reprimand by taking off at a sprint, likely to find another escape route.

"Hello, Mrs. Gianotti," I say, wiping my hands on a tissue. "You're looking well today."

"I look terrible. I am too old for this dumb dog. He will be the death of me." She dresses the part of an old-world Italian *mamma*—the black dress, the white apron dotted with whatever she's been cooking this morning, the gray-and-black hair pulled into a loose bun on top of her head, the dark pantyhose and sensible, slip-proof shoes. The flashiest thing about her are the leopard-print reading glasses that hang from the gold chain around her neck. She says they're "ugly, like pineapple on pizza," but her young granddaughter picked them, so they stay.

And for the record, everything will be the death of Mrs. Gianotti. You should've heard her after last season's winner of *The Bachelorette.*

"How's the deli?" Mrs. G. owns one of Portland's oldest and most famous Italian delicatessens just down the block—my father is one of her best customers. I think she might secretly be in love with Dad, which explains why the fridge here is always stocked with takeout containers from Gianotti's, most of it involving prosciutto, all of it clogging his arteries I'm sure.

"Deli will kill me," Mrs. G. says. "SHERLOCK! Come! We have cannoli to fill!" She turns and shuffles toward the door. Looks like her left hip is still bothering her.

"Good to see you again, Mrs. Gianotti."

"Send my stupid dog home. Maybe I will make sausages out of him."

I hold the door open for her and she flaps a hand at me and grunts as she exits, her thighs *swish-swishing* as she walks. As soon as the bell quiets, Sherlock emerges.

"You're going to be the death of her, you know," I say, moving back toward my desk to answer the ringing phone. Sherlock barks once and then sets to cleaning himself against the throw rug near the front door. Ugh. Just another man to tidy up after. Though Sherlock *is* way cuter than my brother.

"Hawes Photography, Frankie speaking."

"Frankie—it's Gabe. I need you to do me a favor."

"Hey ..." My brother sounds weird. "Are you seriously drunk? It's, like, not even noon. I hope your vacation involves more than boozing it up. Poor Lainie—"

"You're going to have to shoot the Meyer-Nelson wedding."

"What?"

"The Meyer-Nelson wedding. This weekend. Revelation Cove, up in British Columbia. I can't go—"

"Gabe, what are you talking about? You have to go. This wedding is a huge deal."

"Frankie—liiiiisten to me—I crashed my bike and screwed up my leg. I'm at Legacy Emanuel. They gave me morphine. It's awesome."

I bury my face in the hand not holding the phone, but my heart pounds loudly enough in my ears that I almost can't hear my own voice. "Is Lainie there with you? Put her on the phone. You still have time to shoot the wedding—you just need a cast or one of those air-boot thingies, right?"

"I have to have surgery, Francesca. Trust me," he says, on the verge of slurring. "I'd rather be shooting a wedding instead of getting my leg bolted back together."

"Surgery?" My voice squeaks. "Gabriel, please ... please don't ask me to do this. Isn't there another photographer who can shoot it?"

"Frankie, you know I wouldn't ask if I didn't have to."

"Can't Dad do it?"

"And cut short his golf trip?"

Gabe is right. Our dad is in Vegas with his latest playmate. I hope this one is old enough to vote.

"How bad is the break?"

"If I tell you, you'll barf. Blood and guts and stuff."

Oh god, if his broken leg involves blood, it's bad.

"Can I bring you anything?"

"Nah, Lainie is going home to grab some clothes. Lazarus is at the kennel until tomorrow night so we'll keep him there."

"I can go get him—"

"No, you can't. I need you to go deal with this wedding."

"I'm not kidding, Gabe. You cannot ask me to do this."

"The doctor said the surgery will take a few hours and then I have to be here overnight at least. Plus this morphine is *fantastic*."

"Yeah, you mentioned that," I say. "Can't they give you crutches? And more morphine? I can go up with you to assist and hold cameras —all you have to do is point and shoot. You can do that with crutches, right?"

"You can do this, Frankie. You're a super-good photographer."

Now I know he's stoned. I'm an uninspired photographer. Which is why, at Hawes Photography, a full-service, family-owned photography studio, I answer the phones and handle the accounts and sit with bridezillas as they rattle off their ridiculous shot lists that often require unicorns and "A castle would be great" and also "Can you make sure it's sunny that day, not too sunny, but like overcast with some blue sky showing?"

Sure. Let me get my Elder Wand. Please stand by.

"Just pretend the bride is a golden retriever, and you're—ha! Golden!—oh my god, I love these drugs," he says. "I gotta go, sis. All the details are in their event binder."

I turn in my spinny, squeaky office chair. The near-bursting Nelson three-ring binder is on the UPCOMING EVENTS shelf, right where it's supposed to be, waiting for my big brother Gabriel to scoop it up and work his magical magic with his cameras to bring the happy couple—the daughter and soon-to-be son-in-law of one of our dad's oldest friends, practically Portland royalty—all the vivid, shiny memories of their Very Big Day.

"Gabe—"

Beep beep beep.

He's hung up. Probably has to get ready for that surgery or whatever.

"Shit."

Sherlock sits up and whines once at me.

"Yeah, I know, a dollar in the swear jar."

He flops back down and sighs contentedly. What I would give to be Sherlock Bones right now.

I look through our list of freelance photographers. My father, Harrison Hawes, is legit famous for his years as a photojournalist and later for his editorial work of both humans and animals. Like, James Nachtwey, Annie Leibowitz, Frans Lanting famous—almost as well known for his photographic skills as he is for his wandering eye and taste for young models. He shot wars and civil unrest and global chaos, and then Something Really Terrible happened, so he opened this studio when we were kids.

My dad's adventures made for an interesting childhood.

Gabriel inherited the artistry, so Dad paid big bucks for him to go to CalArts and study with some of the best in the field, in the hope that Gabe would take over the family business one day. Still, how anyone with spelling like Gabe's can get a university degree ...

I, however, rely on more practical sensibilities to get through life. Degree from a regular academic university (Portland State), double major in English and history, minor in photography that I only achieved through a miracle of the gods. These days, I participate in things that don't require me to be artistic, given that most ants have more artistic ability than I do.

Okay—I recognize this as negative self-talk. The therapist I saw for four visits at my father's insistence because he thinks I have unre-solved confidence issues stemming from my mother's abandonment—that therapist lady told me I have to challenge negative thoughts with positive ones, so here goes: I am a passing photographer who is actually quite good at photographing dogs.

Yeah. I said dogs.

Not a lot of calls for dog-wedding photographers, and certainly not often enough to pay my electric bill.

But dogs are easy. You hold up a squeaky toy, give them a chunk of hot dog or the specialty bait the dog-show people use, and they give you the world. A dog's eyes are judgment-free, full of heart, and ridiculously eager to please.

Sherlock Bones is living proof. He brings me presents!

I've done some backup shooting in the studio for my dad—mostly kids' portraits—but I get so wound up when the parents are there watching and critiquing ... I actually had one dad tell me he could do my job if he had my camera, and he couldn't understand why I was having such a hard time getting a shot of his kid.

Probably because his kid was trying to climb the backdrop and wouldn't keep his fingers out of his crusty mouth and nose.

And weddings—oh my god, no. I manage brides week in and week out when they come in to book their wedding packages, and they are some of the scariest creatures ever to crawl out of the primordial soup. A few years ago, there was a meme about a honey badger, how they're so badass they can even eat venomous snakes, and I told Gabe that our brides could scare that honey badger right into submission.

He agreed.

So, people, brides included, make me very nervous. They have Opinions with a Capital O. Dogs don't. Like I said, squeaky toy, pat on the head, chunk of meat equals winning shot.

You can see why me shooting the Nelsons' wedding is probably going to be disastrous.

Because last time I checked, the bride is NOT a golden retriever.

Speaking of, I pick up and kiss the small golden retriever figurine sitting next to my phone. My good-luck charm—one of many little statuettes from some unknown source that just appear in random places now and again. Dad swears they're not from him.

I'm pretty sure they are. He's a bear of a man, but he's a good dad.

I spend the afternoon contacting our other photographers; Gabe contracts with a lot of freelancers when we have jobs he can't shoot. Finding someone to take the Meyer-Nelson wedding for an all-expenses-paid weekend up in what is reportedly a gorgeous part of the West Coast—how hard can that be?

Hard. Like, impossibly hard.

Everyone is busy, scheduled to shoot other events from Portland to Seattle. One of our shooters is even on a plane to LA for a destination wedding. Lots of "Oh man, sorry to hear about Gabe" and "Text me when he's out of surgery." Polite sentiments aside, *this is not helping because none of these jerks is available to shoot the Meyer-Nelson wedding.*

I'm going to hyperventilate.

Sparkly lights in the corners of my eyes.

I push my chair aside and lie flat on the Pier One Imports shag rug Lainie picked out for me specially. She said the office was too bro-apartment and needed a feminine touch to bring down the free testosterone in the air. I agree. I love this rug, even if my chair snags on it.

Sherlock comes over and licks my face; his breath smells like salami. "Thank you. That helps," I say. He nudges in beside me on the rug.

The panic attacks don't happen very often anymore, not since university, but the therapist recommended that a calm, cool, and collected life could be the ticket to managing my anxiety.

Routine and structure. Dependability and order. Drama-free and organized.

So, I bought a day planner and canceled my therapy appointments, which leads me to now: Mondays are for movies, Tuesdays and Thursdays are for aqua-fit with my best friend Bryony, Wednesdays are bookstore nights where Bryony and I walk around and dream about the bookstore-slash-pet-rescue we're going to open one day, Fridays are for sushi. Weekends are the only things I freewheel, and not even that much—Saturdays mean chores and laundry, Sundays are for sleeping in and pancakes. I will babysit my dog-nephew Lazarus when he's available (he's a Malamute mix so he basically destroys my apartment but he's also awesome so, yeah, worth it). Throw in the occasional weekender to the Oregon Coast or Vegas, and I'd call this a full-enough life.

The ringing phone startles Sherlock. I push myself up, lean on the desk, and read the caller ID: "Nicolette Meyer Nelson." Oh god, she's already changed her name?

I have to answer it.

She will keep calling until I answer it.

I can't talk to her.

What will I say?

When I told her there were no horses available for the shoot at this Canadian resort, she yelled at me until I cried.

Oh god.

Sherlock barks once, as if yelling *ANSWER THE PHONE, FRANCESCA.*

"Hawes Photography, this is Frankie, how can I help you?"

"Nicolette Meyer here. I'm just calling to let Gabe know that I've sent a courier over with everything he needs for the weekend shoot in British Columbia. Ferry tickets, petty cash, everything we talked about. It's in the binder—you remember," she says, hardly breathing as she speaks, "so the courier should be there soon. We're flying into Victoria tonight because I cannot sit in a car for six hours north and then deal with a ferry and still have a face that will photograph well. Like I need any more stress wrinkles, I swear. I hope their spa doesn't suck." She pauses long enough to, I think, take a drink of something. "Anyway, that's all. Tell Gabe we'll see him Thursday night for the rehearsal dinner, for Friday's prewedding excursion, and then for the big day on Saturday. Between you and me, Frances, I cannot wait for this to be over."

Francesca. Or Frankie. Not Frances.

"Oh, someone's calling through. Probably the caterer. They think they're going to get away with serving Atlantic salmon. Ha! Did you hear how it's filled with sea lice? Ohhhh my god!"

As the phone clicks quiet, the front door of the studio opens, sending Sherlock into investigative mode. A young guy in a sleeveless shirt and bicycle-friendly pants with hair that probably hasn't been washed since he was in grade school yanks his messenger bag around to his stomach.

"Hey," he says. "Cute dog. Yours?" Oh. Wow. He's actually kinda hot. I want to ask him if the eyebrow piercings were painful. That's a lot of nerve endings to be stabbing through. "For Gabriel Hawes. You sign for this?"

"Sure."

He hands over the overstuffed, rigid envelope—it's almost as big as the binder sitting on my desk. I'm terrified to open it.

"Just sign here ... and here. Gotta get two signatures 'cos there's cash inside."

"Right."

He looks around while I sign. Sherlock is very interested in whatever is on the messenger's high-top shoe.

"Nice place. You a photographer?" I hand him the form back. "I always wanted to be a photographer. I'm pretty good with my iPhone." He pulls his phone out of a zippered pocket and goes immediately to an Instagram feed. "I like to get shots of stuff I see in the city. This job lets me do it."

His photos aren't terrible. Then again, anyone with a decent phone camera is a photographer these days. Good thing my father isn't here. He'd threaten to beat this kid with a tripod.

"Those are nice."

"Yeah, they're not for everyone. Not commercial like this place," he says. It doesn't sound like a compliment. "Okay, more stops to make before drum circle tonight." He pats his bag and then Sherlock's head. "See you later, little doggie!"

The bell on the front door jingles his departure.

I take a deep breath and use a letter opener to slice into the envelope. As promised, there are ferry tickets out of Tsawwassen for Wednesday and then Swartz Bay for Sunday, as well as shuttle tickets to and from the resort called Revelation Cove, located in the Discovery Islands, British Columbia, Canada.

"I hear they have bears in Canada, Sherlock. Don't bears eat people?"

TWO

"WHAT IS THAT AWFUL NOISE?" Bryony yells into the phone.

"What? I can't hear you!"

"That NOISE!" The noise stops. "What the hell was that?"

"Did you not get my text?" An elderly gentleman stops and stares at the seat next to me, asking with his eyebrows if he can sit with me. Considering there are exactly one thousand other empty seats, I shake my head no and turn toward the wall.

"I'm on the ferry. I told you all about it." The awful noise—the ferry's powerful horn—ceases.

"I just got in last night and I have the worst jet lag."

"How was the conference?"

"As boring as you would expect it to be. Sitting in a room with overweight, undersexed, greasy men who are all one step short of the heart attack that will send them back to Jesus ... not nearly as exciting as flitting off to British Columbia for a wedding."

"What I would give to have you here."

"You're going to be fine." She practically chokes on the words. Bryony is my oldest friend—we met during freshman orientation at

Portland State, so she knows how mediocre I feel in the bright light cast by my dad and brother. "You couldn't find anyone to do the job?"

"No. I tried everyone. I even offered a bonus."

"Your dad said he'd pay extra?"

"I was going to pay it out of my own pocket." We both know my dad inherited his mother's tendency toward a squeaky wallet. "I instead used the money to get an emergency hair appointment last night."

"Did you go blond yet?"

"Still brown."

"Chicken. Blond makes those baby blues pop!" Bryony says. I've been debating going blond for a while—Bry often reminds me of my platinum phase in college and how we really *did* have more fun. "Well, call me whenever you need me. I'm back in the office training a new girl who just got out of jail."

"Jail?"

"You know how my boss loves her pet projects."

"What was she in jail for?"

"Theft, I think. Apparently, she was a housekeeper and stole some diamonds from her last employer."

"Sounds juicy."

"Maybe she could steal some diamonds for me. Oh, boss is back. Gotta go. And Frankie—remember: you know how to frame a photo. You know how a camera works. You know how to make people smile. You even know how to make them cry."

"Har har."

"I believe in you!" she yells. In my head, I can see her pointing at the framed motivational poster on the wall above her desk, the one with the whale fluke cresting the wave. Her boss hasn't redecorated since 1997.

"I'm going to go find some poutine."

"Not even in Canada yet and you're already speaking French. I'm impressed. *Au revoir, ma chère!*" She disconnects.

But I *am* in Canada, Bryony. My cell phone provider has already texted to remind me how expensive the next four days are going to be. They should just text a photograph of their CEO on his yacht in the Maldives with a "thanks for paying so much for cell phone service the water is great here."

I drove to Vancouver, BC, last night, and today I'm aboard one of their very big ferries that'll transport me and my car to Victoria. There I will somehow find my way into the city's main harbor, locate secure parking, and probably pay a king's ransom for four days of fees. Lastly, I will climb aboard yet another watercraft for the trip north to Revelation Cove.

I'm already tired. Could have something to do with the people in the hotel room next to mine last night. She called him Daddy a lot, and loudly. He said she was very naughty and needed to be punished, also a lot, also loudly.

I put in my earplugs at that point.

I googled the resort, and it looks amazing, owned by a couple of retired hockey players and their families. I don't follow hockey myself, but the Google search brought up the news story from a few years ago about when the primary owner, Ryan Fielding, was attacked by a cougar and his girlfriend saved him. Heroic *and* romantic.

I am neither heroic nor romantic.

And cougars. Oh god, I'd been so busy worrying about bears, I forgot about cougars.

Maybe if I can find one, I can pay him or her that bonus to shoot this wedding. Better yet, maybe they can just eat Nikki Meyer and her too-perfect groom and save all of us a lot of trouble.

THE TRIP aboard the *Spirit of British Columbia* is about ninety minutes, and surprisingly, I manage a short nap before the shuffling and excited twitters of people around me opens my worried eyes.

"There were orca!" a woman next to me says. She must've settled in after I'd nodded off. She wipes snot from the nose of the toddler sitting in the stroller at the end of our four-seat row. "I was going to wake you—we don't see orca on every trip through—but you looked like you needed sleep."

"Thanks." I sit up. There's a kink in my neck from leaning against the wall. I am sad I missed the orca.

"Your first time to Victoria?"

"Mm-hmm."

"Any plans while you're here?"

She has just enough of an accent that I know she's not American. "I'm shooting a wedding."

"You're a photographer?"

I swallow hard. "Something like that."

"Sounds very glamorous. Everyone nowadays calls themselves a photographer, but if you're shooting a wedding, you must be the real thing." Her baby winds up for a scream and lets loose just as the ferry's horn joins in the chorus. "If you need to use the washroom, the ferry will be docking in just a few minutes. Did you drive on?"

"I did."

"Then out you go. If you're late to your car, the other drivers will throw you the stink eye. Slows everyone down."

"Good to know. Thank you."

"Enjoy your wedding!"

I nod and gather my stuff before I burst into tears in front of this woman who seems very sweet. As I slide out of our row, her baby stops screaming long enough to look up at me and reach for the tassels hanging from my giant purse. I do not love this purse, but Bryony bought it for me for Christmas because she said I spend too much time with boys and I need to be more girly so her solution was a trip to the eyebrow bar and this purse. My eyebrows are back to their untidy selves, but the purse has come in handy when I've needed something big enough to carry the state of Oregon with me.

I move quickly enough to stop at the bathrooms and make it down to my car before the overhead speakers advise us that we've arrived at the Swartz Bay terminal. I exit at the first open door off the stairs—and realize I can't remember where my car is. I step aside so as not to raise the ire of the people crowding behind me. Flat against the wall on a very crowded car deck, I close my eyes and try to remember what everything looked like when I got out of my own vehicle.

Big white van. There was a big white van because you thought it looked like a van that a kidnapper would have filled with candy and puppies.

I open my eyes again, anxiety sweat dampening the back and pits of my suddenly too-tight shirt. A scan of this area, and of the cars on the other side of the stairwell structure, does not reveal a white van. Engines are turning on—people up ahead are offloading! Oh my god, I'm going to be one of those people who holds everything up and then all these nice Canadians won't be so nice anymore.

I skip-jog back to the doors for the stairs and go down another floor, trying to remember any other identifiers. Floor number? Remarkable cars?

The announcer is back on the speakers and all I hear are "Oregon plates" and then my heartbeat overrules any other sounds in my ears.

A guy in a hi-vis vest stands right outside the next set of doors. "Do you need some help?" he asks. The cars on this deck are already moving. Oh god oh god oh god.

My throat is so tight—I squeak. "I'm lost. I can't find my car."

"Are you the Honda? Oregon plates?" he asks, his tone not altogether friendly. I nod vigorously. "Come on." He talks into the mic attached to his vest. "Found the Oregon driver."

Sure enough, as we're walking toward the white kidnapper van, I'm treated to the stares and glares of other drivers who've been inconvenienced by my terrible sense of direction. Another guy in hi-vis is trying to angle the cars behind me out of the row and around.

"I am so sorry. I've never been on a ferry."

"Don't worry about it," the guy says. "Just remember for the trip back, hey?"

Again, I nod vigorously and unlock the car and I'm in and then I keep my eyes averted so I don't see that stink eye the mother upstairs warned me of from other drivers and ferry employees. And as I'm driving off the boat and into the foggy morning with the rest of the hurried folks around me, I realize I have absolutely no idea where I'm going and my phone with the GPS helper is buried in the bottom of the tasseled purse on the passenger-side floor.

I'm overcome by a wave of fatigue.

Please tell me the rest of this trip is going to go better than the last twenty minutes.

THREE

I FOLLOW the other vehicles for a few miles—pardon me, *kilometres, dear, you're in Canada now*—until I spy a gas station off the highway and pull into its lot. I definitely need my phone to get me into the city, to find parking, to find yet another boat to take me away from civilization and into the waiting jaws of Nikki Meyer.

Maybe the boat will sink.

Maybe I will contract West Nile virus before we get there and I'll faint and be saved from falling overboard by a dashing, handsome man with no mommy issues and no tattoos professing his love for his last girlfriend. Naturally this dashing, handsome man loves books, and we will carry on meaningful conversations about the mixed messages given to young girls who swoon over Mr. Fitzwilliam Darcy, and he will have an open mind about the importance of romance novels in our literary canon. Also, though he's a conservationist and advocate for animal rights, he does eat responsibly sourced meats, but no bacon because I like pigs. Pigs are super smart. And it's okay that he's saving me because I am a twenty-first-century feminist but I still don't want to fall overboard when I faint from a West Nile attack.

Maybe that nuclear holocaust we've all been fretting over will finally happen, and not even being in Canada will save me, and everyone on the boat will come together and we'll form a band of mercenaries to take out the terrible men responsible for the destruction of Los Angeles and Dubai and Paris. Especially Paris because I've not been there yet.

Or maybe my phone battery won't have died between my brief call with Bryony and now, and I will be able to use my GPS to find my way to Victoria Harbour before the boat to Revelation Cove leaves me behind.

And maybe not.

"Howwwwww?" I whine to only myself and my brother's camera equipment. I charged this phone last night. I specifically remember plugging it in. Welp, evidently not because it's dead dead *dead* now, and I'm screwed until my car battery gives up enough of her juice to make the phone's screen turn on again.

Until that happens, I must rely on pen and paper and, I hope, my pleasing manners. I have to ask someone for directions.

And the clouds have just opened their floodgates. Didn't I pack a compact umbrella in this tasseled behemoth?

I hop out and jog around the front of the small store. The young woman behind the counter is more than happy to draw a map for me to get to the Inner Harbour—except I don't know my north from my south here, and she has a lot of customers needing to pay for energy drinks, small bottles of overpriced maple syrup, and *very* expensive gas.

"You'll be fine! Just drive toward the water," she says, flipping her blond ponytail over her shoulder.

I wave my thanks and saunter back to my car, not caring that I'm getting soaked. As I open the driver's door to climb in, I'm about knocked over by a beagle who zooms past and flies into the car's belly.

"Lila! Come BACK here!" I turn and look—Lila's apparent owner is fumbling with the gas nozzle sticking out of her truck's tank.

"Hey, Lila," I say, leaning into the car. The tricolored beagle sits on the passenger's seat, wagging her tail like this is no big deal. "I think your mom is calling you."

"Oh man, I am so sorry!" The beagle's owner jogs over to me. "I swear she's going to get hit one of these days." She adjusts the Toronto Blue Jays ballcap on her head; the rain is beading on her black Arc'teryx coat. She has a leash in one hand and cookies in the other.

"Does she do this often?" I ask.

"I should've named her Houdini. I've never had a dog who escapes so often," she says, smiling. "I think she wants to go with you."

I slide into the driver's seat and hold out my closed fist for Lila to smell. She licks it. "You're super cute, but I can't take you to Nicolette's stinky wedding," I say. Lila's floppy brown ears are so soft, and her chocolate-brown eyes soften as I pet her head.

"Maybe you can click the leash on?" her owner asks, hand extended.

"Frankie?" a man says to our left. "I thought that was you holding up my line on the ferry. You lost again?"

Oh my god, I know that voice.

"Sam?" I climb out—I've missed my shot with the leash.

"Hey!" he says, resting a hand on my open car door. "Is that your dog?" He bends and wiggles his fingers at Lila the beagle; she bays in return.

"Oh my god—what are you doing here?"

"Let me step in here and grab my girl. Again, so sorry," the woman says, taking the leash from me. She tries to get hold of Lila, but the pup is having none of it. She barks and bays at her mom, jumps into the back seat of my Honda, and then hops into the front, her tail going crazy the whole time. I'm guessing this is a game they play often.

Sam jogs to the car's other side and opens the passenger-side door to try to snag Lila's collar. Instead she escapes past him and runs around the building front, her timing perfect—she shimmies into the convenience store as another customer exits.

"Sorry!" Lila's mom calls, running after her dog.

"Do you need more help?" I yell.

"No, we're good! Thank you!" The woman disappears into the store, leaving me here all alone in the pouring rain with Sam McKenzie staring down at me.

"No, *Hey, Sam, good to see you, fine sir?*"

"Yeah, all that, but why are you in Victoria?"

"A wedding—I'm all for free booze and desperate bridesmaids."

"Wait—what wedding ..."

"Nicolette Meyer, cheerleader, soul-swallower, mean girl with crazy eyes? You remember her?" he says. My stomach flips and my eyes widen. "No shit—is that what you're doing here too? Small world!" He laughs.

I about pee myself. Samuel David McKenzie is my brother's former best friend. Former because Sam was dating Lainie when my brother swooped in for the kill. It was actually pretty heartbreaking.

From second grade on, Sam was the third kid on our family vacations; he camped with us on my dad's outdoor photo adventures to Yosemite and Yellowstone and the Grand Canyon. He was my brother's wingman when they discovered their penises and the magic they could wield on members of the opposite sex.

And then Sam and Lainie had a rough night while my dumb brother was visiting during their senior year at the University of Oregon. Gabe and Lainie drank a lot of cheap wine and shared a lot of sad stories and somehow fell into one another's body parts. That was the beginning of Gabe and Lainie, and the end of Gabe and Sam.

I mourned Sam's departure from our adventures. It was like we were missing a limb for a while there.

"While you contemplate the finer things in life, we're getting drenched."

"Oh, right, sorry. Climb in."

He does, pausing first to swipe the dog hair off the seat.

Sam shakes his auburn mop, sending water droplets everywhere. He's bigger than the last time I saw him—like maybe those Flintstone vitamins his mom loved finally started working. His eyes, still that fierce green. His jawline has sharpened too, dusted with a light stubble. My dad used to tease him that he was the only redhead he knew who could grow a proper beard.

Sam's like a real grown-up man now, and I feel like a dorky teenager as he smiles back at me.

"You look really freaked out right now. Like that time we went bungee jumping."

"This feels a bit like bungee jumping," I admit. I hold up my dead phone. "Battery died. I have no GPS, the girl inside gave me directions I don't understand, and I need to get to the harbor to get on the boat that's taking me to the venue."

He checks his own *charged* phone. "We still have time. Follow me into the city. I've been to this place before. You're gonna love it, F-Stop."

I pause and stare at him. No one has called me F-Stop since I yelled at them as we cracked crabs at Jake's Famous Crawfish in downtown Portland on my seventeenth birthday—my dad, Gabe, and Sam—that no one was allowed to call me that anymore and *especially* not in public because I was a young *woman* now, and it made me sound weird. I think that really hurt my dad's feelings, looking back. He'd always called me that, from the very beginning.

An *f*-stop is the aperture setting on a camera's lens; my name is Francesca, which starts with an F. When Dad was explaining *f*-stop to Gabe and me during one of his many lessons, Gabe made a joke about how they should call me F-Stop because the words "Frankie" and "stop," as in "Stop being a pest," were usually said in the same sentence. So, it stuck.

"Are you seriously going to the Meyer-Nelson wedding?" I ask.

Sam's smile is all Cheshire Cat. "And pass up an opportunity to watch Nicolette Meyer make the second biggest mistake of her life?"

I laugh. Of course Sam would be here. They all went to middle and high school together, and since then, he's done computer consulting or something involving 1s and 0s for her posh daddy. "What was the first mistake, pray tell?"

"Turning me down for homecoming senior year. And then turning down my marriage proposal that famed spring-break night in Fort Lauderdale."

"Right. What a missed opportunity."

"Exactly! Who wouldn't want to live in a Southeast Portland, second-story, overpriced condo I co-own with my mother that's filled with movie memorabilia and shared with a semirabid cat named Zod?"

"You do paint a pretty picture. I can't see why she would give that a pass."

"Ah, but she turned me down flat before all that magic came to be. I don't think she saw the potential."

"Her loss."

"Completely," Sam says, turning on his phone. "Now—why are YOU here?"

"Gabe broke his leg. Mountain biking. He had surgery."

"He always was too reckless on that bike. Does Nikki know yet?"

"Gabe dealt with it, likely under the influence of painkillers."

"Yikes. You didn't talk to her yourself?" Sam says, eyebrows hiking.

"Have you *met* Nicolette Meyer? I think murder is within her skill set."

Sam nods his agreement. "Well, then, let's get going. You have a wedding to shoot."

"This is going to be a disaster, Sam. You've seen my pictures."

His head is already shaking. "This is no time for self-deprecation, or false humility. I *have* seen your pictures. And between the two of us, I'm sure we can grab a few photos of Nicolette Meyer looking like the frosty bride-queen she will undoubtedly be."

"If we're lucky, we'll get a few photos with her forked tongue *behind* her teeth," I say.

Sam laughs, and for a moment, I'm sucked back in time, around the campfire in Yellowstone National Forest, roasting marshmallows in October. Dad was there capturing shots of the bears before they went to bed for the winter. Gabe and Sam, a few years older than me, ate through all the chocolate before we could make s'mores while I caught marshmallow after marshmallow on fire and contemplated if Sam really did have cooties. He didn't seem to in the dancing firelight.

"You look good. I've missed this face," he says, smiling. "You're going to be fine, F-Stop. Follow me in, okay?" His wide hand is on the door release. "Try to stay close—this rain isn't letting up. And please don't rear-end me because that is not a suitable way to get out of this weekend. We already have one irresponsible member of your family in the hospital."

BY THE TIME we pull into the parking garage that will house our vehicles for the next four days, I'm giddy with relief that Sam is here. My phone has gotten enough charge in the last thirty-six minutes of travel that I'll have ample juice to hold me until I can find another electrical outlet. And I have Sam's helpful muscles to help carry equipment. It'll be nice to have another set of shoulders to throw a lens backpack on.

"How were you going to carry all this yourself?" Sam says, pulling equipment out of my trunk.

"I'm mightier than I look."

"I don't doubt that, but you also are not a bodybuilder."

"You don't know that. I'm on a strict diet of protein and the souls of misbehaved children."

"Still a weirdo," Sam says, slamming my trunk closed.

"You have no idea," I whisper under my breath.

We manage to reach the boat that will take us north to this magical island off the BC coast where Nikki Meyer is about to make the second biggest mistake of her life. The guy who greets us—"Tanner Fielding, at your service"—looks suspiciously like the Googled photos of the hockey player saved from the cougar by his girlfriend.

"You're awfully white all of a sudden—don't tell me you've developed a fear of boats," Sam says.

"Do you think this place has wildlife? Like, dangerous wildlife?"

"Probably. But since we're Americans, we can just wrestle them to the ground with our flags and longwinded diatribes about the Constitution," Sam teases.

Tanner helps us stow my equipment up front so we don't take up more than our share of seats. The boat is long and wide with comfortable seating on both sides of the rubber-floored aisle. The rear houses a small galley kitchen where a woman similarly outfitted to Tanner—cargo pants and dark green, long-sleeved shirts with a Revelation Cove logo embroidered over the left chest—prepares refreshments. I don't spy any bottles of wine or champagne or gin, which is a shame, but it's probably best not to get liquored up before we arrive.

Society and its silly rules.

The boat fills quickly, but I insist on sitting near the camera equipment, mostly because I can't bear to make eye contact with any of the people behind us. Odds are excellent that I know at least some of them, if they're wedding guests. Nicolette, Sam, my brother, and me all went to the same Portland middle and high school, and our dads are golf buddies, so there likely are people on this boat who know Harrison Hawes. He's a big fish in a little pond.

And I don't want anyone to see that it's *me*, the offspring who answers the phone, doing this wedding, and not Gabe, the offspring who is an actual award-winning photographer and chip off the old block.

"Do you get seasick?" Sam asks, taking cups of OJ for each of us from the offered tray.

"I don't think so."

"You got seasick that time we rented boats in Newport," he reminds me.

"Yeah, but that had nothing to do with the sea and everything to do with the crappy beer the night before."

He nods and finishes his nonalcoholic orange juice. "Yeah, that was bad beer. So glad we grew up and refined our tastes." He winks and skooches down in his seat to extend his long, denim-clad legs in front of him. "You are going to love this voyage. I've gone up this way and another time on the floatplane, and both routes are beautiful. This part of the world is unbelievable."

"No floatplanes. I can see just fine from here," I say, hoping the orca I missed earlier will make a renewed appearance. Then at least I can tell people I saw killer whales on my big adventure to Canada.

I sip my juice and then take one of the offered treats—a sugar cookie with a dollop of the best jam I've ever eaten in my life—and try to calm my nerves as we finally pull away from the docks and glide out of Victoria's scenic Inner Harbour. Sam leans across me and snaps a photo with his iPhone of a huge boat parked at the very end of the moorage.

"Is that a helicopter on the deck?" I ask, straining to look as we move away.

"I dunno. I was taking a picture of that sign with the Canadian flag on it so I can prove to my coworkers that I am actually in a foreign country and I'm not just taking a random Thursday off."

"Did you really come all this way for Nikki's wedding? Why?"

"She invited me."

I lower my voice and lean closer. "I've seen the behind-the-scenes on this wedding. This place is expensive."

"But remember that I designed some software systems for her daddy, so I got in on the friends & family rate." He tucks his phone away. "Why? Are you worried about my finances, little F-Stop?"

"What? God, no. That's none of my business. I just ... well, if I'd been invited to this wedding, I don't think I would've been able to come."

"You need to ask your dad for a raise. Better yet, you need to go into business on your own," he says, retrieving another of the jam-filled cookies.

"Into business on my own. Sure. Doing what?"

"Writing. Magazine work. You were always fixing our homework for us—why don't you think about writing for a newspaper or something? Use some of those keen investigative skills you used on us when we were kids."

"Because I have no idea where to start with something like that."

"You're telling me the photography articles your dad and Gabe publish are written by them?"

I blush, but my heart also stutters a bit when he mentions Gabe. I know it must be a sore spot—it still is for my brother. He misses Sam, but the two of them have never been able to put this behind them, not when Lainie stands between them.

"You've read those?"

"Now and then ..." His lip tugs into a shy smile.

"Well, thanks. And of course I wrote them. Gabe can hardly spell camera."

"Precisely. Oh! And your Instagram! Lots of dogs on there. There's that one you post all the time, the funny brown-and-white dog—"

"Sherlock Bones."

He laughs. "Nice name. Is he yours?"

"He wishes he were mine. He belongs to Mrs. Gianotti."

"Any relation to Gianotti's Deli? God, I love that place."

I think of Sam popping into Mrs. G.'s deli. "You go there?"

"All the time."

"So close to us. You should've stopped by."

The expression on his face says it all. He would've stopped by, but water under bridges and bygones and such.

"I'm just saying, the photos of the dogs—you're so good at it."

"Should I be weirded out that you've seen my Instagram?"

"I check on you now and again. See what mischief you're up to," he says.

My insides warm as I finish my cookie. Not gonna lie: I've creeped his social media too.

Sam smiles again. "One of these days, Frankie, you're going to get out from behind the shadow of your brother and father and do something really big and awesome."

I sit up rod straight. "I'm not in their shadow."

He arches an eyebrow at me.

"Are you even serious right now? I haven't seen you in a million years, and you're already psychoanalyzing me?"

Sam's face reddens a bit. His Scottish ancestry means every emotion is painted on his face. "Shit, no, I didn't—"

"Not everyone is meant for big and awesome, Samuel. Some of us like quiet and understated." I stand and wait for him to retract his legs so I can pass. My cheeks burn but am I embarrassed? Angry? What the hell am I doing letting Sam McKenzie into my head when we haven't talked to each other since, what—forever?

"Is there a bathroom on board?" I ask the ponytailed, orange-juice woman. She points toward the back of the vessel. We gain speed, the boat's nose angling up slightly with the push from the rear engines.

"You all right?" the woman asks.

"Yeah. Just a little unsteady on the water."

She motions with her hand and I follow as she leads me down the aisle, my eyes fixed on my feet—one step, then another—using the passing seats as support, and then poof! I'm at the bathroom and I didn't have to make eye contact with anyone else who will see right through me.

Door locked, I even avoid my reflection in the narrow mirror. I've had enough examination for one day.

~

WHEN I RETURN to my seat, Sam is bent over a book, his dark blue wool coat pulled taut against his back. He sits up and closes his book.

"Frankie, I am so sorry—I didn't mean for that to come out like that."

"It's fine."

"No, it's not—honestly, I haven't seen you in so long, and it's none of my business. I didn't mean to get under your skin already."

"Just like old times, hey?" Except Sam didn't get under my skin. Sam was the nice one, the Switzerland between Gabe and me. "Are you seriously reading *1984*?"

"*Re*reading it. Feels appropriate right now. I want to be prepared for what's coming," he says, smiling.

He leans back and replaces his earbuds, worrying his lip like he's always done. His hair is longer than I've seen it since we were kids. It suits him. Lets his reddish curls have a moment to breathe.

Growing up, he was teased mercilessly—called everything from Carrot Top to the missing Weasley. (I thought that one was kinda cool, to be honest. Molly Weasley seems like she'd be the best mom.) And it didn't help that it took puberty forever to arrive. When it did, it meant a painful year with eight inches of stretching growth and the onset of acne that required medical intervention.

My dad, famous for assigning terrible nicknames just because he's a dad and that's what dads do, was careful with Sam. I think he could see how much it hurt that every school day was filled with teasing. Dad referred to Sam as Sam, and only occasionally as Samwise, an honorable hat tip to Samwise Gamgee, Frodo's stalwart friend (and arguably the true hero of *Lord of the Rings*). When Gabe brought Sam home for the first time in grade school, my dad didn't blink about adopting this redheaded, freckled kid into our little posse, especially after Sam unloaded his comedy routine on us the first night we shared a pizza.

"Funny kid," my dad said, laughing and wiping pizzeria parmesan off his prized beard. "He can stay." Sam's mom was a single parent, like my dad, so over the years, they'd help each other out wherever they could. It takes a village, I suppose. Even a weird village like ours.

As we zoom out into the Pacific Ocean, the boat eventually turns north and hugs the pristine coastline. We pass cabins tucked into the rocky, wooded shorelines, docks snaking into the water where tethered boats bob in the soft wake. Very occasionally we'll pass a sleeping floatplane, but I suppose you'd need one if you were to live this remotely. Not like you can pop down the block for some milk, or in my case, some of Mrs. Gianotti's fresh cannoli.

One of the bigger islands we pass has a huge ferry terminal and marina—that island is clearly big enough for cars and actual stores. Screeching seagulls flock to a moored boat as a fisherman in yellow waders tosses chunks of something into the air for them to swoop in and fight over.

Halfway through the ride, I slide the window next to me open just a smidge—the air is so fresh. It's one of my most favorite things about the Pacific Northwest—the salty smell of ocean water, the calming aroma of dense forest. It reminds me so much of summers at the Oregon Coast, I'm awash in an unexpected wave of emotion. Those were good days.

The orange-juice woman, who actually has a name—Sarah, Tanner's wife—points out landmarks and creatures and birds and funny stories about fishing adventures. She even tells us about the cougar misadventure her brother-in-law Ryan had on one particular island we pass, explaining that the beautiful, cozy house tucked on the shore belongs to her and Tanner and their little girl.

She says they laugh about it now, but my nervous heart doesn't think a cougar attack is a laughing matter. These Canadians might be hardy folks, but the biggest wildlife run-ins I have are with Sherlock Bones and the neighborhood raccoons who poop on the studio doorstep when I don't leave cat food out for them.

Sarah further explains about Revelation Cove and the amenities offered, how we can take a nature walk with Hollie or spend the day at the spa being pampered by Tabitha and her team of relaxation magicians, or how Miss Betty, the Cove's matriarch, is always ready for an impromptu cooking class with whatever fruits are in season.

"As many of you are here for the wedding, as soon as we arrive, the concierge will provide a detailed itinerary for the events of the next few days," she says.

"What did that iPhone ever do to you?" Sam asks, pulling out his earbuds. I look down. As Sarah talks about the wedding, I am white-knuckling my phone.

"Nothing." I loosen my grip.

"Hey, so, it's been a while since I've done any real photography. If I follow you around and carry gear like we used to do for your dad, can you give me some pointers?"

I laugh under my breath. "Very funny, Sam. Can't you see I'm freaked out enough without you giving me shit?"

"You know how to take a good photo, Frankie. And I need some pointers."

"I've seen your Instagram feed. You're doing fine."

"With an iPhone, everyone's a photographer."

"God, Dad would be so proud to hear you say that," I say.

"Sooo, is that a yes?"

"Have you ever shot with these new Nikons?"

He smiles. "I'm a quick study. And you don't have to pay me. I see the worry crease in your forehead."

"It's permanent."

He smiles at me again. Every time he does that, I remember that bloody campfire. "That's a yes, then? It'll be just like old times."

"I'm sure my dad would be eternally grateful for your help."

"And you might be a tiny bit grateful?" He pinches the air between his fingertips.

"I will allow you to be my assistant if you promise to behave and not flirt with any of the bridesmaids."

"Oh, now, wait a second—what's the point in coming to a

wedding if I don't get to flirt with bridesmaids? And how else will I get them to smile for the camera?"

"We're going to throw chocolate at them. You'll see. It's like catnip. They've been starving for weeks to get into their dresses. A few Hershey's kisses lobbed at their feet and they'll smile plenty," I say, the worry creases easing a little.

"You always were the devious one."

"Don't ever forget it."

Sam laughs quietly, replaces his earbuds, folds his book closed, and leans against the seat in closed-eyes bliss. In a moment of bravery, I pull out a camera, take a quick photo of Sam dozing next to me, and then glue myself to the wide side window in the hopes that an orca will pop by and welcome me properly to this land of cougar-hugging, outdoor warriors.

FOUR

SARAH DROPS inflatable orange boat fenders over the side as the vessel edges against the resort dock. The whole trip north, no orcas, but honestly, some of the most breathtaking natural beauty I've ever seen. Sam was right—this place is unreal. Like the Oregon Coast, only more vivid. Green, green, and more green. Birds everywhere, a few seals watching our boat as it sailed by, even a couple of ginormous sea lions lounging on one of the bigger docks. And the air smells so unspoiled and free of traffic.

On our approach from the south, we could see the rolling lawns of the resort's golf course along the western side. Where we disembark, the dock fingers off in both directions, like an organizational chart, other boats of different shapes and engine sizes anchored so they don't escape. There are rowboats too, oars tucked in their bellies, as well as a wall of kayaks.

Our boat rocks gently against the dock, squeaking against the fenders, as if saying hello to the smaller cabin cruiser parked just ahead. Sarah makes one last leisure-activity announcement that we can take out boats to survey the local islands after a thirty-minute safety session.

Sam waits with me to help carry gear. I thank him three times before we're off the boat, and he stops me and insists that if he's going to be my assistant for the weekend, I'm only allowed to boss him around.

"For old time's sake," he teases.

I'm okay with that. I'm a Scorpio. We love bossing people around.

We follow Tanner and Sarah along the docks, up the stairs surrounded by manicured lawns and trees that are just starting to unfurl their spring outfits. The Revelation Cove lodge sits on the crest of the island's main hill, and like their website photos promised, it's the perfect blend of timber and glass that makes it look like it popped out of the ground fully formed. It's way bigger in real life—at least four chimneys, and that's only on the side we can see. Three floors with balconies, some of which appear to have hot tubs, and expansive windows that, as we get closer to the front doors, allow you to see all the way through the resort's midsection.

I get why Nikki chose this venue. It's magical.

Oh gods of photography, please do not let me screw this up.

When the boat crowd finishes checking in, Sam and I move up to the registration desk, and I recognize the tall, curly-haired guy and blond, bright-eyed woman smiling back at me. "I know your faces," I say. "From *The Oregonian* article."

"It's because my crazy wife here enjoys wrestling wildlife in her spare time," the man says, offering a hand. "Ryan Fielding. This is my wife, Hollie."

Hollie, next to him at the computer, bumps her whole body with his, hardly making him move as he throws an arm over her shoulder. She smiles at us.

"I'm going to guess you're the photographers?" she asks.

Sam speaks before I can. "That would be us. This is Francesca Hawes, and I'm her lowly assistant, Sam McKenzie."

Hollie leans against the desk's upper ledge. "Are you here for the Meyer-Nelson wedding?"

My heart thuds. "Yesss ...unfortunately."

"Nicolette Meyer is a little scary," Sam adds quietly.

Hollie laughs and looks around us before speaking. "My spa manager Tabby has been in tears twice today, and it's still too early for wine. Please let Ryan or me know if you need backup. We're used to these sorts of creatures."

"We have tranquilizer darts back here," Ryan says, winking. "As well as wine."

Ryan excuses himself to the concierge desk behind us—a guest is playing the little silver bell like he's auditioning for an orchestra—and Hollie checks us in, apologizing that our rooms are on separate floors. We stash our gear behind the desk so she can give us a tour of the facilities—the spa, the bridal suite, the banquet hall that will host both the rehearsal dinner and after-wedding reception, and the outdoor lawn area that will host the actual wedding. Finally, she gives us a glossy pamphlet detailing the venue for the Friday prewedding excursion, just a leisurely boat trip away to one of the surrounding islands.

We then follow Hollie into the main dining room and she offers coffee and sandwiches so we can go over the shot binder to see if there's anything else we might need to keep Nikki from tearing the place apart.

"It's not nice to talk negatively about our guests, but you guys are in the hospitality business, so we're on the same team," she says, stirring a third creamer into her cup. "Wasn't a guy named Gabe supposed to shoot this wedding?"

"My brother. He broke his leg mountain biking last weekend, so hooray! Here I am!" I stop short of telling her how completely unprepared I am for the terror rushing toward me.

"Between the three of us, I'm sure we can keep Nikki's claws from doing any lasting damage," Hollie jokes. "I'd say I've seen worse, but that would be a lie. Ryan is way more laid-back than I am, so if things get too hairy, we can call him in for interference."

"He played hockey, yeah?" Sam says.

Hollie nods. "And he coaches now. Which is why brides are

child's play to him." She pops the crust of her tiny sandwich into her mouth. "So, shall we get you settled? Maybe a quick stop at the bar for a shot of good-luck whiskey?"

I think this Hollie person is my new best friend.

ONCE SAM and I have delivered the bulk of the gear to my room, I grab each of us cameras to scout with. It only takes a heartbeat for Nikki to smell me on the premises.

"Francesca Hawes!" Nikki's voice bounces off the wide hallway walls. "Stop where you are."

Sam lifts a brow at me. "Brace for impact," he says.

"What in the living HELL is going on here? We hired your *brother* to shoot this wedding and we get you?"

"Good to see you again, Nikki," Sam says, offering his hand for a shake. She takes it tentatively.

"Gabe said he talked to your dad last night and explained everything," I say, scrolling through my texts, preparing to show her the one from my brother detailing his conversation with Donovan Meyer.

"Yes, I know all that but I am VERY concerned about your qualifications to shoot MY wedding. Do you have any idea how big of a deal this is? Was there no one else—"

"I'm sorry, Nikki. I did try to find another photographer to take over for Gabe, but it was too short notice."

"Nicolette. Please do not call me Nikki. I'm not a child anymore, *Francesca*." She slowly drapes her long hair so it falls down her back. She looks like a blond Angelina Jolie, but Angelina from *Maleficent*— after she started wearing the horns. "So, I'm just supposed to make do with you? God, you are so much shorter than your brother." She looks me up and down, her upper lip curled like she licked the snotty side of a slug.

"As Frankie's assistant, I'm tall enough to make sure we get the roots of your hair with every shot."

"You most certainly will not. I want the photos of my *face*. I just don't want all the photos looking up my *nose*."

"There will be plenty of photos of your face, not looking up your nose," I say.

Nikki's eyes are still on Sam. "My dad invited you because of whatever bromance you two have going over software. That doesn't mean we're pals."

"God, Nikki, seeing you is like a breath of fresh air," Sam goads. "I've missed your sunny disposition."

"I'm not the same person I was in *high school*, Sam McKenzie. Seems you haven't changed a bit," she says, turning her laser gaze on me. "Meeting tonight, 6:00 p.m. In the banquet hall so I can update the shot list, now that we're stuck with you." She turns back to Sam. "And he's not welcome."

I turn on the sugar. "Actually, he is. Sam's my assistant for the weekend. We're going to have a great wedding, Nikki!"

"*Nicolette*." She spins on her heel and tries to stomp down the hall, her efforts comical because the plush carpet underfoot absorbs the impact of her freakishly thin frame.

"Why are some women so *mean?*" I ask when the elevator has swallowed her.

"She probably needs a snack."

"Warn all the warm-blooded creatures on the premises. Hearts are the chosen sustenance of Nicolette's kind."

My phone dings in my pocket. I pause and pull it out—office email. Shit, I'm going to have to deal with all that at some point today too. While I'm covering for Gabe, there's no one covering for *me*. Maybe I'll call Lainie before the meeting tonight and ask her to handle some of the office crap.

"Everything okay?" Sam asks.

"Yeah. Studio emails." We head toward the stairs. "The guy she's marrying is probably just as gorgeous as she is. And rich. She wouldn't marry below her station."

"You mean Nicolette Meyer who told Dave the Star Quarterback that she couldn't go to prom with him because his parents drove an American-made minivan?"

"Exactly. Ohhhh, it would be so much cooler if she'd marry someone, like, thirty years older than she is. At least then I could ease my ragey high-school envy knowing that she'll be changing adult diapers before her firstborn graduates elementary school."

"You're twisted," Sam says.

"Like you didn't know that? Come on—I learned from the best." Sam pushes the door open to the stairwell.

I think about my dad, his affinity for youth akin to the queen from Snow White who inhales the youthful radiance of the girls in the kingdom. The longest girlfriend he's ever had was nearly twenty years his junior, and when he started passing kidney stones and couldn't party or hold her bags while she shopped, she quit coming around. She also said his hair plugs looked fake. I did agree with that. He looks much better these days—bald.

We head outside, first stopping to snag two of the Revelation Cove umbrellas sitting in a wire basket near the door. We need to scout possible locations to take some shots of Nikki and her financier, er, I mean, fiancé.

Perhaps to spite the threatening gray clouds overhead, Sam checks the weather app on his phone. He holds up the screen so I can see it—two of the three days have little lightning bolts protruding from bellies of their cartoon clouds. "This is going to be interesting," he says, radiant with mischief.

"Getting electrocuted is not part of the plan," I say. "Too much water around for that."

"It would make a great picture, though. Like Baked Alaska, only Baked Nicolette," Sam says. "Or maybe the lightning can defibrillate her groom when he sees how much this wedding is going to cut into their retirement fund."

"Oh my god, stop. If she hears you ..." I punch his arm.

"Ow. No abuse or I'll file a formal complaint with Human Resources."

"Tell me when you do—I'd like to file a complaint of my own," I say, staring at a rocky mound jutting from the perfectly manicured lawn. "Come on. That might work up there." We follow the path, our steps on the tiny gravel serenaded by the chatter from so many different birds, I'd need an Audubon field guide to identity them all.

The *lack* of "busy" sound is so soothing—no cars, no buses with faulty brakes, no mopeds or motorcycles, no neighbors screaming at each other over whatever sporting event has them riled up today. I'm a city kid, born and raised, but my favorite memories are always situated in places where the city noises fall away, replaced with the quiet only open nature can provide.

"Something else, isn't it?" Sam says, barely above a whisper.

"Gabe is still not forgiven for being a dickhead, but this place is all right." Camera at my eye, I take a deep breath and reassure myself that there is no pressure, it's just a picture, a moment in time, that I can retake or delete if I need to. I know the technical settings for the light we're in; I know how the camera works; I know there are two memory cards in the slots that will hold thousands of photos.

The camera is just an extension of your eyes and your arm, F-Stop, my dad says.

Sam clicks away beside me, and it's then that I realize I've forgotten to give him a tutorial on how the camera works. I step closer as he scrolls through his shots and see that I don't need to teach Sam McKenzie anything. "These okay, you think?" he asks.

I nod. We're saved.

"I guess being your dad's packhorse all those years wasn't a waste," he says.

"You did not learn how to use *this* camera by doing that—this is a digital camera. My dad uses film. This one has more bells and whistles."

"Stick to the basics. Isn't that what he always says?"

Yes. My father does say that.

Sam shrugged. "I bought a camera a few years back for hobby shooting."

"Why didn't you tell me that earlier? Here I've been freaking out that you wouldn't know what you're doing—"

"And I'm telling you to stop freaking out because I know enough of what I'm doing." He offers his hand for a high five.

I follow him up to the rocky mound, down the stairs carved into its opposite side that lead to the beach, up the shoreline, and then back toward the golf course. By the time we're climbing the concrete-and-timber staircase that leads to the pool deck, my legs are shaky and I'm a little short of breath.

"You forget how physically taxing photography can be," Sam says, winking as he offers a hand to pull me up the last stair.

"Shut up. I sit a lot in my job, remember?" I follow him through a rear door and back into the dining area, currently about half full, the huge room warm and welcoming with the low hum of pleasant conversation and the occasional clink of silverware on plates.

"We have an hour before we have to meet with Nikki," Sam says, sliding onto a stool at the bar on the north end of the room. "Let's have a beer."

"I don't want to show up drunk," I say.

"You are not such a lightweight that one beer will put you down." He motions to the bartender. We decide on a spring ale from a Vancouver brewery, and with that first sip, I concede that this was a good choice.

Sam and I catch up on pleasantries—what his mom is doing, who my dad is chasing, where I'm living, even a very brief tiptoe through how Lainie and Gabe are doing. I shift quickly and ask if he really has a semirabid cat named Zod, and indeed he does, inherited from the downstairs neighbor who got a tech job overseas and couldn't take the cat with him.

"Zod. What kind of name is that?" I ask.

"From Superman. The bad guy."

"Ah."

He pulls out his phone and scrolls to a picture of an intimidating, overstuffed tabby with an exposed fang. "He looks like a Zod, don't you think?"

I zoom in on the photo. "I don't know what Zod looks like, but this cat looks like if you fall asleep, he will snack on your face."

Sam laughs. "Nah ... he's a sweetie now. I've only had to have one rabies series so far." He raises his glass, only an inch or so left of his beer. "We're supposed to do this at the beginning, but for good measure, I propose a toast: here's to a successful weekend of keeping Nikki—"

"*Nicolette*, Sam. She is not a *child* anymore."

"—to Nikki Meyer from burning our effigies on the shores of Revelation Cove," he says. We clink our glasses, but Sam's eyes twinkle with beer and trouble. He used to get that look when we'd sneak out of tents or cabins to get into the really good food my dad would hide in the camping bins. Dad told me once that he knew if he hid our favorite treats, and we went searching for them after he was asleep, then we were still kids. The day would come when we'd be looking for his liquor stash instead.

Speaking of liquor, my head is spinny. "You were wrong," I say, setting my empty pint on the bar. "One beer is definitely enough to put me down."

"They make it a little stronger up here," Sam concedes. "I forgot to mention that."

"Well, Nikki better not give me any trouble because I'm feeling just loose enough that I might remind her that she's human like the rest of us." I pause and try to think of a moment when Nikki seemed human like the rest of us.

Sam and I shake our heads at the same time. "No, you're right. Not human," I say.

A raised voice behind us catches our attention. "Oh, what a surprise," I say to Sam. "Bridezilla brought Mothra along." A dark-haired woman with a pin-up girl body—tiny waist and wide hips, white top, black pants, red lips, but cold eyes—is pointing animatedly at the buffet spread, squawking about allergies or something.

"Is that Adalynn Burnett?" Sam asks.

"Not Burnett anymore. She got married. Can't remember what her new name is. Gabe shot her wedding a couple years ago," I say.

We're quiet for a moment as Adalynn's escalating agitation garners attention from more of the early diners. "We absolutely cannot have *any* shellfish anywhere near the bride. You have an entire spread here of clams and mussels and—and—and whatever *this* is! If she even breathes near this table, she will puff up! She's getting married in, like, forty-two hours and you are dealing in instruments of death!"

The poor kitchen staffer under attack tries to reason with Adalynn, explaining that they are very careful with allergies and the kitchen has been made aware of the bride's intolerances and that the resort has Epi-Pens on site at all times as well as trained medical personnel should something go amiss, but *please rest assured no one wants to kill your bride friend.*

"She *was* the darling of the drama department." I lean back against the bar. Drinks AND a show!

"Maybe she'll revive her performance of Ophelia and drop into the water and float away from us."

"She could take Nikki with her," I say.

"No, there are shellfish in those waters. She would puff up."

"Like a puffer fish."

"*Fugu.*"

"Pardon you?"

"*Fugu.* Puffer fish. Did you know that if your sushi chef doesn't know what he's doing and he cuts the *fugu* wrong, it could kill you?"

"I don't think they serve *fugu here.* But if they did," I say, pulling my ponytail tighter, "I'll bet Nikki would be allergic to it."

"And she'd puff up," Sam adds.

"Very unsightly."

"They should stay out of the water at all costs."

"Or they could float in the pool until they shrivel into raisin husks and the sweeper cleans them out," I say. The bartender chuckles under his breath.

"You guys need a mic. This is good stuff."

"Glad to be of service, good sir. Stay for the nine o'clock set," I say, tipping my invisible hat as he takes our empty pints.

"If we sat here until nine drinking *this* beer, they would have to use the Epi-Pens on us," Sam says.

"We'd better save all the epinephrine for young madam," I say. After my horrifying adolescence of living in the shadow of the popular kids, this banter with Sam directed at Nikki Meyer and her lead henchwoman Adalynn Burnett is making me less afraid of them.

Or maybe it's just the beer.

I wish I could have more, especially since Adalynn has finished skinning the kitchen staffer and her pinpoint focus is now narrowed on Sam and me. She sashays vigorously across the short expanse and stops, hands on hips.

"Enjoying the show, are you?" she snipes.

"Hey, Adalynn," Sam says. "You're looking as fierce as ever."

"I am the maid of honor—"

"Matron," I correct.

"Excuse me?" She gives me a once-over. I shrink into myself. It's freshman year all over again and she's a senior and I am a crumb on their coveted corner table.

"I said, you're the *matron* of honor. Because you're married."

Adalynn crosses her arms over her ample bosom, wrinkling the white button-up, Oxford-style shirt that would make me look like I was playing dress-up in Dad's clothes. On her, it looks like fashion. "I don't even know why you are here, *Francesca*," she spits my name, "but I am warning you both that if Nikki gets anywhere near a shellfish, she will puff up like a—like a—"

"Puffer fish," Sam offers.

Adalynn glowers at him and takes a half step closer. "If anything screws up this wedding, there will be hell to pay. We are all on Team Nikki—"

"Nicolette. She prefers to be called Nicolette these days," Sam says.

That shakes Adalynn for a second. "Whatever. We are all on the same team this weekend. My best friend must be married before we leave this confounded island or I will personally murder anyone who stands in her way."

"The shellfish technically are already dead," I say. "So, you couldn't murder them."

"Murder is a strong word," Sam says.

"I agree, Sam," I say, nodding and trying to hold the grin in my cheeks.

Adalynn's pointy, manicured finger is inches from my nose. "Your brother promised her a beautiful wedding and he's not here. Do not speak to me again unless you are asking me to rearrange her train."

As if it's a move they all practice at each other's posh homes in front of wide, gilded mirrors, Adalynn spins on her heel, her thick, brown waves bouncing behind her as she storms out of the dining room.

"She seems fun," Sam says, swiveling toward me.

"God, nothing changes. It's like high school all over again."

"But it's not. You held your ground today, F-Stop. Well done." He bows his head reverently between us.

"It would probably be best if I put some of that beer in a water bottle and just keep it with me all weekend."

"I'm sure that can be arranged," Sam says, pulling his wallet out to pay the bartender.

"No, don't. Just charge it to the room," I say. He's already shaking his head no.

"Booze is on me. Because the entertainment is free." He smiles again, wide and softened by the beer.

Yeah, Sam McKenzie definitely does not have cooties anymore.

FIVE

AS PROMISED, Nikki is holding court in the banquet hall. The round tables are already draped in their Sunday best, just waiting for the shiny silverware and expensive floral centerpieces to make them complete.

"No severed heads. So far, so good," Sam says close to my ear.

Adalynn sits to her right, flanked by seven other women I've yet to meet. Sam squeezes the back of my arm as we move toward the table.

"They're humans, Frankie. Just like us," he whispers, reminding me of my own words from earlier.

"Only in the scientific sense."

"Questionable."

As we're five steps from the table, Nikki checks her nonexistent watch. "Cutting it a little close, aren't we?"

"Hello again, Nikki," I say. "These are your bridesmaids?" I paste on my business smile and say a collective hello. They all look a little stunned.

She slides a folder across the table toward me. "Their names and the order they appear in the bridal party are attached to their individual sheets. I updated this from what you have in the binder, so throw those other pages out."

"I shall do that."

Nikki nods toward the two open seats in front of us. I guess that's our cue. I can feel my pride slipping down my throat like a raw oyster.

"Now, you have the shot binder, and I suppose it's a good thing you were present when we put it together"—news flash: I put the whole thing together. Gabe never does them because he's an idiot—"but now that we're here, I'd really like it if we could get some wildlife in some of the shots."

The table is quiet. "Right ... I think we talked about this before, didn't we?" I ask.

"We talked about *horses*. But this is British Columbia, Francesca. There is wildlife everywhere."

"Soooo, you want me to wrestle a bear for your wedding shoot?"

She sighs and rests her interlaced hands on the table. "*No*, I don't want a bear for my wedding shoot. But the girl who works at the front desk—"

"Hollie Fielding? One of the people who owns and runs this place?" A little respect, if you please.

"Yes, whatever. She said she does nature walks, that there is a lot of wildlife in this area. She said something about otters and eagles and other birds. Maybe ask her what she might be able to recommend."

"We didn't arrange for a falconer this weekend," I say.

"See what you can DO, Francesca," Adalynn cuts in. "This is supposed to be Nikki's special day. Can you try to be accommodating just once in your life?"

I don't know what the fuck she's talking about, but as Sam clenches a hand around my wrist under the table, I am reminded that the proper response here is to grin and just say, "Yes, Nicolette."

Nikki then launches into the music she wants playing during the outdoor photo shoot to help everyone relax, that she has everything loaded onto an extra phone that she'll give to one of the staff members to connect to their outdoor speaker system.

"Only if this music is kept low," Sam says, sounding very official. Nikki opens her mouth to protest, but he cuts her off. "We need to instruct people where to stand and what to do. No loud music."

Nikki slides her hair over her shoulder. Score one for Sam.

The rest of her demands are more for her beleaguered bridal party than us, though she has added a few shots—she wants to be in one of the rowboats "Because I didn't even know they had those and it's so romantic, like a fairy tale!" and then her on the carved rock staircase that leads down to the beach, and of course some of her on the beach but "My dress absolutely cannot get wet. Do you have any idea how much I *paid* for my gown?"

Sam appears to be taking notes on his phone, but in truth, he's typing an ongoing unspoken response to everything Nikki says. I lean over as if to prompt him to add something and it takes everything I have to not laugh at what he's writing.

"Are you even listening?" Nikki asks.

"We're taking notes," I say. "No stone unturned, Nikki. I know how important this weekend is to you."

She squints at me. "I can't tell if you're being patronizing or ..."

I offer my most honest face. "Nicolette, seriously, weddings are a huge deal. It's going to be a really beautiful ceremony. Bert is a very lucky man."

She smiles, and for a fleeting second, fear and maybe regret flashes in her blue eyes, but she recovers quickly, averting her gaze to the dangerously heavy engagement ring on her left hand.

What some people will do for money.

～

"HER FIANCÉ'S NAME IS *BERT*?" Sam says to me in the elevator. "Bert definitely sounds like an old dude." The doors slide open.

"I was always too chicken to ask when she came in to demand I control the weather for her special day. I do know there are no adult stepchildren in the bridal party," I say. "I only wish I were quicker on the draw with the Ernie jokes, but in between worrying about not getting her bazillion-dollar dress wet and finding her an eagle to pose with ..."

"She didn't seem in the mood for jokes," Sam says. "Which is a shame because I have many." He wiggles his phone in front of him.

I stop before my room. "What are we doing for dinner?" As soon as I ask, it dawns on me that maybe Sam doesn't want to be a "we," that maybe he wants to just chill in his room and read or sleep or raid the minibar, which I must ask him to go easy on because it cuts into our tip.

"Honestly? I don't want to be in the dining room tonight. I think I've had enough theatrics for one day, and we still have three days to get through."

"Well, technically only two. We're not booked for Sunday."

"Oh, thank the gods. Then we should definitely spend Sunday entertaining the bartender." Sam grins. His is an excellent plan—I'm going to need all the rest-and-recovery time we can get before heading back to the studio to deal with whatever we shoot in the next couple days. Dumb Gabe can do the editing—I'm sure I'll be plenty busy blocking the door to keep Nikki from barging in to see her photos.

"Room service it is, then. You wanna hang out, or ...?" I ask.

"Yeah, let me change into snack pants," Sam says. I laugh—that's what we called them when we were kids. The best snack pants have an elastic waist and deep pockets to fill with all the junk food a single human child can carry. "See you in ten?"

"I'll warm up Netflix," I say, pushing my door open.

Once inside, I nestle my camera into its bag and dig my phone out to log in to the resort's Wi-Fi. The connection isn't awesome, but it's enough to see all the missed messages from Bryony, including the overtly sad-faced photo from aqua-fit that she's attending alone since I'm here. I pull the sliding glass door open and snap a photo of the utterly majestic surroundings, texting it in response.

OMG. I'm on my way. Let's move there forever, she texts back.

Gorgeous. No words.

I hope you find a gorgeous man to get naked with while you're there too.

BRY, I AM WORKING. NO WIENER TIME.

It's always WIENER TIME.

BYE, BRYONY. Off for dinner. xo

She follows with a series of inappropriate emojis involving eggplants, and though it makes me giggle, I do feel sorry for the eggplant to be assigned such a "prickly" affiliation.

I click on the TV and search what's available, settling on a movie channel that is playing one of the *Fast and Furious* movies. The Rock, lots of cars, and a pasty, brooding Vin Diesel in a tank top. I'm stuffing my second leg into my own snack pants when there's a knock at the door.

"One sec!" I mute the TV and throw the room service menu on the bench at the end of the bed so we can decide what foods we shall be stuffing into our faces tonight, and then hop to the door.

The face standing on the other side is not Sam's.

"Hey, Frankie."

"Uhhhh …" is the sum total of my response. Flashes of senior year, of a first date at a football game between our rival high schools, followed by pastries at a downtown *Star Wars*-themed café, my first (and only) trip to a comic book store, hours spent in the bookstore lounging through the stacks and how impressed I was when he'd buy me books, of reading while he played his video games, my legs across his lap and how he'd stop playing every few minutes just to touch my knee, of making out in his mom's Corolla in the parking lot of his high school at midnight, of losing my virginity in a hotel in Cannon Beach, Oregon, after my senior prom ...

Of him dashing my heart to bits when he broke up because he wanted to be single when he went off to college. Of the unrelenting silence that followed, until he'd get lonely and FaceTime or email, only for us to play the game all over again. Of my dad putting a stop to it all and telling that boy if he didn't leave me alone once and for all, he'd put a hit out.

"Rob? What are you doing here?"

"Can I come in?" he says. His dark brown hair has a touch of early gray at the temples, but we're both turning thirty-one this year, so that's not so early, I suppose. He's leaner and fitter than the last time I saw him. Guessing he's not eating pastries or playing many video games these days.

I step aside to make way for him to enter the room, but the words in my brain are looking at each other with upturned palms murmuring, "What the hell do we do now?"

He gestures to the bench. I nod, rushing to pick up the room service menu. "How have you been?" he asks as he sits. I remain standing.

"Fine. Good. Yeah, good."

"You look great."

I scan my outfit. "We're just settling in. Finished with my client for the day."

Recognition flashes in his eyes, accompanied by a stiff smile. "I saw you earlier—I was going to say hello then, but it felt a little weird. I didn't want to put you in an awkward spot in front of your boyfriend."

"Sam? Sam McKenzie is not my boyfriend."

"That's Sam McKenzie?"

"The red hair didn't give it away?"

"He's bigger than the last time I saw him," Rob says.

"Well, that's what puberty does."

He smiles again, though his lips quiver slightly. He's nervous.

Under all this sheen and polish, dorky, Zelda-playing Rob is still in there.

"So, why are you here?" I ask. My armor is slowly clicking into place as the fog of chaos clears and I remember the last time we spoke and the shitty things he said to me.

"Ah, well, first, I wanted to say hello, but really, I wanted to ... apologize. We didn't part on good terms, and I never really had the opportunity to say how sorry I was—"

"It's fine, Rob. It's been years."

He steals a glance at my bare ring finger of my left hand; I stuff my fists into my pockets.

"I was an absolute douche back then. I could make all the excuses about being young and stupid, but mostly, I was just a huge dick."

"You're right. You were."

"And you didn't deserve that, Frankie. I just really wanted you to know that."

"Okay. Cool. Soooo, are we done here?" I need him to leave. He didn't just tear my heart out once; he did it over and over again, and I let him. I'd get the damn thing duct-taped and superglued back together, and then Rob would call and leave voicemails about how lonely and suicidal he was without me.

And I'd fall for it because I was afraid of being alone. I didn't want to end up like my dad, flitting from one hollow relationship to the next.

"There's another reason for my visit—I was hoping we could make peace, you know, since we're going to be working together this weekend."

"Do you work *here*? At the resort?"

Rob folds his hands in his lap, nestled between thighs that have seen a lot of gym time in slacks that came from the expensive section of downtown.

"My wedding."

The floor is watery underfoot.

I think there's only one wedding here this weekend. Right? Would they book in competing bridezillas?

In my peripheral vision, a car explodes on the television. Plumes of red and orange flames and carnage. Smoke and shrapnel.

A knock at the door. "Open up! I'm starving!" Sam says.

"Who are you marrying, Rob?" My fingertips are ice cold.

He pauses before answering. "Nicolette Meyer."

I shake my head. "She's marrying a guy named Bert. Bert Nelson. You are Rob Whitford."

Sam knocks again. "F-Stop, I swear, if you fell asleep in there, I'm going to go order all the cheeseburgers on this island and not share a single one with you."

"You should probably get that," Rob says, nodding at the door.

Numbly, I move toward it and pull it open. Sam, dressed in snack pants and a smile, has a bucket with four sweaty bottles of the ale from earlier tucked under his arm. "I thought we'd get good and drunk on Canadian beer to prepare ourselves for—"

He doesn't finish his sentence, eyes fixed and then narrowed on the body behind me. "What the hell is he doing here?"

I look up at Sam and whisper, "Please come in and help me. Please."

He nods and follows me into the room, setting the bucket down on the wooden dresser.

"Hey, Sam. Long time, no see," Rob says, his voice sheepish. Good. I like sheepish.

"Why are you here?" Sam says. His tone emboldens me—Sam and Gabe took turns sewing me back together in those post-Rob days.

"He's marrying Nikki Meyer."

Sam's eyebrow lifts. "I thought she was marrying a dude named Bert."

"Bert is her pet name for me," Rob explains. "She wanted something ... different. From who I was before."

"But your last name is Whitford," I repeat.

"Mom and I decided to change our last name right after I graduated from college. We went back to her maiden name because she divorced my dad. Finally," Rob says on an exhale. His dad was a horrible man back when we were dating. Alcoholic, knocked Rob's mom around. It was a bad scene. And I wouldn't have known about the name change because we stopped communicating once and for all by the end of college junior year.

"You're looking pretty posh these days," Sam interjects.

"I came into some money."

"You're gonna need it," Sam says under his breath.

"Anyway, thank you for letting me know that you are the Bert she's marrying. This weekend, I just need you to do your job and smile for the camera. Whatever happened with us was a lifetime ago," I say, lying through the old scars that seem to never heal properly. "Sam and I have a lot of planning to do tonight, so if you'd be so kind ..." I position myself sideways and motion toward the door, arm outstretched.

Rob smooths the front of his button-down shirt. "Yeah. Of course. But maybe if we have a sec, we could grab a drink—"

"No."

"Right." He nods. "Well, it's great to see you both. Thanks for stepping in for Gabe. Nikki said he had to have surgery?"

I stare at Rob. He's not getting another kind word for me that I am not professionally obligated to give.

Sam starts toward the door. "We'll see you tomorrow, *Bert*."

With that Rob—Bert—whatever the hell he's calling himself now—nods quickly and skedaddles.

The door clicks closed. Sam steps closer and places a warm hand on my arm. "You okay?"

"How did I not know this?"

Sam twists the cap off a beer and hands me the bottle, followed by a second for himself. "If he never came into the studio with Nikki for the planning sessions, how would you know? He has a different last name, for Christ's sake." Sam takes a long drink. Another explosion on the TV lights up the darkening room.

"He said he came into some money? Had you heard anything about that?" I plop down on the bench at the end of the bed.

"The only thing I know about Rob Whitford is that he broke your heart a million times, and there was nothing I could do about it," he says. His jaw clenches and clouds move into his eyes. It warms the cold chill wrapped around my heart.

"It wasn't your job to do anything about it," I say. He sits next to me, leaning back against the bed on his elbows. His snack pants are screen-printed with the Seattle Mariners logo.

"Gabe wanted to go break his geeky little legs for the way he treated you. We may have waited outside his school once or twice to encourage him to leave you alone."

"You did not!" I say. The thought of Sam and my brother going to bat for me ... Rob never mentioned that. Then again, when Rob spoke to me after that first breakup, it was only ever about him—how he was so lonely and depressed without me and how he'd made a mistake and if I didn't take him back, he might kill himself. Fearing he'd follow through with swallowing all the pills the school medical clinic had prescribed, I'd take him back. We'd communicate long-distance nonstop for a month or two (we were at different universities), and then he'd call me, usually at two in the morning, and leave a snippy, intoxicated voicemail about how he just couldn't see this working long-term and he was going to have to cut me loose but he wished me all the best.

We repeated this pattern for all of freshman and sophomore years, and every time, Sam and Gabe and Bryony would tag-team to put Humpty back together again. And then, finally (and in hindsight, thankfully), March of junior year, some girl texted me a photo of her with Rob, the two of them naked, and that was the end of it.

I only ever showed it to Bryony, but if Gabe had seen it, he'd be in jail right now instead of laid up on his couch with rods and pins in his leg.

"Don't let him back into your head, Frankie," Sam says, sitting up. He pulls the room service menu onto his lap.

"It would be easier if he looked like shit and was living in his mom's Corolla."

"It's even better—he's marrying Nicolette Meyer." Sam holds his beer out between us, and I clink my bottle against his. "Repeat after me: This is going to be a great weekend."

I take a deep breath. "This is going to be a great weekend," I say, my spirits lifting at the sparkle smiling back at me in Sam's eyes.

MY PHONE SHRIEKS from the bedside table. I fumble for it, groaning as it flips onto the floor and I have to roll to my side to grope for it. I squint through tired eyes at the screen, quickly deciding that second bucket of beers last night was probably not the best idea.

Nikki is calling me. On my cell phone. Not the hotel phone. And it's only 8:00 a.m.

"I cannot deal with this yet ..." I moan. I let the call go to voicemail, sit up, find a water bottle, swallow two Advil, take a pee, and rinse with mouthwash. *Now* I can call her back.

"Good morning, Nicolette," I say.

"Why didn't you answer? Did you listen to the voicemail?"

"I was indisposed. What can I do for you?"

"You'd know if you'd listened to the voicemail. Now I have to say it all again?"

"Is everything all right, Nikki?"

"I was hoping you could come downstairs and grab some casual shots of me and the bridesmaids at the breakfast buffet, before we go in for our spa session."

"Uhhh ..." Did we talk about me photographing them at breakfast? I can't remember. Beer brain.

"It's just that we all look really cute, and the light is beautiful this morning—I know it's not part of what we arranged in the binder, but I could pay you a few dollars extra for some casual shots. They'd be great for Instagram and my lifestyle website."

Nikki has a lifestyle website? And she wants me to shoot photos for her, basically for free, to use on her social media sites. If Gabe were here, he'd tell her to shove it up her posh little butt.

"Okay, cool, so if you could be down here in like fifteen minutes—"

"I'll need half an hour."

Nikki sighs. "Fine. Hurry up or you'll lose the light." She hangs up. I flip off her name as it fades from my screen.

I text Sam. **Her Royal Highness requests our presence to take photos of her eating her oatmeal**. It takes a minute, but then the wavering bubbles indicate he's texting back.

Nothing would please me more. How long?

I told her I needed 30.

Sounds good. Meet you at your door in 28.

U rock. xo. I flop onto the bed and will my circulatory system to make haste with the magic of ibuprofen.

It's going to be a long day.

NIKKI WAS RIGHT—THE light in the dining room is nice this morning. Not too bright, just enough cloud cover that graciously serves as a giant softbox. We use on-camera flashes with diffusers and bounce off the high ceilings to fill in the light from the ginormous dining room windows. Thinking ahead—more like thinking about herself ahead—she'd asked the hostess for a spot near the back corner where not only is the light maximized but where no other guests are seated.

It does all look quite glamorous to see eight gorgeous, perfectly coifed women nibbling on their breakfasts, but the reality is, none of them are actually eating. Adalynn stares at the mini quiche on her plate like she might propose to it; all but one of the other bridesmaids are taking small bites followed by hefty swigs of black coffee.

"A life of beauty is too much for me," I say to Sam, our backs turned as we change settings on the standalone flash units.

"You make it look effortless. If not for those rosy cheeks, I'd hardly know you drank your weight in beer last night," he teases.

"Says the kid who turns into one giant freckle the minute the sun kisses his cheeks."

"Some girls like freckles," he says. The corner of his mouth lifts, and I know exactly what he's talking about: the trip after the one with the campfire. We were at a place in Arizona, the rare hotel stay because my dad was short on time for some magazine deadline and he needed to concentrate on work, not making sure his three "assistants" weren't getting lost or bitten by rattlesnakes in the Grand Canyon. This hotel was nice—all-day buffet, a huge pool, even a gift shop, and we made full use of everything while Dad was out working. We were at the pool, me eleven or so, my brother and Sam both on the edge of fourteen, and these two other boys started giving Sam shit about his red hair. When one of them made a crack about how no girl would ever want to go out with someone so ugly, I lost it.

Because Sam McKenzie, even then, was never ugly, inside or out.

I attacked that kid by jumping on his back and launching us into the pool, me still hanging on like a bucking bronco. The hotel lifeguard pulled us out, him covered in scratches from my ragged nails and me with what would become two decent bruises around my wrists where he was trying to get me to let go. I was banned from the pool, but the three of us wrapped towels over our wet bathing suits and then sat on the bed where we stuffed ourselves with the spoils of our latest vending machine raid. In between inhaling my Butterfinger and Baby Ruth, I traced a Little Dipper pattern on Sam's back in his freckles and told him that girls like freckles and that he shouldn't listen to that dickhead.

Gabe chided me for cussing; Sam blushed with his whole body.

Not so different from right now, when his green-blue eyes lock with mine. Yeah, Sam McKenzie is the opposite of ugly.

"*Francesca*, could you please grab a photo of us toasting?"

Right. Yes. Focus. Literally.

Camera poised for action, I turn and see Nikki and her friends with their long-stemmed mimosa glasses aloft. Sam moves without even asking, and the two of us snap the photos of Princess Nicolette as she and her starving friends share one maudlin toast after another.

Finally, it's done, and the bride and her party make a hasty retreat toward the spa. "Remember that I can't photograph you in the spa itself—against privacy for other guests—but we still have the excursion today, and I'll be ready to grab some shots as you all get ready for the rehearsal buffet this evening."

"But what about tomorrow?" Nikki stops and puts a hand on my arm. We've moved as far as the dining room's entrance, and she is now partially blocking the way for other people coming in.

"Nikki, let's move out of the—"

"Are you not going to be able to shoot me getting my hair done in the spa? Because that is definitely in the binder," she says, oblivious to other hungry guests moving around her like creek water around a fixed stone.

"I'm sure we can work something out—"

"Go. Work it out right now. And then come and tell me that they're going to let you photograph us in the spa. I paid a lot of money to be here, and I'll be damned if some second-rate hotel manager is going to tell me I can't have my photo taken on the most important day of my life!"

She joins her minions who wait on wobbly legs filled only with mimosas. They disappear around the front desk area, headed toward the spa. I should send up some sort of emergency flare to let the poor staff know Nikki Meyer is on her way.

The tall, good-looking guy who checked us in the other day—Ryan—watches as Nikki storms past the front desk. His smile is too wide for this early in the day. "I heard her little speech. I'm sure photographing her while she gets her hair done will be fine. I'll tell Tabby, the spa manager."

"Thank you," I say, flattening my hands on the cool marble check-in countertop. "Seriously."

"I hope the chap who's marrying her knows what he's in for."

"I'd almost feel sorry for the poor schmuck, but he's just as delightful," Sam says, added emphasis on *schmuck*.

"Let us know if you need reinforcements, yeah?" Ryan says, scooping a pile of snow-white folded bath towels under one arm. "And for later, we have plenty of beer."

"Ryan ... you wouldn't, by any chance, have a falconer on site?"

He laughs. "She already asked. The best I can do is a rather sweet golden retriever owned by the chef. Or maybe a goat? We do have a few goats. They're great lawnmowers." He leans closer. "Just keep them away from Hollie. They hate her." He winks, and then he's off.

"Welp, I will go share the good news with the prin*cess*. No falcons. Only goats," I say.

"And a sweet golden retriever."

"We could dress it in a bear suit and tell her it's a Canadian bear, very rare and dangerous, not to be trifled with."

"Sounds like we have a plan," he says, smiling. "Should we get breakfast before ...?" Sam adjusts the camera bag over his shoulder. The borrowed Nikon hangs from around his neck—he looks so natural with it there. Reminds me of my dad. Like a camera is just a part of his body. I always feel like it's an alien attaching itself to me.

"Yeah. Breakfast would be good. I'll be right there."

He nods and slides into the dining room. I pause just long enough to take a deep, cleansing breath, and then I walk toward the spa and into the mouth of the waiting dragon.

SEVEN

EXCURSION: defined as "a short journey or trip, especially one engaged in as a leisure activity."

Yeah, I looked it up. I'm also looking up tips on how to bury bodies without getting caught because Nikki Meyer might be complaining about the spilled contents of her nonalcoholic-mimosa glass for the last time ever in her life.

Water. Water seems to be the best place to bury bodies. It works for the Mob.

And this area of the world has had a weird rash of severed feet washing up still tucked in their shoes over the last decade, so maybe in a few years' time, they'll find Nikki's dainty bones washed up in her Michael Kors boot.

Even Rob—Bert—has the decency to look embarrassed.

That is when he's not stealing glances like he wants to talk. He edges onto the bench next to me at one point and I turn so it's obvious I'm not interested in pretending we're friends. He takes the hint.

The boat is good-sized but today it's only the bride, groom, and the wedding party. No parents, thankfully. I'm nervous enough as is and I'm glad to not have extra critical eyes watching us, especially since the vessel bouncing on the rough chop is not lending itself to great photos. Nikki and Rob don't seem like they're super in love—they only smile and kiss when Sam or I lift the camera. As soon as we get the shot, Nikki pivots to her bridesmaids, and Rob's face dims a little.

I scroll through the photos—I don't feel confident in what we've caught so far, mostly due to the boat's jostling—but Ryan Fielding assures us there'll be plenty of time for photos when we stop. When he quietly jokes to me about dumping the bride overboard, I know I'm in good hands.

Ryan takes us up to a place he calls Rock Bay and then points out tons of different bird species nesting in trees that have grown in accordance with the wind's moods. Even though Sam's weather app promised rain and possible electrocution, the heavy clouds have parted a few inches, and I *think* that's the sun I feel on my face. Maybe.

It looks like one of those thrift-store Jesus paintings for a minute—the sun beaming itself from the heavens in rays so bright, you could reach out and touch them. The green of the towering Douglas fir and shorter, stouter pine trees shine in Technicolor contrast against the dark blue-gray of the pregnant clouds, and the quieting wind means the deep, greenish-blue water isn't decorated with the earlier white-caps that looked like cupcake frosting.

"You're a little green around the gills," Sam says.

"Better now that we're not bouncing."

"Better for everyone." He nods toward the back of the big cabin cruiser where Nikki and her bridesmaids nibble saltine crackers and these round, flat biscuits Sarah Fielding called Digestives. It's probably the most the bridesmaids have eaten in a year.

"Is it just me, or do those two seem a little ... stiff?" Sam says quietly.

"I'd chalk it up to nerves if it were anyone else," I say. "I don't care what's going on behind closed doors. I just need them to smile pretty so we can get through this in one piece."

It's been enough years since Rob and I were a thing that I don't feel any jealousy that he's marrying Nicolette, but it bugs me how he tries to be so attentive to her, and she brushes him off. Maybe she knows something now I didn't back then—maybe the trick to getting Rob to be nice is to treat him like shit.

Thing is, Rob *was* nice for most of the time we were together, at least until that part where we kept breaking up and then I'd go running back. He was a real comedian, fun to hang out with, and he didn't seem to care what people thought of him. He was my introduction to fandoms and geek culture and doing what made you laugh, even if other people thought you were weird. We had some good times.

But this guy now, in his expensive shoes and wrinkle-free shirt, this is Bert. He cares too much if other people think he's weird, so he's bleached all of that color out of his personality.

If I feel anything for him right now, watching him try to get his beautiful fiancée's attention, it's pity.

Ryan pulls slowly alongside a dock attached to a small, rock-faced island with a beige-sand beach. He disembarks just long enough to drop anchor and tie us off. Farther up on shore is a white gazebo with a large round table at its center and a tall black cabinet attached to the gazebo's side.

"Archery," Sam says, pointing toward the far end of the beach. Sure enough, against the rock wall are stacked hay bales awaiting their targets.

"Are you serious?" I look up at him. "They're giving her arrows? Why does this seem like a really bad idea?"

Ryan's back on the boat, hands on his denim-clad hips, his voice loud enough to interrupt conversation. "Ladies and gentlemen, Sarah and I will help you ashore, offer refreshment, and then we will move right into our safety lesson so you can throw yourselves at today's activity. Everyone will have plenty of time to nock and shoot arrows, but today we're booze-free, for safety."

One of Rob's groomsmen pats the flask in his inner pocket and smiles, like it's some big secret and we haven't all seen him sipping from it over the last hour.

"Before we disembark," Sarah says, "I'll ask you to respect the land we're about to walk on. This area belongs to the Kwakwaka 'wakw people, dating back some nine thousand years, with a treaty history that would confuse non-historians," Sarah explains. She points to the bluffs overlooking the beach. "The First Nations people of British Columbia very much treasure the natural world, including creatures, plants, trees, mountains, you name it—so no funny business. This is their land—we will respect it while we're here."

With Sarah finished, Ryan pulls two long bags from under the front benches. Sam offers his help. "Bows. I keep them at the resort or else the critters find a way into the onshore cabinet and chew the bowstrings."

"They don't chew the arrows?" Sam asks, sliding one of the bags aside to make room for the third.

"Not since we switched to plastic fletchings. Plus we only keep supplies here when we have events. We bring out the hay bales at the start of the season, and unless we get a bad storm, they're usually good for the summer. During the quiet months, everything is taken back to the resort."

"Ever had anyone shoot anyone else?" I ask.

Ryan's eyes crinkle handsomely at the corners when he smiles. His teeth are very white—I'm guessing they're not all real, given his former occupation. "Not yet." He knocks on the wooden accent on the boat's side. "Bad for business if guests start nailing each other with arrows."

There's a first time for everything. Let's hope it's not today.

Ryan throws all three bow bags over his shoulders—not heavy, just awkward, he says—so Sam pulls his camera out of our gear pack.

Mine's already around my neck—I was ready for orca, just in case. On the way here, Ryan told us a story about how before he and Hollie were a couple, she was a guest at Revelation Cove and one night, she went out in a rowboat by herself, got caught in a storm, and met three of the orca from the local pod.

"Hollie Porter is the reason for a lot of our safety rules at the Cove," he said, laughing. "Good thing she's cute."

"She saw actual orca?" I asked.

"People never believe her—or about the cougar—but what people don't get is that we see these creatures a lot. And the cougar can swim between islands. It's how they hunt."

I looked wide-eyed at Sam. "They can swim between islands?" Gulp.

"We do perimeter checks every day and have staff who serve as lookouts for big-cat activity. So far, so good," Ryan said. "Plus, the cougar who got me was sick. That was really unusual behavior."

"I still want to see some orca," I said quietly, looking out the boat's window. "I can't imagine seeing some up close and personal."

"If ever in doubt about the truth of the wildness in British Columbia, go to YouTube," Sarah said, smiling. "We've got it all up here."

Cameras at the ready, Sam and I get to work without even speaking to one another—and I'm so glad he intuitively knows what Nikki might want here. Shots of the bridal party offloading from the boat, walking up the dock, walking onto the sand and complaining about how their expensive shoes are (mostly Nikki and Adalynn), complaining because there is no cell signal, complaining because the refreshments Sarah quickly prepares are nonalcoholic and accompanied by yet *another* reminder that Nikki is allergic to shellfish, complaining while Ryan sets up targets and unloads the bows from the bags and arrows from the cabinet, complaining because the glove-style grips Ryan has provided will damage their fresh manicures ...

Ryan handles them like a pro. I guess a few whiny bridal party members is nothing compared to what he faced on the ice.

He uses Sarah to demonstrate the proper way to hold a bow, nock an arrow, and loose toward the target. When he finally shoots, he hits just left of the red on the paper bullseye affixed to the hay bales. Adalynn claps her hands together excitedly and *whoops*, earning her a glare from the bride.

"Ryan, you're like Robin Hood!" Adalynn says, running her hand down his arm. Sarah then takes the bow from her brother-in-law, nocks, and looses—it lands dead-center in the red.

"Little sisters can be so annoying," Ryan teases, winking at Sarah and ignoring Adalynn's repeated attempts to get closer to him.

"She does realize he's *married*, right?" I whisper to Sam.

"I don't think she realizes *she's* married," he says. His whisper against my ear sends a frisson of happy through me, like when you hear a beautiful song and you feel it in your skin.

"Okay, let's come closer and choose our bows. Pick it up, see how it feels in your hands, practice pulling the bowstring back. If the bow feels too heavy to hold upright, pick another. These are carbon-fiber bows, so they're pretty light but you want it to feel like an extension of your arm," Sarah says.

"The NUMBER ONE SAFETY RULE: When one in our party goes down to collect arrows, all bows must be in the down position. There is zero wiggle room on this. If you're nocking arrows while we're collecting from the targets, you are done. Are we clear?" Sarah looks around the gathered half-circle. Yeah, she's definitely a mom. "And you—with the flask?"

The groomsman looks at her, like he's surprised he's been caught. "You will be watching today. No arrows for you."

Bert gives his friend a dirty look and shakes his head. I'm glad Sarah benched him. What a knob.

As Sarah helps everyone choose a bow, Sam and I check with Ryan about the safest places to stand to catch the action. Everything will have to be from the sidelines—no way I'm getting front and center with these weapon-wielding geniuses.

Adalynn is the first to step up to shoot, trying her hardest to get

Ryan to put his arms around her and demonstrate. When Sarah steps in to do this, I'm not ashamed to admit that I captured the look on Adalynn's face with my camera. Sam and I will enjoy reviewing these later.

Once she gets the hang of it, Adalynn is actually pretty good. The Rob I knew was never an athlete, but this new-and-improved Bert is strong and surefooted at the firing line. He tries to get Nikki in to shoot with him, his body wrapped around hers, the arrow pulled back together. She only agrees when I tell her it would make a great series of pictures.

She obliges, turning on the charm, giggling as Bert kisses her ear, giggling more and smiling as his left arm wraps lovingly around her waist while she pulls back the bowstring. They even kiss once her arrow is loosed, and the smiles really do look genuine.

Until I thank them and the camera stops clicking. Nikki's demeanor changes, as if the director has yelled "Cut!" She pushes away from Bert, plodding through the sand toward her bridemaids.

I lift an eyebrow at Sam; he returns the sentiment.

The remaining members of the bridal party each give it a go but their arrows fall point first into the sand, far short of the targets. This brings some much-welcome laughter, especially when the groomsmen step in and try to be manly heroes to "help the fairer sex," and then miss the hay bales themselves.

Soon, everyone's laughing, and it's perfect for our lenses. At last! Some levity!

About an hour in, the archers take turns coming off the beach and tucking under the gazebo to enjoy the new spread Sarah has laid out —fresh boards of meats, cheeses, sliced fruits, and Canadian chocolates, as well as French presses with strong coffee and a battery-operated kettle with an assortment of teas.

So far, the weather has cooperated—the divine sunbeams of earlier have faded and the clouds continue to look mildly threatening, but the lack of bright sunlight is quite helpful for Sam and me. Like the sky is a giant softbox, which means we can get away with using only the small Nikon flashes to provide extra boosts under the gazebo. It's always a good thing when you don't have to drag expensive strobe and softboxes onto beaches—sand is brutal for camera gear.

"How you doing?" Sam asks, stepping next to me. He hoists his camera between us and scrolls through some of his shots. After about twenty images, I throw my arms around him in unbridled relief, my camera bumping against his.

"Thank you. Thank you so much for being here. For helping me."

"And miss all this fun? This is like having a backstage pass to a really bad play," he says, winking.

I drop my arms and watch as he continues to scroll. He's gotten some beautiful shots. "You're doing me and Hawes Photography a real solid, ya know."

When his screen times out, his eyes meet mine. "I'm really glad we're hanging out. I've missed you." And he looks sad for a second with the words he's not saying—he misses Gabe too. When they had their falling out, we all grieved the hole that Sam's absence left behind.

"My brother is an asshole," I say quietly. "I've really missed you too, Samwise."

He bumps me with his shoulder. "No one has called me that in a looooong time." His grin reminds me of when we were kids. I love the way it feels. "Let me see the ones of the lovebirds shooting the arrow together."

"Did that look as fake to you as it did to me?"

"Fake—like carob-isn't-real-chocolate fake."

"Oh man, your mom doesn't still eat carob, does she?"

"Thankfully, that phase passed," he says. I lift my camera and click on the screen. "Damn, yeah, Frankie, those are—"

"OWWWWWW! JESUS CHRIST! WHAT THE HELL?"

Sam and I spin like timed dancers and jog around to the gazebo's front. A few feet into the firing area but far from the hay bale targets,

Rob—BERT—lies on the ground, screaming like a … well, like a guy with an arrow protruding from his calf.

There's a first time for everything.

God, I hate being right.

EIGHT

RYAN AND SARAH descend on Rob, hollering at everyone to put their bows down immediately. The back of his denim pant leg is quickly darkening with blood, and my knees are quickly weakening at its sight.

"Don't you dare faint," Sam says. "I know how you are around icky stuff." He leads me to the gazebo steps and sits me down. "Breathe. I'll see what I can do to help."

Contrary to Ryan's barked orders, Nikki stands with her bow still in her hands, her eyes wide, face pale. "I didn't mean to. Oh my god, I didn't mean to, I swear."

"What the HELL, Nikki? Aaahhhhhh!"

"I didn't *mean* to! It slipped!"

"Bow DOWN!" Sarah says, again like she's talking to a toddler. Nikki drops the bow onto the sand.

Adalynn steps in, dropping to her knees next to Rob, Ryan, and Sarah. "Don't remove the arrow. We need to secure the shaft—cut it if we can—and stabilize it. There's no way of knowing if it's hit the bone—"

"I THINK IT'S HIT THE FUCKING BONE, ADALYNN!" Rob yells.

"—until we can get him to a hospital—where's the nearest hospital?"

The look on everyone's faces ... who is this person and where did whiny, prissy Adalynn go?

"I'm a registered nurse. I just don't work anymore. That's how I know what to do."

"Thank god someone does OWWWWW!" Rob moans.

"Stop moving." Adalynn rushes back into the gazebo and grabs the huge first-aid kit Sarah brought off the boat. She returns with scissors, gauze, medical tape, and an automatic blade. "Okay, Bert, we're going to slice your pants along your calf. *Hold very still.*"

Sam stays next to me, chatting away to keep me distracted from the blood darkening the sand under Rob's leg. But sneaky guy that he is, Sam is also taking photographs of Adalynn being heroic. "Never thought I'd see this side of her," he says.

"Right? It's like she really is a human being."

"Super weird."

Nikki is surrounded by her remaining bridesmaids, the lot of them grimacing at the scene before us, offering soft words to keep Nikki from freaking out. Oddly, she's not crying. For a moment, she even looks annoyed that her fiancé is lying on the ground with an arrow shaft sticking out of his leg.

Once Adalynn cuts Rob's pant leg away, it's clear the arrowhead is completely buried in his fleshy bits. She opts to stabilize the shaft rather than try to cut it shorter. While they work on that, Sarah enlists the help of the bridesmaids to quickly clean up the refreshments. She sends the groomsmen—except the drunk one who gags every time he looks at Rob—to clean up the targets, repack the bows into their bags, and collect all the arrows.

It's a surprisingly smooth operation. Up until the part when we're loading Rob onto the boat and the arrow knocks against something and he starts with the howling again. His cries bounce off the surrounding rock faces, echoing back like a soundtrack from a B-rate horror film. I'd say I feel sorry for him ...

"Stop smirking," Sam says, bumping into me as we wait our turn to load. "They'll see you."

"Let me enjoy this. For just a second."

"Next you're going to tell me it's just deserts for all the arrows he shot into you all those years ago?"

"Something like that. You know how I love a good metaphor."

The drunk groomsman—now sober—actually has a name. "Edwin," he says, offering his hand to Sam and me. "Do you think he's going to die?" he asks.

"I'm sorry—what?" Sam says.

"The arrow. Do you think it will kill him?"

"Only if the hospital is closed and we have to take him out back and saw off the leg with one of those Christmas tree saws. They usually have tetanus on them ..." I nudge my arm against Sam's—Edwin is clearly not in any state to think about bones and saws and tetanus. Normally I wouldn't be either, but again, this is sorta fun.

The shell-shocked faces around us don't make for great photographs, but Sam catches a few anyway, discreetly while Ryan and Sarah help Adalynn position Rob onto his stomach along one of the cushioned benches. Adalynn asks for them to drape a damp towel over Rob's turned head and face to keep him calm—we do that with Lazarus when he goes to the vet.

She then sits with Rob's leg stabilized with more towels and held firmly between her hands as Ryan and Sarah prepare the boat for movement. I don't realize I'm staring at Adalynn until she catches me.

"I'd say to take a picture because it would last longer, but that's a little obvious," she says. Aaaaand she's back.

"I'm really impressed with how you're handling this, that's all."

"What, you don't think pretty girls can have brains?"

"I know a lot of pretty girls with brains," I say. "You included."

Her mouth opens as if the next words are waiting to be launched, but then they freeze. Her shoulders drop, and Adalynn smiles. A real smile, not the fake one she gives Nikki every time Nikki squeaks at her.

I take the photograph.

"Can I see it?" she says. I nod and move across to her, kneeling on the floor next to the bench. When the screen lights up with the photo, she smiles again. "I miss it. Nursing, I mean. My husband makes a lot of money, so he told me I could stop working. He *asked* me to stop working. He didn't like my long shifts because we couldn't just drop everything and fly to Paris for the weekend."

"Yeah, I hate that," I say. She chuckles.

"I miss it, though. The hospital is like a big, weird family." Rob moans as the boat picks up speed. "I felt like I was needed when I was there." Adalynn looks around us, like she's checking to be sure no one else can hear her. Nikki is at the other end of the boat with the rest of the wedding party, Edwin's arm wrapped reassuringly around her shoulders while her bridesmaids pet her hair and hold her hands.

You'd think she was the one with the arrow sticking out of her body.

"Why don't you go back to it?" I ask.

"We're trying to have a baby," she says under her voice. "My husband wants children."

"Your *husband* wants children."

"A rich man's wife has certain ... obligations."

"So you can't have a baby and a career at the same time?"

"And keep all this up?" She gestures at her shapely figure, her perfect hair and makeup, her outfit coordinated to match the day's adventures. "I envy you ... in a way."

"Me?"

"You get to be whoever you want. Dress in regular-people clothes." I'm not sure if that's meant to be a dig. Shopping off the rack at Target works for me; I'm frugal with my fashion choices. I'd make a terrible rich man's wife because I would never spend $800 on a purse. Do you know how much dog food $800 could buy for a local animal shelter?

"I just mean that your family doesn't have a lot of crazy expectations for you. I remember when we were in school, your brother took the photos for the school paper and the yearbook and how he'd miss classes when you guys were going with your dad on his photography jobs. With your dad being who he is, it's not like you didn't know what you wanted to be when you grew up. And you're not married, obviously"—she nods at my ring finger—"so you get to be whoever you want. You get to do *whatever* you want."

"Well, not really. I work for my dad because my English degree is useless unless I get a teaching certificate, and children terrify me." And also because I'm too chickenshit to do anything else.

She laughs again, but it sounds sad. "I worked in pediatrics. There's nothing so inspiring, or heartbreaking, as watching children fight the shitty diseases eating at them. They're such brave little warriors." Her eyes glaze with tears. "It's why I don't want to be a mom."

"Are you scared?"

She nods, her dark, lustrous swirls of hair bouncing with the effort. "What if it got sick or something? I can take care of other people's kids, but my own?" She shakes her head.

"You'd be a great mom," Rob says, sliding the towel free and looking back at us.

"You're not supposed to be listening to girl talk, Robert," Adalynn scolds. "Close your eyes and relax so you don't throw up."

I'd almost forgotten he was there—well, except for that arrow shaft pointing skyward just a foot from Adalynn's shoulder.

A two-way radio crackles from the front of the boat as Ryan speaks to the staff at the resort. Sounds like the plan involves getting Rob into a floatplane for the trip to the closest hospital.

Adalynn sits up straighter, the tension returning to her face. "Anyway, it's good you have a job with your dad. We need hard-working people like you in the service industry." She looks out the window at the passing landscape, and just like that, our bubble of heartfelt sharing has ended.

"Good talk," I say, standing and moving carefully to where Sam is sitting on a side bench. His long legs sprawled in front of him, his head is tilted against the window, eyes closed even though the bouncing boat makes his head wobble too much for him to actually be asleep.

"Look at the images," he says quietly as I sit down. I set my camera aside and pick up his, resting on his stomach, the strap still around his neck. The most recent shots—the bridal party hovering around poor, poor Nikki. "Do you see what I see?" Sam sings under his breath.

Well, either Edwin is again drunk, or he's making a play for Rob's bride.

"Is he kissing her ear?"

"I'm no expert in ear-kissing, but I'm going to guess he wasn't whispering instructions on how to make a pizza."

"Mmmm ... pizza." My stomach growls. I continue scrolling through Sam's photos—he really did capture some beautiful shots—but it's the ones where Edwin and Nikki look a little too familiar that make me uneasy.

Rob—Bert—is her fiancé. He's bleeding all over the back of the boat due to an arrow protruding from his flesh, an arrow Nicolette Meyer put there not even an hour ago. And currently, she's cozied up to one of the groomsmen at the other end of this waterborne vessel.

"Do you think ..."

"That she shot him intentionally?" Sam asks, his green eyes opening. "Let's just say that maybe our buddy Bert should add a food taster to his house staff."

"And why isn't she sitting back there with him? Maybe show that she's a little bit concerned?"

"Maybe because she's not?" Sam says. I click the screen off and sit back against the bench. "You have a nice chat with Nurse Adalynn?"

I turn so there's no way she can see my face—in case she reads lips.

"She just opened up and shared real thoughts and feelings with me."

"Maybe you should consider a career in counseling. You do have that kind of face."

"What kind of face is that?"

"The kind that says you look like you give a shit about my problems."

"Hardly." I lean in closer and lower my voice. "I kind of feel sorry for her. It's like she has to keep up this facade for all these other people—"

"Her 'friends,' you mean." Sam air-quotes.

"But because we knew each other for a minute a million years ago, I'm somehow the safe choice for her to spill her guts?"

"Maybe. It's not like you're going to run and tell anyone."

"Well, anyway, whatever her reasoning, she was nice for 0.9 seconds, and then the viper was back."

"People are so weird," he says, crossing his arms over his chest and leaning his head back again. But his eyes are fixed on me.

"Stop chewing on your lip. It's not food," he teases, echoing what my father has been saying to me since I was old enough to understand words. "Uh-oh, I know that look."

"I feel like we should tell Rob. Bert. Whatever."

"That his bride is probably banging his groomsman? No. Definitely no."

"But what if—"

"Put your armor back on, Joan of Arc. We're here to shoot a wedding. Rob Whitford or Bert Nelson—he's still the guy who tore your heart out of your chest over and over again, who *cheated* on you over and over again. You owe him nothing except a memory card full of photos."

I look over my shoulder at Rob—he didn't replace the towel per Adalynn's instructions, but his eyes are closed. The constant wincing tells me he's not enjoying our trip back to the resort. I am thirty years old now. Thirty-one this fall. I should be *over* this heartbreak—it was years ago!

"What is wrong with me, Samwise ..."

"Nothing is wrong with you, F-Stop. But you also don't owe that little prick any loyalty. His marital woes are not your concern. They are paying you to be here. You are not their friend, and they are not yours." He nudges my shoulder with a closed fist. "Armor back on. We still have a rehearsal dinner to get through before beer o'clock."

Shit. The rehearsal dinner! "Do you really think they'll go through with it? Won't they need the groom to do that?"

The boat slows as we approach Revelation Cove, and my phone in my pocket goes nuts with notifications now that we're within spitting distance of a cell tower. "I think if Nikki wants to hold court at a rehearsal dinner for her fairy-tale wedding, the groom is almost an afterthought."

Sarah uses the on-board intercom to explain that we'll be pulling to the dock in a moment and if we could all wait to unload until Bert is taken to the floatplane, which is waiting and ready to transport him down to Victoria. "That's the best and closest facility to deal with this sort of injury," she says.

"Will he need surgery?" Nikki asks, as if Sarah is all of a sudden a doctor.

"That will be up to the trauma staff—"

"What about the rehearsal dinner? It's in three hours! Will he be back in time for that?" Nikki whines.

Ryan takes over. "Bert will be missing the rehearsal dinner, but I'm sure the medical staff will do all they can to get him back to us for the wedding tomorrow."

"Nicolette, will you be going with Bert to the hospital?" Sarah asks, the intercom mic back on its hanger. "His mother is already on board the plane waiting, so there's plenty of room for you—"

"No. I will not be going to the hospital. Adalynn can go—she's a nurse. I have to stay here and entertain our *guests*." She doesn't even look at Rob as she's talking.

The boat pulls alongside the dock, and waiting Revelation Cove staff spring into action, tying off the boat, opening the side door, and stepping on board with a stretcher for Rob. The whole process only takes a couple of minutes. Adalynn does volunteer to go to the hospital with him, which is probably for the best since Rob's mom, whom I haven't seen in *years*, is not on the plane waiting for her son but instead fretting on the dock. I don't get a chance to say hello, but I will tomorrow.

Despite the motherly panic written all over her face, she looks good—even though I don't like her son, no woman deserves what she endured throughout Rob's childhood. I'm happy she got away from her terrible husband. Rob was a jerk while we were together, but he never hit me.

Nikki stomps toward the resort, barking commands over her shoulder about what they're going to do with no groom at the rehearsal dinner. Sam and I watch them load Rob and take off.

"I think this is working out exactly as she wanted it," I say. "Now *Bert* won't be there to steal her spotlight."

"And I'd say you're absolutely right, Detective Holmes." Sam offers a bent arm. "Come. We need nourishment before the next act begins."

"Is it too late to ask for a refund? This performance is not living up to expectation."

"Are you kidding? The bride shoots an arrow into the groom's leg the day before the wedding while canoodling with one of the grooms-men? Someone get Scorsese on the phone," Sam says.

"Oh man, Gabe's gonna be so sad he missed seeing Rob Whitford take an arrow."

Sam pauses, pulls out his phone. His thumbs fly, and then my phone buzzes in my pocket. "Send it to him," he says. I look at the screen—it's a photo of Rob lying face down in the sand with the arrow in his calf, total agony on his face.

"You're going to win a Pulitzer for this," I say. "And I'm sure we're being completely unethical but so is cheating on me eighty-four times."

"Eighty-four, is it?"

"Once, twice, eighty-four times—does it really matter?"

Sam takes my elbow so I can text and walk and leads me up the paved path toward the resort—I send the photo to Gabe, and of course to Bryony. It'll be a meme before day's end. Good thing Bry's dad is a lawyer so he can represent us in the inevitable civil suit to follow.

Worth it.

It dawns on me how much sand is in my shoes. I hate the way it feels between my toes, in my socks.

"I need to wash my feet."

"Well, you're going to have to do it later. Look."

I glance up from my phone and my stomach drops. Nikki and her mother are storming toward us, and I think I hear the wail of woodland creatures as they flee in terror.

"Be bold and mighty forces will come to your aid," I say under my breath, pasting on my armored smile.

NINE

"WHAT IS your plan to deal with tonight?" Mrs. Meyer asks me. As if this whole debacle was from the inner workings of my evil empire.

"Well, certainly no groom is not ideal," I say, "but think of what a great story this will make for your grandchildren."

Mrs. Meyer's face wrinkles like I've just handed her a fresh pile of dog poo. "Even if I were to ever have grandchildren, I would *never* tell them such a horrible story."

"Oh, you mean, because your daughter shot your son-in-law in the leg with an arrow the day before their wedding?"

"Sam McKenzie. I thought that was you," Mrs. Meyer says, pivoting to face him. He smiles cheekily. "You were an odd-looking boy, but I'm glad to see you've grown into a man who knows when to zip his lip."

"Always a pleasure to see you, Mrs. Meyer. It's been too long." He offers a hand to shake, but she snarls at it. Clearly, he's dipped it in the typhoid of peasants.

She then steadies her gaze on me. "I'm sure a discount will be in order since your brother is not here to do his job?"

"No discount will be necessary, or offered," I say. "Especially since Sam is working for free as my assistant, and he is an excellent photographer."

She *hmmphs* at me. "Let's just hope all those years of tagging along after your philandering father has taught you a thing or two about that camera."

Before I can slap her frigid face, Sam wraps a tight arm around my shoulder. "Hawes Photography looks forward to servicing the remainder of your special event with unrivaled professionalism and artistry. We wish you all the best for an unforgettable evening."

"With what we're paying you, you'd better hope so," Mrs. Meyer says. She snaps her fingers and I swear Nikki jumps a foot.

And with little more than a pinch of wind that smells strangely like barbecue, they're off to primp and preen.

"Do you smell meat?" Sam says next to my ear. We're still watching the iced royalty walk away; we don't dare move until they've been ingested by the resort for fear they sense our heartbeats.

"I thought it was the smell of my laser eyes burning a hole through Mrs. Meyer's Botoxed cheeks."

"Well, that too, but I *think* they might be making food meant for human consumption, food that involves barbecue sauce and a lot of napkins."

The front doors to the resort close behind Nikki and her mother. Concurrently, some of the tension melts out of my shoulders, though not enough to ease the growing headache creeping up my neck and over the back of my skull.

Instead of risking more delightful discourse in the lobby, we follow the path around the huge building's left side, past the heated pool that's filled with brave families risking inclement weather for some gleeful splashing, and to the rear door we discovered this morning. Sure enough, on the deck just outside the main dining room, a young man in chef's garb reigns over a ginormous barbecue.

Speakers affixed under the eaves play soft rock while other resort guests relax in small huddles around individual tables, electric votive candles at their centers. Some eat, some drink, that guy over there is reading. And as the stingy sun pokes her head through a cloud, everyone stretches for the rays like they're hoping to recharge their personal battery packs.

But Sam and I are ruled by our stomachs. He opens the door for me, and I lead us to an open, four-seat table. We should go upstairs and unload the camera gear and start downloading pictures, but we still have a long evening to get through, and I'm going to require energy in the form of messy, artery-clogging calories.

My phone is again going crazy in my pocket. On top of all the Hawes studio business that keeps pouring into my inbox, Bryony and Gabe received their respective texts. And as promised, Bryony is busy turning the photo into memes. Rob lying on the ground clutching his thigh, the arrow embedded deeply in the muscles of his calf, its feathery bit pointing toward the heavens, captioned with:

When you tell her she has enough shoes.

When you spoil the ending of the last episode of Game of Thrones.

When you say that Tauriel the Elf from The Hobbit *movies is stupid and not canon.*

When you cheat on my best friend and are about to marry a pit viper.

That last one is my favorite.

Sam and I order, knowing "rehearsal dinner" does not include plates for us. We agree to abstain from more of that delicious beer until after the event tonight, but by the time we're done wiping the barbecue sauce from our fingertips with one of a zillion premoistened towelettes, Sam looks like he needs a nap. His phone buzzes face down against the tabletop; when he grabs it and reads the screen, his eyes cloud over a little.

"Everything okay?"

He clicks it dark and offers a fake smile. "Yeah ... yeah, just a work thing."

The look on his face suggests it's not a work thing. "Should we go unload these shots and prepare ourselves accordingly?" I ask.

"Why am I so tired? I work way harder than this in real life."

"It's Nikki. She's sucking your life force from you. All brides do this—as soon as they get a ring, their fangs grow in."

"Remind me to never find a bride." He glances at his phone as he says it.

Ah. The text—it's not work. It's from a woman. Does Sam have a girlfriend?

Why do I care? It's none of my business.

Something twinges in my chest, a wholly unfamiliar and uncomfortable sensation. "You never want to get married?"

"I fear I would not be so brave if an arrow found its way into my calf," he says. He has a smear of barbecue sauce on the corner of his lip. I tap my own lip in the same spot; he smiles and wipes clean the sauce, nodding his head.

"Not every bride shoots her groom with an arrow. I don't think anyone on our staff has ever photographed a wedding that involved bodily catastrophe, other than fainting grooms."

"Archery did seem like an odd choice, given the company."

"Just think how bad it could've been if we'd gone to a rifle range," I say, finishing the last of my ice water.

"Thank heavens we're in Canada." He stretches like a lion as he stands. I sign the slip to charge the meal and tip to the room, and Sam follows me out, up the elevator, and down the hall toward my room.

"We should probably spend some time going over my shot lists for tomorrow, making sure every detail is covered," I say.

He checks the time.

"Can I have one hour? Just one hour to close my eyes."

"Yeah. I have studio email to deal with—"

"No. Just take a break. Studio email can wait. Text Gabe and tell him to deal with it."

"Ha ha." He really *has* forgotten what Gabe is like.

I unlock my door and Sam trails behind me, dumping his camera bag on the table. He then flops on my bed—rather than retreating to his own room—drops his phone beside him, and grabs one of the extra pillows. "Set your alarm. Take a nap for sixty minutes, Frankie.

We've had a trying day already." He squishes the extra pillow over his face, just like he used to do when we were kids.

Funny how the little things never change.

Except I only have the one bed in this room. Am I supposed to take a nap next to him? Or in the plush, overstuffed chair in the corner?

What am I supposed to do here?

It's just Sam. I *know* Sam. He's like a brother.

Except he's not. He's nothing like a brother.

So as not to disturb, I slowly slide onto the bed next to him and set my phone alarm for one hour from now. Sam was right. It feels good to rest for a second, to think about what a completely weird day this has been so far. Why isn't Nikki more worried about Rob? Did she really mean to loose that arrow? Is Mrs. Meyer blaming me for what went wrong on the archery range today? And what the hell is going on with Nikki and Edwin the Drunk Groomsman? Does Rob not *see* that? If he does, why is he even going through with this wedding?

It's all so bizarre—the Rob I knew would never have given a woman like Nikki a second glance.

Or maybe he did and I was just clueless. When I knew him, he was a nerdy, soft-bellied gamer geek who didn't care if he wore a *Star Wars* T-shirt to a nice restaurant, and by nice restaurant, I mean Red Robin. Now he's all muscle and expensive shoes and cufflinks and I'm guessing he hasn't seen a bottomless basket of steak fries in a very long time. Maybe when he was just Rob, he was Francesca material, but now that he's Bert, he's Nicolette Meyer material.

My ego grabs an ice pack from the fridge for her bruises.

All this overthinking is not what I'm meant to be doing right now. I check my phone—I've burned through six minutes of precious rest time thinking about stupid Rob and stupider Bert.

I fire off a quick text to Gabe: **Can you please answer some of the emails waiting in the studio inbox? I'm kinda busy here doing YOUR job.**

Phone down, I close my eyes. Deep breathing, exhaling to a count of ten, visualizing the release of the tight muscles in my shoulders, neck, and head. My attempt at a moment's peace is interrupted by a mild but continued vibration between Sam and me on the bed.

My phone is quiet—it's clearly Sam's. And therefore none of my business, especially when he doesn't adjust the pillow over his head to check who's calling him.

The vibration stops, but then starts again.

The next sequence of buzzing isn't a call but rather someone on the other end who is firing texts like they might a gun. *Buzz. Buzz. Buzz. Buzz.*

How does a person text so fast?

"Sam ..." I whisper. Not a word, not a movement from under his starched white bed pillow. "Sam." A little louder. No response.

I sit up. I can't help it. I look at the screen. Three missed calls and a flurry of texts that keep coming, every new one displacing the one at the top as it rolls in:

Pick up the phone.

PICK UP THE PHONE.

SAM! You can't ignore me. Stop being a child.

SAM I WILL CALL YOUR BOSS AND TELL HIM WHAT YOU'VE DONE IF YOU DON'T ANSWER MY FUCKING TEXTS AND CALLS.

You think running off to Canada is going to keep you from dealing with this?

SAMUEL MCKENZIE, you will do the right thing and CALL ME or you will hear from my lawyer.

All of the messages ... from someone named Lisa R.

I can feel my heartbeat in my teeth. Whatever is going on, Lisa R. is *very* unhappy about it, and my red-haired friend is snoring under the pillow that covers his face.

Like a true ostrich.

I set his phone back down and flip onto my right side, trying to ignore the continued vibrations. I'm not sure when they stop—the next sound in my ears is the tinkling of my own phone alarm, pulling me from a restless break that has left me feeling even more drained.

I slither off the bed and into the bathroom to take care of business and floss my teeth and inspect how much touchup my face will need before the rehearsal dinner. Perched on the edge of the tub, I yank my socks off and wash the sand off my feet. I should've done it before the nap—my toes are itchy now.

Sam's voice from behind startles me. "I hope I didn't get sand on your bed."

"I'm sure it's fine. Nice rest?"

"A little. I could sleep for a month. I think it's all this fresh air." He hands me a towel as I turn off the faucet.

"Your phone was blowing up while you were asleep," I say, drying in between my toes without making eye contact.

"Sorry about that. Yeah, it's work. No big deal. They can manage without me for a few days," he says. When I do finally look up, his neon-sign complexion is blotchy, offering a different version of the truth.

"Soooo, you said you wanted to go over the shot list. Why don't I start uploading the earlier photos while you finish with your elf-sized feet, and then we can nail down a plan for a groom-free rehearsal dinner."

I nod, feeling super weird because if Sam and I are friends, I should be able to ask him who Lisa R. is. But we're friends who've only just been hanging out again over the last twenty-four hours after years of distant politeness on social media.

Maybe Lisa R. is one of his software developer friends. Maybe they're working on a project together. Maybe they are in a work spat.

Maybe she's his girlfriend and something has happened and he's not stepping up to the plate to deal with it. Oh my god, she's *not* his girlfriend but maybe a coworker and she's *pregnant* and he's the daddy and he's shirking his responsibilities. Oh man, she sounds so mad, I'll bet she's pregnant with twins.

Which is why he looked at his phone earlier when he made the offhand remark about never wanting a bride.

It's none of my business.

Maybe if I say it a thousand times, I will eventually start to believe it.

Or maybe Sam McKenzie is a big fat jerk like the rest of them.

WE MANAGE to sharpen the list in an hour. Good thing too because my phone dances with text after text from Nikki making changes and asking for this or that and then finally requesting that we come to the bridal suite for more photos of her and the bridal party getting ready for dinner.

Not a single word about Rob, his condition, or when he is due back.

Is Bert OK? I text. Her very short response pings back.

"Rob is fine, according to Nikki. He's coming back late tonight," I tell Sam.

"Wow, so I'm guessing no surgery." Sam wipes his freshly washed face on one of my clean hand towels.

"She wants us in the bridal suite for more photos of them getting ready."

"Let me guess: more lifestyle website?"

"Who knows. Why does someone need so many photos of putting on clothes and makeup? It's not the Last Supper, for Pete's sake," I say, pulling the memory cards from the reader and reinserting them into the camera.

"It sort of is, though."

"You really think this is the only time Nikki Meyer is going to get married?"

Sam chuckles. "No, I don't, but I do think this is the last time our friend *Bert* will be acquainted with so much of his money."

"I'd call you a cynic, but indeed, she will take her cut, won't she?"

I say, double-checking my lens inventory in my gear backpack. I pull out the speedlights to check their batteries.

"Then again, she should get a little something having to be married to that slug," Sam says. "No offense to slugs."

"I'm sure they didn't hear a word." Batteries are still good. "But will he be on crutches for the ceremony, do you think?"

"If he didn't need surgery, that means the bone probably wasn't involved. So maybe just bandages? He does have a lot of muscles these days."

"Now we will hear about how all those hours at the gym building his radiant calves were good for something. *Ha ha ha, joke's on you, Fate,*" I say. Never once did Rob want to go to the gym when we were together—in fact, one New Year's Day, we went to a doughnut shop, got one of those pink boxes filled to the brim, and then sat on a bench outside a local gym stuffing our faces so the sweaty, crying people on the cardio machines could sneer at us. Of course, I was seventeen so what did I know about the importance of cardio, and also I really, really like doughnuts.

"You ready?" Sam loops his camera over his neck.

"Yeah. Sorry. One sec." I text my dad to remind him his prescription refill is waiting for him when he's back in town; I text Gabe with the password to the studio email so he can stop being such a jerk and help out a little; and I forward next week's schedule to Lainie because trying to explain to Gabe where to find it once he logs into our studio scheduling system ... Just easier if I send the whole week at a glance so they both know what's coming at them when Gabe is able to stand upright again.

Finally, I make sure the latest download is in the cloud storage folder and then close my laptop. My own camera around my neck, I quickly paint my lips with gloss, stand, and take a deep breath.

"Don't worry, F-Stop," Sam says, a reassuring smile on his face. I wish I could tell him that I'm now less worried about photographing Bridezilla, and more than curious about this Lisa R. and what terrible sequence of misdeeds Sam has committed to earn such a barrage of acid.

We take the stairs rather than risk getting stopped in an elevator by wedding guests wanting us to take their photos—Gabe warned me about this. Guests will see the cameras and assume "Oh, wouldn't it be great for X and Y to have candid shots of everyone" so then you're stuck taking pictures of people for free, and it's like a contagion—if you photograph one set of humans, they'll tell the rest of the guests, and pretty soon, you're shooting free headshots for a bridesmaid and free baby pictures for a cousin's kid during what's supposed to be your dinner break.

Standing outside the bridal suite, I raise my hand to knock and find that it's shaking. Sam gently wraps his own warm hand around my wrist.

"A few pics, in and out. Then the rehearsal dinner. We know what we're doing. When it's all done, we undertake a vending machine raid. Deal?"

I nod. Lisa R. aside, I'm so grateful he's here.

Inside, it's obvious the bridesmaids have spent more than their fair share of time with the champagne. Empties litter the suite. A young woman who I think is a cousin—named Blaire?—sings along to the music playing in the background, a hairbrush as her microphone, her hair already perfect. A few of the other women provide backup, but Nikki looks like she's going to throw up. And since Adalynn is at the hospital with Rob, she's not even here to hold the barf bucket for our darling bride.

"Finally," Nikki says, moving toward us with yet another piece of paper in her hands. The green tinge of her face fades a bit as she sips from a small bottle of juice.

"You all right, Nikki?" I ask. She ignores the question and stabs a finger at the paper she's just handed me.

"I made you a cheat sheet with the names of the important people who'll be there tonight." I look down the list—certainly enough, she's got herself and Bert (though Bert's name has been crossed off), her family, her bridal party, a bunch of other names, and then wayyyy down at the bottom is Rob's mom's name, all by itself, also crossed out.

My eyes back up, Nikki's already nodding at me. "His mother is the worst. I would've done just about anything to get out of inviting her, so in some ways, this whole situation has worked out perfectly."

Worked out perfectly for whom, Nikki? I bite my tongue.

Yeah, Rob could be a dick, but his mom was a sweet, quiet woman, afraid of her own shadow after years of living under the brutal hand of her ex-husband. And if she's made the trek all the way up here to Canada to see her only child get married, I give her bonus points.

"She'll be in the group shots tomorrow, of course, but I have no idea what she's wearing and she refused to join us at the spa, so her hair is probably a wild mess. I just don't want her to ruin the aesthetic, you know? Once these shots are up on the lifestyle site, I won't be providing a very good example for my followers if there's a weird church lady in the middle of everything. I'm sure you understand," Nikki says, placing an icy hand on my wrist. The polish on her nails might actually be real human blood.

"Also, I talked to the concierge, the tall guy with the broken nose—honestly, why don't people fix things like that—

"Ryan? The guy who helped with Bert's accident today?"

She waves a hand at me. "—and he said they don't have any wildlife here for us to use." She finishes the last sip of juice and dabs her lips with a tissue. "I didn't trust that you'd remember to ask him, so I handled it."

"They did say the chef has a golden retriever," Sam says.

Nikki leans back on one popped hip and folds her arms over her boobs, her face hardening. "I do not want a stupid dog in my wedding photos. God, Sam, you're just as annoying as you were fifteen years ago."

"But not nearly as annoying as that lipstick on your teeth," he says, pointing at her mouth. Her hand flutters to her lips. "Shall we get started, Francesca?" Sam bobs his head once and we set to photographing the scene as Nikki checks her makeup and clucks at her increasingly rowdy bridesmaids to clean up the champagne bottles.

Sam photographs all of it, the scurrying of bodies in their coordinated, tight skirts as they scoop up bottles and drain the last few drops of every glass they stack on the silver service cart, the pillow fight that doesn't quite get started because Nikki shrieks like a wounded harpy, the two bridesmaids near a long table spread with food who are taking turns throwing doughnut holes at each other's open mouths. So much for not eating until the wedding is over.

Nikki manages to regain some control and pulls everyone closer to the windows covered with sheers that provide just the right amount of afternoon light. She barks orders:

"Hair over one shoulder only!"

"Don't pose straight on at the camera—it doesn't look natural."

"Remember your angles like we practiced."

"No double chins!"

"Laugh like you're having the best time of your life."

When a Prince song blasts out of the speakers, it takes exactly three words in for chaos to reassert itself.

"Why won't they listen to her?" I ask Sam, just loudly enough for him to hear me over the blaring music.

"If things carry on like this, a mutiny could be on the horizon," he says.

The suite door opens and in a cloud of expensive, nauseatingly strong perfume, Mrs. Meyer strides into the fray. Four of the eight bridesmaids have arms slung around each other and are shrieking about Prince's crying doves, oblivious to the arrival of the newest wasp, at least until she stops all the merriment with her stinger against the top of the wireless speaker.

"When we go downstairs, the lot of you will not be drinking another drop," she says, eyes scanning the tipsy women. "Nicolette, one would think you'd have better control over this situation. I will not be embarrassed by your thoughtless friends who can't handle their wine."

"Mother, it's fine. They're just nervous." Her bridesmaids giggle behind their hands. Except Blaire the cousin. She's shooting looks of admonishment at the other women, as if just seconds ago, she wasn't the ringleader. Traitor!

Nikki's mom locks eyes on Sam and me, and my heart skips a beat. Her stick straight, ice-blond hair that earlier stretched down her back has since been folded into an updo that looks more like an elegantly frosted cake. Her glacial-blue eyes and demeanor could refreeze icebergs. She must sleep in a hyperbaric chamber because she looks the same age as her daughter.

"Hello, Mrs. Meyer," I say. "You look lovely tonight."

"What will be *lovely* is if we can get through this evening without me pushing any of these morons into the ocean." She closes the distance between us and holds out a hand. At first I think she wants me to shake it, but she nods at the paper rolled in the small black apron I've tied around my front. Useful for holding spare batteries and handheld flash units and single-use tubes of lip balm for those folks with dry, crusty lips. Nothing ruins a photograph faster than crusty lips. Except maybe a booger.

I pull out the shot list and hand it over. She scans it, nods, and then returns it. "I'm sure Nicolette mentioned the situation with Robert's mother?"

"How she's not as pretty as the rest of you so we shouldn't take her photo?" Sam says. *Oh god, Sam, don't poke the Beast.*

"Let's just say that Ms. Nelson has been reticent to accompany us to the spa and she was unwilling to share what she's wearing tomorrow, so I have no idea if it coordinates."

"I'm sure everything will be fine," I offer. "Ms. Nelson is very understated and conservative in her styling, so I'm sure she won't steal any spotlight."

"How do you know Ms. Nelson?" Mrs. Meyer asks. Nikki is close enough that she turns to listen in on the conversation.

Uhhhh ... does Nikki not know that Rob and I used to be a thing? "Before your future son-in-law was Bert, he was just Rob, and we were friends. I knew his mom years ago."

Mrs. Meyer's left eyebrow twitches and I think she's trying to hike it up in distaste, but again, Botox.

"Let's just get on with it. There are a hundred-odd hungry people downstairs and I need a drink," she says, her spinning form leaving behind a cloud of money.

The green tinge is back on Nikki's face, and for the quickest flash, I feel bad for her. I don't remember much about my mom, but I can't imagine growing up with someone like Mrs. Meyer for a mother. She's cut from a whole different breed of arctic.

Sam plucks the shot list from my hand and we put on our photographer faces to finish shooting in the suite. The faster we get this done, the faster we can get downstairs and set up for dinner.

Nikki stops me just as I'm about to change out my memory cards. "I want to see."

"I'm sorry?"

"Show me some of what you've got so far."

I look to Sam for help; he's busy chatting with Blaire and two other bridesmaids who are posing with empty champagne bottles.

I hold up my camera so she can see the screen, and I click through the images.

"Wait—go back."

I do.

"I look demented in that one. Delete it."

"Nikki, I can't delete anything. It all goes into the computer so it can be edited—"

"Are we paying you for your opinion, Francesca? No. We're paying you to take photos that make me look good. *That* does not make me look good."

The screen times out. I click it back on and delete the photo as ordered. Nikki then unwraps the strap from around my wrist, takes the camera from me, and clicks through the images. "Where's the delete button? Seriously, you'd better hope that Sam got some better shots on his camera."

"Please don't delete anything—there is so much we can adjust once we're in the editing studio."

"Can you make me not look like that slug thing from *Star Wars?* God, Bert loves that those stupid movies."

So she *has* seen his geeky side.

"That slug thing is called Jabba the Hutt, and you couldn't look like him ever in a million years." I hold my hand out, waiting for her to return my camera.

Her lips purse as the camera screen goes black again. "When Gabriel called my father and said you'd be coming to shoot the wedding instead of him, I had to get out my old yearbooks. I didn't even know Gabe had a little sister."

"I've been to a party at your house before, Nikki, with my brother and Sam. In high school."

She hands me back the camera. "Some of us are more forgettable than others."

~

I TURN AWAY and dab at the unexpected emotion Nikki's vicious words evoked, pretending I'm just going through my shots.

"Shall we head downstairs?" Sam asks, the back of his hand against my upper arm.

"Yeah. Sure, let's go." I sniff and push my shoulders back as I face him.

"Everything all right?"

"What? Yeah, I think I have an eyelash in my eye. Hazards of shooting with mascara on sometimes," I lie. Sam watches me for a beat.

"You sure?"

"Come on!" I move away from him, away from the windows and

the box of Kleenex. "We should get set up before it gets too nutty down there."

Too late.

The banquet hall is clotted with humans. Panic tickles my throat. "It's darker in here than I thought it would be." I pull off my pack and open two of the small softboxes that we can mount onto the speed-lights. We don't have time or space to set up light stands with strobes and umbrellas—that will be tomorrow—so I hope this works.

"Crank up your ISO a little, aperture as wide as you can get it. Let the flashes and softboxes do the work." Sam takes a quick photo of a couple chatting amiably at one of the candlelit tables. He shows me the picture. "See? We have plenty of light. And we can still get the flame dancing."

He's right. I can do this. It ain't gonna be art along the lines of Dad or Gabe, but the event will be documented.

We take turns knocking required shots off the list: tearful toasts from Blaire the cousin, Edwin the Drunk Groomsman who is actu-ally Rob's best man—surprise!—and then from Nikki's dad, Donovan. As we stroll around the room, I find Rob's mom's placecard at a table along the side, instead of up front where Nikki's hard-plastic family holds dominion, and I'm relieved for her that she's not here.

In that instant, I hate Rob's guts even more. He is his mother's world, and he doesn't even have the balls to make sure she's seated at the main table with the rest of his new family.

Gross.

Once toasts are concluded—ripe with plenty of jokes about Nikki shooting Bert in the leg with the arrow—diners are happy to sit and be served by the waitstaff in their black pants, pressed white shirts, and forest-green aprons. Glasses are refilled and clinked, food is devoured, conversations are shared, desserts are ogled. Even for a control freak she-demon like Nikki Meyer, there's only so much vari-ation in events like this. Eat the free food, hit the free bar, repeat until management kicks you out or until someone drunkenly trips into the front table and does a face plant into the groom's cake.

Which is exactly what happens just as we're rounding the bend on our last shots of the evening.

Drunk Edwin is covered in frosting, laughing his ass off with the frat-boy idiots who take up handfuls of the mangled cake and start flinging it at one another like monkeys. Nikki looks like she might die on the spot; Mrs. Meyer looks like all the blood in her body is about to explode out of her face.

"I knew this was going to be a good weekend," Sam says, ducking as a handful of cake does a fly-by of his head.

TEN

SAM POKES a fork in the direction of my plate. "Can I have your mushrooms?"

"Please. Eat all the mushrooms."

We've survived the rehearsal dinner, though one of the softboxes did take a direct hit of groom's cake. Now that it's washed clean and Nicolette Meyer is tucked safely away in her suite, Sam and I are stuffing our faces with a late dinner in my hotel room while our cameras take turns downloading the night's images.

An image pops on the screen of Nikki's face contorted in open-mouthed despair just after a blob of groom's cake has landed on her bare shoulder.

Sam snorts. "Now *THAT* is the weekend's Pulitzer," he says through a mouthful of steamed asparagus.

"I probably shouldn't have taken that shot, but ..."

"We are here to document. That is our mandate. And document we are."

"Aye-aye, captain."

More photos flick past on the screen. "These are good," Sam says. "And you say you're not a photographer."

"I'm clinical. I'm not an artsy shooter, not like Dad or Gabe."

"Not true. I've seen your puppy portraits."

"Does she look like a golden retriever?" I say, pointing toward the screen.

Sam tilts his head. "More Irish setter, I'd say."

I nudge him under the table.

"That's not a clinical shot. That's one of the realest moments from the entire night."

"I can't believe they had a food fight."

"They're friends of Rob's. What did you expect?" Sam asks.

"Not that."

"I kind of feel sorry for Bert Nelson née Whitford right now."

"You mean beyond the fact that he had to be airlifted to a hospital to have an arrow removed from his body?"

"Yeah, besides that." Sam takes another parmesan-dusted bread twist from the basket in the table's center and tears it in half.

"I don't feel an ounce of sorry for him." I grab the last bread twist. "Do you think Nikki is sleeping with Drunk Edwin?"

"Well, if they're not yet, they will be soon."

"Then why is she marrying Rob?"

"She's marrying *Bert* because she has expensive taste in shoes, and he has the coin."

"Now who's the cynic." I take a long drink from a sweating bottle of delicious Canadian ale. "I need to move to this country. They have excellent beer."

Sam offers his own bottle and we *tink* the necks against one another.

"That smirk looks devious, F-Stop."

"I'm thinking about Mrs. Meyer sewing a skin suit out of Rob's hide in recompense for his terrible taste in groomsmen."

"Ooooh, dark. Even for you."

"You saw the look on her face. And who the hell was she texting while it was all going down?" I ask, ejecting my camera and motioning for Sam to hand me his memory cards. Per my dad's instructions, though our cameras can send the photos to the computer using Wi-Fi, he insists we do it manually, just in case. Spotty Wi-Fi, like they have here, can mess with a photo's data. Last thing I need is a bunch of half-downloaded or pixelated images when Nikki starts harassing me from her honeymoon suite in Bali.

"The speech from the uncle was pretty good, though, you gotta admit," Sam says, pushing his plate away. He picks an errant grain of rice pilaf off his shirt and drops it into his napkin.

"He was such a pervert!"

"What? Come on! Who doesn't want their drunk uncle talking about how hot his niece is or how Bert is going to have to really 'deliver the goods' in the sack if he wants to hang on to his nubile young bride and how all the Meyer men are known for their prowess in matters of the heart?"

"You mean matters of the penis."

"Your words, not mine."

"No, those were his words—he thrust his arm up like a giant boner! I cannot believe they didn't arrest him on the spot."

Sam's laugh echoes off the hotel room walls. "I cannot believe you just said boner."

I tear off a piece of my bread and throw it at him. But only one piece because it's divine and I'd have eaten the whole basket without sharing if I weren't worried about getting into my slacks tomorrow. "Samwise, this is why I'm never getting married." I point at the laptop screen with a butter-slick pinkie finger. "Look at all this time and money spent, the worry and anxiety and stress ..."

Sam takes a swallow from his beer. "You'll get married. One day. You'll find Mr. Right and the siren's call of smooth, white satin and baby's breath will be too much for you."

"I'm allergic to baby's breath," I say, finishing my bread twist.

"Liar."

"Makes me puff up ... like a puffer fish."

He cackles.

And just like that, the earlier messages and calls from Lisa R. come galloping back. I'd nearly forgotten.

I lean forward on the table to switch out the memory cards again. "What about you, Sam McKenzie? Are you really going to be a bachelor forever? Or is 'The One' out there waiting for you to swipe right as we speak?"

He doesn't answer, no smart-ass retort or comeback. When I look over at him, his crooked smile does a weird thing to my heart. And then I feel stupid—I've probably just scraped off the Lainie scab. Again.

"Sorry. I know the whole thing with Gabe and Lainie ..."

"Is a thing of the very distant past." He sets down his beer and rests his hands on the arms of the plush overstuffed chair. "I'm glad they're happy. Lainie and I were so young, and yeah, it sucked, but it wasn't meant to be."

I snort. "You're so evolved these days, Mr. McKenzie."

He shrugs. "Nah. Both of those people have played a huge part in my life, in who I am as an adult. I want them to be happy. Just like I want *you* to be happy."

"I am. I'm perfectly content."

"Again with the lies," he teases. "It's okay to admit that you want more. That maybe one of these days, someone might catch your heart and keep it for themselves. Not all guys are Rob Whitford."

I dig at my cuticle until it stings. "Sam, there have been guys since Rob."

"It's none of my business, but you are more than just my former best friend's little sister—you were always the third side of that triangle. Our third Musketeer. I want you to be happy."

"I am."

"Yeah, your social media profile would suggest otherwise."

"Stalker!" I say.

"Hardly," he says. "Part of the job."

"I think you're taking this big brother thing to a whole new level," I say.

He shudders. "I'm not your brother. But I worry about you. And an Instagram feed filled with nothing but pictures of dogs and doughnuts and takeout sushi—"

"But I love doughnuts and takeout sushi."

"So do I. But I don't take a photo of every maple bar or plate of sashimi I eat. I'm just saying, you should get out more."

I do get out. Bryony and I have our routine. Bookstore, sushi, movies, aqua-fit. He doesn't even know about aqua-fit because I never take my phone into the pool.

Sitting up, I wipe any remaining butter off my fingers and grab my phone. "Well, Mr. Life Is an Adventure, let's have a look at YOUR social media feed, shall we?" Sam entwines his fingers across his flat midsection. I want a man's metabolism. Putting it on my Christmas list.

Maybe I'll find this Lisa R. in his Instagram feed. I scroll through the more recent shots I've not seen—friends, art, and places. The Oregon Coast, the Hollywood sign, the Statue of Liberty—but also a park bench with a dedication to a lost love, a cluster of flowers in the middle of a sidewalk, a stray kitten that makes my heart ache. Fine. Sam gets out more than I do.

And then a few interspersed photos of me and Sam and Gabe when we were kids. Sam and his mom then, and now. (Sam looks like the before and after of Captain America, I swear.) Even Sam and me and my dad, holding up the fish we caught on that trip to Newport, the one with the terrible cheap beer. Sam and I are both green with nausea, but the trout we had on our lines were the funniest part of the picture that took twelve attempts to take because Gabe was laughing too hard. And then as we were offloading at the dock, I tripped and fell and broke two fingers and we spent the rest of that afternoon in the ER getting my fingers set and casted.

I hold the screen between us, twisting so he can see it.

"That was probably the best trip I've ever taken," he says.

"Until the part where I broke bones."

"Especially then." He sits up and leans forward on his forearms.

The dock I fell onto was made of old, tarred logs, so in addition to fingers breaking when they got jammed in between the logs, I took plenty of splinters home with me. Without hesitation, Sam handed our fishing creel and the small cooler of snacks to my dad and scooped me right up. My dad gets a little panicky in situations involving blood or bone—which is where I get it—so Sam directed traffic, so to speak. He asked the dock master about the nearest hospital and then led my white-as-a-sheet father there. Sam held me in his lap the whole time while Gabe held the emptied cooler so I could throw up, and once we pulled into the tiny ER, Sam carried me in so I wouldn't have to walk.

Our eyes meet. I set the phone down on the table and hold up my left hand, the ring and middle fingers that I broke, wiggling them for good measure. "All better these days."

Sam stretches and takes my hand in his, lying it open in his palm before turning it over and inspecting my fingers. I hope he can't see that I'm shaking. "Good as new," he says, returning my hand to me. His face is beet red, and a fine line of perspiration beads on his upper lip. He slaps his hands on his denim-clad thighs and looks out the window into the inky night. "I should turn in early. Big day tomorrow."

I clear my throat, grabbing the last swig of my beer because my brain is a desert and my throat its sandy expanse. "Right. Of course. We should sleep."

Ask him about Lisa R.

My lips won't move.

"Do you want some help tidying this?" Sam moves to scrape and stack our plates before I answer. We put everything on the delivery tray, and he carries it toward the door. "I'll see you at eight for breakfast in the dining room?"

"Sure. Yeah, eight is good. Must fuel up and prepare for the onslaught."

"We can go over any last-minute stuff then," he says, moving aside so I can open the door. He steps into the hall, the tray of dirty dishes between us. "F-Stop, get some sleep. You're going to be great tomorrow."

I cross my fingers and hold them up in front of me. "For luck."

Sam smiles and stares at me for a long second. "For luck. See you in the morning." He then turns and walks down the hall, stopping only to place the tray on a silver cart tucked next to the ice machine. The fluttery, warm, gooey burn in my chest glues me to the spot, watching him walk down the corridor.

Turn around. Look at me. Look at me before you turn the corner.

He does, just before the hotel hallway takes him away.

ELEVEN

"DID you even close your eyes last night?" Sam asks, scooping scrambled eggs onto our plates. As we move through the breakfast buffet line, I'm holding onto our tray like it's a life preserver ring. I know I have to eat, for energy, but anxiety is cutting an angry waltz through my guts.

"Fruit?" His hand is mid swing from the bowl. I nod, soothed by the smell of pineapple and orange. He obliges, followed by buttered toast on both our plates. He grabs two glasses of fresh-squeezed orange juice from the round table at the end of the buffet line, and then I follow him through the buzz of humanity to a spot near the window.

"God, this place is beautiful," he says, sliding onto his chair. With full plates on the table before us, I chew slowly and indulge in a few moments to see this place through Sam's eyes, and not through my own—I'm too freaked out.

Sam's hand lands on my left wrist. "Francesca, look at me."

I do.

"In two hours, you will photograph a beautiful bride getting her hair done. Two hours after that, you will photograph her walking down the aisle. Then family photos, shots of the bride and groom—whom I have been assured is here and ready for action—and the reception. During all this time, *I am going to be right by your side.* I know this is scary, but you got up on stage when you were fifteen and sang 'Somewhere Over the Rainbow' in front of four hundred people when the original Dorothy lost her voice. Remember that?"

My smile wobbles. "That was pretty terrible."

Sam laughs. "Well, it was better when Toto joined in, but you were brave that day, and you're going to be brave today. You are a professional picture-taker. You can do this."

"I'm so grateful you designed that software for her dad so you could get on the guest list," I say. "And I swear to Hades, if you start singing about blue skies and bluebirds today, I will push you into the pool."

He presses his hand over his heart. "I am nothing but a Cowardly Lion, awaiting your orders."

"Lion. Oh god, don't say that. What if a mountain lion swims to this island and eats the bride?"

"Then she will get the wildlife she wanted, and we will all get a reprieve."

The remaining seats in the dining room fill quickly. A gaggle of older ladies sneaks in with their hair in rollers to grab plates of food and then disappear again. A family of five settles at the table next to ours, the parents looking harried as they make sure their three young, curly-haired daughters have exactly what they want on their plates and that nothing is touching or that one sister didn't get more syrup on her waffle than the other. Drunk Edwin and his band of merry cake-throwers wander in looking less polished than perhaps they should on The Big Day, but if my experiences around idiot frat boys are anything to go by, they'll be fine once they eat and take a shot of the hair of the dog.

As we're finishing up, a flash of golden fluff careens in from the main entrance, tail wagging excitedly. I swear I can hear the dog's thoughts: "People! Food! People and food!" She has a pink bandana tied loosely around her neck and the prettiest golden coat—Nikki should definitely be careful inviting this pup to her wedding today. She'll upstage the bride!

An older woman in a Revelation Cove uniform and long white cardigan hurries in, calling what I assume is the dog's name (unless there's a human in here named Acorn), but the dog is happy to give chase and wind her way through the tables, pausing where hands are outstretched for a pat or an offered chunk of bacon. When she makes it to our table, of course I have to get out of my chair and onto my knees so I can give Acorn a proper hug. She obliges, licking my face just long enough for me to grab gentle hold of her scarf so the staff member can catch up.

"Ah, thank you," she says. "The chef's dog. I'm supposed to be dog-sitting. Clearly not going to earn my wage today." The woman's name tag reads Miss Betty.

"No problem," I say, ruffling Acorn's head. "Goldens are so friendly. She just wants to hang out with the people who have all the delicious food." The little girls at the adjacent table are losing their minds over the new arrival.

"Yes, well, this little missy gets all the delicious food she needs and then some." Miss Betty reaches down and takes over control of Acorn's collar. "I hope she didn't disturb you."

"Are you kidding? A dog around this one?" Sam says. "She's a canine magnet."

"I have one of those in the family," Miss Betty says. "Off we go, Acorn. Leave these people to their eggs." She waves and the dog happily trots next to her babysitter, though if that grip loosens at all, Acorn will gladly return and clean up the syrupy mess the youngest child next to us has deposited on the floor.

A server strolls past with a silver trolley, offering tea and coffee. I ask for the largest cup she has. Sam's spoon tinks against the side of his cup as he stirs in cream and sugar, and with both hands around the steaming caffeine, he sips, smiling at me over the brim of the mug.

"What," I ask. "Do I have food on my face?"

"It's just funny to see how some things never change," he says.

"What are you talking about?"

"Sherlock Bones. That beagle at the gas station in Victoria. Now Acorn."

"So? I love dogs."

"And dogs love you," he says, setting his cup down. "Do you remember that year Gabe and I were going to meet some girls downtown for the Starlight Parade? Your dad made us take you with us because you found out there were dogs in the parade line-up and you wanted to take their photos."

"I also remember how those girls stood you up."

He nods, face widening with a smile. "They totally did, but can you blame them? Blind dates with Ron Weasley and the Archangel Gabriel?"

"I think you may have lost them when you invited them to the Dungeons & Dragons meetup," I say, slurping my own coffee.

"Nothing wrong with D&D. You missed out, kid," he says. I snort. "*Anyway*, you were so excited about the dogs, so Gabe and I followed you through the whole parade route as you trailed them. You got some incredible photographs that night."

"Yeah, and my dad picked them apart because they weren't people AND they weren't technically perfect."

"He picked them apart because he wanted you to learn," Sam says.

"My dad always made it seem like me wanting to photograph dogs was dumb. Like it was less important than him chasing an endangered marmot or a desert fox."

Sam's already shaking his head. "Your dad is tough on you because he wants you to be the best you can. He doesn't give a shit if you take pictures of dogs or rodeo clowns."

"Or brides, it would seem."

Sam takes another sip. "You're good at it."

"Shooting brides?"

"There's a distasteful joke in there somewhere," Sam says. "No. Dogs."

"No one gets famous photographing dogs."

"Well, first, that's not true," Sam says, "and second, who said anything about getting famous? Is that what you want?"

"God, no. I've lived with my dad's career, and now Gabe's. I don't want anything to do with that spotlight."

"Which is why you waste your talents by answering phones and dealing with bridezillas."

Even though there are still people in this expansive room with us, it's like a vacuum has sealed off my hearing. My face superheats, and my fingernails embed crescents into my palms.

"Again? Really? You don't know anything about my talents."

"I do, and I know you're not happy doing what you're doing."

"*How* do you know this?"

Sam's shaking his head again. "Because I've known you since you were six. I remember when you wanted to be a veterinarian and then a dog breeder and when you'd glue yourself to the TV when the dog shows were on over Thanksgiving and then that one in New York City—"

"Westminster Kennel Club. It's the biggest dog show in North America."

"See? That's what I'm talking about! I remember when your dad gave you one of his first digital cameras and you started charging the neighbors five bucks for photos of their pets just so you could save for your own puppy."

"A puppy I never got because of my dad's stupid career."

"Frankie, listen to yourself. The world deserves to see what you see. I would bet a hundred bucks that if you put Nikki Meyer and Acorn in the same setting, the photos of Nikki wouldn't stop traffic, but the shots of Acorn would."

"It's a *dog*, Sam. I know my worth."

"But do you?" Sam folds his hands across his front and leans back in his chair. His eyes don't leave my face.

Nicolette's voice from last night rings in my head: "*Some of us are more forgettable than others.*"

Shit. Is she right? Am I forgettable?

Is Sam right? Am I unhappy working for Dad and Gabe?

My heartbeat thuds in my ears and my cheeks might be smoking. Napkin plucked from my lap, I drop it theatrically onto my half-empty plate. "And what about you? Are you living your fullest life? Dodging calls and texts from Lisa R. because she's a 'work thing' and you can deal with it later?"

The light drains from his eyes, like a bulb has been shut off. "She's a colleague. Nothing more. And how do you know about Lisa?"

"Your phone. Yesterday when you were napping. It was blowing up, and you slept right through it. I didn't mean to look, but it wouldn't stop buzzing the bed."

He nods and looks down at his hands, now clasped on the table-top, his plate pushed out of the way. "It's a complicated situation."

"So complicated that you are okay to dissect my life, but you won't tell me a thing about yours?"

His mouth opens, and then closes again.

"It's fine. Like I've been telling myself for the last eighteen hours, it's none of my business." I stand, my chair snagging on the carpet and almost dumping me on my ass. Not the graceful exit I was going for.

I dig into my pocket and pull out a second key card for my room, thrusting it in his direction. "I'll meet you outside the salon in an hour. Grab your gear from my room. Camera, two speedlights with Gary Fong diffusers. I'll have a reflector and small softbox. Make sure there's a memory card in the slot and a second one in your pocket."

"Frankie, wait—"

"See you in an hour." I'm off, weaving through the tables, eyes on the exit. I'd intended to stop by the front office to see if I could get some more face time with Acorn, just to calm my nerves, but the unexpected stinging in my eyes pushes my feet forward.

I am *not* going to let Sam McKenzie crawl into my head and tell me what's wrong with my life. I didn't let him do it when we were kids, and I'm sure as hell not going to let him do it now.

And I will ignore that little bitch of a voice that tells me he's already in there.

TWELVE

THE SHRIEKS REACH my ears before my feet reach the door.

"I specifically said that I wanted an updo with carmine-red lisianthus wrapped into the curls—these obviously are *not* lisianthus! They're not even red! Baby's breath is so 1985—I *cannot* have this in my hair! Is there something wrong with you?"

I slip into the salon, not surprised to see that Nikki's face is flushed and blotchy from her tantrum. Clearly she hasn't made it as far as makeup yet. Before she notices I'm there, I snap a photo of her angry reflection in the mirror. I am not above blackmail.

The woman she's going off on stands with a comb in hand, waiting for the wave to settle, but the look on her face is stern. She's listening respectfully, but she's not cowering to Nikki Meyer. I like her.

"We were not able to get lisianthus in *any* color, and certainly not carmine-red, which is pretty rare. Our usual floral supply outlet in Vancouver had a bad run of fungus gnats, so they didn't have any fresh stock. Flying it in from the States would've been very expensive and not in the budget you provided. I thought this would be a reasonable alternative. It's lightweight, it photographs nicely, and it doesn't wilt."

"Well, you thought wrong. No baby's breath," Nikki says, crossing her arms over her chest.

Today is going to be the longest day of my life.

IN THE END, Nikki's hair is sans flowers, but the resulting updo is spectacular—any embellishment, other than the small tiara tucked into the sculpted hair (of course she has a tiara) would be too much. She tosses orders at Sam and me throughout the spa session—"Get photos of the girl doing my makeup."

"Grab shots of the bridesmaids being cute."

"Can you take an artsy shot of all the makeup and stuff on the counter?"

"Get one of me in the reflection. Make sure to get my good side."

"Take a photo of my feet."

"Take a photo of my hands."

"Take a photo of my demonic personality that you can see if you look at me out of the corner of your eye."

Sam and I let the shot list guide us, throwing a little checkmark next to the contracted photos we've grabbed. Every time Nikki throws in a new angle, my editing time for these photos increases. Alas, a problem for next week, a problem for idiot Gabe who can prop his pinned leg on a cushioned stool and fix whatever detritus I capture with his cameras today.

As we're nearing the last bobby pin insertion and the last stroke of the contour brush over Nikki's perfect cheek, I excuse Sam to grab shots of the exterior setup where the actual ceremony will take place. "It'd be nice to get some images without all the humans in it yet."

"On it," he says, camera bag thrown over his shoulder.

Once the spa staff are finished with Nikki and her bridesmaids, the lead stylist, Tabby, helps arrange what actually turns out to be a lovely photo. Nikki sits in the chair, and her bridal party stands around and in front of her. Gabe will be so impressed by the symmetry and lines in this photo. I even get the lighting right, though it is made easier by the lofty skylights that bathe us in soft morning hues.

Once I've got that shot in the camera, Nikki stands, barking orders at what's next and at Adalynn who just cannot stop digging at her own updo. Something about a pin stabbing her in the scalp. Just as Tabby moves to inspect, an insidious grumbling issues from over-head, a bit muffled as we are in the heart of the building, but present nonetheless.

"Is—is that *thunder?*" Nikki asks, eyes wide. "Do NOT tell me it is thundering. Oh my god, seriously. Of all days?" She spins and glares at Tabby. "Do you get a lot of thunder up here?"

Tabby, still fussing with Adalynn's painful hairpin, shrugs her shoulders. "No. Hardly ever, in fact."

I lift my camera high enough to pretend I'm looking at the photos so Nikki doesn't see the smile on my face.

"I cannot *believe* this. We are getting married outside! In an hour!"

"I'm sure Ryan and his team have contingencies in place. Did you not discuss this as part of your wedding package?" Tabby pats Adalynn on the shoulder; Adalynn nods and thanks her, mouthing "Much better" before taking her place next to Nikki.

"I wanted to get married outside, which is why we chose this place."

Tabby looks skyward. The clouds above are still white and puffy. "No rain yet. Might just be a single roll, a couple of clouds wishing you a happy wedding day," she says. "Now, you all go upstairs and get into your wedding clothes, and I will look into what's happening down here. I'll send Ryan and/or Hollie and their people to your suite in just a few moments, once we do a walk-around of the cere-mony space, just to make sure everything is A-OK."

Nikki's nodding her head, the pout on her face more appropriate for a five-year-old than a grown woman about to be wed. She flinches as another peal of thunder detonates overhead. "I cannot believe this," she mutters, pulling the belt of her robe impossibly tight and charging out of the salon.

Once the last bridesmaid has cleared the door, Tabby steps to her station, hands moving independently as she tidies. "Ninety percent of the time, I love this job," she says, smiling at me. "The other ten percent is reserved for days like today. Agony."

"Why can't you control the weather, you beast? One star on Yelp for you!"

"It wouldn't be the first time," Tabby says just as my phone buzzes.

Text from Sam, with a photo: ***It's thundering. Also raccoons like wedding flowers***.

"About those ten percent days ..." I hold up the photo of a raccoon nibbling contentedly on a blush of flowers pulled off the end of one of the aisles of white ornate wooden chairs.

"Did I ever mention that raccoons are my very favorite?" Tabby says, walking me out of the salon. "Good luck to you for the rest of today." Another roll of thunder.

"Do you suppose she's angered the gods?"

"And probably the demons too," she says.

I stop against the far wall and text Sam. **Tell me they've shooed it away**.

LOL. Raccoon is gone. Nikki will never know.

Going upstairs now. Meet me at the suite. Time for shots of bride in dress.

He replies with the generic thumbs-up. What do I expect after I was so rude to him in the dining hall? I know he's just trying to help—and he's right. He knows me from way back, years before we were troubled by the pressures of adulthood. He knows the *real* me who did want to be a vet and who did want to be a dog breeder, but who chickened out and took the easy way because she also didn't want to disappoint her father.

I hate that Sam sees all that.

But I also kind of like it.

But I also kind of hate it. What business does he have, prowling around in my motivations and ambitions when he clearly is leading his own messy existence?

Everything is perfectly fine as it is. As I click through the photos from the salon, I reassure myself that Bryony and I have a comfortable system worked out that keeps us both from falling prey to broken hearts and other maladies and side effects of romantic pursuits. The last date I had was with a client who came in to book a photo session. Super handsome guy, very polite, even impressed my dad. But when Gabe came blasting into the studio after the session with a camera full of shots of this guy—and his mistress, and his wife who happened upon the photo shoot after receiving a tip from a mutual friend— welp, that took that guy right off the proverbial table. Just as well. Gabe reported there were accusations of genital warts thrown into the air at the park where they were shooting, in between bouts of hair-pulling and pine-cone throwing.

So Sam picking at me that I'm not meeting my potential, or whatever he said ... did he even use the word potential? Oh god, is he getting to me already? Is he right? Am I not meeting my potential working for Dad and Gabe? But they need me ...

Even if working for them makes me "forgettable."

"Hey, Frankie." My head snaps up and a shiver washes over my arms. Not the good kind.

"Rob. Or Bert. Sorry. How's your leg?" I don't see any crutches, and his pant leg looks stretched to its max, I'm assuming from underlying bandages. He's holding a plate with fruit and a bagel smothered in cream cheese.

"It's okay. Sore as hell, but it missed the bone. Just a few layers of stitches. Good thing I have strong calves," he says. *Ding! Ding! Ding!* I wish Sam were here to hear this. We should've put money on how quickly Rob/Bert would mention his muscles.

"That's good. Crutches would've sucked for today."

"Yeah ..."

"Why'd she shoot you?" I don't even mean to ask it.

"I'm sure it wasn't on purpose."

"Yeah, you're probably right." I think for a millisecond about mentioning Drunk Edwin, but nahhhhh.

The lobby is filling with people in wedding finery. Serving staff ply guests with hors d'oeuvres and demitasse cups of coffee served from handheld trays; Ryan and Hollie direct folks to choose seats outside, assuring everyone that a canopy has been erected to protect the ceremony from any potential rain.

"What are you doing down here?" I ask Rob. "Shouldn't you be polishing your gold in preparation of your coming nuptials?" Scrooge McDuck pops into my head.

"I'm about to get dressed. I was just coming down to get my mom something to eat. She's a bit tired after our long night, plus she's nervous." *Nervous because her new daughter-in-law is little more than a playground bully.* "She'd love to see you—Mom, that is. I told her you're the photographer today."

"I saw her briefly waiting on the dock yesterday. She looked worried, but wow, she's a whole different person. I look forward to photographing her today," I say.

"I'll tell her you said so," he says, looking down at the plate, which shakes ever so slightly. "If you decide you want to talk—"

"About what? We've said everything we needed to say. And you're getting married in an hour."

"I just want to know if maybe there's a chance we can be friends going forward."

"Rob, this should be the least of your concerns right now. Focus on one woman at a time today. Make that Nikki. No use digging up ghosts."

A warm body sidles up next to me. "Everything okay here?" Sam asks, standing closer than necessary. He's taller than Rob; I'm weirdly grateful. I need Rob to feel as small as he's made me feel over the years.

Rob reaches out and clamps his clammy hand around my wrist. I stiffen. "Your forgiveness would mean a lot to me, Frankie."

Sam moves a half step forward, and Rob lets go, as if I've burned his flesh.

"You run along now and put on your wedding suit, Bert. Wouldn't want anything to mess up this perfect day, especially after yesterday. You need all the luck you can get," Sam says. Rob casts one more hang-dog look at me and then limps away, just as another roll of thunder booms overhead, bringing a stab of lightning with it.

"I'm a big girl. I can fight my own battles, Sam McKenzie," I growl.

"Thunder, lightning, but no rain," Sam says, as if I haven't spoken. The space between us breathes again. "Seems weird."

"Seems perfect," I say, brewing in my own storm as I head to the elevators, Sam hot on my heels.

THIRTEEN

THE BRIDAL SUITE is more of the same—Nikki barking orders, a harpy in a white dress. I keep the camera at the ready in case she takes flight and shoots flames from her orifices. Bryony's voice echoes in my head, telling me to be nicer. "We women have to support each other, Frankie. Don't be judgmental."

Of course, Bryony is right. But I'm *nervous*. And I'm not even really sure Nikki qualifies as woman *or* human. I feel so sorry for her bridal party. All except Adalynn look like they're about to: (a) burst into tears; (b) commit murder; (c) both.

Nikki's dress is stunning, and while I'd pinned her for a sleek mermaid or slim-fitting silhouette to show off the body she clearly works hard for, I was wrong. She's full-on princess today, sweetheart neckline with ample but tasteful cleavage. The absence of sequins is more than made up for by the exquisite bodice lace and a tasteful belt with a clasp that probably is real diamonds and not rhinestones. The mile of fabric on the white, petticoat-supported skirt is embossed with a similar lacy pattern.

It's a big dress, the kind you see debutantes trying on during those cable TV wedding-dress reality shows—but it is *gorgeous*. Nikki looks like a Barbie doll, the one I coveted as a kid but my dad refused to buy me because he felt that Barbies sent an anti-feminist message to impressionable young girls. I now see he was trying to protect me from hating my woefully underperforming physique, comparatively speaking, but I still want that damn Barbie.

Sam and I do our best to capture the moment without intruding. We get Donovan Meyer, Nikki's father, as he strings a lush pair of new pearls around his daughter's neck, when Mrs. Meyer helps her into the matching earrings, the rare moment of tenderness when her red-faced dad has put his martini down and her sharp-angled mother has retracted her claws, and the two of them don't look like they're going to tear each other to bloody shreds.

We capture as Tabby, on a tall stool, finishes pinning the light-weight, midback-length veil into the tiara, and as Adalynn and the other bridesmaids pose, as if they're buttoning up the back of the dress (it's actually a zipper). Despite Nikki's contrary attitude that one can only attribute to nerves at this point, I do get her to lift the dress to show off her garter belt and white satin Louboutin heels.

The furniture has been rearranged to give us space to photograph the bridal party against the fireplace wall, the bricks and surrounding all painted a soft eggshell that reflects the light beautifully.

We pause so Nikki can have her face powdered and her lips touched up; Sam and I double-check we're not missing anything. The primary reason I have avoided wedding photography all these years: If you forget ANYTHING from the big day, it's impossible to recapture it. Brides are very unforgiving when it comes to stuff like that, which is why I've instituted policies and built checklists and spreadsheets for Gabe, and even my dad—he was so used to shooting the outdoors that when finances dictated he had to specialize on humans for a while, he needed that guidance to be sure we'd keep clients happy.

Rob's mother, in a well-tailored, mint-green pantsuit and not church lady at all, smiles behind her hand like she used to. Before, it was because she had a missing tooth from a blow to the face. And then it's like she catches herself, drops her hand, and smiles more fully. The tooth has been repaired, and she looks beautiful.

Surprising since the way Nikki made her sound, I thought she'd have a third eye or a ragged stump in need of tending.

She sees me watching her, walks across the suite, and wraps me in a warm hug. She even offers one to Sam, remarking how much he's grown and changed since we were kids. We only have a moment to chat as we're meant to be photographing the ongoing drama, but I promise her that tonight, once the cameras have been put away, we'll catch up. Her eyes sparkle when she smiles, and it warms my stomach. It's so good to see Mrs. Whitford—or Ms. Nelson, I suppose—looking so happy and healthy after all the traumas she sustained in years past.

Hollie knocks and enters with a plate of tiny puff pastries, I'm assuming as a means to soften the news that their team has in fact unfolded the earlier erected canopy so that the guests are completely protected from the temperamental elements.

"I did not want to get married in a *tent*," Nikki complains.

"It's not a tent. Well, I guess technically it is, but it's top of the line. I know it's not what you wanted, but the front end where you and your groom will be standing is constructed of one hundred percent clear vinyl, so you can see right through it to the stunning landscape behind. It'll make for some beautiful photos, if past weddings are anything to go on," Hollie explains.

Thunder rolls overhead, and she places the tray of pastries down on one of the painted-wood side tables. She steps closer to Nikki, bending to fluff the corner of Nikki's stunning dress. A hush falls over the room.

"Nicolette, you look amazing. You are going downstairs in a few minutes to marry the man of your dreams. It doesn't matter if you're in a tent or on a beach or in a tin shack. All that matters is this moment, how breathtaking you look, how beautiful your bridesmaids are, and how much that man downstairs loves you."

Nikki's posture softens. She reaches out and takes Hollie's hands in hers. "Thank you. Thank you for saying that. You're right, of course," she says through a hiccup, tears threatening to spill over. Adalynn thrusts a lace-edged handkerchief in Nikki's face.

Hollie releases Nikki's hands and turns to all of us. "Now, shall we let these fine photographers finish their shots so we can get you downstairs and into the waiting arms of your groom?"

Sam and I shoot and shoot to make sure not a single moment of the prewedding excitement is missed. Hollie is the perfect stage manager, passing out bouquets, helping with last-minute makeup, straightening bows and ribbons where necessary.

Knowing we have covered all that can be covered and with the grand moment imminent, we march downstairs to the tent ahead of the bridal party.

And Hollie understated this tent—it's very cool. Plastic windows framed into the canvas walls, high-pitched roof, light fans circulating the heavily perfumed air, and sparkly lights along the framework that bathe the entire space in fairy dust. A string quartet seated in the northeastern corner plays softly. This whole thing looks like a movie set.

Sam and I huddle in the back corner for a moment. "Check your battery. And we're going to need flashes in here," I say, pulling out my silicone flash diffuser. He echoes my movements.

"Battery is at three bars," he says.

"Put a spare in your pocket." I pat the server's apron tied around my waist; my spare batteries are tucked right where they should be. Sam fumbles with the diffuser over the end of his speed-light. I help him secure it so it won't sproing off mid ceremony and smack some unsuspecting guest in the back of the head. "Plenty of white in here, which is perfect. It's like working in a giant softbox. Position the flash at an angle to bounce off all these white surfaces," I say.

I run through a few tests to make sure shutter speed, aperture, ISO, and flash settings are in sync, and then dial in the same numbers on Sam's camera. I don't know how much experience he has with flash shooting in an enclosed area, so I must be particular. This is when being a clinical shooter helps.

"I know how to use the camera, Frankie," he teases.

"I just want to make sure."

Thunder explodes again, followed by a juddering flash of light.

An older woman at aisle's end near us, her outfit more appropriate for a drum circle than a wedding, grabs the seat back in front of her. "Ooooh, this storm is right over us," she says, eyes wide. "Bad luck to get married in a thunderstorm."

"Hush now, Mariah. No one needs to hear that," her companion says. On closer inspection, her companion is her twin. Like, *identical* twin. "It's bad luck enough to be marrying into this ridiculous family," the twin says.

I don't have time to engage these ladies, plus it's not my business, but I quickly ascertain that we're standing on the bride's side of things. The primary difference between Mariah and her twin, beyond their taste in hairstyles—the second lady's hands are dripping with diamonds and gemstones.

"Nice that they've put us all the way at the back, isn't it?"

"Crazy aunties are best at the back," the second twin says.

"We're not crazy. We're eccentric," Mariah says. She reaches a veiny hand toward me. "They call you eccentric if you're rich, so my advice to you, young lady: get rich and *then* lose your marbles."

"Nah, you're just *weird*, Mariah," her sister teases.

"Maybe, but I'm still rich." Mariah drapes her palm over her sister's jeweled hand and then looks up at me again. "I'm two minutes older, you see, and for twins, two minutes means you're the boss." They cackle wickedly as another roll of thunder unfolds. Mariah turns her head and winks at me; I hear the click of Sam's shutter near my head and realize quickly that she's not winking at me at all.

"Where can I get one of those?" Mariah nods toward Sam.

"Let's sit at their table," he whispers.

"You always did have a thing for patchouli oil," I say, my back turned so the sisters can't hear me.

"It's the beads and little bells on her skirt. I'm a sucker for beads and little bells."

I laugh and shake my head just as the music changes. "Oh, we're up! Groom's coming in."

Sam and I split like we've been caught with our hands in the cookie jar. I take point near the front. Glorious wildflower arrangements are perched atop white pedestals, dripping with ivy and white lacy flowers I don't know the name of. The officiant walks quietly past and takes his position under the white, flower-decorated arch at the front. Next, a markedly limping Rob, Drunk Edwin, and the other groomsmen start down the aisle. I shoot them from the front, Sam from the back, and then we move opposite each other, like opposing magnets, to the respective sides of the guest seating to capture every possible angle before the music changes again to announce Nikki's arrival.

I nod toward the door to let Sam know I'm going out to follow her into the tent.

Enough distance stretches between the tent exit and the side doors of the resort that a canopy to protect from the elements wouldn't be practical, and as I step onto the gravel pathway, a heavy drop of rain hits me right where my hair parts. I skip-run toward the building, and through the glass double doors, I see Nikki freaking out, her hand not holding the bouquet gesturing wildly.

As soon as the door opens, the raised voices roll over me like a wave as Adalynn and bridesmaids try to reassure Nikki with the stack of umbrellas sitting in a pile on a tablecloth-covered table. Nikki's father finishes the drink in his martini glass, slides it onto the table, and picks up an umbrella.

"Stop being a spoiled brat. It's hardly raining. Right?" He looks at me.

"Yeah. Yes. Just a few drops. And the tent is miraculous. You're going to love it."

Nikki sniffs at me. "Hold that over my head. I swear to GOD,

Adalynn, if any part of my hair or dress gets wet, I will never speak to you again."

"Before you open the umbrellas, I need to get some shots of you here, before you enter the tent. Your last moments as a single girl, Nikki!" I say, trying to infuse sincere enthusiasm. It sounds fake even to me. But the umbrellas are put aside for a second and everyone pastes on their best wedding faces—it's sort of alarming how quickly their faces morph from angry and biting to smooth and pleasing.

And once I announce I have what I need, the angry/biting faces resurface.

"Don't scowl, Nicolette. Your face will get stuck like that," Mrs. Meyer says.

"And Botox isn't cheap," her dad says under his breath.

My hand involuntarily touches the worry lines between my eyebrows, the lines my dad says have been there since I was born.

More thunder. Another blast of lightning.

"Let's move, shall we?" I say, hoping we can get from one structure to the next without getting zapped. Pretty sure umbrellas conduct electricity.

For once, everyone listens. The bridal party lines up, umbrellas are opened, two Revelation Cove employees open the doors while four others hold umbrellas over the bridal party. One even follows alongside me, umbrella lifted to protect my camera, so I can I walk backward ahead of them as they move up the path. I click like a maniac to get THE moment before Nikki enters the tent and wows her guests, washing people in that weird, soft "everything will be okay after all" feeling that comes when one attends a wedding.

Once we reach the "porch" of the tent—a wide, covered area just outside the main entrance—umbrellas are collapsed and handed off, the bridesmaids are lined up, and Mrs. Meyer is escorted to her seat by an usher (Nikki wanted to walk down the aisle with both of her parents, but the aisle is too narrow and the dress is too ginormous to accommodate three human bodies). The veil is arranged; the train is fluffed and straightened. The music changes again, and then one at a time, the seven bridesmaids and Adalynn, the *matron* of honor, take their leave of the bride and sashay into the tent, coordinating bouquets clutched against their fronts.

"You ready to do this? You can always back out," Nikki's father says, hiccupping.

"Have another martini, Donovan," she snarls. "Just a few more minutes, and I won't be your problem anymore."

"You will always be my problem, dear girl."

I keep taking photos to hide how completely awkward it is to be listening to them. Isn't this a moment when a father and daughter are supposed to have that last moment of happiness, where the dad will share some sage advice as his baby girl walks into the arms of another man?

Weddings are bizarro. I'm going to elope.

The satiny curtains are again pulled aside, this time to invite the bride and her father into the tent. I move ahead down the aisle, hoping I don't trip. I'm damp with nervous sweat—while I *know* people are looking at the bride, me being dressed all in black in the middle of the very white aisle and around all these very white, pinched faces makes me feel like everyone is staring, waiting for me to screw up.

Worry shoved aside, I throw myself into capturing every angle of Nikki and her dad as they move down the aisle. A quick look toward Sam—I see he too is doing his best to make sure no memory goes uncaptured.

I turn my focus on the bridesmaids and groomsmen, and on Rob, whose eyes glisten with emotion as he sees Nikki walking toward him, a wide smile pasted on his face. How does a person get teeth that white?

Nikki and Donovan Meyer reach the dais. "Who gives this woman to this man to be wed in holy matrimony?" the bald officiant asks as he pushes his wire-framed glasses up his bulbous nose. Looks like a proper pastor in his white robe and purple sash.

"Her mother and I do." Donovan Meyer stretches his daughter's hand toward Rob. "I hope you know what you've signed up for, kid."

Nervous titters—not quite laughter—vibrate through the tent, tailed by another huge boom of thunder. The pastor makes a joke about God offering his blessing for this union, and I'm grateful for his quick efforts at relieving the tension. No one photographs well when they're tense.

Nikki steps up onto the dais next to Rob, and they face one another. The pastor embarks on a lengthy speech about love, honor, responsibility, which is great and wonderful, especially when punctuated by the loud snores of Weird Aunt Mariah. Turns out this tent has very good acoustics.

Someone across the aisle gently shakes her awake. "Is the priest still talking? Jesus, they talk a lot," she mumbles, her chin dropping to her chest again. Grinning mouths are politely covered with hands to hide their shared amusement.

But Aunt Mariah's right—this guy talks *a lot*.

Finally, he gets to the part about "Does anyone here have any objections as to why this man and this woman should not be joined forever in the sacred bliss of marital harmony," and dammit, I should've been faster on the draw to catch the surprise on everyone's faces when Drunk Edwin moves to the front of the dais and raises his hand like he's in first grade again.

"I do. I object."

And the thunder overhead drowns out the eruption of human lava inside this very white, very expensive vinyl volcano.

FOURTEEN

SAM IS next to me in a literal flash. Of lightning, that is.

"What the hell is happening right now?" he says, leaning to the side so he's right next to my ear.

"I have no idea. I need to text Gabe. I don't know what to do—"

Sam stills my hand as I dig for my phone in my apron. "Don't text Gabe. We can figure this out." Our voices are just above a whisper, but still low enough that, I hope, the closest guests can't hear us. The front of the tent is a cacophony of yells and insults and spirited finger-pointing, and thank heavens Rob's other groomsmen have the presence of mind to step in between him and Edwin before someone throws a punch. Though I doubt Rob would put up much of a physical fight—he's awfully pale, hopping a bit to take the pressure off his injured leg.

Nikki is off to the side, surrounded by Adalynn and Blaire the Cousin and the other bridesmaids; the sole flower girl, about six, sits on the edge of the whitewashed-wood dais, legs swinging as she picks her nose and wipes her treasures on the nearest folds of satiny décor.

I lead Sam to the back of the tent so we can be out of the way but still positioned to get a wider shot should the shit really hit the fan. More than it already has.

"What in the bejesus is going on up there?" Aunt Mariah asks. She's definitely awake now.

"Uhh, when the pastor asked if anyone objected, the best man did. So now they're fighting," I say.

"I told Monica that this family is cursed," she says, nodding to her sister before looking back at me. "That dumb young man should run as far and as fast as he can."

"He can't run, Mariah," her twin, Monica, chimes in, smile bordering on wicked. "The bride shot him with an arrow yesterday."

"Like I said before—cursed."

Donovan Meyer grabs Drunk Edwin by the scruff and throws him off the dais; his landing on the laps of shocked front-row guests is accompanied by shrieks and hollers. Then fists are unleashed, Donovan Meyer going after Edwin, half the groomsmen trying to pull them apart, the other half throwing awkward punches at a scrappy, muscled guy who looks distantly related via the icy Meyer eyes and hair. Even two of the bridesmaids are after Edwin, nails and teeth bared—one looks like she might be a kickboxer.

Rob makes to hop toward the carnage but his mother uses her outside voice from the front row and demands that he freeze. Smart move—he looks like he can hardly stand up—so instead, he just hurls insults.

Seems to me he should be hobbling over to talk to his bride.

"This looks like one of those European soccer games," Aunt Mariah says. "Hooligans, they call 'em."

"It's called *football* in Europe, Mariah," Monica scolds as she stands, her own phone poised to record the action. In fact, most of the guests now have their phones out and held aloft, recording the show. Well, at least those who aren't scrambling for the exit to avoid being caught in the melee.

Sam lifts his camera, and one eyebrow; I nod.

And we start shooting. You never know—they might need documentation for the coming depositions.

THE FIGHT IS RUDELY INTERRUPTED by the sound of an airhorn battering our ears. Ryan stands in his dark-green-and-khaki ensemble with his hand raised high at the back of the tent, flanked by four of his beefiest staff members, including one huge guy all in black who must be their security guard. Everyone up front freezes.

"THIS WILL STOP NOW," Ryan commands. Grown adults in expensive wedding clothes clamber to their feet, shaking out their bruised hands and dabbing at their bleeding cuts with offered handkerchiefs and tapping at blossoming bruises on cheekbones and sucking on bloodied lips. Nikki's veil is torn and her bouquet ruined —she used it to beat against her father's back as he pinned Drunk Edwin to the ground and slapped at him. Fights on TV and in the movies are so glamorous and choreographed—in real life, fights look, well, ridiculous, all flailing arms and uncoordinated, unmet punches and scratches and unbalanced kicks. No one looks like Bond or Jason Statham or Wonder Woman when they throw a punch.

"This is gonna go viral," Aunt Monica says to her sister, not even attempting to hide the glee in her voice as she taps at her screen to finish up the video.

"Link it to my favorite animal rescue page. They could use some donations," Aunt Mariah says.

"If this wedding is over, then parties need to disperse. I don't want to call the RCMP, but I will—they have units on the water and can also be here by helicopter in minutes." The tent quiets. The pastor, huddled behind the booger-covered curtain, steps into the light.

"Are we to continue with the ceremony, or would the parties like to regroup and consider their options?" he asks.

Rob looks at Nikki, and she looks back at him—and in that moment, I swear we all hear his heart break.

Looks like he won't be getting his happily-ever-after today.

"Anyone who is injured, please report to the front desk and our first-aid attendant will see to you," Ryan announces. "Everyone else—the reception will carry on as scheduled, commencing in two hours. The food's been paid for, you all need dinner, and I refuse to let it go to waste after my staff has worked so hard to prepare it."

The guests murmur to one another—I think they're relieved they will indeed get fed tonight.

"Mr. and Mrs. Meyer, Ms. Meyer, Mr. Nelson and Ms. Nelson, a word, if you please?" Ryan says, gesturing for the wedding party to accompany him to more private environs.

Mrs. Meyer stands. "If you please, ladies and gentlemen, give us a moment and we will return to you with an update on what the rest of the day shall look like." She glares at her daughter, and then at Drunk Edwin crouched on the edge of the dais with a pocket square against his bleeding nose, before turning back to the gaping crowd. "This is most unexpected, but we appreciate your patience, and your discretion, as we seek an acceptable resolution."

Discretion. I bury my laugh in Sam's arm—there are no fewer than a hundred cell phones recording the mayhem.

Rob's mom helps him from the dais and down the aisle, his limp so bad he can hardly walk, followed by Mrs. Meyer, her frigid eyes straight ahead. Donovan Meyer reaches to take his daughter's hand, but she slaps him away and stomps past, her father following reluctantly behind, his formerly white pocket square soaked red where he holds it against his lip. Drunk Edwin really got his licks in—Mr. Meyer looks more hamburger than human at this point.

Three bridesmaids and two groomsmen form a single line—two of the guys help Edwin off the low stage—and file down the aisle and out of the tent, not at all ordered or reverent like they were when they entered just a short while ago.

Once the wedding party is gone, the gossip machine cranks into full tilt.

"Now what?" Sam asks.

"I have noooo idea."

"You always did have a nose for adventure," Sam says. "Remember that time at Magic Mountain when Gabe and I went on the Superman Escape ten times but the only time you went on it, it broke?"

"That had nothing to do with me."

"Or when we took you with us to the last night of that under-twenty-one dance party thing in downtown Portland and someone let off tear gas?"

"Again, nothing to do with me, Sam McKenzie."

"I'm just saying ... when you're around, things have a funny way of going sideways."

"You're suggesting *I* cursed this wedding?"

"Not at all. This wedding was cursed the day that Rob Whitford said yes to a date with Nicolette Meyer," he says, his smile wide. "I'm just saying that hanging around with you never fails to disappoint."

"You're welcome." I pat my phone in my apron pocket. "I should call Gabe."

"Why?"

"Because he's going to *freak out* that I screwed this up—my first wedding gig, and look!" I say, gesturing toward the disordered front seating and smashed flower arrangements.

"That wasn't your fault. Are you going to tell me you feel guilty it's thundering too? Did you have control over that?"

I bite my cheek. "Sam, I was supposed to be able to show my dad and Gabe I could handle this—clearly I haven't."

"Again, not your fault. You were doing great—*still* are doing great. Nicolette's poor choice in grooms has nothing to do with you."

"Still ..."

"Hold off on calling Gabe until we know what's going on. And stop biting your cheek. You're going to make it bleed," he says. "Come on. While we're waiting, let's go find Acorn." He pinches his lens cap into place.

"We should probably wait and see what's going to happen here."

"Nothing's going to happen here. Do you really think they're going to go through with the wedding now?"

I shake my head. "Do you think that maybe Nikki and Drunk Edwin will get married?"

"Here? Today? This isn't a Hallmark Channel movie, F-Stop. Besides, I saw the cake top—it has a blond bride and a brunet groom, and Edwin and his blond, surfer-boy hair doesn't match. Come on. We'll be back in five minutes, ten at the latest."

Hmmm ... I pause next to the eccentric aunties. "Ladies, if I give you my cell phone number, will you text me if and when the bride and groom return? I'm going to step out and take some exterior photos, just in case they reconcile."

"Certainly, dear." Aunt Monica hands me her phone. "And I'll send you this video too. You get insider access." She winks awkwardly—the false eyelash on her left eye is coming unglued.

"Thank you so much," I say, giving back her phone and then following Sam out into the persistent thunderstorm.

Inside the main building, Sam and I start toward the front desk but then I spy Acorn asleep on a huge dog bed just behind the concierge counter. The woman from earlier—Miss Betty—stands next to her, the phone handset against her head. I gesture toward the dog; she nods and smiles.

"Acorn, hey, sweetie," I say, kneeling. She springs to her feet. She's gotta be quite young—her golden-yellow coat is still puppy soft. Her excitement at new friends suggests she can't be more than a year old.

Miss Betty hangs up. "What in the world is going on in that tent?"

"Not a wedding," Sam says.

"Ryan and our security guard, Thomas, and three other guys went flying by and then a few minutes later, the bleeding wedding party came through the lobby and disappeared into the ballroom. I had to shoo all the staff out. Never seen the like," she says, shaking her head. She leans forward on the counter, resting on her elbows. "Then again, I've never seen a bride and groom more ill-suited for one another."

"Really?" Sam asks.

"Oh, yes. That bride has been hiding in corners all over the building with that other sandy-haired man. I thought he was the groom until Hollie corrected me."

I stand, my hand resting near Acorn's head as she licks my palm. "That would be Drunk Edwin, the best man."

"Well, I think that young bride chose the wrong groom. And this is proof," Miss Betty says, her hand flattened toward the hall where the ballroom resides.

"Hey, would it be okay if we played with Acorn for a few minutes? Frankie here is obsessed with dogs, and she's got quite the eye for photographing them," Sam says.

"Oh, now that would be lovely. I'm sure Acorn's dad would happily pay you for some photos—"

"Absolutely not," I say. "It would be my pleasure. If I get some cute ones, I'll send them on over, no charge." I rub Acorn behind the ears; she licks my cheek. "It would be doing me a favor."

"I wasn't sure when Joseph brought that pup to the resort, but I swear Acorn has become everyone's emotional support animal," Miss Betty says, smiling. "Is it raining?"

"No, just thundering."

"That's so odd. Do you want to take her outdoors?" She bends slowly behind the concierge desk and grabs Acorn's leash, handing it over. As soon as the dog sees it, she bounces on her bed, nearly sending it flying from underneath her.

"I'll maybe play with her in the lobby to get some photos—does the thunder scare her?"

"Nothing scares Acorn." She hands Sam the leash, a little pouch of doggie treats, and a couple of poop bags. "If you go outside, probably best to take her to the side opposite the wedding tent. There's plenty of lawn over there and no stairs to the beach. She loves the beach. You won't get her out of the water once she's in!" Miss Betty's laugh makes me wish I had a grandmother.

"Come on, Acorn!" I say. She follows me across the lobby and behind the front desk area where there's more space, and some awesome skylights. Sam doles out the treats, which I use to get Acorn to be adorable, snapping photos that are—yes, really good. When Acorn starts sniffing around, we opt to snap on her leash and brave the thunder so she can do her business.

Acorn leads the way, showing us to her favorite pee spot, and once she's done, Sam unclicks the leash and spots a lonely tennis ball next to the shrubs. As soon as the dog sees it, she barks like mad, already running in anticipation. It all happens so smoothly—Sam throwing the ball, Acorn being awesome, as dogs are—I grab some photographs that will not only thrill Acorn's dad but that also make me a little proud.

"Is that a smile I see on your face?"

"Sshhhh, don't scare it away," I say, clicking a shot of Acorn in midair, jumping for the ball. "If only brides were this easy."

"Maybe you should keep a pocket of cookies and a manky tennis ball with you from now on," he says.

"For the record, this will be the last wedding I ever photograph." *Click. Click. Click.*

"And it's the Wedding That Never Happened. You must have a guardian angel watching over you."

Acorn flops panting onto the grass, jumping as a roll of thunder booms overhead. The storm is moving away from us finally, but it's still loud as it bounces off neighboring mountains. Sam reattaches Acorn's leash and nods toward the resort.

Neither of the Weird Aunts has texted me in the thirty or so minutes to say we're back in action, but we should probably check in to see what's happening anyway. And Acorn looks like she needs water.

"I don't even know what to do with the wedding photos I have," I say, taking Acorn's blue nylon leash from Sam. "Like, will they even want them now?"

"I'm sure Nikki will want the ones of her being glamorous for her lifestyle website," Sam says.

"But do we photograph the reception, or are we, like, done?"

"Dunno. But they'd better feed us. I'm still an invited guest to this wedding, and I didn't come all this way to get cheated out of a piece of that cake," Sam says, holding the door open for us.

Miss Betty directs us toward the kitchen so Acorn's dad can get her some food. I show him a few previews of the photos we took, and I swear he looks like he's going to cry.

We leave Acorn with Joseph, though I promise to come back for a proper goodbye before I leave Revelation Cove. Our timing is impeccable—as we're walking out of the kitchen, Nikki and the rest of the wedding party have just exited the ballroom. While the obvious external bleeding has stopped, the red faces and stained mascara suggests that the party is definitely over.

There's no way through it except through it, I hear my dad saying in my head. "Let's get this over with," I tell Sam, walking toward the group, now stopped at the front desk.

"So, just that we're on the same page here—"

"The wedding is off," Donovan Meyer announces, before his wife or daughter can utter a word. Rob and his mother stand to the side, both looking like, well, like this dream wedding day has been smashed to a million pieces by a cheating bride.

"Oookay, soooo, do you want me to continue taking photos or—"

"No more photos. Whatever you have, we can deal with next week when we get back to the city," Mrs. Meyer says coldly.

"I want the lifestyle shots," Nikki says, black tears streaking her face. I can't figure out why she's crying. "For my website."

"Whatever." Donovan Meyer flicks the air with his hand.

Sam steps in. "And you will remit the remainder of the photography package fee to Hawes Photography, plus tip, with no problem, correct, Mr. Meyer?"

Donovan Meyer blinks, as if just now seeing Sam McKenzie for the first time. "Hey, Sam," he says, offering his bruised-knuckled hand for a shake, his blustery exterior calming for a beat. "Yes, of course, it's not the little photographer's fault my daughter is a moron." He gives me a curt smile.

Nikki sniffs at her father's insult. I sort of feel bad for her, her dad calling her a moron ... but not really. She is sort of a moron. Plus she's not very nice, so there's that.

"Let's go make an announcement to the guests," Mrs. Meyer says. "I'm sure the lot will expect to be fed."

"Well, they did travel all this way expecting a wedding," Rob says. He sounds angry—this is good. Rob *should* be angry. He drapes his mother's hand through and over his forearm and hops toward the tent, making eye contact with me for a quick moment as he passes.

Sam and I trail the party back outside, our cameras quiet while the announcement is made that the wedding will not proceed as planned, that any gifts brought to the venue can be collected "with our apologies" while those sent beforehand will be returned in the weeks to come. Lastly, "Please convene in the ballroom for an early dinner."

Rob and his mother lead the procession of their half of the tent. Once they've cleared and are back in the main building, Nikki's side slowly empties, though I'm surprised at how many people stop and pat Nikki's cheeks or the back of her hand, as if she's the victim here.

I guess no one really knows what to do in situations like this.

No one except the Weird Aunts who are still in their seats, passing a silver gemstone-encrusted flask between them. "You owe me a hundred bucks," Aunt Mariah says to her sister.

"For what?"

"I told you she wouldn't go through with it."

"You and those stupid tarot cards," Aunt Monica says. She

catches sight of me looking at her and offers the flask. I smile but respectfully decline.

"Well, me and those stupid tarot cards were right, so pay up, sis," Mariah says, her softly wrinkled palm flattened between them. I'm shocked when Aunt Monica digs into her Louis Vuitton wallet and pulls out a crisp one-hundred-dollar bill that Mariah promptly stuffs into her ample bosom.

"So, Mariah, do you think the bride will marry the best man, then?" Sam kneels and asks.

Mariah looks at Sam, her old eyes watery but still sharp. She looks up at me. "Girlie, if I were *you*, I'd take this ginger snap out behind the barn and do unholy things to him."

I'm not sure who is blushing harder between Sam and me, but Aunt Mariah's face lights up with devilish glee.

"Okayyyy, on that note, ladies, do you require an escort into the ballroom?" Sam asks, standing and offering his bent elbow.

"Well, if the short one isn't gonna take you out behind the barn, maybe I will."

"Pahhh ...," Monica scolds, shaking her head.

"What? I'm old, not dead—and this ninety-two-year-old goat has a few things she could teach this little red-haired stud." Mariah grabs her carved cane from the back of the seat in front of her and wraps a gnarled hand around Sam's arm. Aunt Monica, still shaking her head, takes my arm, though it doesn't look like she needs it. She's not as bent as her sister.

We escort the sisters indoors—thankfully, the ballroom is already open and staff have plenty of hors d'oeuvres on offer. At the studio, I'm used to retrieving lunch and coffee orders for Gabe and Dad, so I move on autopilot, directing Sam to help me put plates together for the sisters. I send a server over with a teapot. Sam sits for a second to make sure they've got everything they need, and I step out to make a call.

"Gabe, you are not going to believe what's happened ..."

FIFTEEN

SAM FOLLOWS me into my room so we can unload gear and put everything back in its respective home, now that there's no wedding to shoot.

"I think I'll keep my camera with me tonight, just in case," I say.

"At the non-reception?"

"Yeah, I mean, I could get some photos of people and then just grab their email addresses to send them on, if they want."

"Too generous. You're going to get sucked into doing family portraits for everyone who eats." He's right. "Why don't you leave the camera here, and let's just enjoy the unexpected night off? There'll be free food and dancing and probably more of that amazing Canadian beer ..."

"Dancing?" I unzip my case and tuck my camera inside. "How about just the beer part."

"How about the beer part and *then* dancing?"

"I thought you said you came to this wedding to find babes."

"I don't think I ever said that." He hands me his camera.

"You did! You said something about hitting on bridesmaids."

"That was before I saw the bridesmaids."

"I thought that's what all single guys did at weddings." As soon as I say it, the name "Lisa R." flashes in my head. If she's been blowing up his phone, he hasn't been obvious about it.

"Well, I'll have some stiff competition down there tonight now that *Bert* is single again," he teases.

"Man, his mom looks so sad."

Sam nods, stretching his long legs in front of him as he sinks into the overstuffed chair in the corner. "I remember his mom was a bit of a mess when we were younger."

"Yeah, her husband was an abusive dick. He'd hit her for burning his toast."

"A winner. Maybe Nikki dodged a bullet after all." Sam reaches for a hotel-provided chocolate, the wrapper echoing in the very quiet room. That's one of my favorite things about Revelation Cove, actually: the silence.

"Nah, Rob's not a hitter."

Sam pops the candy into his mouth, his cheek bulging with it. "Is there any tiny part of you that sees this as karmic retribution for what he did to you?"

"If I were a narcissistic brat, then yeah, I'd say he got what he deserved," I say, curling onto the end of my bed. "But mostly it just sucks all around. I don't like seeing people upset, even people who've hurt me. Enough years have passed, now Rob just looks like a guy who got dumped at the altar."

"You're a better human than I am, Frankie." Sam leans forward and tosses me a candy. "Why didn't we ever hook up?"

I freeze with my hand halfway to my mouth, the chocolate already softening between my fingertips. "Uhhh ... because you were my brother's best friend? Because you were with Lainie? Because that would've been weird?"

"Would it have been, though?" He leans forward, elbows on bent knees. "We've known each other almost our whole lives. We know each other's dirty little secrets and idiosyncracies and hopes and dreams."

"We *did*. And then incommunicado for basically a decade. Remember that bit?"

The chair exhales as he sinks back into the cushions. "I guess. But it really bothered me when Rob hurt you. I wanted to break his stupid neck. And not because I was Gabe's best friend." Sam's eyes sparkle from across the room, his cheeks pinking with his honesty.

Saved by the buzzing phone. "I should answer this ..." Sam nods. "Hello?"

"Frankie? This is Aunt Mariah. You still got that camera handy?"

"I'm just up in my room—"

"Well, come down from your room and bring your camera and that hot clansman with you. You're not gonna wanna miss what's going down."

She hangs up and I stand to pull out the cameras. "Something juicy is happening in the ballroom."

Sam laughs and slips his shoes back on. "Like I said, never a dull moment around you."

SIXTEEN

WE HEAR it the second the elevator doors open. Music. Loud music —and hollering, and I'd guess dancing.

"We were gone for a half hour," I say, camera around my neck as we approach the pulsating ballroom doors. "How did it go from casual snacks and wine to full-blown rave so quickly?"

Sure enough, the ballroom is in meltdown mode. I don't see Rob or his mom, but Nikki and Drunk Edwin are making up for lost time —time when she was engaged to another man—which is super gross and terrible because Edwin is supposed to be Rob's best man. By the display of roving hands and tongues, neither seems to care that everyone can see.

"It's clear who got Edwin in the divorce," I say to Sam. He cups his ear, indicating that he can't hear me.

Adalynn, changed out of her matron of honor dress into something black and *much* skimpier, is on one of the tables, dancing. Sam starts taking photos of everyone and everything. I follow his lead. You never know ...

"If you wrote a book about this, people wouldn't believe you,"

Sam says right into my ear to be heard above the din. "Blackmail smells so good in the afternoon." He cackles wickedly.

"She didn't even wait for the body to go cold!"

The stage where the DJ was going to set up at the proper reception is, at the moment, occupied by a group of young unknown males who I assume are members of the bride's side, all of them bent over an open laptop that must be controlling the obnoxiously loud music.

Aunt Mariah sees me and waves us over. She pats the unoccupied seats next to her and Monica and yells, "We saved you space!"

"Any sign of the groom?" I ask against her head.

"Nooooo. But they have plenty of free champagne. Bottom's up!" Aunt Mariah says, draining her delicate crystal glass. I doubt Sam can hear her, but he sets his camera on the table and disappears into the throng, returning with two sweating bottles of that awesome Canadian beer we're growing too fond of.

"Put your camera down, F-Stop. We've got enough dirt to fund our bungalow in Bali." He taps his bottle's neck against mine. It's strange to be day drinking when I'm supposed to be working, but by the time the bottle is near empty, it feels less strange and more awesome.

I pull out my phone and snap photos of the chaos to send to Bryony. The Wi-Fi here still sucks, and I'm probably going to regret sending so many photos once I see my roaming data overages, but whatever. Like Sam said, you gotta see this shit to believe it.

"Come on," Sam says, plunking his empty bottle on the tabletop. "Dance, we must."

"No. Please, no," I say. "Let's get some food. I'm hungry—"

"Dancing first, then food."

"Doesn't it feel wrong to dance, though? Like, Rob's upstairs nursing a broken heart and we're down here partying?"

"Are you serious? Can't you see the evil beauty in that?" Sam clasps his hands before him in mock prayer. "Pleeeeeeease," he begs.

But I can't—I am a terrible dancer, and I don't want him to see that I haven't improved since he and Gabe tried, and failed, to teach me basic dance moves a million years ago. Sam went through a phase when he was really into this dance-centric video game, so he and Gabe concocted a scheme that if they could learn some sweet routines, they'd be the hit of the eighth-grade spring dance and all the girls would want them.

I have no idea if it worked out, but I do know they finally stopped asking me to play the game with them because it was more frustration than fun.

"One dance," Sam says next to my ear. I can smell the ale on his breath. It is not terrible.

I shake my head, but before I can protest, his gentle finger under my chin turns my head toward his.

And he kisses me.

And I let him.

Because he tastes good, and his lips are soft, and it's *Sam*, and he's beautiful, and he's saved my butt this weekend for sure …

"Wait—" I push him away. "What are you doing? It's just the beer talking."

"We've had one beer, Frankie."

I flatten my hand against his chest as he moves into me again. "Wait, wait, *wait*. I have to think about this—"

"No, you don't. You don't have to overthink everything. We're here, there's music and free food and drink, we're young and single, and—"

I squeeze out of Sam's arms. I just need a second to breathe; I need to be able to hear my own thoughts racing through my head so I can pick apart the alarm bells and red flags from the balloons and fireworks. Because that kiss was way more fireworks than alarm bells.

"Young lady," Mariah's voice cuts through the noise. Her arthritic hand is waving me over. "Help me to the powder room." I look at her, and then Sam, and he nods.

"I'll get us some food."

I'd make a joke about no shellfish, but it's too loud in here and my brain is too freaked out to be funny.

I move alongside Aunt Mariah, help her with her cane, and make sure she's not stepping on her very long, broom-style skirt. The thin tassels hang almost to her knees as we shuffle toward the door. Once we're out in the lobby, the quiet punches us in the ears.

"Well, *that* little shindig got out of hand quickly," Mariah says. Out here, I can hear the bells on her skirt tinkling with every slow step. "And I didn't have to go to the powder room. You looked like you could use a moment." She nods at me, her frizzy, wild hair the opposite of her twin's tame, well-coifed white helmet. "I don't meet many girls your age who are as short as me."

"Yeah ... I'm the shortest in my family by a longshot, so I hear that a lot."

"Never underestimate the power in a small package." She points toward a padded bench next to a huge window that overlooks the rear of the resort. "Every husband I had started out thinking I'd be a pushover, easy to control, because I was small—the only thing he controlled was how quickly he shaped up when he learned who really wore the pants in the family."

"Every husband?"

"Four. Is that a lot? Between my sister and me, we outdid Elizabeth Taylor." I help her scuttle onto the high-backed bench; she hands me her cane. "Don't worry, dear. I wasn't one of those girls with loose morals."

"I would never suggest such a thing."

"The first one died in World War II—we married when I was only seventeen, back in '44 when Hitler was tearing things up. Reggie died after his ship went down, hit by a U-boat torpedo."

"I'm so sorry."

"That one hurt the most. I learned to guard my heart after that. Took me a while to remarry. But I did, when I was twenty-five because back in those days, you were a spinster at that age if you didn't have a husband and babies." Mariah talks about her life, pausing only when one of the Revelation Cove staff stops to see if we're in need of anything—surprisingly, Mariah asks for a cosmopolitan.

Her second husband died in an industrial accident, so after that, deciding her heart couldn't take anymore, she resolved to only marry for money. Which she did. "Now it's just me and Monica—we outlived them all. The last fella was a good guy. He didn't have children either ... old Sol and I met at a Jewish community center dance that those places sometimes hold for old people. I didn't want to go—we're not even Jewish!—but one of Monica's rich old-biddy friends invited us, so I went as backup. Sol needed someone to help him spend his money, and I needed someone to laugh at my inappropriate jokes. It was a match that lasted fifteen years. I miss him every day."

When the staff member returns with her cocktail, Mariah smiles and promptly hands it to me. She digs under her blouse and pulls out the hundred she won from her sister back in the wedding tent and offers it to the young woman whose name tag reads "Shelly."

"That's too much, ma'am. It was just a drink," Shelly says.

"Take it. Put it somewhere safe for a rainy day." Mariah mimes like she's tucking the money into her bra and shoos the girl away. I try to give her drink back. "Nope. That's for you. You looked like you needed it after that boy kissed you."

I don't think I've ever had a cosmopolitan.

"So, spit it out. What's the deal with that beautiful hunk of man meat? He has to be Scottish. He looks like that actor on the show with the time-traveling nurse." I laugh. *Outlander*—Bryony's favorite book series and show, the books we have road-tripped to many cities chasing after its author. "Your Sam is a cutie. Have you known him long? You work together?"

And I don't even know where the tears come from, but come they do. I divulge all my secrets: that the groom, "Bert," is my ex-boyfriend when I knew him as a completely different, way-geekier guy named Rob who broke my heart forty-two times; that Nikki was as horrible in high school as she is now; that Sam was our third Musketeer until my stupid brother stole Sam's girlfriend and how Gabe broke his leg in a mountain-biking crash last week, which is why I'm here instead of him; and how Sam was always so kind to me when we were growing up, and this weekend has made me realize just how very much I've missed his presence in my life.

"Where's your mother, dear? Can you not ask her about these things?" Mariah hands me a white cloth hankie.

"No mother. She left when we were little. Gabe and I were raised by my dad."

She *hmmphs* and thinks for a second, and then taps a gnarled finger against her red-painted lips. "Do you have feelings for Sam?" She rests her hand over her midsection. "The kind of feelings that would let him see you nekked?" Her watery blue eyes are so sparkly when she smiles.

"I don't know. He kissed me—you saw that—and yeah, it was really nice."

"Sooo, what's the problem, other than you're not drinking that cosmopolitan so you can have the guts to tear off all his clothes?"

"Mariah, you sure have very progressive ideas for a woman your age."

"Sweetie, I've lived through just about every revolution there's been over the last century—the kind with bullets and bombs, and the kind with birth control pills and burning of bras. Women have always run the world, kid. Without this"—she hoists her sagging bosom with both hands, and then, both hands together in a V pointing toward her seated nether region—"they would have nothing. They do everything for *this*. If men would think with their brains and not their Wee Willie Winkies, think how much could get done!"

I laugh and sip the very strong cocktail. She's right—if I finish this, I will definitely be ready to tear off Sam's clothes.

"This is not a speech about women's lib—this is about you being a strong, independent woman who takes what she needs. I can see it on your face—you like that boy. I've watched you the past couple days, and you fit together. And he watches you with those soft eyes a cat gets before they fall asleep." Mariah places a warm hand on the back of my wrist. "Let him kiss you. Let him be kind to you. Let him tear Bert's heart out and serve it as pâté."

"There might be another woman, though. Maybe someone he's not telling me about."

"Is he that kind of fella?"

"That's just it—I don't know. We lost touch after the Gabe incident. Honestly, I don't know what he's like now, other than what I see him post on social media. I just know what a great guy he was when we were kids, up until the part where Gabe stole his girlfriend."

"Don't forget that the girlfriend allowed herself to be stolen. Sometimes the heart wants what it wants, and it sounds like Sam and your brother were just kids themselves."

"My brother is still with Sam's ex—her name is Lainie. She's an event planner—she's actually really great."

"See? It worked out for everyone."

"Well, except Sam. It broke his heart."

"Sam is a big boy. And you're a grown woman. You're not the little sister tagging along for rides on the back of their scooters anymore. What are you, twenty-six? Twenty-seven?"

"I'm turning thirty-one this year."

"Pahhh ..." She flops a hand at me. "Child, you need to get busy. Life doesn't last forever, and you will reach a point where the years are going too fast for you to remember your own name. You squeeze every last ounce out of it—whether that's with Sam or if you want to climb that crazy high mountain in the, the, the—"

"The Himalayas? Mt. Everest?"

"That one. See? Don't wait until your brain starts skipping like a scratched record. Go in there right now and grab that boy and show him who's boss. Come right out and ask him if there's another woman. Watch his eyes while he talks to you. If he blinks or looks away or turns a funny color—and I'm guessing young Sam turns a lot of funny colors with that complexion—then you know he's lying. Trust me, Frankie." She plumps her boobs again. "Women run the world."

She winks and grabs her cane, wobbling to stand upright. "I'm going back in now. You finish that cosmo, and I will flirt with your man until you slide back in to steal him away. Deal?"

She offers her hand for a shake. I take it. "Thank you, Mariah."

"And you've got my number now, kid. When you're back home, you call me. You can come hang out at my very expensive Laurelhurst house that Sol bought me before he kicked the bucket." With another wink, she shuffles back toward the ballroom, the quiet shockingly interrupted when the ballroom door opens and thrusts its noise into the peace.

THE SKY on the other side of these immense windows is deciding what it wants to do—the rain finally arrived, but the thunder and lightning left a while ago, likely figuring its job was done here. I will never get over how incredibly beautiful this place is. And tomorrow, before I leave, I'm going down to put my toe in that water, even if it freezes off.

The ballroom door opens and closes behind me, but I'm too enraptured by the view ahead, too warm from the pink drink in my hand to pay much attention.

"Is this seat taken?"

Sam. With our cameras.

"Mariah said you were still out here sipping some liquid courage."

"Yeah, she's cunning. Ordered the cosmo for herself and then forced it into my hands."

"That little old thing?" Sam smiles and sits. "I believe every word."

He faces the window, crosses his ankles, and breathes deeply. "This place is unreal."

"Yeah ... it kills me that there's all this beauty, and yet the idiots in there are treating it like their personal mosh pit."

"Rich people, am I right?" Sam eyes the now-empty glass in my hand. "You hungry?"

My stomach growls on cue. "I could eat. But"—I nod toward the ballroom—"not in there."

Sam stands, loops his camera over his neck, and offers his bent elbow. "Mademoiselle, allow me to escort you into Revelation Cove's fine-dining area."

"Why, thank you, sir. How very gallant." I hand Sam my glass, grab my own camera, and take his arm. The dining room still has tables available—with the bride's side of the wedding party living it up in the ballroom, the groom's family and friends are in here, gathered in a markedly more somber affair.

I spot Rob and his mom in the corner. He offers me a tired smile when we make eye contact—yeah, he looks terrible. Which is to be expected.

"I should probably go say hi to Rob's mom."

"After we eat, Frankie. This isn't your disaster to fix," Sam says, pulling out my chair for me. That he's chosen the chair that puts my back to Rob may be strategic. Either way, I'm glad.

As we're sitting, my phone buzzes in my pocket. "It's Gabe," I say, reading the screen. "He and Lainie are at the studio and he can't find —I don't even know what he can't find because his spelling is so terrible. I should call him—"

Sam takes my phone and places it facedown out of my reach. "Your brother and your father are grown-ups. You've been taking care of their crap all weekend. They can find whatever they need right this second without you."

"It's just that I know the studio like the back of my hand, so they always rely on me to help out."

"Yeah, they do. And tonight, they can help themselves."

Sam's got a point, but I worry that Gabe might actually need something, and if he's at the office, on a Saturday—shouldn't he be at home resting? He just had surgery! What could be so important that he's there now? "Maybe I should call him. He's only a couple days out from his surgery. He should be at home with his leg up—"

"It's a broken leg, Frankie, not a heart transplant. Let Gabe figure it out. I'm going to be selfish and demand my own Francesca Time without the Hawes men butting in. For once."

Sam wants Francesca Time? He never calls me by my full name.

"So—surf-and-turf, or something a little lighter?"

I smile and relax into my chair. "As long as it involves more of those bread twists from last night, I don't even care."

We order dinner and a pitcher of the good beer and we catch up and laugh and reminisce about the old days and for a little while, I forget that there are even other people in the room. The anxiety and pressure I've been feeling since the fateful phone call that put me in this faraway location melts off my shoulders. The alcohol loosens my neck, and although I'll likely have a headache tomorrow, right now, I'm feeling about as chilled out as I have in a long time.

As our plates are taken away, Sam orders dessert—"Two plates of whatever you have in chocolate"—lamenting that we aren't getting any wedding cake, so we should fill our boots otherwise. Another pitcher of beer over the chocolate torte cake that is so rich, I'll need to have my teeth cleaned as soon as I return to Portland. More laughs.

And when Sam reaches across the table and rests his hand on mine on the tabletop, I don't pull away. "Did it bother you ... that I kissed you? Was it weird, I mean?"

The beer has made me bold. "No. I liked it."

"It didn't feel brotherly or whatever? You keep making jokes about how it always seemed like you had two annoying brothers."

I shake my head. "There was a time when I stopped thinking of you as a brother ..."

"And?" He leans forward but doesn't release my hand.

"And I started to think that maybe you didn't have cooties."

Sam laughs loudly. "All boys have cooties. You know that."

"Well, I started to think that maybe our cooties could be friends."

His eyes blaze as he finishes the last sip in his pint glass. "I think *that* is an excellent idea."

"Are we intruding?" The woman's voice from my right catches me off guard, popping the bubble Sam and I have been floating in for the last—oh shit, almost two hours. "I wanted to stop and say hello, before Robert and I leave the resort in the morning."

I slide my hand out from under Sam's, standing to greet Mrs. Whitford, er, Ms. Nelson. Rob looks at Sam, at his hand where it was holding mine just a few seconds ago, and then nods curtly. I swear he's shrunk just since this afternoon. He's no longer in his tux, but his dress shirt and slacks hang on him like he's borrowed a bigger man's clothes.

"Hey, Rob," I say.

"You look well, Frankie. So good to see you again," Rob's mom says. "Sam, good to see you too." She looks back at me. "When Rob said that Hawes was doing the photography, I expected it to be Gabriel up here."

"So did I. He broke his leg mountain biking last week, and we couldn't get anyone else on such short notice."

"That's what Nicolette mentioned," Ms. Nelson says. "Well, it all worked out anyway, didn't it? I'm sure your photos turned out beautifully. Not like we'll be needing them now." Her lips pull in a tight smile, but her jaw is clenched.

"I'm so sorry about today. For both of you," I say. "And how's your leg, Rob?"

"Bourbon has helped," he says, swirling his drink glass.

"Bourbon helps everything, doesn't it?" Sam says, standing to offer his hand for a shake. "What the hell happened in there today?"

Ms. Nelson jumps in. "What happened is we dodged a bullet. And now Robert can go on with his life and find someone who wants him for who he is, and not his bank account—something he has worked *very* hard for, mind you."

"Mom, stop. Nikki has more money than God."

"Nikki's *father* has more money than God. Doesn't mean it's hers."

"The way she spends it?" Sam interjects. "Well, Rob, I know this sucks right now, but spend some time with the bourbon, get back to the gym, and you'll find your legs again."

"You ever been left at the altar, Sam?" Rob says, his words harsh. He sounds like he did twelve years ago, in one of those late-night calls he'd initiate all sweet and whiny after breaking up with whomever he was sleeping with. The call would end up with him being angry that I wouldn't come over to his place right at that moment to "console" him. He's not going to get an ounce of sympathy from me, especially if he's going after Sam.

"Ms. Nelson, it was so good to see you again," I say, stepping next to Sam and looping my arm through his. "You look amazing. I'm thrilled to see the changes you've made in your life. You really are an amazing woman." I let go of Sam long enough to wrap Rob's mom in a heartfelt hug. Let her son be a douche—he means nothing to me.

"Sam and I were about to head up to our rooms for the evening, but I'm so glad you stopped to say hi. I hadn't been able to break away to do that quite yet. Again, I'm so sorry about today," I say to her. "I'm not sure how the situation will pan out with Nikki and the photos, but if you call or email the office next week, I'll be sure that you get access to the online albums. I did get some nice shots of you and Rob together before ..."

"Thank you, Frankie. You always were such a considerate girl. Take care of yourself now," Ms. Nelson says. "Tell your father I said hello."

She gestures for Rob to move ahead, and when he does, his injured gait is even worse with the beloved bourbon on board.

"Are we done here?" I ask Sam. The mischief returns to his eyes.

"I would say we are definitely done here." He gives me back my phone. "And do **not** check your messages, *Francesca*."

"You're so bossy."

His left eyebrow hikes.

I try to sign the meal to the room, but Sam won't allow it, instead carrying the leather folder with the bill up to the bar. "It's not a date if I don't pick up the tab."

"Was this a date?" My cheeks warm.

"I'd like to think so, yes."

"But this is the twenty-first century. Equality is en vogue. I can pay for dates too."

"You may pay for the next one, if it would please the lady." He bends at the waist in an exaggerated bow. *The next one? We're going to have another date?*

The bartender returns Sam's credit card. As he tucks it away, I scan the dining room to see if in fact Rob and his mom have left. I don't want any more awkward conversations or to end up sharing the elevator. I'd like to go upstairs and leave this whole fiasco behind me.

But am I going alone? Will Sam deposit me at my door and that will be the end of our cooties being friends?

"After you," he says, camera hanging from one shoulder. He wraps his free arm around my shoulders and leads me to the elevators. As we pass the ballroom, it's clearly still quite the party behind the closed doors. I hope the twins made it to their room all right.

"They'll be fine," Sam says, as if he can read my thoughts. "They made it to ninety-two without you babysitting them."

"It's just so loud in there."

"They're surrounded by family members. Someone will make sure they get to their room okay."

The elevator dings open. We load in, alone, thankfully. The butterflies in my stomach break out in a jig atop the sloshing beer as we climb toward the third floor.

I don't have to ask if Sam's coming with me—he exits the car, arm still draped over my shoulders.

I stop in front of my door but before I can invite him in or say good night, Sam has my face cupped in his hands and he's kissing me again and he smells so good and I can taste the chocolate from earlier on his lips and honestly, this is a perfect moment.

Even with my phone buzzing in my pocket.

"If you answer that, I will throw it into the ocean," he says against my mouth. "Open this door, woman, before I break it down."

I laugh and pull my face away just long enough to find my room key. Once the little green light on the lock flashes, Sam pushes me inside, his hands on my shoulders, takes the cameras away from both of us, and kills all but one light. He then takes my phone, and his, wraps them in a towel, drops the bundle on the bathroom counter, and closes the door.

"Our phones can have their own private party as I will require your undivided attention for the next few hours, Ms. Hawes," he says, stalking toward me, pausing only to kick off one shoe, and then the other. When he moves his fingers to the buttons on his shirt, I reach up and still his hands.

"Let me." I hear Mariah's words in my head, urging me to rip off all Sam's clothes. But it's a perfectly lovely shirt—may not want to rip it.

Though I may have overestimated my fine motor skills, given the amount of alcohol in my bloodstream right now.

"Buttons are hard," Sam teases, reaching to pull my thin knit sweater over my head.

"Are we really doing this?"

"If we're not, then it's weird I'm in your room taking all my clothes off."

"But—"

Sam quiets my questions with his lips against mine again. "No. Overthinking."

I stop him and push back gently, putting six inches of distance between our faces. "I don't want this to just be a fling, Sam. We've had a lot to drink, and we're in a beautiful resort, and I don't want this to ruin our friendship."

"Would you rather I go?" he says, pushing back a little farther.

"God, no—I *really* want this ... but I'm scared."

His finger is gentle under my chin. "I'm not Rob, Francesca. I'm not going to do what he did to you."

I bob my head and then look up at Sam, the faint lamp light reflecting the kindness in his eyes, the kindness I've always loved about him. "So, do you have, like, other things you can do to me, then, or ...?"

His smile burns like a freshly lit match. "Oh, you have no idea."

SEVENTEEN

I HAVEN'T WOKEN up naked next to a man in a very long time. The last guy I dated, Joel, we never got to the sleeping-together bit because there was too much about him I knew I'd never get past—how he talked with food in his mouth and only tipped waitstaff 10 percent, even if they were really attentive, and how he would slap my ass when we walked through Costco and tell me, "More squats, less pasta," and how all he ever talked about was his sports-betting site and how rich he was going to be once it took off.

I only went out with him because every time I'd pop by to meet Bryony for lunch, Joel would come to the front desk and *flirt* like a dying man. And he was good-looking. He had a good job, drove a BMW (that I later learned was his mom's), and he talked about how amazing the dogs were at the rescue where he volunteered every weekend.

He volunteers at a dog rescue? Awwww!

But then one Saturday afternoon, he invited himself over to use my cable so he could order a pay-per-view UFC match (that I ended up paying for). "Make us some sandwiches, hey, Frankie?"

Insert confused emoji here.

I couldn't get the new jar of dill pickles open and he teased me about being the "weaker sex," until he couldn't get the jar open either. And then Gabe dropped by with my dog-nephew Lazarus, half malamute, half *T. rex*, and Joel freaked out and jumped on the couch like he'd seen a mouse, and it slipped out that he was terrified of big dogs, "Er, ah, okay, maybe all dogs and I lied about the dog rescue because Bryony said you liked dogs and I thought you were cute so I lied."

As such, Gabe opened the pickles and I booted Joel out and then I took Lazarus for a walk with my brother and upon returning home and kissing my nephew goodbye, I opened my emergency tub of Chunky Monkey and watched *Pride and Prejudice* for the eight millionth time. It was an excellent night.

But this ... Sam is pressed up against my back, his arms around my front like he's protecting me from unseen evils. Yes, I can save myself from unseen evils, but he has really nice arms and a broad, muscular chest with just the right amount of hair and beautiful, broad, strong hands, and I feel so safe at this very moment—safer than I've ever felt, to be honest. I wish I could bottle this feeling and keep it in my pocket forever. Or I could bottle it, sell it, and retire to the Scottish Highlands where I'd find an old castle I could fix up and fill with twenty awesome dogs and the locals would teach me to drink proper Scotch in exchange for pictures of their own awesome dogs.

The sun is peeking through the split in the curtains. Sun! No rain and no thunder and today should be Nikki-free! And even with the low-grade, post-beer headache thrumming behind my eyeballs, at this very second, life is good.

Deliciously, blissfully good.

And I don't even care that I don't know what time it is—our phones are still concealed by a plush towel in the bathroom for their own night of sharing of the circuitry. I wish I'd thought ahead and thrown some breath mints on the nightstand so I don't assail Sam with morning breath, but for once, I resolve to not overthink and instead appreciate this situation for what it is.

I nuzzle tighter against Sam, my back against his chest, and when he stirs and kisses my bare shoulder, my skin goose-bumps with delight.

"Good morning, F-Stop," he says into my hair. "Is it super cheesy to admit that I have always wondered what it would be like to wake up next to you?"

I laugh into the back of his hand wrapped around my own. "We've woken up next to each other a hundred times."

"Always in a tent or around a campfire or in an RV with your dad and brother too," he says, pulling me closer into him. "And never naked." Evidence of his nakedness, and the fact that it's morning, is obvious against my bare backside.

He pulls his hand free and moves my hair aside, kissing my neck. "I think we should perhaps fulfill that age-old ritual that if you want to have a good day, you should give yourself to the person whose naked body lies next to yours in the very warm and cozy resort bed."

"Age-old ritual, hey? Is this some sage wisdom Aunt Mariah whispered to you?"

"Right after she handed me the sheep knuckles and her vial of dragon tears," he says, biting playfully into my neck, chills racing through me. And then he's kissing the tops of my shoulders and nibbling my earlobe and telling me how beautiful I am and then some other stuff and then he again shows me just how perfect our bodies fit together, even if he is a foot taller and has some real power here to dash my heart into a thousand unrecoverable pieces.

WHEN WE WAKE AGAIN, sticky with dried sweat and sore body parts, the sun is higher in the sky and it's not an alarm that pulls me from my stupor—it's the door. Someone is knocking. Persistently.

"Sam ... Sam, someone's at the door." He stirs but pulls me tighter into his side. "Sam, I gotta answer the door. They won't stop knocking."

"What time is it? It's probably housekeeping. Maybe we slept through checkout."

I untangle my legs from his and push off his bare chest, scooting to the edge of the bed to grab one of the fluffy, hotel robes, so long it almost reaches the top of my feet. What a surprise.

"One sec," I say, quickly rinsing with mouthwash and pulling my very matted hair to one side. My hand on the doorknob, I fully expect it to be Nikki waiting to pounce.

"Good morning, Ms. Hawes," Ryan says. "I am so sorry to disturb you—"

"Did I sleep through checkout? I am so sorry—"

"No, not at all. It's only ten."

"Right. Okay, sorry. I had my phone off."

Ryan nods and then reaches toward me with a piece of paper. "Your brother phoned. He's been trying to reach you?"

"He probably can't find the scotch tape," I tease, opening the paper, my stomach dropping into my feet as I read the message.

"He just phoned again a few minutes ago with this, so I came right up to tell you, rather than ring the room line."

"Did he say anything else? Shit, I don't even know how I can get back there—"

"My brother can fly you down to Victoria, as soon as you're ready to go. Just meet us in the lobby and we'll get you back to the mainland."

"Okay. Jesus, okay, ahhhh, I need to wake Sam. I need to think for a second—"

"Frankie, who is it? Is it housekeeping?" Sam calls from behind me, his voice sleepy.

"Get yourself together and we'll see you downstairs in a bit," Ryan says. "I'll have the kitchen put together a quick to-go breakfast for you both."

"Thanks, Ryan. Thanks for this."

I don't remember shutting the door. I don't remember much after handing Sam the piece of paper that reads, "Frankie, please call me. Dad's in ICU. Massive heart attack. Come home ASAP. xo Gabe."

~

SAM and I make quick business of showering, dressing, and packing all my gear. He runs back to his room and throws his things together, and then helps me carry everything to the lobby where Ryan and Tanner Fielding then hurry the camera gear down the dock to load into the floatplane while I check out.

I don't even have time to be terrified at the prospect of flying in a plane that takes off and lands in water because my phone—my phone that had been wrapped up with Sam's in the bathroom while we charted each other's territories—is absolutely clogged with voicemails and text messages from Gabe and Lainie as they tried to reach me last night.

Dad had a stroke or heart attack while golfing in Bend. They're airlifting him back to Portland.

Frankie, CALL ME.

FRANCESCA, WHERE ARE YOU?!

Frankie, it's for sure a heart attack. Your dad is in surgery. Gabe is freaking out. Call us. Love you. xo Lainie

And on and on over the ten or so hours I was luxuriating in Sam's attentions.

"Francesca." Aunt Mariah's voice whistles behind me, and I turn to Sam, pleading with my eyes: *I cannot deal with this right now. Help me.*

He nods once and moves quickly toward the aunts, Mariah's face lighting up when she sees him smiling politely at her. He stops them before they reach me, and it's clear what he's saying—the light on Mariah's face darkens, and for the first time since I've met her, she looks serious.

She removes her hand from Monica's arm, places it on Sam's, and points toward me. "Hurry now, Sammy." I see them in my peripheral vision as I sign the room charges to the Hawes Photography corporate card.

"I'm so sorry to hear about your dad," Hollie says. "My father is a nurse, and he would tell you that if your dad is in surgery, this is a good sign." Maybe she's right? If he was too sick to have his heart fixed, he would just be on life support or something, right? They wouldn't try to fix whatever caused the heart attack?

"I hope you'll come back up here to see us just for fun. No bridezillas next time." She offers her hand; I take it, holding on for a moment but resolving not to start crying. Not yet.

"Francesca, I'm so glad I caught you," Mariah says next to me. I release Hollie's hand and turn to the nonagenarian. "Sammy has told me what happened to your dad. You need anything? Do you need money to get home?" She moves to fumble with her leather cross-body purse.

"No, thank you. We're going to fly back right now and then ..." I don't even know what then. We still have to get from Victoria to Vancouver, and then the drive to Portland is, like, six hours. *Six hours!*

"I'll make sure she gets south to see her dad," Sam says. "Don't you worry."

Mariah steps closer and takes both my hands in hers once again. "When you get home and settled, will you send me a message on the phone and tell me how he is? I don't want to be one of those nattering old women everyone gets annoyed by, but I think we're friends now, and I will worry about you."

I sniff and nod. "Yes. I'll text you and let you know how he is. Thank you very much for your kindness."

"When he's all better, you come over to my place. I'd love to introduce you to my dogs." She pats my cheek, and then resumes her position on Monica's arm.

"Take care of yourself, young lady. We'll be thinking good

thoughts for you and your family," Monica says, helping her sister, again in a long, dangerous skirt, toward the dining room.

My business at the front desk finished, Sam and I take our leave. As we load onto the tiny plane that I swear to all the gods is made out of one of those hobby-shop model kits, I pull out my phone and reread the messages from Gabe and Lainie. Sam sees me scrolling.

"I am the worst daughter ever."

"You are not. Don't start with that shit. Your dad will be okay. If he's still alive and was stable enough for surgery, then he's going to be fine."

"Hollie just said the same thing. Her dad is a nurse."

"So she would know. And they flew him to Portland, to OHSU, which has the best heart doctors. He's not stuck in some small-town hospital in the middle of nowhere."

I nod, trying to keep the tears behind the rims of my eyes. I don't want to lose it yet. I need to be strong. I need to be strong for my dad because he's always been strong for us. He raised us after my mom left, and even though balancing single parenthood and his huge career was a Herculean task, he never once complained. He never once spoke an ill word about my mother or about how hard it was to deal with parent-teacher conferences or after-school activities or the perils of raising teenagers.

I have to be strong for my dad because Gabe is a total weenie when it comes to stuff like this. In some ways—a lot of ways—I've stepped into the role that a mom would normally occupy.

I take care of the Hawes men, because they are *my* men.

And Gabe won't know what to do without my dad there directing his every step.

Harrison Hawes has to be okay. He's all we have left.

EIGHTEEN

TURNS out Sam had flown to Vancouver for the wedding and rented a car to get to Victoria, rather than drive his own car from Portland into Canada. Which means once we're back in Victoria, we're able to turn in his rental, take the ferry back to the mainland, and drive together to Portland in my car.

When he slips behind the wheel, I don't protest. He insists I need to relax and breathe and be available to answer my phone should Lainie or Gabe call.

The subsequent six hours—more like just under five (even with the shitty Seattle traffic) as Sam risks hefty speeding fines by sailing down Interstate 5—are a blur. Gabe calls with news that Dad is out of surgery and stable, but he's in the cardiovascular ICU and pretty groggy from the medication. The doctor said they did an angioplasty and placed stents because his arteries were blocked, and that he's going to have to change his lifestyle if he wants to avoid future incidents.

I laugh to myself. Harrison Hawes, change his lifestyle? He lives as he pleases. Death will have to try harder.

By the time Sam pulls into the lot at Oregon Health Sciences

University, I'm jittery with nerves and too much gas-station coffee. He parks and grabs my hand, refusing to let go as we find our way to registration and inquire about my father's whereabouts. We're sent to the twelfth floor in the Kohler Pavilion, and it dawns on me in the elevator that Sam and Gabe—and Lainie—are about to see one another for the first time since their big blowout and breakup.

"You don't have to come up. If it's awkward," I say as the elevator dings skyward.

"Don't be ridiculous. Harrison is like my dad too." I look up at him, and he leans down to kiss me softly. "Gabe and Lainie and I are grown-ups. This isn't time for petty bickering about old wounds."

Sure enough, when we get to the family waiting room outside the cardiovascular intensive care unit, or CVICU, Lainie is on her feet, immediately offering hugs to me and then to Sam. Gabe is asleep, stretched on one of the vinyl couches, his casted broken leg propped on a stack of pillows. His hair's a calamity and the purple bags under his eyes dark, even as he rests to try to erase them.

"He's a mess," Lainie says under her voice. "Not been a great week, clearly. And he won't take the pain medication the doctor gave him because he's afraid he'll miss your dad waking up."

"He's still asleep, then?"

"Yeah. He woke up briefly after they brought him out of recovery, but he wasn't making much sense."

"What the hell *happened?*"

"He was golfing and collapsed." Lainie turns and nods to a woman who looks to be in her fifties—well dressed in dark jeans, ankle boots, a button-down blouse with a light cardigan, her hair a shoulder-length bob of blond and silver, thin silver bangles on her wrist. Her head rests against the wall, eyes closed. "She was with him, thank heavens, which is why they were able to get him to the hospital so fast."

"Her? Is she an old friend or something?"

"Apparently, she's his new girlfriend. Her name is Diana. And she's actually really nice," Lainie says.

I almost laugh. The woman dozing against the CVICU wall is *not* my father's type. She must be an old friend or something. I shake my head. "No way. Not enough cleavage or crocodile tears to be one of Harrison's women," I say. As if she knows we're talking about her, the woman named Diana wakes up, looks around the room, and then smiles when she sees me.

She stands, smoothing her shirt and fluffing her hair, and walks toward us. "You must be Frankie," she says. "I'm Diana—a friend of your dad's." She nods and looks to Sam. He introduces himself too.

"Sam. Old friend of the family."

"I've heard stories about you both."

"Good ones, I hope," Sam says. I jab him with my elbow. *Don't be nice to her. We don't know who she is yet.*

I take her offered hand. Handshake firm, but not aggressively so. "You were with him when he collapsed?" I ask.

"We were golfing. He'd had a few drinks, so I thought maybe he'd had one too many, but when I saw his face, I knew."

"Diana is an ER nurse, so she knew what to do," Lainie says.

"How long have you known my father?" I ask, feeling territorial—and guilty. She was there for him when his children were not. When I was cavorting in my undergarments with Sam in a foreign country.

"We've been friends for years. He golfed with my late husband, so that's how we met," she says. "But we only reconnected after your brother shot my son's wedding about five years ago."

There's no way they've been dating for the last five years. I've booked my dad's travel plans, hotel and restaurant reservations, and couples' massages, and they've never involved a middle-aged ER nurse named Diana.

"A few months ago, he called and asked me to dinner. We've been 'hanging out,'" she air-quotes, "ever since."

"Right. Okay. He's not mentioned you, is all," I say, hoping that out loud, that doesn't sound as shitty as it does in my head.

"We were waiting to tell you and Gabe, and my son Derek. Thought it would be nice to have a family dinner. Maybe this summer or something, to be sure *we* were sure about what we're planning."

"And what are you planning?"

She hoists her left hand. The ring finger holds a heavy diamond in a platinum band.

I pay all the credit card bills. I definitely would've noticed a charge for this.

Sam wraps an arm around my shoulders just in time to prevent one of two things happening: (1) My legs giving out from under me; or (2) Me tearing Diana the ER nurse's face off.

"Okay, we can talk about this all later. Frankie, let's go get some coffee and check in with the nurses and see what's happening with your dad," Sam says. I don't even have time to argue as he steers me out of the waiting room and down the hall. We stop in a quiet section of the corridor and he turns to me, his strong hands gentle on my shoulders.

"You are going to be just fine, and your dad is going to come home, and you can talk to him about Diana and engagement rings and big plans later, but today"—he lifts my chin so I can't look away—"today we're going to focus on getting your dad the care he needs and letting him know we're here for him. All of us. No drama today. Not with you and Gabe or you and Diana or me and Gabe or any of it. Okay? Our mission, should you choose to accept it, is to get Harrison healthy and behind the camera again." I nod. Sam's right. I have to focus on Dad.

Sam reaches down and feather-kisses my lips. I feel stronger knowing he's by my side, that he has a vested interest in my family's well-being, and in mine.

It's a foreign, scary, wonderful feeling.

And I'm glad for it.

∾

WE TAKE turns going in to see Dad, still asleep, and we take turns retrieving coffee and bottles of sugary fruit drinks for each other and we take turns going to the cafeteria for dinner so that there's always someone in the CVICU waiting room, just in case. It's not terrible time spent, to be honest. Gabe and Sam and Lainie joke about old times, and it's almost like my father's misbehaving heart might be the salve these two numbskulls needed to end their decade-old blood feud.

We laugh until we cry about some of the crazy shit we did as kids when Dad would be out photographing his creatures and we'd be left to our own devices; we even make fun of some of Dad's former female conquests and the ridiculous things he's done for women over the years. Granted, we're polite enough to wait until Diana leaves to "freshen up."

We sit until Dad's cardiologist insists we go home and get some rest. The sun has long gone to bed, and the city lights outside the hospital windows sparkle in the midspring evening. It would almost be magical if it weren't tinged by the smell of cleaning fluid and anti-septic and the sound of muffled sobs of family members in the waiting room and down the halls.

Before we head out, though, I insist on going in again to see my dad. Every time we enter his room, every person must don a paper gown and hair covering and shoe covers. It's tedious, but not nearly as tedious as lying in bed post heart surgery.

But I have to whisper to him that I'll be back in a few hours and he'd better be awake so I can give him shit about what a lousy golfer he is. His face is puffy and he's got a lot of wires and tubes coming from everywhere, but he's nice and pink, which is reassuring, and as per usual, his goatee and bald head are perfectly managed. I'll need to call his barber next week and cancel his standing Tuesday appointment.

It's this that makes me break down. Having to call Dad's barber.

I sit next to his bed for a while and hold the hand with the temperature monitor thingie clamped to his index finger and I beg for him to not be a selfish jerk and leave me behind to manage my dumb brother all by myself. I apologize for being tough on him when it comes to eating the right foods and not drinking so much and not buying new lenses just because they're pretty when the old lenses we have work just fine and he can buy as many lenses as he wants as long as he promises to just wake up and come home and we can figure out all the other stuff later.

A nurse I didn't hear come in slides a box of tissues next to me and pats my shoulder. "He's going to be just fine. He's sleepy right now from the medications. Tomorrow he'll be awake and ready to cause more trouble."

I laugh and nod and dry my nose and eyes. If the nurse says he'll be okay, I have to believe her. One more kiss to Dad's forehead, and I leave, pausing outside his door to peel off and discard my sterile hospital layer and take a deep breath so I don't start bawling again.

"I can't believe the bride did that!" I overhear Lainie say upon my approach to the waiting area.

"Yeah, seriously, you saved my ass going up there, man. I owe you." My brother. "I mean, I know Frankie could've taken some photos of, like, pets or whatever, but I was so worried. She just doesn't have that *thing* when it comes to taking pictures of people, no matter how hard we've tried to teach her over the years."

"She did really well. I think you're going to be impressed. She didn't need me at all." Sam. He's defending me? "It worked out. I wasn't going to go, but when you called—I'm glad to have had a few days away from ... everything. And that venue—"

I step into the doorway. Their faces freeze as they all look at me. "You only went up to that wedding to make sure I didn't screw up the photos?"

"Frankie, no—" Sam stands to move toward me, but I stop him with my hand in the air.

"Gabe? You called him to come and make sure I didn't mess up?"

"It's just that I know how nervous you get photographing people

—" Gabe tries to shift in his seat but winces with pain when he moves his leg and his foot bumps against the floor.

"You know how much I *suck* at photographing people. I was standing right outside the door. I heard what you said."

"I know I put you in a terrible position," Gabe says.

"And you were afraid I'd screw up one of Dad's best clients, so you sent Sam for backup but then—" I look at Sam and my stomach turns over. "Was any of that real? Were you really there for me, or because Gabe was paying you to babysit?"

"Frankie, come on, you're blowing this out of proportion," Gabe says. "We were just looking out for you."

My eyes are trained on Sam. "Except we spent the weekend working side by side, and then last *night*"—I swallow hard, tears stinging my eyes again—"and you didn't say ONE WORD about this. You let me believe that you were there for the wedding only, that it was a lucky coincidence that you found me on that highway and that you just happened to be heading in the same direction so 'come on, let's hang out, oh, sure, give me a camera too.'"

"Francesca, please ..." Sam says, his face bright red.

"You lied to me."

"And if he'd said he was there to make sure you got the shots, wouldn't that have undermined your confidence even more?" Gabe says, the prior softness in his voice hardening. "The job needed to be done. I fucked up by breaking my leg, and no one else could fill in. I knew you'd be totally freaked out, and I knew Sam had been invited to the wedding, so I called him to make sure he'd keep an eye on you."

"How did you know Sam had been invited?"

"Because the guest list is in the binder? You put it together. Did you not read it yourself?"

I did put the binder together, but I never read the guest lists. Why would I? I never shoot these weddings, so why would I give a shit who the bride and groom invite to watch them break each other's hearts?

I look up at Sam and my chest squeezes so much, I almost go ask the nurse to check me in to the bed next to Dad's. "You lied."

"I didn't lie. I just didn't want you to second-guess yourself, which you would've done if you'd known why I was really there."

"Omission is still a lie," I say, flashing all of them my dirtiest look before grabbing my purse and jacket, spinning on my heel, and near sprinting to the elevators.

"Frankie, wait!"

I don't. I keep walking, and even when Sam catches up to me, I'm still moving.

"Can you stop for one second and *listen?*"

I press the elevator button, biting my lip so I don't yell or cry. I'm so tired. *I'm so tired.*

"Francesca, please," Sam grabs my arm before I can step into the elevator car. The doors open, and then slide closed again, going to its next customer. "When Gabe called, he made it sound like you needed a friend. I didn't do it for him"—Sam jabs a finger down the hallway—"I did it because it was the perfect way to get to see you again."

"Instead of just calling me or sending me a message?"

"It felt weird! Like you wouldn't want to talk to me after everything that happened."

"Sam, that was between you and my brother, NOT me. You left me too," I say, not able to hold the tears back anymore. "I mourned when you left us. I was so fucking sad when you and Gabe broke up. But you tossed me out too."

"Why didn't you ever try to get in touch with me?"

"Probably because the parting words when you and Gabe had that blowout were something along the lines of 'I never want to see or hear from you again,'" I say. "You looked at me and Dad when you yelled it."

Sam runs a hand down his face. "We were so young. I was hurt, Frankie." He steps closer and reaches out to touch me; I flinch away. "I've missed your friendship so much all these years, and for what?

Over some heartbreak a million years ago? I was a KID. I didn't know shit. I didn't know what I was throwing away when I flipped out. But when you and I started talking the other day, it brought back all the good stuff. It brought back all those awesome years we spent together—"

His phone rings. It's not on silent. He shuts it off but then the elevator opens again, so I step into it. I need to get out of this building, into the fresh air, away from sick and dying smells and memories of how much it hurt when Sam and Gabe stopped being friends and how amazing this weekend was even though it started out pretty terrible and how Sam's hands feel on my body and how his lips feel against mine and how it was all based on a lie and how fucking bizarre it is that my father has a girlfriend—a fiancée!—he hasn't even told me about ...

Sam follows me onto the elevator, but we're not alone so our conversation is halted. And although he's silenced the ringer, his phone goes off again, and he ignores it again. He stands so close to me, I can smell the Revelation Cove bath wash he used when we were scrambling to get downstairs to the waiting floatplane.

The elevator drops us on the lobby level, Sam close behind me. He stops me again, this time his grip firm around my elbow. "Please, Frankie, please just wait."

I pause and turn to him. His hands are soft on my neck, on my cheeks, as a broad thumb wipes away the tears I can't get to stop. "Let's get something to eat. It's been a long, exhausting weekend, and now that we know your dad is okay, we can go drop off the gear and get some food and *talk*. Just the two of us."

"Last night? What was that, Sam? Was that even real?"

He tightens his hands ever so slightly on my cheeks and bends down to kiss me. "Every single second was real, Frankie. It was like a dream come true. I swear to you—I will go Tom Cruise and jump on that ugly yellow couch over there and tell everyone how real last night was—"

"Please don't. That would be weird, even for you."

"I swear, Frankie, I *swear* that I only went up to that wedding to see you. It was an opening I couldn't afford to miss. I had to—"

"SAMUEL McKENZIE!" a woman's voice shrieks across the busy lobby and registration waiting area, scaring people to a standstill.

Sam's hands slide from my cheeks to my shoulders and then he's not touching me at all. The blood has drained from his face, his eyes wide and scared like he's seen a ghost. I turn to look in the direction of the shrieking party just as a very angry, very *pregnant* brunette knocks me on my butt.

"Lisa, hey!" Sam yells, separating her from kicking at me.

"Who the hell is this? Is this the slut you've spent the weekend with?" She tries to kick me again.

Lisa. Lisa R. The name on his phone ... Is this that Lisa? The woman who was allegedly just a "work thing" he could ignore? This very pregnant woman trying to kick a new hole in my face—is she his girlfriend, and oh my god, *is that Sam's baby?*

"How did you even find me?"

She throws her cell phone at him; it bounces off his chest and hits the floor. "GPS, stupid. I always know where you are. You're a software geek—you should know better than that." She reaches out to slug him.

"Lisa, STOP lashing out. Jesus, control yourself," Sam says, pushing her gently aside.

"Don't touch me or I will scream." She flails away from him as I scoot backward. A security guard has appeared out of nowhere and helps me up.

"I have been calling and calling and texting and you seem to think you can just run off to another country with some **whore**!" Lisa yells, her finger repeatedly jabbing in my direction. She looks wild—hair unbrushed, makeup smeared like it was put on a few days ago but never washed clean, blemishes on her face that look picked at, soiled sweatpants, no socks in unlaced running shoes, unzipped sweatshirt with one sleeve nearly ripped off, and her ill-fitting shirt barely covering her very swollen stomach. "Does she even know about me? Does she know about the baby?" Lisa cackles—it sounds like a demented fairy-tale witch. "Yeah, I'll guess by the look on her face she doesn't know about the baby, does she, *Sam* ..."

The security guard steps in and warns Lisa to keep her voice down and requests they take this little situation outside or he'll call the police. He asks me if I feel safe to leave the premises.

I look to Sam—his face is hard and unreadable. Which tells me he's not following me to the car, and we're definitely not going to dinner to talk.

"Frankie, I gotta deal with this," he says, voice barely above a whisper, his words sending Lisa into a new tailspin of shrieks and yells that earns her a strong-armed escort out of the building. She hollers about police brutality all the way to the whooshing automatic doors, and I can see Sam is torn between me and following her.

"Go. Looks like she needs you more than I do right now," I say. My ass hurts from where I landed funny on the hard tile floor from Lisa's push, and I'll have a decent bruise on my shin where her foot met bone.

"Let me get her settled, and then I'll text you. I can meet you at the studio, if you'd feel more comfortable talking there."

"You have enough to deal with right now. I'm assuming Lisa can give you a ride home?" I don't wait for him to answer, instead pushing past, away from the curious eyes of the crowd spectating this latest bout of weirdness.

As the doors slide open, I reach for my phone to call Bryony, and all I can think about is going back to my quiet life, my aqua-fit and bookstore and sushi nights and no men and no drama and no pregnant girlfriends who appear out of nowhere.

Bry answers right away, and I try to explain in gulping sobs as I'm running, Lisa still carrying on outside the main entrance.

I'm only able to speak in broken sentences—"Dad is okay," "Sam is a fraud," "Gabe set me up," "Sam has a pregnant girlfriend," "Found us at the hospital."

"Frankie, stop where you are." I do, right beside the exterior concrete stairs connected to the parking garage, under an LED lamppost that buzzes with flying insects. "Take a deep breath so you don't hyperventilate."

I pause and follow her instructions. "Bryony, everything is falling apart. Sam *lied* to me. He spent all weekend acting like he was a knight in shining armor, and now this wild, VERY PREGNANT woman just came screeching into the hospital—"

"Is it his girlfriend?"

"I don't know! I was still trying to deal with the fact that he fucking LIED to me about being at the wedding." Another sob breaks out of my chest. A woman walking past gives me a sympathetic smile.

"Okay, go to your car. I'm coming over. Have you eaten?"

"No," I squeak.

"Let's get you to your car first, and then I'm bringing dinner. Everything will be okay," she says, which makes me cry harder.

I slog up the three flights to the floor where we left my car, Bryony still speaking in reassuring tones, but as I reach the ass end of my blue Honda Accord, it is not in the state I left it.

"Bry ... oh shiiiiiiit."

"What? Frankie, are you okay?"

"The car ..."

"What about the car? You don't sound okay. Where are you? I'll come get—"

"My car. The trunk is open. Someone has stolen everything."

I can hear Bryony's breath through the line. "What do you mean, *everything?*"

I walk along the driver's side—the window has been broken out, shattered safety glass all over the steering column and driver's seat, the trunk popped open and empty.

"Everything as in *everything.* The cameras, speedlights, stands, lens backpacks, gear bags, the laptop with the weekend's wedding photos. It's all gone."

"Oh my god," Bryony says. "What hospital are you at? What

garage? I'm on my way. Call security, and then they'll call the police. We have to file a report for the insurance and it'll be theft over $5000 so that's a felony, I think ..."

And she keeps talking but I don't hear her words because my stomach tilts with cafeteria coffee and my ears are overcome with that roar that happens right before I throw up and pass out.

NINETEEN

I WAKE up in the ER.

Because I *did* actually pass out, and apparently someone driving out of the parking garage found me on the ground next to my barf and my trashed car, so here I am, alone on a gurney with people checking my heart and my head that I bashed against the concrete floor and they're asking me questions about if I know who and where I am.

It only takes a few minutes for them to figure out that I'm not dying but basically in the grips of an impressive panic attack (and likely a mild concussion) but that I need to follow up with my family doctor to rule out possible epilepsy. When they learn my dad is upstairs in the CVICU, well, that seals the deal on the panic attack idea. So, they give me a gurney in a quiet corner with the lights low and blankets fresh from the warmer and the curtain pulled and a lovely injection of Ativan to make everything feel fuzzy and soft like the first time you pull on new bedroom slippers.

Gabe and Lainie come down and I try to tell them everything that happened with Sam and that Lisa woman and the car but Gabe gets stuck on the part about the stolen gear and goes into his own rage spiral where he hobbles as angrily as possible on crutches, slapping the long blue-green privacy curtain out of his way, phone against his ear as he calls the police and demands a patrol car show up.

Lainie sits with me, stroking the back of my hand, and then Bryony appears and we all agree that Lainie will drive my broken car back to the studio tonight and then Uber back to get Gabe and their car, and Bryony will take me back to her apartment so I'm not alone because "That's a decent bump on your head" and "You've had too much Ativan to drive or be by yourself overnight."

It's a good plan, I suppose. I just want to sleep and wake up when everything isn't stupid.

THE NEXT MORNING, I wake with a headache, and the good relaxation drugs from the hospital have definitely worn off. I'm cozied up in Bryony's delightfully plush queen-sized bed in her quaint second-floor apartment in an old refurbished house in Northwest Portland. It's raining, fat drops pattering against the window, though the curtains are closed so it's hard to tell what time it is. I roll over and squint at the alarm clock on the shabby-chic dresser across the room: 9:47 a.m.

"Rise and shine, Princess Francesca." The door creaks as Bryony pushes it open with her backside, and she enters carrying a tray complete with a tiny blue vase holding a white, broad-petaled daisy ready to share its pretty face. "Bagels, cream cheese, Red Rose tea with milk, and some delicious Advil, for your dining pleasure." I slide up against the metal headboard and she places the tray on my lap. "How are you feeling?"

"Everything."

"And that means …?"

"It means I'm feeling *everything*. I'd like to go back to whatever they gave me in the ER last night."

"Well, that cute ER doc did give you a prescription." She shakes an amber-colored pill bottle with a smattering of tiny pills in it. "But you probably need to be coherent today so let's save these for night-time, shall we?"

"Aren't you supposed to be at work?" It's a Monday.

"I can take a day off to make sure my best-best-best friend isn't going to die."

"I'm not going to die," I say, sipping the tea. "It just feels like it."

"First of all: Gabe called. Your dad is awake and talking, and he wants you to call him as soon as you can. Second: The police finally showed up at the OHSU parking garage and took prints from your car because it is a pretty big theft, almost $30,000 worth of equip-ment, Gabe estimates, so they're taking it a little more seriously than they might otherwise. Lainie said they decided to have the car towed to their guy to get your window replaced and the car detailed. It'll be ready for you by tonight and you are to call her when you're ready."

"That Lainie ..."

"And third: Sam has called and/or texted no fewer than three million times, to the point where your phone battery died so I plugged it in but then put it in airplane mode to stop the incessant buzzing."

It comes rushing back to me—the scene Lisa R. made in the hospital lobby, the screaming and physical violence, the angry stripes on her stomach when her shirt pulled up and the wild scratching of fingernails marred by old polish. "That woman—Lisa—something is definitely not right with her."

"Sam's girlfriend?"

I nod. "I don't know if that's who she is, but she thinks he belongs to her."

"And she's super pregnant, you said, so we have to wonder what kind of life that kid is going to have if its mother is as unstable as she sounds."

"Could be drugs ..."

"Could be not your problem too, Frankie." She hands me two Advil and a small glass of OJ. I swallow them down.

"Sam and Gabe lied to me. Gabe called Sam and asked him to

follow me up to the resort to make sure I didn't screw up the wedding photos."

"Sounds like the bride did that all on her own." Bryony takes the empty juice glass and slides onto the bed next to me. "So, what are you going to do?"

"About what?"

"About Sam?"

"Sam has bigger fish to fry right now."

"Not according to the flurry of text messages. He seems pretty frantic to talk to you, Frankie."

I shrug. "I need to go see Dad."

"I'm going with you. I want to see this mythical Diana person in real life."

I sniff against a new wave of emotion. "She seems really nice. Maybe even normal. Her boobs were covered and everything."

Bryony gasps in feigned shock. "I won't believe it until I see it."

"But engaged? Why didn't he tell me? And did Gabe know about it? Why are the men in my family so stupid and sneaky?"

"Maybe because they know you'll worry?" Bryony places a warm hand over mine.

"I worry because they don't."

"They're big boys, though, Frankie. At some point, you're going to have to stop taking care of them."

"Clearly not today," I say. "When you talked to Lainie, did she mention if Gabe has calmed down about the stolen equipment?"

"He's pissed, but you guys have insurance."

"I don't think I got all the photos uploaded to our cloud. Everything sort of fell apart at the actual ceremony, and then Sam and I decided to have dinner, and then ..." My insides are all messed up and aching and sad thinking about how perfect Saturday night was.

"You should call him, Francesca," Bryony says, squeezing my hand. "I can see it on your face that you care about him."

I do care about him, but I'm also furious. "Sam needs to deal with his life right now, and maybe someday, we can get together for coffee and talk about why he lied to me about, well, everything."

She nods once and tucks her loose bob behind her ear. "Fresh towels in the bathroom, and you have clothes in your drawer." Bryony and I have sleepovers often enough that we keep clothes at each other's apartments, just in case movie night turns into wine-and-movie night and we don't want to endanger human lives by driving home.

"Thanks for the breakfast," I say. "Thank you for taking care of me and not giving up on me, even when I make all the worst decisions in the world." Bry moves the breakfast tray aside and wraps me in a big, warm hug, letting me cry until I'm ready to face the world again.

TWENTY

DAD IS ENTERTAINING his nurse as I pull on my sterile gown and booties—it's the story about that time he was stalking a very ferocious three-inch Eastern collared lizard and it turned on him, attached itself to the lip of the camera lens, and wouldn't let go, so he had to go find it some bugs and then the lizard let go and sat with my dad and ate its bugs before posing for a photo that won him some funny-wildlife photography contest. (I think he actually won the contest with the photo of the lizard on the lens taken with his backup camera. It's a funny shot.)

My dad has won a lot of awards—I'm glad to hear him talking about one of them. And for all the strutting about he does in his usual life, he never brags about the big wins; he only makes fun of the smaller ones. People don't know about Pulitzer and National Geographic and International Photography Awards because he never mentions them.

I stand just out of his view at the edge of the open door, watching his animated face as he makes the nurse laugh. I love him so much— he was the best dad he knew how to be, especially after our mother left us on our own.

Harrison Hawes turns his head just enough to see me. "F-Stop! Don't skulk in the hallway, kid, come see your old man."

I laugh quietly to myself. He hasn't called me F-Stop in years. Warmth blossoms in the sad bits under my sternum.

"Hey, Dad," I say, sliding into his room. The nurse is still laughing as she puts his chart away and slips past me with a polite hello. I hoist the plastic shopping bag in my hands. "I brought bacon."

His eyes widen. He loves bacon.

"Dad, no—I'm kidding. You just had a heart attack. NO BACON." I set the shopping bag on the bed. It's actually shaving cream, the razors he likes, and some warm socks. My dad hates having cold feet. "Gabe been in yet?"

"They're just downstairs having a bite. How are *you*, Frankie? Nice shiner, by the way."

I gently move my finger to the purpled skin around my eye. When I went down, I hit at an angle that has generously gifted me a goose-egged forehead and a blossoming black eye.

"How long are you here?" I ask, deflecting his question. "You look amazing for someone who had heart surgery mere hours ago."

"I feel amazing." He pats the bed next to him and moves over. "You're the one I'm worried about."

I sit, biting the inside of my cheek and reminding myself to be an Ice Queen so the tears don't spill over and soak his bed.

"Gabe told me about the car getting broken into."

"Dad, I am so sorry—I was just freaked out about you being here so we didn't stop at the studio first—"

"Kid, we have insurance, both car and business property, and Gabe told me the wedding was a disaster anyway. I don't give a shit about any of it."

"I got most of them uploaded onto the cloud while we were at the resort, like you always tell us to do, so there's at least something for the clients."

"When I'm back on my feet, I'll give Donovan a call. I'm sure he doesn't give a shit either. His daughter is a handful."

"Seems your daughter is a handful too."

"All children are handfuls, some more than others," he says, smiling. I rest his hand on my bent leg, palm up, the plastic vital-signs monitor still clamped around his index finger. His big hands are rough and calloused—like a man who's worked for a living, who's seen stuff. He's had run-ins with cougars and bears and deadly snakes and dive-bombing birds of prey and enterprising desert lizards, but he also was embedded in Iraq (in the early '90s and again with the second invasion) and then Afghanistan, taking photos of Saddam's burning oil wells, the endless poppy fields and their Afghani workers turning flowers into opium, and later, the bodies of children and women killed by Taliban mercenaries and American drone strikes.

These shots earned him big attention, and relentless criticism. It was an orphaned Syrian child and the child's kitten that finally sent him home to us permanently. He won't talk about it, but it was bad enough that he stopped taking calls from the big news agencies and turned his attention to domestic photography, "Events where people don't die and animals aren't mutilated for sport."

"You're thinking so hard, there's smoke coming out of your ears," he says.

My dad knows me better than anyone.

"It's been a weird few days."

"I second that emotion," he says, taking his hand back and pulling the sheets a little higher. "You met Diana?"

"I did ... are you really engaged?"

My dad has a lot of smiles, depending on his audience. This one on his face right now is the one he saves for Christmas mornings and graduations and when Sam and Gabe and I would put on impromptu talent shows around the campfire.

"So it's serious," I say. "Is she a good woman?"

"She's the best woman. Way too good for me," he says. "She reminds me of your mother."

"I don't want to talk about my mother. She left us."

"She *didn't* leave you, Francesca. She *died*. She didn't want to, but she did. She would've given anything to have stayed, to have watched you become a woman."

"I'd be a disappointment, I'm afraid."

My dad pretends like he's playing a violin, wincing when he lifts his left arm to hold the invisible instrument. "Are you done yet? Or should I get the nurses to bring snacks for your pity party?"

My dad isn't averse to emotions or talking about our problems; my dad *is* averse to us feeling sorry for ourselves, especially in the middle of the day when it's not socially acceptable to drink.

"Anything you want to tell me about Samwise? I hear he's back in town."

"He never left town, Dad."

"He left *our* town. I hear maybe the two of you spent some time together this weekend?"

"He was at the resort. He helped me take photos. You taught him well," I say. I am not going to tell my father the sordid details, although the look on his face suggests he might already know them.

My phone buzzes next to me on Dad's bed.

"Sam?" my dad asks.

"He won't stop texting."

"Talk to him."

"I will. You and all of this"—I gesture at the wires and machines and my dad's hospital gown—"is more important than anything else right now."

"You're stalling. You used to do this when it was time for a math test too. I always knew when you'd have a big exam coming up because you'd clean out all the closets or suddenly reorganize the boxes of Christmas decorations."

"This is *not* the same."

He clamps his hand over mine. "Answer his texts. Samwise is a good guy. Don't let the rift between him and Gabriel ruin your shot at happiness. Just because your brother is an idiot doesn't mean you have to be too."

"Aww, stop saying such sweet things about me, Dad," Gabe says, hobbling into the room with Lainie close behind, tying the neck strings on his paper gown. I stand and thank her for dealing with my car, offering a big, papery hug. I don't know how Gabe landed her, and how he's managed to hang on to her for so long. But even ten years into their relationship, they're still like newlyweds, so something must be working.

I plop into one of the hard vinyl-and-chrome chairs, and I want to tell my dad what Gabe did—how he undermined me by asking Sam to help me shoot the wedding, how he made me look incompetent and stupid by sending a babysitter, how Sam had some crazy pregnant lady screaming at him in the lobby and I don't know who she is or what Sam's relationship is to her and why did Gabe call him in the first place because now I'm all confused and discombobulated and I just want to go back to routine and order. But my father has just had a major heart attack. The last thing I should do is burden him with my whining.

I'll take my pity party back to the studio instead. I'll get back to work. Work is good. Keeping busy is good. Not thinking about Sam is good.

The room's conversation is light and medically relevant—Dad recalls the few details he can remember about the golf course, Gabe provides a colorful description of the sound of his lower-leg bones snapping after that sweet jump on his bike that he should've landed. My black eye and bruised forehead seem like I didn't put in much effort, comparatively speaking.

The tap of knuckles on the closed glass sliding door draws our attention from Gabe's rambling about pins and bone-setting.

Diana.

The door opens. "Hello! Hello! Am I missing the party?" She finishes tying herself into her gown and walks in, a green smoothie in one hand. I notice the other hand pinching at her slacks, and her smile wobbles a little.

Is she nervous?

She leans over Dad and kisses him chastely on the cheek.

"Looking handsome as ever, Harrison, though you could use a shave," she says, grinning as she hands him the drink. Okay, points for the green smoothie, points for calling him by his full name—he hates being called Harry.

"How is everyone today? Francesca, oh dear, look at your face!" She leaves Dad's bedside and comes closer to me. "Does it hurt? Did they give you anything for it?"

"It's fine. I feel more embarrassment than pain."

"Don't you feel that for even a second. You've had a very stressful week—your clumsy brother and your dad who eats too much red meat and then the car getting broken into. It would be a lot for anyone." She turns my head slightly to inspect the damage. It hurt too much to put makeup on, so my colorful handiwork is on full display. "Do you have a GP? A family doctor?"

"Sort of. I hardly ever go."

"I'm going to set you up with my brother. He's got a wonderful family practice. Good doctor who will retire when he dies standing up in an exam room. You've had these fainting spells before?"

I nod slightly.

"Have you ever been tested for them? Cardiac, epilepsy, that sort of thing?"

"They always just said it was a panic attack. They did a bunch of stuff in the ER yesterday."

"Even if it is, Francesca—"

"You can call me Frankie."

She pauses her nurse mode and smiles, her eyes sparkling. Is she going to cry because I told her she could call me Frankie? Her voice is softer when she speaks. "Even if it is panic attacks, we can figure that out so you don't end up fainting somewhere dangerous. Okay?"

"Thank you. For caring. That's really sweet. You don't even know me."

"I know a lot *about* you, though. Enough to know how important you are to your dad." And before I can object, she gives me a tight hug. I'm waiting for the moment that the veneer cracks and a forked tongue slithers out or her eyes flash with evil vampiric intent as she spies my dad's wallet, but I think Diana might actually be a decent human being.

Which is a huge step in the right direction for Harrison Hawes.

"Frankie, can you stay for a bit? We want to talk to you kids about a few things," my dad says over Diana's shoulder as she releases me from the hug. "Take a seat."

I sit next to my brother and Lainie, my stomach unsettled by Dad's need to talk to us kids. That doesn't happen unless something else is about to happen, usually something big and uncomfortable.

We already know they're engaged—she's too old to be pregnant. Oh god, are they adopting a baby or moving to some faraway locale where the nearest airport is a three-day trek on donkeyback through militia-infested territory or are they applying for that one-way mission to Mars and so they have to enter a biodome in the middle of Arizona to prepare but this is goodbye forever?

"I'm closing the studio," Dad finally announces. The machine above his bed monitoring his heart rate beeps twice in rapid succession and then quiets again.

"What?" Gabe and I say in unison.

"I want out. I've been thinking about it for a long time, and this little performance is the nail in the coffin, so to speak."

"Harrison, don't talk about nails and coffins," Diana says.

"We own the building, and the real estate—it's worth a fortune. I'm going to sell the building and then you two can have the proceeds from that now, rather than waiting until I kick the bucket, so you can get yourselves established somewhere more accessible, more reasonably priced, if the photography is still what you want to do." He looks at me. "Frankie, you do the books—you know how ridiculous the property taxes are on that place, how they go up every year because it's prime downtown real estate. You're the one who deals with clients who bitch and moan because there's no parking and the nearest garage charges four bucks an hour. Market's good right now— let's sell the building and get out while we can."

"But you're closing the business?" Gabe asks. "What about all of our clients?"

"I'm selling the building. If you want the clients, they're yours. You can set up elsewhere."

My phone buzzes again. I look down to scroll off what I assume will be another of Sam's messages, but it's Aunt Mariah texting with just a single line: ***Thinking of you. Hope your father is OK. Love, Auntie M.***

"I've been taking pictures for a long time. I want to go see the world without the pressure of deadlines or client satisfaction." My dad lifts his tethered hand and Diana takes it. "We want to travel. I want to teach Diana to take photos. It's time for me to see places on my own terms, not because AP or NatGeo have sent me."

Where the hell am I going to get a job? I've been taking care of Dad and Gabe for so long, my résumé literally has one line on it. I worked for Dad before university, and then the day after graduation, I came back and reclaimed my office chair and have worked for Dad ever since. My health insurance is through Hawes Photography. How will I pay my rent without a regular paycheck? Sure, Dad has made some money but we're not filthy rich, not compared to Nikki and her family—and he still makes us work for a living. No handouts.

Where I am stunned silent, Gabe is purpling with anger. Lainie speaks close to his ear, low enough that I can't hear from where I'm seated, but Gabe is shaking his head obstinately. That's his forte— being impossible.

"Dad, forgive me, but you can't just quit the business. You have upcoming contracts that need to be fulfilled. We have shoots booked."

"I had a massive heart attack, Gabriel. Either you can take the jobs, or we refund their deposits and those clients can find a new photographer. I'm not going to kill myself over another family's annual portrait or their daughter's wedding," my dad says, a little more vigor in his voice. "And if you want to keep the business going, then you can. We will need to sit down with the lawyers and hash it all out, see where you both fit in here, if there's a future for Hawes Photography or if you go off on your own."

"I can't rely on Frankie to help shoot clients," Gabe says, his short laugh harsh.

"Wow. Another vote of confidence. Thanks, Gabe," I say.

"You're a secretary, Frankie! That's what you do! You answer phones and do paperwork and smile at the customers—"

"Enough." My father's voice echoes off the walls, and his heart monitor responds in kind.

"Gabriel, Francesca, I know this is a lot to take in," Diana says, "but I'm going to speak as a medical professional here and ask that you both take a five-minute timeout away from this room. You see that little blinking number on the screen? We need to keep that from going above 75. It is currently at 112."

"Sorry, Dad," I say. I stand and go to him, giving him a kiss on the cheek. "You rest. We can deal with this when you get out of here, yeah? I'm sure everything will work out. It always does."

Dad kisses me back. "I'm not going to dump you on your butt, kid. We'll sort this out."

"I trust you." I give him one more quick hug, grab my bag, and say goodbye to everyone except Gabe.

I wish Harrison and Diana's news was that they were selling Gabe and adopting a shiny new sister for me instead.

TWENTY-ONE

THE AQUA-FIT INSTRUCTOR took one look at my face and asked me if I had medical clearance to be here. She then lowered her voice and asked if I needed help, like, was my boyfriend beating on me or something, and I laughed and explained to her that no, I do not have a boyfriend and if I did, he certainly wouldn't be beating on me.

We're not supposed to talk during class, but Bryony and I always find space in the back of the pool, giving the side-eye to anyone who tries to take our spot.

The first question out of her mouth once we're in the water: "Have you called him back yet?"

"Eyes forward, Bryony," I say. She splashes me.

I follow along, though the bouncy exercises still rattle my brain a little so I just do the arm exercises and underwater leg stuff minus the bouncing. The first time I got into this pool and realized I was the youngest by forty years, I thought Bryony had made a mistake about the class time and started to get out. But because she's so tall, she's got an early arthritic situation going on in her feet and knees, so this low-impact, water exercise is easier on her than the personal trainer I hired who dragged us around the gym until we barfed.

And don't underestimate the intensity of a solid hour of aqua-fit—this shit's tougher than it looks.

"You have to call him back, Frankie, or he's going to lose interest and move on."

"Really, Bry? He'll lose interest? I'm not a puppy or a plot of land."

"You know what I mean."

"Seems Sam McKenzie has enough to keep his interest right now. That Lisa woman was so pregnant, I'd be surprised if she hasn't burst since last weekend."

The change in the music means it's time to do the exercises with the pool noodles. Bryony grabs two off the pool's side and hands me one. "It's Thursday—four days since you've been back from Canada, since you saw him at the hospital. He's probably going crazy with worry. If you'd just meet him for coffee so he can explain his side of the story—"

I stop treading water and stand still. "Whose side are you on?"

Bryony stops too. "I will always be on your side. But I also know how stubborn you can be when you come within an inch of anything that might be remotely painful."

"I don't have time for a relationship right now," I say.

"You are the worst liar," Bryony says. "What, because your social calendar is filled with dates with me? Aqua-fit and sushi? And your job is so overwhelming that you have to work nights and weekends just to keep on top of things?"

I give her a dirty look and kick my feet harder, punishing the water.

"I've known you for too long to listen to your self-sabotage anymore, Francesca. I'm worried about you. I can see how unhappy you are. And now with your dad closing the studio, you've got this amazing opportunity to go and do something that YOU want to do, free of Gabe and Harrison, and you're frozen. I heard you on the phone with Gabe in the locker room—you cannot possibly want to keep working for him. I love you, but your brother is a jerk and always has been. Stop begging him to keep you on as staff and go find what makes you happy."

"And are you happy, Bryony? Working at that insurance agency? What was your major at school anyway? Art history? What happened to that big important job you were going to get curating for museums? What about your dreams of working at LACMA or the Met? Instead you're selling car and health insurance and dealing with dickheads who ask you how the weather is up there and then grab your ass. Are YOU happy?"

The music is still playing but everyone in the pool has paused and is watching us.

I don't say anything else—mostly because I can't. If I talk, I will cry, and that doesn't solve anything. It's impossible to stomp out of a pool, damn water, so I swim to the side, slapping the surface as hard as I can, which doesn't hurt the water at all but does in fact make the sides of my hands and arms sting. I climb up the stairs, quickly grabbing my towel off the railing because I know everyone is still watching and they just saw my flabby butt but I don't even care.

I just want to go home.

Bryony doesn't follow me to the changing rooms, and behind me I can hear the class resuming where I so rudely interrupted. I skip the shower—I don't want to take any longer than necessary, to give Bryony time to reconsider. Wet bathing suit kicked off, I dress as quickly as I can. A little girl in a flower-and-unicorn suitie watches me while waiting for her mom who's on her phone complaining very loudly that the Starbucks barista screwed up her flat white and "only morons can't make a decent flat white."

I thought flat white was a paint color.

I pull on my shoes and check my phone, more out of habit than anything. There's a text from Gabe: ***Nikki Meyer is coming in tomorrow at 10 to see what we've got. FYI***.

Awesome.

∼

FORTUNATELY, Nikki comes in with her parents, *sans* Drunk Edwin, and they have the reins tight so she behaves. Donovan Meyer talks with me and Gabe, asks about my dad, mentions that he'll wait a week or two for Dad to settle in and then give him a call.

He also pays the balance on the wedding package. I provide them with a USB drive with every shot we took that I'd uploaded to the cloud. Gabe edited the stuff Nikki wants to use on her lifestyle site, nearly choking on his own tongue when he had to admit the photos were nearly as good as he would've taken—and when Nikki starts in on me about being irresponsible enough to leave *her* photos on *my* laptop in the trunk of my car, Donovan shuts her up. His raised voice makes Sherlock Bones lift his head from the rug under my chair, but the pull of his nap is too much to resist.

"Her father had a heart attack. The last thing she gave a shit about was photos of you prancing around like a spoiled brat after ruining a six-figure wedding so you could canoodle with the best man."

Jesus ... six figures?

"Edwin and I are in *love*, Daddy."

"You were supposed to be in *love* with Robert." Donovan looks at me. "Next time, she's eloping."

Donovan and Mrs. Meyer then stand and thank us for our time and energy, and Donovan repeats that he'll call my dad soon and get him out for a walk around the green. I have a hard time reconciling a friendship between my father, who wears Fruit of the Looms from Target, and Donovan Meyer, who probably owns Target.

Once they leave, Gabe hobbles back to his desk, whining as he props his leg on a pillow-topped stool. "Are we carpooling to the lawyer's this afternoon? We have to be there at four," he asks. Sherlock follows him and pushes into circus pose, hoping Gabe will drop a bite of the half-eaten sandwich on his desk.

"I'll drive myself." I plug in my earbuds, route the calls to voicemail because what's the point in taking client calls if all the clients are going to vaporize in the next month anyway, and proceed to do the month-end books.

Routine and structure.

Dependability and order.

Drama-free and organized.

Until the front door jingles open and Sam McKenzie walks in.

TWENTY-TWO

"CAN I HELP YOU?" I ask.

"Really?"

"Hawes Photography is here to meet your needs, to capture those memories most important to you, those life events you absolutely don't want to miss. Like the births of your children. We have a special package just for that—"

"Stop, Frankie. Just ..." Sam nods at Gabe, pats Sherlock's back as he sniffs this newcomer, and then grabs one of the chairs from the waiting area. He plunks it down on the opposite side of my reception desk. On his lap rests an old Nike shoebox, held closed by two thick rubber bands that look stretched to their limits.

"Why are you even here? If you want your bag, they didn't take that from the car. It's in the back room—" I stand, as if I'm going to retrieve Sam's overnight bag from the wedding weekend. I guess the thieves weren't interested in pajamas and dirty underwear—they left our clothes but took everything else, including a fresh tube of toothpaste and my half-finished packet of birth control pills.

"Frankie, I'm not here for my bag. Please ... I just want to talk."

"So, talk."

"I didn't lie to you about being at the resort for the wedding. I already told you—when Gabe called, I saw it as an opportunity for us to reconnect."

"We certainly did that, didn't we."

Sam blushes, hard, just as Gabe's chair rolls out from his desk. "Come on, Sherlock," he says, snapping his fingers. He then grabs his crutches and makes himself scarce, the dog trotting after him. Guessing Gabe's not too keen thinking about his little sister sleeping with his former best friend.

"Aren't you late for a Lamaze class or something? Honestly, you don't have to explain anything to me. I'm good. It was a fun weekend, but now we're back to reality."

"Her baby—"

"Her, as in Lisa R. The 'work thing' you spent all weekend ignoring."

Sam takes a measured breath and sets the orange-and-white box on the floor at his feet. "Lisa Reynolds is her name. She's a colleague, in the loosest sense of the word. She's a freelance developer who's done some work for my boss. We went on a couple dates months ago—"

"I'd say, oh, about nine months ago?"

"She was newly pregnant when we went out, but I didn't know that. We had dinner and drinks, a lot of drinks, and yeah, we slept together. But then she told me she was already pregnant and she really wanted to work it out with the baby's father—we were basically friends with benefits, and I had zero interest in stepping into the middle of her relationship. We parted ways. I thought that was the end of it."

Sam readjusts in his chair, clearly uncomfortable. "She showed up one night late and said he beat her up and kicked her out of their apartment. She stayed with me for a couple weeks until she could get her own place, but something in her head sort of snapped. I didn't know her that well, but I've since learned from her sister that Lisa has schizophrenia and the pregnancy meant she had to taper down her meds."

He reaches into his back pocket and pulls out a folded paper—a legal document.

I unfold it. "You had to get a restraining order?"

"Not just me—several people in our office." Sam leans back in his chair while I scan the page. The RO was issued three months ago, set to expire three months from now. "She had a situation about a month ago where she showed up at the office, clearly not in her right mind, so we—myself and my boss, Alysha—we transported Lisa to the nearest hospital and they admitted her on a psych hold until her sister could get here from back east."

"What about her baby? Oh my god, what if she hurts it?"

"I'm not going to tell you that doesn't keep me up at night. It's not my kid, but it's an innocent baby. My boss and another woman in the office do some outreach work with a women's shelter, so they're trying to help Lisa get ready for the birth, to make sure she has a support system in place—the sister has her own family in New Jersey or something, so she can't stay out here indefinitely."

"Will she take Lisa's baby?"

"I don't know. I've tried to stay out of it—I can't be near her. It got violent before, but now she's even worse," he says, and then his face looks so sad. "When I got home from Canada ... Zod was missing. She broke into my place and kidnapped him. Said she took him to the pound because we couldn't have a cat near the baby."

"Jesus, Sam ... Did you go look for him?"

"She refused to tell me which shelter she took him to. I checked with Multnomah County Animal Control and the Oregon Humane Society, but they don't have him. I honestly don't know if she maybe just dumped him in the woods or something. He's got a microchip, so maybe someone will find him eventually." He drops his head, eyes down.

"I'm so sorry, Sam." I should offer to help him look for his cat. "Does she think you're going to be living together?"

"She thinks a lot of things, Frankie, and a lot of those things involve surveillance from the CIA and alien worlds."

"Are the police or Social Services involved? Does anyone know her history and that she's about to have a baby?"

"Yeah. She's probably going to lose custody as soon as it's born."

"And she's going to blame you for that," I say.

Sam pushes his fingers into his eyes, like he's trying not to let any emotion escape. He used to do that when we were kids and he was trying to keep Gabe from seeing him cry.

His chair squeaks as he sniffs and leans forward to take the restraining order back, folding it and replacing it in his back pocket.

"I wasn't cheating on anyone, and I didn't mean to deceive you about the wedding," Sam says, his voice quiet. "I've missed you. I've missed this family. You were *my* family too." His eyes are nothing but honest, the green irises bright like damp spring grass.

"I don't know what to say."

"You don't have to say anything," Sam says, standing abruptly and then leaning to pick up the shoebox. "I just needed to let you know I didn't cheat, on anyone. I would never do that to you, Frankie." He moves the chair back to its place with the others against the wall but stops again in front of my desk, handing me the box. "This is for you. Do whatever you want with it."

The little bell on the studio door announces his departure.

He doesn't look back.

"He's a good guy, Frankie," Gabe says from the breakroom doorway. "He's loved you since we were kids."

I laugh, but not because he's funny. "Seriously? Says the guy who stole his girlfriend and broke his heart," I say. I stare at the shoebox, now sitting in the middle of my desk. Its corner is pressing a button on my keyboard, causing the computer to holler at me in a series of staccato beeps. I move the box, but I don't want to open it. No idea what's in it, but whatever it is, I don't want to share it with Gabe.

"I'm taking a sick day. Make sure Sherlock gets home, will ya?" I yank my purse out of the bottom drawer of my desk and tuck the shoebox under my arm.

"Lawyer at four! He charges by the hour!" Gabe hollers after me just before I slam the studio's heavy back door.

My car is back to its former self, thanks to Lainie, parked in its usual space behind the building. God, Gabe doesn't deserve a woman as good as Lainie, but I'm so glad that she's in our lives.

On the driver's side, under the windshield wiper, is a paper bubble mailer.

I yank it out, the paper part limp from a recent shower. I tear into it. Inside is another doggie figurine—a Boston terrier. I don't have a Boston terrier yet. This one's cute.

Dad must've coordinated with Gabe to leave it out here for me. He'll deny it. I'll thank him at the lawyer's.

I tuck the dog into my pocket and set Sam's box on the front seat, staring at it like it might be filled with tarantulas. I can't open it now. What the hell could it possibly be?

I instead check my phone: two voicemails. The first is from the Portland Police—they've already had a hit on one of the stolen cameras from a pawn ticket submitted to their records department. The serial numbers match so I can contact Tracy at blah blah blah and they'll talk to me about next steps after the thirty-day hold has passed and if it's not needed as evidence of a crime committed. No information on its condition, if it'll even be usable, or if we'll ever get it back. Whatever. I've already filed an insurance claim for the stolen gear. Let it sit in the evidence room forever.

The second voicemail is from Aunt Mariah, who talks to the message service as if she's carrying on a live conversation with me. She's invited me over for drinks, "Coffee if you want but I have something stronger," and to meet her dogs. "You said you like dogs, didn't you?"

Yeah, Mariah, I do like dogs.

TWENTY-THREE

THAT THERAPIST from long ago told me I had a tendency toward avoidance behaviors, i.e., I tend to engage in tasks that are not central to what I should be doing but rather are activities that sidetrack my forward momentum. For example, instead of looking for a new job after Dad's bombshell about closing the studio, I cleaned out my closets until three in the morning and spent too much money online ordering organizational baskets and tubs. Or instead of talking to Bryony to make up after our tiff at aqua-fit, I scheduled a dental cleaning and a Pap smear for next week.

Instead of preparing for the meeting at the lawyer's in four hours when we'll talk about the studio closing ... I just can't. It's too much. It's *always* been here. Our lives have revolved around it. What am I without Hawes Photography?

My whole life has been shaped by my father's skill—and my mother's, if I'm being a hundred percent honest—with the camera.

It's also why she's gone.

Sam's orange Nike box stares at me from the passenger seat. But I can't sit here in my car stewing about Sam and all the confused emotions stirring in my head and heart either.

I call Mariah back.

"Dahling, so good to hear from you. How's your papa?"

"Better. Home now to recover but already up and moving around, more than his doctors would like," I say.

"Yes, soon they'll send him to some smelly gym full of old people where he has to walk on a treadmill and listen to soothing music. Been there, done that," she says. "So, bring your camera and come over immediately. I will order us lunch—do you like dim sum? We have a great place on speed-dial." She gives me her address, and Monica in the background yells for me to Google Map it so Mariah doesn't get me lost.

This visit will serve perfectly.

I sneak back in through the studio's rear entrance to grab one of the spare cameras to photograph Mariah's dogs. Once returned to my car, I stuff Sam's box under the front seat to be dealt with later. I then open Google Maps and commit to feeding my avoidance behaviors steamed dumplings, rice noodle rolls, and Oolong tea.

AUNT MARIAH WASN'T EXAGGERATING when she said her Sol bought her a huge, expensive house.

The exterior looks like something right out of *Architectural Digest* if they were doing an article on the most impressive, old-money houses of Portland. The view is fantastic—right across the way from the duck pond and lawns green with the spring rain at Laurelhurst Park—but the front yard is ginormous with the house set far back on the property and gates blocking unwanted guests from snaking up the cobblestone driveway that leads to a proper servants' entrance. I park where I think is appropriate and follow the paved path around to the double-wide, carved-wood front door.

A maid answers the bell, introducing herself as Christina. She's dressed in a light-blue dress with a white apron tied over the front and sensible shoes. She welcomes me into the madness, her long, black braid bouncing between her shoulder blades as she leads me to the kitchen at the back.

The inside is just as beautiful as one would expect driving by, the décor a clear mix of the twin sisters. Huge windows let in a ton of light and crystal chandeliers abound. Monica's refined taste is reflected in the whitewashed wainscoting and refinished hardwood and parquet flooring, the lush Persian rug runners in hallways and on the grand staircase, the expensive, twenty-seat teak dining set, vases and artwork everywhere, interspersed with Mariah's wildness—crystal balls placed on corner tables draped in colorful, gauzy cloths, bowls full of raw crystals, the almost overwhelming aroma of incense, wall hangings of naked goddesses and Georgia O'Keeffe paintings that I'm pretty sure are not prints, and of course, dogs.

Like, seven dogs, of all shapes, sizes, and mobilities, including a scruffy little white thing with floppy, serrated ears who has a wheeled-harness device supporting his back end.

"That's FDR. Named after the thirty-second president who was paralyzed," Christina explains. She races through the names of the other dogs as they clamber around us, but they're barking too loudly to hear much of what she's saying.

Yeah, I fit in here. Maybe Aunt Mariah will adopt me.

"Francescaaaaa! Perfect timing! Christina will get you a plate," Aunt Mariah says, waving me over with a hand holding a wonton. "Hurry up before Monica eats all the good stuff."

Monica flaps a hand at her sister and pats an open chair between them.

For the next ninety minutes, we eat until we can't move and laugh until we can't breathe. Mariah tries to ply me with another of her favorite martinis—turns out Christina is an expert mixologist—but I explain I have to deal with family business this afternoon, and showing up sauced at the attorney's office may not play in my favor.

Conversation eventually turns to how my dad is doing, what's going on with the photo studio, and inevitably, Sam.

I tell them about his visit this morning—about the mystery box—

and about Lisa Reynolds and her mental illness, how Sam seems to have been roped into all of it.

"I knew the second I laid eyes on him that he was a keeper," Mariah says.

Monica rolls her eyes. "You were just wishing you were a few years younger so you could give him a test-drive."

"She's not wrong," Mariah says as she cracks a fortune cookie open and laughs. "Ha! Even the cookie knows: 'You will meet a beautiful stranger for long walks in the park.'"

"Be careful. Sounds like a serial killer to me," Christina says, clearing plates.

"That's the problem with this generation," Mariah says. "No romance. Everything is so serious. You kids and your social media and sneaky ways and swiping right."

"It's always been like that, sister," Monica chides. "We just didn't talk about it or announce our every move on the Twitter."

"What's in the box, do you suppose?" Mariah asks.

"No idea. It's an old Nike shoebox, held together with tape and thick rubber bands."

"Maybe it's his heart," Mariah says.

"Or maybe it's a token he's taken from one of his victims," Christina adds, pouring wine into Monica's glass. "Maybe a hand or an eyeball."

"You have to forgive Christina. She's studying criminology so everything to her is a potential murder."

"You want to be a police officer?" I ask. She's young—maybe twenty-two?

"FBI. Working on my degree right now. I have a little boy so I'm taking night classes."

"And she's the top student in her program, but she won't tell you that," Mariah says.

"If you need to disappear, Christina is your girl," Monica adds.

"Disappear?"

"She took us completely off the grid," Monica says. "She taught us how to use VPNs and protect our bank accounts and hide ourselves from the outside world, digitally speaking."

"It's important—these ladies are here alone, and my *abuela* was targeted by online scammers. They took all her money. I want to make sure these two are protected."

"Christina knows all the tricks," Mariah says. "She's a real Jane Bond." She giggles.

"That's her favorite joke about me," Christina says. "And I could help you. You'd be shocked to know how much Big Brother knows about you."

"You should let her look at your accounts," Monica says.

"Our Christina is the best," Mariah says, picking a discarded baby corn off her sister's plate. "And her little Aidan ... oh my goodness, he is just the cutest." She pauses and studies me for a second. "You know, with your bone structure and Sam's coloring, you would make very cute babies too."

"Mariah, stop it," Monica says, dropping another dumpling onto her plate. "Forgive my sister. Her own loins failed to produce so she's busy trying to make sure everyone else's compensates."

"Don't talk about my loins like that, you barren wasteland," she says. Monica howls at her sister. These two have the weirdest sense of humor.

Mariah then turns to me. "Your Sam—because he *is* your Sam, whether you admit it now or wait fifty years and lose precious, precious time—he doesn't seem like the sneaky type who is swiping right."

"I taught them about Tinder," Christina says, hiking an eyebrow.

"You were just hoping one of us would get murdered so you'd get an A in your forensics class," Monica says.

"Nothing gets past you, Auntie Monica," Christina teases as she refills water bowls for the dogs and then doles out cookies, but only if they sit. The dogs know what's up—they listen to Christina.

Mariah takes my hand, the back of hers blue with prominent veins through the paper-thin skin. The look on her face tells me we're moving on from jokes and into more delicate territory. "There's some stuff going on with you that I think needs working out before you're ready to be with that Sammy. Where is your mother, child?"

"I told you at the resort. I don't have one."

"You came from somewhere. Where *is* she?"

I can't speak. My throat has closed off. My nose and eyes sting. I shake my head.

"Don't torture the poor girl, Mariah," Monica says. "If her mother has left her, she doesn't want to rehash it with you over pork buns."

I shake my head again. "She left. When I was three. Like, she died."

Mariah hands me a cloth napkin embroidered with "M & S."

"How did she die?"

"Why does everyone always want to talk about this?" I say, trying to sound flippant.

"Because we learn how to become women by watching our mothers," Mariah says softly.

"Then I guess I'm not very good at being a woman," I say. "I just had my dad and brother to watch."

"And by watch, you mean watch *over*."

"I'm good at it. Watching over. Taking care. It's sort of my thing," I say, stuffing my mouth full of cashew chicken so I won't have to talk.

Grocery shopping from the age of ten on with all the coupons I'd clipped from the Sunday paper. Homework never late. Clean closets. Organized kitchen cupboards. Socks arranged in rainbow order. Dental cleanings every six months. No scuffs on the studio floor. Backdrop paper replaced immediately after even the smallest tear. Taxes filed on time. Hair appointments for Gabe, every third Thursday at 9:30 a.m. Annual eye appointments for Dad. Cholesterol medication refilled on the last Friday of the month.

"Your father closing his photo studio is a huge opportunity for you. What is it *you* want?"

I shrug. I have no idea. I've always only just taken care of my dad and Gabe. I've only ever just been the one they ask for stuff because they know it'll get done.

Mariah waggles a bony finger at me. "Tonight, after the lawyer business, I want you to sit with paper and a nice, sharp pencil—write down everything you've always wanted to do, your wildest dreams and your most practical ones. Write it all down. Then put stars next to those things you love most."

Aunt Mariah asks Christina to come over. The maid does, bending so Mariah can whisper in Christina's ear. When the young woman stands, she's smiling. "Be right back."

"You want me to write a bucket list?" I ask, doubtful.

"Call it whatever you want. I'm not saying this is a list of things you will do before you die," Mariah says. "This is a list to help you get straight in your head what you would do if nothing else mattered. And because we live in the modern world, money must be considered, so let's find a happy medium—what would you spend your days doing so that you could still afford to feed and clothe yourself? Are you going to follow your brother to his new studio and answer his phones until you're old and wrinkly like me? Or are you going to follow your own path?"

"But that's just it. I don't know where my path is."

"That's why you start by making the list."

Monica, who's been mostly quiet nibbling on fried rice, sets her fork aside and flattens a hand on the soft white linen tablecloth. Her fingers have fewer baubles today, but whoever married and then widowed her had expensive taste.

"Normally I do not subscribe to my sister's airy-fairy view of the world, but this list-writing—she made me do it back in the '70s. I never had my own children, and I was living as a surgeon's wife, spending his money and organizing his charity events while he slept his way through the OR nursing rotation. On my fiftieth birthday, Mariah made me sit down and write a list of everything I would do if I could.

"So, I did. And I went back to school—the oldest student by far back then—and got my master's degree in English literature, which was good for nothing except teaching spoiled brats who would rather make fun of Jane Austen and the Brontës instead of examine their progressive attitudes toward sexism and classism. But I was so proud of my master's degree that I got a PhD with a specialty in post-Regency, nineteenth-century literature, specifically the three Brontë sisters. I met a beautiful Spanish man who hardly had two cents to rub together and then divorced my surgeon husband. Yes, I was lucky in that I had his money to sustain me before and after the divorce, but I was no longer indentured to him. I was free."

"Well, free with a delicious payout from the surgeon's many bank accounts," Mariah teases.

"I had an excellent attorney. The best his money could buy," Monica says, lifting a penciled-on eyebrow. "But we're talking about you, little Francesca: this is *your* life. You need to find what 'free' means to you."

And then my sobbing body is encased in a hug from the nonagenarian twins who feel like a clamshell of expensive perfume mixed with incense and dog slobber.

When they finally let go, Christina is waiting patiently, a wine bottle showcased in her hands. Mariah thanks her, takes the bottle, and then hands it to me.

"This is a Domaine Serene Monogram, a Pinot Noir from the Willamette Valley, vintage 2011. You can open and drink it while writing your list, or you can save it for that first day in your new, 'free' life. Share a glass with someone," she winks, "or save it all for yourself. This bottle is about *you*."

She sets it on the table and I hug her again. "Thank you for this. For everything."

"You are always welcome here, at least until we're dead. I can't say whether the new owners will want you hanging around, eating their dim sum." She pats my cheek and sits back in her chair, feeding FDR the last chunk of her fortune cookie.

"So—enough with the heavy stuff. You brought a camera?

Because I'd really like some photos of these dumb dogs before I'm too blind to see them, and we're running out of time before you go into battle for your freedom." She taps the huge Apple Watch on her frail wrist.

I dab my face dry, finish the lemon water in my glass, and stand. Camera bag unzipped, I hoist the Nikon out of its resting place. "Come on, FDR. I'm gonna make you a star."

TWENTY-FOUR

"BUT IF YOU sell the building, our regular clients, the ones who we rely on for the business's foundation, will get annoyed and confused that they have to find a new place."

"That's what GPS is for, Gabriel," my father says. "That real estate is worth a fortune, way more than the cumulative value of the business itself."

They've been arguing about this for an hour. The lawyer has detailed reports about what we could get for the building, as well as the card of his most trusted real estate agent (read: his wife) ready to list it as soon as Monday.

"It'll sell within a week, I can almost promise you—in this area of downtown? If you were interested in redeveloping it yourselves, you could easily get the zoning permission and remodel the existing structure into high-end loft housing. It's all the rage in downtown. A very popular option for some of these older buildings, and then you have a passive rental income stream for life."

My dad is shaking his head before the lawyer even finishes speaking.

"Sell. Then we can divide the assets fairly so the kids can have their fresh start, and I can have my clean break."

"Harrison's cardiologist has strongly recommended he take time off from work to recover, so this is the right opportunity for him to make this decision," Diana says. Ordinarily I'd be pissed that this woman, basically a stranger, is sitting in on our very personal business. But she's been quiet, only chiming in where Dad's health is concerned, doing her best to maintain a neutral stance. By the looks of her (and yeah, I googled her so what shut up that's what we do nowadays), she's not here for Dad's money—she has a lot more green than he does.

"Taking 'time off,'" Gabe says, "is not the same as throwing in the towel."

"It's my towel, Gabriel. I'll do with it what I want."

The lawyer waits a beat and then with Dad's nod of approval, he pushes another folder toward Gabe. "We've prepared printouts of comparable, suitable properties for you to reestablish Hawes Photography—or whatever you choose to call it, if you rename—out of the downtown core. A few are in the suburbs, which would be an excellent option. I think you'll see the rents—"

"Rent? I don't want to rent. We *own* this building!" Gabe whines.

"Oh, for Pete's sake. You stand to walk away with at least a million bucks here, Gabe. That should be enough to set you up for a while. Stop your grousing," Dad says. His face is redder than I'd like.

A million dollars. I do the books for Hawes, and there's no way the business is worth that much. Location really IS everything—the building and its position in downtown is where the value is.

"And think, Gabe—a place out of downtown means parking," Lainie says. "What's the biggest thing people complain about when they call or come in?" She looks to me for confirmation.

"Parking," we say at the same time.

"It's expensive to park downtown," I say. "We lose a lot of potential clients because they get too stressed out about driving into the maze of one-way streets and then having to find parking on top of that, what limited parking there is where we are."

"People are wimps," Gabe says under his breath.

"People are your business, kid," Dad says.

"An address in the suburbs makes us look like Walmart," Gabe says.

Dad laughs. "Okay, well, you're going to have to figure this out on your own, then. I'm selling the building. Jerry, call your real estate lady. I want it listed by Monday." Dad flattens his hand on the shiny tabletop. The back of his left one is still greenish-yellow from the healing bruise where he had his IV. It's a subtle reminder about why we're here.

We want Dad to live, not be stressed out about work and keeping his children afloat.

"It's either we do this now, when I'm alive to pay for the damn attorney, or you wait until I'm dead and the two of you fight over my will." He turns to me. "What do you think, F-Stop? You've been awful quiet."

"I just want you to be healthy and happy, Dad. Gabe and I will do whatever we can to make sure you're not stressed. We don't want you to have another heart attack," I say.

"Harrison, did you want to ..." Jerry the lawyer pulls out yet another folder, this one stained with time. My dad meets Jerry's eyes and then nods, sitting back in his high-backed, brown-leather chair.

"Your father also wanted to address this while we're all here today. Your mother had a life insurance policy, plus there was a payout from the Associated Press because she was killed while working for them. Those funds have been in trust accounts since you were children, gathering interest, waiting for your father's approval to release the money."

Jerry opens the folder and passes over stapled documents, first to me and then Gabe. It's a bank statement, listing Dad's name first as the trust account holder, my name on the second line.

And then a balance, nearly equal to what we'll get as a payout from the sale of the building.

I slide the document back. "I don't want this." I grab my jacket and purse off my chair and stand. "Are we done here? Have we decided we're selling the building?"

"Francesca, please," my dad says.

"I have an appointment. I gotta go."

Which is bullshit. It's nearly six o'clock on a Friday night.

Before anyone else can object to my leaving, I pull the heavy frosted-glass-and-chrome door toward me and do my best to not run through the office and down the four flights to the parking garage.

I'M STILL KINDA FULL from the dim sum with the twins, but this cheeseburger is too delicious and melty to not eat and I think it's in the Bible that throwing away sweet potato fries is a sin. Plus it all pairs beautifully with this Japanese whisky the guy at the liquor store recommended. Friday nights are usually sushi with Bryony, but neither one of us has broken the stalemate, so cow it is, and alone at that.

Across my kitchen table sits Sam's Nike box. We're having a stare-down.

So far, I'm winning, rearranging all my dumb dog statues in order by breed rather than opening the box.

Hound group, working group, toy group, sporting group ...

This whisky is super nice and my cheeks are warm and I'm feeling much lighter and fuzzier than I was this morning when dumb Sam just whisked into the studio with his sad tale about that crazy Lisa R. and how he's missed me and *look here's the restraining order and also she kidnapped my cat*—

Okay, that part really, really sucks. I can't even make a joke about it because cats are innocent creatures and it sounds like Zod was really cool and even though cats aren't dogs, they don't deserve to be kidnapped by assholes like Lisa R., so now I'm crying for Zod and I can't chew this bite in my mouth because I'm crying too hard and I'd better spit it out or else I'm going to choke to death, all alone, drunk at my dining room table with an unopened box of what could be body-part trophies from Sam's serial-killed victims.

As I'm leaning over the garbage to lose the bite in my mouth, my body shaking with sadness for Zod who could be out in the woods all by himself, scared and alone and cold and hungry, someone knocks on the door.

I spit and rinse at the sink. I can't talk to anyone right now. I'm too sad. Poor Zod.

"Frankie, open up. It's me."

"What do you want?" I shuffle over and say from the other side. Bryony is so tall that when I look through the peep hole, I only see her boobs. She has nice boobs. I've always been jealous of her boobs. Mine are pathetic.

"Just let me in. Please?"

I undo the deadbolt and open the door a couple inches, but I can't stop crying. "Zod is gone," I announce.

Bryony has a cloth grocery bag over her shoulder and a pink pastry box in her hands with the legendary Voodoo Doughnuts logo on its top. She nudges her way into my apartment, sets her packages down on the hall table, and bends down to wrap me in a hug. "I don't know who Zod is, but I'm sorry he's gone." She pushes back, sniffs in the region of my face, and examines my eyes. "You've had a little drinky-poo tonight?"

"It's Japanese. It's really good. Come have some." I relock the front door. Serial killers lurk in dark hallways waiting to prey on young single women, or at least that's what Christina said.

Bryony lifts her grocery bag and the doughnut box from the table.

"I'm sorry we didn't do sushi tonight," I say, a fresh wave of tears buffeting into me. "I had a cheeeeeeseburger instead," I sob. "It was really good but I'm so sad about Zod, I can't eat anymore. There's some left if you want it."

"Thank you for the offer," she says, eyeing the half-eaten mess of a burger on the table. "You sit and I'll make us something warm to drink. Coffee or tea?"

"I don't care. You pick."

I plop back onto my chair and finish the sliver of whisky left in my glass. I don't want any more cheeseburger or fries. *Sorry, Bible. I can't finish my sweet potato fries. Zod is gone and I'm sad.*

Bryony brings over a plate of the weird doughnuts that made Voodoo famous. Some people call it a tourist trap, that you can get better doughnuts just about anywhere else—my favorite pastry place is called Piewalker's but it's only open until seven and it's now, like, ten, so I'm just glad Bryony thought to bring me maple bars with bacon because maple bars are my favorite and I really tried to stop eating bacon but bacon is delicious. I should make that my New Year's resolution for next year: stop eating bacon.

"You okay, Frankie? What's going on? Who's Zod?" Bryony slides a cup of peppermint tea in front of me. The steam warms my chin. It's nice.

"Zod is a cat. Or was. Maybe he's dead. Oh my god, he might be dead."

"Okay ... whose cat is—was—he?"

"Sam's."

"So, Sam's cat died?"

"Kidnapped," I say. Bryony hands me a wad of tissues from a box on the windowsill. She knocks over, and then rights, a Great Dane in the process.

"Who kidnapped Zod?"

"Lisa R."

Bryony holds her cup in front of her face for a second. She's thinking. "Lisa R.—is that the pregnant friend of Sam's?"

"Only she's not his friend. She's terrible and she took poor Zod to the pound or maybe dumped him all alone and scared in the woods, we don't really know. She said cats are bad for babies."

"So the baby is Sam's."

I shake my head. "He had a restraining order." Through my fuzzy head, I see Sam sliding the unfolded document across the reception desk.

"I'm confused. Lisa R. had a restraining order against Sam?" Her face pales.

"NO. Lisa R. is violent and mean—obviously, if she kidnapped little Zod—so Sam had to get a restraining order against *her* because she broke into his apartment and kidnapped his cat and threatened him too."

"Whoa."

"Poor Zod," I say, crying into the tissues. "He was just a cat. He didn't know anything about people problems."

"Okay, so is Sam okay? Did Lisa R. hurt Sam?"

"Nuh-uh. He's fine. He came to see me this morning."

"And that's when he told you about Zod and the restraining order?"

"Yeah ... he also brought me this." I plunk my hand on top of the Nike box; one of the old rubber bands finally gives way and splits itself in half.

"What is it?"

"A shoebox."

"Yes, but what is inside of it?"

"Dunno. I haven't looked."

"Do you want to look?"

"No. Christina said it could be body parts."

Bryony sets her teacup down. "Who is Christina? And why would Sam give you body parts?"

"She's going to work at the FBI. She would know this stuff."

"Mm-hmm ... okay, well, I think we've had enough of this fine Japanese whisky"—she takes the bottle and puts it on top of the fridge —"and I think a nice, hot bath will do you some good. How does that sound?"

I nod. That sounds really nice. Then I can cry about Zod and my tears will just melt into the bathwater but I have to be careful not to cry too much or I'll flood the apartment and float down the street in my bathtub, naked for the whole world to see.

The next thing I know, Bryony is nudging my shoulder. I must've fallen asleep with my head on the table. She helps me into the bathroom and into the tub. I don't even care if she sees me in my birthday suit because we're best friends and we're both girls so it doesn't matter.

The water is so warm and lovely. "This is really perfect, Bry. Thank you," I say, sliding until the bubbles from the bath bomb tickle my neck.

"I'm going to set up the couch. It's okay if I sleep over?"

"That would be cool. We could go for breakfast in the morning. Ooooh! Elmer's! Let's go to Elmer's and get German pancakes. Those are sooooo good ..."

"Let's just get you through tonight first. See if you're up for actual food by the time this whisky wears off."

"Good plan. I love you, Bryony. Thank you for being my best friend. We're like those awesome doctors on that hospital show—"

"*Grey's Anatomy?*"

"I am Cristina Yang and you're Meredith Grey and we're each other's *people*."

"That is a good show."

"You're my person, right, Bry?"

"Of course, Frankie," she says, leaning over to kiss my forehead. "Don't drown. I'm coming to check on you in ten minutes."

"Whatever you say, boss." I salute her. My arm feels heavy and splashes water over the side of the tub when I drop it back into the water.

Poor Zod.

TWENTY-FIVE

"SOOO, are we still going for German pancakes?" Bryony asks, carrying the whole pot of coffee to the table. She's moved my figurines back to the shelves where they usually sit without a single word of teasing me about why a grown woman has toy dogs in her apartment.

"Please do not talk about food." My stomach flips over itself. "I'm never drinking again."

"Well, at least not until tonight," she teases.

"No, I mean it this time."

"Mm-hmm." She pushes a glass of orange juice and two extra-strength Advil in front of me, as well as a plate with a plain buttered bagel. "Down the hatch."

I swallow the pills with the OJ, which has clearly been spiked. "What the hell? I just said I was never drinking again!"

"It's a finger of vodka. Hair of the dog. You'll thank me when your head stops pounding."

"Oh god, why did I drink so much?"

"You were sad about Zod."

Riiiiight. My throat tightens. "I'm still sad about Zod."

Bryony sits down across from me. "Do you think maybe you were sad about more than just a cat you've never met?"

I look up at her but the light coming in from the curtained window next to the table is so bright. "We met with Dad's lawyer yesterday. He's selling the building—they're listing it on Monday. Gabe is freaking out."

"Wow, that's fast. And Gabe is always freaking out about something. How do *you* feel about it?"

"Honestly, I have no idea what to do with my life."

"Is Gabe asking you to work for him?"

"He just assumes I'll follow wherever he goes, like a lost puppy who does his filing and answers his phone," I say, finishing the rest of the OJ cocktail, grimacing as that last gulp hits my unsettled stomach. "I went to see the twins yesterday, before the lawyer."

"The old ladies from Nikki Meyer's wedding?"

"They're so cool. You have to come with me and meet them. Aunt Mariah has seven dogs—one of them is named FDR and has a little doggie wheelchair—anyway, I photographed all of them. It was awesome."

"What does this have to do with the studio closing?"

"Oh. Yeah, right. Sorry. Aunt Mariah said I need to make a list of all the things I want to do, like, what I would do for a job if I could pick my future."

"Have you made the list?"

"I drank the whisky instead."

"We should do this together. Today. I'll make a list with you. It'll be fun." Bryony walks over to my desk, easily locating pens and paper because my tidy apartment is a perfect display of my avoidance behaviors.

She hands me a set, and then sits, the old wooden chair creaking under her. When she sees my face, though, she sets her pen down. "Did something else happen yesterday? You don't look like you're done feeling sad."

"The lawyer had some paperwork. About my mom. There's

money from her life insurance and a death-benefit payout from the Associated Press. My dad has had it in trust all these years, earning interest."

"Well ... that's good news, isn't it?"

I look at her sharply. "Good news that my mother is dead?"

She tips her head at me. "You know what I mean, Frankie."

"I don't want the money."

"You might someday. Let it sit for a while. Think about it. Talk to your dad when it's just the two of you and no Gabe and no lawyer." She nods toward the Nike box. "Aren't you the least bit curious about what's in Sam's box?"

"I can only deal with one upheaval at a time right now, Bry."

"Right. Okay." She uncaps her pen and refills her coffee cup, in that order. "So—shall we write some lists?"

We spend the next few hours sipping our way through the pot, pausing only for Bryony to make scrambled eggs that I barely nibble on because *whiskyyyy*. Otherwise we hunch over our respective pads of paper and write weirdly shaped lists of everything from climbing mountains to space travel to a year in Scotland to more practical things, like working in a big, important museum and being out from under the weight of student loans and leaving the insurance job due to exhaustion stemming from explanations around why flood insurance is so expensive, and not having to work for our dumb brother anymore and taking more photos of dogs and maybe one day owning a farm that's filled with rescue dogs and the occasional cat, but only if the cat is cool, like Zod undoubtedly was, and maybe going back to school to get a master's so I can get a respectable job that people don't look down their nose at.

"So, if you don't want to work for Gabe anymore, what's your plan?" She spins my list around so she can see it. "You really want to go back to school?"

"No. Not really. But I also don't want to be a secretary anymore, not for Gabe or anyone else. And that's basically all I'm qualified to do with an English degree. And I'm tired of people treating me like the hired help."

She leans back against her chair. "Hey, you said you photographed the aunts' dogs yesterday. Can I see the photos?"

"They're dogs."

"Lemme see 'em. I love dogs."

"You do not love dogs."

"Okay, well, I tolerate dogs because YOU love them, and that's what you do when you're someone's person." Bryony has a nasty scar on her left hand and wrist that justifies why she may not love dogs. And no matter how many times I tell her that a dog's behavior is a reflection of how it's been treated by its owners, she can't get past the fear that's been with her since she was seven. Being a chew toy for a rogue Rottweiler will do that to a person.

I grab the camera and my laptop, and plug in the card to download yesterday's shots. It's an older DSLR, so no Wi-Fi—gotta do this the "old-fashioned way," which always makes my dad laugh because he used film for most of his career. *"When you had to know how to actually take a picture,"* he says.

Bryony scoots her chair over so she can watch the images pop up on the screen. I grabbed some photos of Mariah and Monica and Christina too, a few posed as a group, then individually, and most of them candids, showcasing the joie de vivre that oozes from these women.

"These are amazing," Bryony says.

"You have to meet them. Mariah is hilarious—like the friendly neighborhood witch, all mystical and new agey. She wears broom skirts and tons of bracelets whereas Monica's a bit more serious, Chanel suits and the like, even at home, but it's obvious they adore each other."

"They've been together since the very first moments as clumps of cells."

"Isn't that crazy? It makes me worry ..."

"About what one will do if the other dies first."

"Yeah," I say. "They're ninety-two."

"No way. Okay, we need to ask them about their skincare regimen."

"Right?" I point at the screen. "This is Christina. She lives in the house with them—she and her little boy. He was at daycare yesterday so I didn't meet him, but the sisters talk about how cute he is."

"Is she related to them?"

"I don't know … neither of the twins had their own kids, so unless she's a niece or something. But she wore a uniform and she seemed very devoted and patient."

"And she's the one who wants to work at the FBI," Bryony adds. "The one who said Sam's box probably has body parts?"

I laugh and look at the Nike box, which has since been moved to the bar that separates the kitchen from the dining area. "I suppose it would have blood seepage or something. Unless the pieces are wrapped in Ziplocs."

"I'm pretty sure Sam isn't a serial killer." Bryony sits back in her chair. "Those are amazing shots, Frankie. I know you don't want to believe you're a good photographer, but you are. It's in your blood."

A very cute shot of FDR flashes on the screen. The deep breath crawls out of my chest like it's been waiting there for a year to come out. "She chose photography over us, Bry."

Bryony gives the screen a confused look, and then picks up what I'm saying. "She didn't. Your mother loved you."

"Not as much as the job. Not as much as she loved putting herself in warzones so she could chase some fucking award that just sits on a shelf to collect dust."

"I don't know what to say, Frankie. But I'm glad you're talking about it. Finally."

"Mariah asked me at the resort, while we were waiting to see what would happen with everything—she asked me where my mom was. I hate it when people ask me that. Usually I can just slough it off but this was different."

"You were in a vulnerable spot up there—you were already

feeling nervous about shooting the wedding, but then Sam showed up and there were sparks and you were surrounded by people who have family … It's only natural that the pond might get stirred up a bit."

As much as I don't want to admit it, watching Nikki with her mom, even as brutal as Mrs. Meyer is—it made me think about my own wedding day and how much it sucks that my mother won't be there to help me buy a dress or get ready or put on my veil. And then Sam was there, and those dreaded sparks that have left my heart short-circuiting, even as I avoid that box sitting on the counter.

He hasn't texted me since yesterday, which I guess is good. At least he's not being a weird stalker dude.

Maybe Bryony's right. Maybe the Meyer wedding stirred up sediment that has sat dormant for too long.

"You should be proud of your mother, Frankie. She seemed like an amazing woman. She'd have to be—look at her daughter!"

Hmmph. "I *am* very good with a copy machine, I won't deny it."

"Smart-ass," she says, sipping her coffee, now likely cold. "I'm glad you're joking about it. This is all progress. I think I like Mariah the Good Witch."

With the last photo downloaded, I unplug the memory card reader and close my laptop. "Why does this still bother me all these years later? I hardly even remember her! Why am I so *angry* about it?"

"I don't know. I'm not a shrink." She flattens her hand over my list, still sitting near her on the table. "I do think that if you look through this, if you *really* get to the heart of what you've written down here, you might find something on it that would make your mother proud. It's human nature to want our parents to be proud of us." She reaches over and takes my hand. "I think you should show your dad these photos. See what he says."

"He'll just pick them apart. My dad photographs important stuff."

"Do not look at the photo of poor paralyzed FDR with his gnawed-off ears and say he's not important. You could do a lot of good photographing dogs who need families. And I'm not going to let you whine about how mean your dad is—he's an internationally recognized, award-winning photographer. If he's giving you feedback, that's because he wants you to be better." She gives me a stern look.

"Francesca, forgive me for saying this, but you sound like a brat right now—do you know how many up-and-coming photographers would give their left arm for feedback from someone like Harrison Hawes?"

"Sure, but that's because he's not their dad."

"And you're afraid of disappointing him," Bryony says, releasing my hand. "Which is exactly my point. No one can find this for you." She taps her fist over her heart. "No one can find what gets you out of bed in the morning except you."

Bryony leans over in her chair and wraps me in a hug. She really does give the best hugs.

"You claim to not be a therapist, but you're really good at it," I say against her shoulder. "Thank you."

She pushes back, both hands on my shoulders. "Think nothing of it. Now—about those pancakes," she says, lifting an eyebrow.

"I could eat."

"Hair of the dog," Bry says, lifting her hand for a high five. "Works every time."

TWENTY-SIX

THE HAWES PHOTOGRAPHY building sells right away. I didn't want details about what the new owners were going to do with it. As soon as the ink dries, everything happens fast—within a month's time, all our photography gear has been inventoried, packed up, and moved. Gabe found another location quickly, thanks to the Jerry the lawyer's wife and her mad real estate connections. It's still in Portland but in a cool redevelopment with other businesses, a storefront like before (Gabe insisted upon this), and, yes, tons of parking.

Dad and Gabe and I spent our last evening at the old studio, just the three of us, sitting on the floor, eating Thai takeout from the containers, sharing a few beers and a few more laughs, our voices echoing off the space that had been emptied of our equipment, of our lives over the last two decades.

And then saying goodbye to Sherlock Bones, and yes, Mrs. Gianotti—gahhhh. Ouch. She gave us a ton of fresh meats and hard cheeses wrapped in white butcher paper as well as a party tray of cannolis, "So you eat—you must eat," she commanded. Then she started crying and hugging Dad, alternating between pinching my cheeks and then Gabe's. She'd wipe off her tears, and then it would start all over again. We tried to remind her that we're not leaving Portland, that Gianotti's is the only deli for the Hawes family, but she just flapped a hand at us.

"Francesca, you have to come and take this dumb dog for a walk. He will be the death of me," she said, and with a final wave, she limped out the front door and down the block, Sherlock Bones barking at her heels.

When our avoidance to leave became almost comical, Dad ripped off the Band-Aid and kicked us out. A tearful final walk-through, our arms loaded with Mrs. Gianotti's presents, and then we clicked off the lights and closed the door forever.

It only takes a few days for Gabe, Lainie, and me to get the new place in working order. We have a guy coming in tomorrow to finish installing the new automated rigs for our backdrops, and then it's back to business. Good thing too—people are very excited about the new location, and after hearing about Dad's heart attack and subsequent retirement, a bunch of our longtime customers called to book shoots to support Gabe and me in our new venture.

So imagine Gabe's surprise when I give my notice.

"But the studio's not even open yet. You can't quit!"

We're at their place, an open, airy, modern loft apartment with plenty of room for their insane dog. I brought dim sum from Mariah's favorite restaurant because I knew we needed to have this conversation in private, in case Gabe lost his shit.

"I'll give you a month. Once we're really rolling again, you can hire a new person and I'll stay long enough to train them."

"I'm not going to find someone who can do everything—marketing, Photoshop, accounting, keeping the customers happy, shooting when I need ..."

I wish I could bottle the look on Gabe's face as he's speaking. It's like as the words fall out of his mouth, maybe for the first time he realizes that he needs me, that I bring value to this family business.

"Frankie, you're buying a house. Mortgage lenders kind of like it when homeowners have jobs."

"I'm not taking out a mortgage," I say. It's true. The money from the sale of the building was in cash, shockingly, so Dad didn't waste any time doling out what he said he would to my brother and me. He and Diana left yesterday for their ten-day European river cruise—to take pictures, no doubt—so he wasn't kidding when he said it was time to do something different with his time.

And no, we still haven't talked about my mother's money. He said we could do that when he gets home from Germany.

"So, what, you're just going to be alone in that big house all by yourself and watch soaps and wear your pajamas all day?"

"I don't watch soaps, but maybe I'll start. Pajamas all day sounds tempting," I say, biting into a wonton.

"Ooooh, Netflix. We could spend weeks watching everything on Netflix," Lainie says.

"We could catch up on the Oscar nominees we've missed all these years working for this overlord," I say.

"No ganging up. We talked about this," Gabe whines.

"Hand him a fortune cookie so he doesn't cry, Lainie."

Gabe sits up and pushes his plate aside so he can rest his weight on the table. "What do I have to do to make you stay?" he asks me. He looks at Lainie and she nods supportively.

"I want to photograph dogs."

"Dogs? Like woof-woof?"

"Very good, Gabriel. Doggies say woof-woof! Gold star for you," I tease.

"So, like, you want to have dogs running around the studio."

"No, I want to make this a thing where people can bring their dogs, or cats, in for portraits. Families are changing. A lot of people, especially millennials, are choosing to either not have kids or to have dogs as their first kids, and then human families later. There's a huge market for people who want nice pet portraits."

"And you've done market research on this?"

"Only informally. I don't have a spreadsheet or PowerPoint for you, if that's what you're asking," I say, pushing a few grains of rice around with a single chopstick. "I want to photograph dogs. We know I'm not great with human subjects, but I've been busy"—I dig out my phone, open my weeks-old, dog-centric Instagram account, and hand over the phone—"and I think we could make a lot of people really happy with this."

The account already has over a thousand followers.

"These are amazing, Frankie," Lainie says, watching over Gabe's shoulder as he scrolls.

"And I want to be able to go to local shelters and photograph their dogs and cats and rabbits if I have to, with proper lights and everything, so that we can help those animals find homes. An awesome picture will help a homeless creature find its family."

Gabe clicks on the screen and holds up my phone to show me what is probably my favorite picture ever. "Is this dog in a wheelchair?"

"That's FDR. Named after President Roosevelt. He is the coolest." Lazarus barks. "Okay, except for you, Laz."

Gabe continues scrolling. "These are really beautiful, Frankie."

The bloom of warmth inside me almost makes me sweat, it's so intense. "Thanks, big brother."

Gabe clicks my phone closed and hands it back. "Okay, so if we add a submenu to our photography offerings with devoted packages for people's pets—within reason, no horses or whatever—"

"I can go on location and photograph horses or bigger animals that can't be brought into the studio."

His head bobs and he bites the end of his chopstick in thought.

"And I want to be made a partner, rather than just a secretary, because even you admitted that I do a lot of shit in my job and I'm tired of being treated like I'm only there to make doctor and hair appointments and to freshen up the coffee. If I'm going to be photographing more, I don't want to be doing all that other crap too."

Lainie refills everyone's wine. "So we hire someone. Someone who wants to learn everything they can about the business of photography from the ground up," she says. "For the next month, Frankie can train them to do the business side of things that she handles, and then she can start scheduling herself based on the demand."

"Also—you have to start giving more of the business operation stuff to the accountant. I do all that now, but we should be using a proper CPA," I say, "instead of just relying on her to do our taxes."

Gabe's eyes are distant and he's bouncing slightly in his chair. Lazarus bounds over to the table, looking to see if anyone's going to give him anything delicious. Gabe drapes an arm over the huge dog and rubs his gray-and-white head. "What do you think, big guy? Aunt Frankie wants to take pictures of other doggos. What's your take on it?"

Lazarus hoists his front half onto Gabe's lap, no small feat, but he's very clever—there are steamed dumplings left on the plate at the table's center.

"Okay, so if I bring you in as partner, you'll still do the administrative stuff until you can get a decent schedule of clients. Once you get to an average of ten clients a week, we can hire someone to replace you," Gabe says. He relents, grabs a pork bun, and hands it to Lazarus, who grips it daintily in his front teeth and hops down to enjoy his treat in peace. He's the weirdest dog. "And you can have Fridays to shoot photos at shelters or whatever."

"Really?"

"Isn't this what you're asking for?"

"Yes! But I didn't think you'd go for it," I say.

"We do have one other condition," Lainie says. She fumbles under the table with something; when her hands reappear, she hands me a small sea-foam green box wrapped with a matching bow. She nods at me, her smile expectant.

I pull the silky ribbon and open the hinged box. Inside is a beautiful set of pearl and diamond earrings, and a small card with Lainie's lovely handwriting on it that reads: "Will you be my maid of honor?"

My head snaps up, and Lainie lifts her left hand over the top of the table. On her fourth finger sits an engagement ring—a square-cut diamond in the middle surrounded by a bunch of other diamonds set in white gold or maybe platinum and it's so sparkly and not too big and it just screams *Lainie*.

And then I'm out of my chair and Lainie and I are hugging and Gabe even stands long enough for a hug and then Lazarus is in on it and he's barking and howling. "You're getting married! You're getting married! I'm so excited! This is amazing!" I love Lainie so much. I'm so happy she's going to be my sister.

Gabe disappears for a beat, his walking boot clunking against the floor with each step. He returns with a bottle of champagne. When the cork *pops*, Lazarus takes off in his bonkers lap run around the center of their open-concept apartment. My brother pours three glasses and offers a toast, his eyes fixed on Lainie.

"To the world's most perfect woman. I will work every day of my life to deserve you." We clink glasses, and they kiss, and her diamond catches the light on the modern chandelier hanging over the dining room table and throws a million sparkles around the dimly lit ceiling and walls.

"And one more thing," Gabe says, glass again in the air. "To my little sister, F-Stop, who will take the best photos of our wedding any brother could ask for."

I freeze. "What? No. I'm not taking your wedding photos." And my dumb brother laughs, which makes Lazarus crazy all over again. It's good they don't keep anything breakable within reach of this dog and his wide, sweeping tail.

"Nah, Dad will do it. I just wanted to see the look on your face. And also, you're still a pretty great little sister, but I'm only going to say that again the day you get married and maybe on my death bed so don't get too used to me being nice."

We again tap glasses and drink. "No threat of that, Archangel."

WITH THE MEAL done and the moon high overhead, it's time for me to leave my newly engaged brother and his bride-to-be and their crazy-ass dog and retreat to my own quieter abode. I've been slow to leave because tonight is my last night at my apartment. Walking into the place that's been home for the last eight years, my life stuffed into cardboard boxes, is equal parts sad and exhilarating.

I carry the remaining dinner dishes into the kitchen as Lainie packs up the leftovers for me and slides a boxed tiramisu into my cloth grocery bag.

"For later," she says. "In celebration of your new house. I forgot to bring it out."

"Thanks, Lainie."

"There's one other thing Gabe wanted me to tell you ..." She leans against the counter, fingers fidgeting with the engagement ring.

"Are you pregnant? Oh my god, are you pregnant?"

Lainie laughs. "No, thank heavens. No babies. Not yet. I have my hands full enough with your brother and Lazarus." She takes a step closer followed by a deep breath. "You know my mom is sick, so we're going to be getting married soon. Like, in a month."

"Whoa! Can you plan a wedding that quickly?"

"It'll be a small affair. Just family and a few close friends. I'm scrambling to find venues but we have a lot of friends in the wedding business, as you know, so it's time to call in a few favors."

"Hey! You guys should go up to that resort in Canada! Oh, Lainie, it's gorgeous. You wouldn't believe how beautiful it is up there."

"We'd like to go up there to visit eventually, but for the wedding ... my mom, she just can't travel right now. Chemo has made her so weak," Lainie says. She looks heartbroken—Lainie and her mom are really close—so I throw myself against her in a tight hug and let her just hang on for a moment.

"I'm so sorry, Lainie."

She bobs her head; I pluck a tissue from the box on the counter and hand it over.

"Wait—if I'm the maid of honor, does that mean I get to plan a bachelorette party? Wow, this is only slightly intimidating." I hope my smile reminds her that this time in her life is meant to be fun and special too, and her mom will be so happy if her daughter is happy.

"Nothing fancy. But *no Vegas*. I've seen those movies. I know how those trips end."

"What happens in Vegas ..." I wiggle my eyebrows.

"We're staying in Portland. We can go to Powell's and get expensive cocktails after or something."

"You are *not* going to a bookstore for your bachelorette," I say. I love Powell's too, but yeah, no, we are not having a hen party in the History section of a bookstore.

"Because everything is happening so quickly, we wanted you to know now, so it wouldn't be awkward when the day comes—well, there'll be the rehearsal dinner and stuff too beforehand, but you know what I mean."

"Okayyyy ... Unless you're planning a deep-sea scuba wedding, which you know I won't do because I am terrified of deep water and I'll choke and die and that would not be a fun wedding memory for you, I'm sure whatever you're planning can't be that bad."

Lainie takes a deep breath and rests her warm hands on my crossed arms. "Gabe has asked Sam to be his best man."

Oh. Shit.

"Is scuba diving still off the table?"

TWENTY-SEVEN

ON THE DRIVE HOME, I decide I'm not going to let Sam's involvement in my brother's wedding get to me. This is *their* special day—this is not about me. *Grow up, Frankie.*

Though it is weird that after all these years of not speaking to one another, all of a sudden they're good enough friends that Gabe has asked Sam to be his best man. Maybe they've had long, heartfelt talks that I'm not privy to. Maybe they've worked everything out via email or over a pitcher at their favorite brewpub.

Maybe I don't know about this stuff because I don't answer when Sam texts or calls or emails.

Maybe I don't even know why I'm ignoring him.

His last email from two days ago said that Lisa Reynolds had her baby, a little girl, but that the child went immediately into foster care because Lisa threatened to kill the baby and herself to save them from the "CIA-sponsored chemical rain that will bring a biblical apocalypse on Portland and Seattle."

Lisa R. is now in psychiatric care, and her baby is somewhere out there in the world, waiting for the court system to find her biological father to see if he wants the child. Sam's email sounded so sad ... it's not even his baby, but he's one of those guys who would save a baby bird fallen from its nest. He was always the kind one, and that's why he and Gabe worked as friends. He kept Gabe from being a dick. Well, most of the time.

I should've asked Lainie about Gabe and Sam making up. But that makes me look like a sixth grader with a crush. I should just ask Sam myself.

And say what? Why didn't you tell me you were at the Meyer wedding to take photos because Gabe asked you?

Why were you there to help me when we haven't properly talked to each other in years?

Why were you there to be *nice* to me?

I park, stop at the community postbox to check my mail, and zone out until I'm at my front door, trying to remember what pocket I put my keys in. Inside, the leftovers go into the fridge and then I grab one of the two forks I've left unpacked. Mmmm, tiramisu. I clear off a space on the dining room table, currently messy due to stacks of collapsed moving boxes and packing tape and my endless lists.

Sam's Nike box still sits on the counter between here and the kitchen, though the second rubber band holding it closed gave up its will to live and split into powdery, tired chunks a few days ago. I've been avoiding it in favor of filling other boxes with my life.

But now I'm out of other boxes to pack. And I still don't know what's in this one.

Maybe I should look. Will it answer some of the questions I can't bring myself to ask Sam?

If I open it now, and it's yucky, I can leave it behind. I can wrap that Sam part of me in his box and put it in the dumpster. And then tomorrow night, I'll sleep in my very own house, Sam surgically removed from my heart.

A fresh start. A new beginning. A blank chapter.

Stop stalling.

Both hands on the box, I move it before me like maybe there's a baby bird inside.

Lid off. Inside smells like time, the hint of moisture and dust but not dead, rotting flesh, so I'm pretty confident Christina's estimation of body-part trophies from murder victims is no longer a reasonable guess.

Maybe something in here will remind me why I'm mad at Sam and make that surgical excision a bit easier.

On the top of the stack of items, I find the piece that should do the trick: an article Sam's printed from *The Oregonian* about my mother's last photographic mission. It's apparently just one in a series the paper did on war photographers whose work has made a significant difference in the lives of the people they photographed.

My mother Lara was killed in action in Iraq in 1991, working on assignment for the Associated Press. It was right after a bombing in Fallujah, meant to take out a bridge over the Euphrates River but that actually hit a market and killed hundreds of civilians. She reportedly was embedded with the Marines in the south at first, but then somehow broke from their protection to report on the growing humanitarian crisis evidenced by the mass exodus of Iraqis, nearly 1.5 million of them Kurds, from Iraq's major, war-ravaged cities.

Lara, her handler, and a translator snuck away, without the US government knowing where they were. My mother was brave, and stupid, that way. Her specialty wasn't just war photos; it was documenting the impact of Hussein's regime, and the American invasion, on the people of Iraq, specifically the women. She managed to score an interview with an underground group who were hiding Iraqi Kurds—women and children—to smuggle them out of Baghdad, and even out of the country if they could.

And then she and her handler were killed when their hotel was bombed. AP said it was pro-Saddam rebels; my dad thinks it was an American bomb that did it. Some children might want to investigate this further, to find someone to blame.

I don't care. A bomb is a bomb is a bomb. My mother made a choice to go there instead of staying home with me. Finding out whose initials are signed to the bomb casing isn't going to bring her back to life.

But this article includes an interview from an Iraqi Kurd named Zerya Salar who now lives in Salem, Oregon—she was one of the women my mother photographed. The article reports that my mother's attention to what Salar and her fellow refugees were going through helped them get out of Iraq.

According to Salar, my mother's work with an NGO based in southern Turkey, just across the border from what is now commonly called Iraqi Kurdistan, saved the lives of nearly two hundred women and children.

Whoa.

My mother's work did this?

And I never knew. I never knew because I refused to talk about her with my father or Gabe.

But Sam knew. And now he's telling me.

I sit back in my chair for a second, the printed article resting on my lap. This is heavy shit. My mother's actions saved lives. Have I ever done anything remotely heroic? I've spent so many years squelching my anger and resentment because I feel like she left me here to take care of my dad and Gabe.

But now, things are finally starting to change. Dad has Diana and is off on a new adventure; Gabe and I are going to be partners instead of me just taking care of his dry cleaning *and* I get to photograph dogs.

That's maybe not heroic, but it *is* progress. Right?

I hold up the article again and stare at the grainy black-and-white photo—my mother and some of the women and children she met in Iraq. "Are you proud of me? If I try harder, will it make you proud that I'm your daughter, even if I'm not saving the world?"

Yet, Frankie. You're not saving the world yet. My dad's voice in my head ... because I can't remember what Mom's sounded like.

I blow my nose and take a few bites of tiramisu. The tears make it a little saltier, but it's good.

The article set aside with all the care given to a relic, I dig deeper into the box. There are a few other pieces about my mom, some printed on copy paper and others clipped directly from the newspaper when people still did such things. The handwriting at the top of those articles looks like it might have been Sam's mom. Given the amount of time that Gabe spent at Sam's house, and vice versa, it doesn't surprise me that she had an interest in what happened to Lara Williamson Hawes.

Ha! The Polaroids! They're starting to crack with age, but they still make me laugh, not only for the funny antics of the much younger Three Musketeers in the shots but because I remember when my dad gave us two Polaroid cameras to share, with, like, ten boxes of film, on the first trip we took into the desert. It became a thing—he'd give us proper film cameras if we wanted them, but the Polaroids were supposed to be for fun stuff. Hanging out in the tent or camper, in the car, at the pool, in the boats we'd rent to fish or crab.

"Ahhhh!" I say to no one but myself. It's a shot of me and Sam, my newly set fingers in a bright-pink cast, hoisted in Sam's arms after we've just come out of the ER in Newport, Oregon. I'm a little loopy from the painkillers they gave me before they set the broken bones, but we're laughing like it's the funniest thing we've ever done.

Under the various photos are random pieces of our shared past—bottle caps and seashells and polished rocks and a dark-green "worry stone" from this incredible glassblower at the Oregon Coast and the severed house key that Gabe broke off in the deadbolt at Sam's that led to my dad having to pay for a locksmith so Sam and his mom could go through their front door again and unspent arcade tokens and a friendship bracelet I made for him when I was going through my friendship bracelet phase ...

This box is soaked in the years we spent together growing up and turning into real human beings.

But there are also birthday cards, to me, that he never sent, one for every year after Sam and Gabe had their falling-out. I open one after another: "Thinking of you on your birthday. I miss your friendship and I hope you're staying out of trouble." Variations on the same theme, for ten years' worth of cards he never sent.

It's not like he didn't know where to find me. Then again, after he and Gabe "broke up," it was weird and sad and awkward, and with Lainie sort of in the middle of everything between the two boys, it was probably best for everyone to just go off into their lives and let the trauma settle into the soil.

After everything else has been emptied out, one business-sized envelope remains that reads "FRANKIE" across its front. The envelope looks new, and sure enough, when I open it and pull out the letter, with it is a printed selfie we took while at Revelation Cove.

F-STOP ...

I hope you don't mind the nickname—it feels weird to call you Francesca after all those years of thinking of you otherwise.

I know you're mad. I should've told you about why I was at the wedding and that Gabe had called me and I should've told you about Lisa R. the second you saw her name pop up on my screen and I probably shouldn't have allowed myself to want you the way I did, the way I still do, but I'm not going to apologize for that because I'll never regret the time we spent together at Revelation Cove. Also I'm glad you found all this stuff out after we left so that you didn't pull a Nikki and shoot me with an arrow.

So, if we're going to start with confessions, to clear the air in the spirit of no more secrets or whatever—well, this box is a good start. I almost didn't give it to you because I didn't want you to think I was some weirdo stalker. Having the box and keeping this stuff together was how I dealt with life after I lost the Hawes family. It wasn't just about Gabe—sure, he was my best friend and had been since second grade, but it was also the loss of your dad, who was like a father to me all those years (and still is) ...

And I'd lost you.

I was with Lainie in high school and for that first part of college. I know that.

But here's where the truth is: I've loved you since I was fourteen.

And I know that in itself is creepy because you were only eleven and I'm sorry if that's just too icky, but truth and honesty and all that jazz, right? As we got older, I couldn't just admit my feelings for you—what if we broke up, as young people tend to do, and things got messy? I'd have lost you AND Gabe AND your dad. I couldn't risk it. Plus, Gabe probably would've broken my neck if I'd laid a hand on you. I know he acts like a pain-in-the-ass big brother, but he is your fiercest protector.

And then when you were with Rob—or Bert or whatever we're calling him these days—GOD, I wanted to kill him. He treated you like shit and it made me so, so mad, madder than I've ever been at anything in my life (except when my mom wouldn't let me drive to LA to see Garbage in concert when I was sixteen). I was always ready to go with Gabe every time he wanted to go break Rob's legs. We never did anything more than stare him down and maybe throw a few threats, but what I would've given to punch his mean little rat-whiskered face.

I digress. Forgive me. Seeing him at that wedding stirred up some shit. And I'm glad Nikki dumped him at the altar because that newly muscled dickhead deserved it. Karma.

Back on topic: Yes, I was with Lainie through high school, and I loved her. I did. And I was devastated when she and Gabe hooked up—everything I'd worried about if I'd pursued you came to pass, which sucked so much. It made your absence in my life even harder to take. But it was more than just my girlfriend cheating on me—it was the betrayal of my best friend. I got over Lainie as any twenty-one-year-old guy does, with beer and going to the gym and focusing on work.

But the pain of losing Gabe's friendship was overwhelming because I knew if Gabe and I were over, you and I probably were too. And then it happened. Everything I'd been afraid of happened.

I was a coward. I should've been braver and called sooner. I know that now.

Slowly, life found a way to not kick me in the face with reminders of how much I missed the Hawes family ... of how much I missed you.

And in all these years, despite my efforts, I've never found anyone like Frankie Hawes. Quirky, funny, talented, crazy little F-Stop.

No offense on the little. I know you hate short jokes. Which is a shame because I have been saving all my short jokes for the last decade. I've got some great material if you'd like to hear it sometime ...

I'll wrap it up as I've rambled long enough, but I just wanted you to know how sorry I am that I wasn't transparent from the get-go. I was just excited to see you again, and that weekend is one I will remember until they throw my ashes into the ocean where my melted mercury fillings will poison the fish for the next millennium. (Just kidding. The planet won't be here in a millennium. Probably because of my melted mercury fillings.)

If you decide you want to grab some coffee or food and talk, I'll bring the Polaroid in case any bones are broken while we're out. I still have a box of your dad's film.

All my love,

Samwise

P.S. If I can get Garbage tickets, would you be interested in going? I think they're still a band ... xo

I FOLD his letter carefully and slide it back into the envelope, but the photo, I slide into my purse. When I get to the new house, I'll attach it to the front of my new fridge with one of my doggie magnets. I wouldn't mind seeing that photo every morning when I come in to make my coffee.

Knock knock knock.

It can't be Bryony. She's allegedly on a date.

Unless the date didn't go so well and that would mean she's here with ice cream and her boxed sets of *Outlander*.

I check through the peephole, but the face is obscured by flowers of unnatural colors, made by florists who think blue and purple daisies are cool.

It couldn't be Sam—he wouldn't just pop over unannounced.

"Who is it?"

"It's me, Frankie. I just want to talk." The flowers lower, the peephole view unobscured.

It's Rob.

TWENTY-EIGHT

"WHAT ARE YOU DOING HERE?"

"I thought we could talk—"

"How did you know where I live?"

"I was here years ago, when you first moved in. I took a chance that you hadn't left yet."

I don't remember Rob ever being here. This is very strange. "Rob, seriously, what do you want? If this is about rehashing old times," I say, nodding at the flowers, "we covered that up in Canada."

His face is red and tired, like he's about to burst into tears and/or he's had too much to drink. He doesn't smell drunk, but the flowers dangle from his hand, like he's about to drop them.

"Come in—I swear to god, if you try anything weird, I'll hurt you."

"Nothing weird. I promise." He flattens his free hand over his heart. I wave him inside the apartment and close the door. He offers me the flowers.

"Thanks." I set them on the bar. All my vases are packed.

"I didn't want to show up empty-handed." He looks around the space, and my heart skips a beat when I realize the guts of Sam's Nike box are still sprawled all over the table. "You're moving?"

"Yup. Come in and have a seat." I direct him away from Sam's treasures and toward the couch, which is basically the only free spot to sit in the whole place. I'm not going to offer him coffee or tea or booze—I don't want him staying.

"Why are you here?"

"We didn't get a chance to really talk up at the resort, and I wanted to make sure your dad was okay. My mom sent flowers over."

"Yeah, that was nice. Thank you. I was glad to see her happy."

He nods. "It was tough. My father was really bad there at the end," he says, his voice dropping. "He almost killed her."

"Wow, I'm sorry, Rob."

His head bobs. "He's in prison now. We've changed everything, obviously—our names, location, everything—he's due to get out in another year and Mom is scared, but he wrote a letter and it was forwarded to her from the court, and he says he's a changed man."

"He's said that a lot in your life, hasn't he?"

"Yeah ... but maybe a decade behind bars will have fixed him. Who knows."

"Will you try to reestablish a relationship with him?"

"Noooo. He almost killed my mother. She's my priority, always," he says, leaning back against the cushions, "which is probably why Nikki left."

"She left because you were taking care of your mom?"

"My mother looks good, on the surface. But there's a lot of damage there. She has PTSD, and that manifests in nightmares and blackouts where she doesn't know what she's doing. It means she needs a lot of looking after."

"And Nikki got jealous."

"And Nikki got jealous," he says.

"Rob, that's weird. She's your *mother*. Nicolette is a grown woman."

He laughs. "Okay, that's a stretch."

"Why on earth would you want to marry her?"

"She was pregnant." He picks up a roll of masking tape on the couch next to him and fidgets with it. "You met her father—he's very old-fashioned and said if she was knocked up, we had to get married."

"Wait—she didn't *look* pregnant."

"She isn't. She had a miscarriage. But we were too far in the planning stages to call it off, so we decided to just go ahead and get married."

"I'm sorry. About the miscarriage. That's really sad. For both of you."

"Yeah, I'd like to be a dad someday. And this is going to make me sound like a total dick, but I don't think the baby was mine."

"You think it might have been Edwin's?"

Rob nods his head. "We've all been friends since university, and her dad really does not like that guy. It was a major ordeal just to get him approved for the wedding."

"'Approved'? Man, these people ..."

"Money makes people shitty," he says. "Anyway, enough about me. I didn't come here to tell you my sad tale."

"Then why did you come here?"

"Well, two reasons: One, I wanted to apologize, for everything, from the past. We were young and I was stupid and I know I treated you horribly. I'm so embarrassed about the way I acted back then. I would give you some lame excuse about how I didn't know any better, but it would literally be the truth. I'd only had my dad as a role model, and I was trying to find a way to be a man on my own. I didn't hit you, but I was still emotionally abusive, and there's no excuse. So, I'm sorry."

He looks sincere. Even though his face is thinner, his angles harder, and he's not wearing a Legend of Zelda T-shirt but instead an expensive button-down and casual sport coat, he almost looks like the Rob of old. A few more wrinkles, but still that haunted look in his eyes.

"We're cool, Rob. We were kids. And I'm glad you're not

marrying Nikki. I think you're going to find someone out there who treats you like you deserve."

"Someone like your Sam, maybe?"

The blush starts in my toes. "Yeah, Sam and I are good friends."

"'Friends,'" Rob says. His smile has a tightness to it—he used to get that whenever I'd mention any interactions with other guys. But my dalliances are no longer Rob's business, and haven't been in a *very* long time. "Sam's a good guy. Tried to break my arm a few times when I was being awful to you, so I can respect that." Rob's veneers are bright in the low light of my apartment. White, and fake.

"You said there were two reasons for your visit?" I ask, deflecting.

He takes a deep breath, sets the roll of tape down, and leans forward, elbows resting on his bent knees. "You were robbed, right? Your car?"

"Uhhhh, yeah ...? How would you even know about that?"

His hands, now clasped in front of him, are shaking.

"Rooooob ... how did you know my car got broken into?"

"Don't get mad, Frankie—I just didn't want her to have all those photos after what she did to me, to everyone who traveled all that way, to my poor mom—"

"ROBERT WHITFORD! Did you do it? *Did you break into my car and steal all that gear?*"

His eyes are so big, it's more white than iris. "I didn't—I mean, not me personally."

"So, what, you *hired* someone to do it? How did you even know where the hell I was? How did you find the car?"

"I knew you were at the hospital, so I gave the guy the make and model of your car with your plate number—"

"How the fuck did you know my plate number?" It dawns on me at this very moment that Rob has *never* been to this apartment because we were long broken up when I moved into it. "Rob, have you been stalking me?"

"Now, come on, that is a loaded word—"

I stand. "You've never been to this apartment before. You know my car make and model AND my license plate. You knew where I'd be. And then you hired some thug to break into my car and take all my gear? And some of it was pawned! Was that you?" With most of my life packed up, bookshelves empty and walls freed of their décor, my voice has nothing to absorb it so it echoes back at me.

"God, no! I would never do that. It must've been the guy ..."

"You need to get out. NOW. Before I call the police."

He bolts up from the couch, and even though it scares me, I stand fast. He reaches into his back pocket. "I know your dad must have business insurance to cover the losses, but I wanted to pay you personally, because I feel like an asshole."

"Rob, you *are* an asshole."

He nods again and drops an envelope on the coffee table. "There's twenty-five thousand in there. Should cover what we took."

"Get *out*."

He looks pathetic as he slinks to the front door, but I couldn't give less of a shit. I'm so angry, it's all I can do to not throw something at him. Lucky for him, all the good, heavy bookends are already packed.

He slides his shoes back on. "I know this is all really strange, but—"

"It's so far beyond strange, Rob. This is unhealthy and freaky and you need some serious counseling," I say, grabbing his flowers from the counter and thrusting them against his chest. "If I ever see you near me or my family again, I will call the police and tell them every-thing. Got it?"

His face pales. "I could get fired—and my mom. Please ..."

"Should've thought of that before you went all psycho stalker dude. Time to go, Rob."

"Wait ..." He reaches into the pocket of his sport coat and pulls out a tiny dog figurine—a Chihuahua. "I was going to leave this for you."

My stomach drops into my feet. "These ... these are from you? All these years?"

"I know how much you like dogs, so when I'd see one, I couldn't help picking it up for you."

I'm shaking—I'm *terrified*—but I open the door so if he tries anything else, my neighbors will hear me scream. "Goodbye, Rob. For real this time."

He nods and looks down at his expensive Italian leather shoes. My heart pounds so loudly in my ears, I can hardly hear anything else.

"Take care, Francesca. I wish you all the best."

As soon as his body clears the threshold, I slam the door and lock the deadbolt and the flip-lock. Then I slide a chair under the doorknob, just in case. I'm trembling so hard, it takes a few tries to get the chair to stay in place.

I really should call the police.

I can't call my dad because he's in Europe.

Gabe is celebrating his engagement tonight.

I could call Sam ... but what good would that do?

I can't believe Rob knows all that shit about me. Where I live, my car, my license plate—oh my god, what else does he know? He hired a bad guy to break into my car! Oh man, if the men in my life didn't have a reason to break Rob's legs before, they certainly do now.

Laptop out, I navigate to all my social media accounts and make everything as private as I can. The only thing that stays open to the public is my doggie Instagram account, and that's because I need it to help me drum up business so I can stop looking after Gabe 24/7.

But I hear a familiar voice in my head: *"You'd be shocked to know how much Big Brother knows about you."*

I grab my phone and hope I don't wake little Aidan. This job calls for Jane Bond.

TWENTY-NINE

I NEED to go to sleep. Tomorrow is a big day.

But every single noise—amplified by the apartment stripped of her personality—makes me jump. I consider having a small drink or maybe one of those panic-attack pills from the ER to calm my nerves, but I feel like I need to be on my guard in case Rob goes full psycho and shows up again or throws himself through my window with an axe.

I have the meat tenderizer under my pillow and my trusty softball bat from the one high school year I played softball just to prove to my brother that I was athletic. News flash: I am not athletic. But I could swing a bat into Rob's head if he was coming to do murder on my person.

All this time I've been worried about Sam storing body parts in an old shoebox.

Seems I've been barking up the wrong worry tree yet again.

At quarter after eleven, I know I'm not going to be sleeping anytime soon.

I pick up my phone. **I'm sorry it's so late. I finally opened the box, and it was really great. Thank you,**

Sam. Maybe we can get pancakes and have a chat in real life?

My heart flutters with anxiety when the little bubbles shimmy, indicating he's replying.

I love pancakes. I could eat.

What—now?

Are you otherwise engaged?

I pause. I'm not otherwise engaged. And I could use a friendly voice to calm me down.

Meet me at the Original Hotcake House? On Powell?

Leaving now. See you soon, F-Stop.

I THROW on essence of makeup to hide the purple circles under my eyes, a little lip gloss to make me look less pale.

When I pull into the lot, my insides do a happy-scary dance—Sam has already arrived, leaned against the trunk of his car. Dressed in jeans and a dark sweater that accents his fair coloring so nicely, he's as handsome as ever. Why did it take me so bloody long to text him?

He looks up from his phone and waves as I take the empty spot next to him.

When I grab my purse, I note my shaking hands. *It's just Sam. You're fine. Everything is okay.*

"Hey," I say.

"Hey yourself." I follow him up the walk and he holds open the restaurant door for me. Once seated, I order tea; he orders coffee. The waitress offers us a few minutes with the menu, and we scan politely, the air between us a little tense with as-yet unspoken things.

When the waitress reappears, we tell her we're here about the pancakes. "Coming right up," she says, taking our menus and disappearing.

I wrap my nervous hands around my tea. "Thanks for meeting me so late," I say.

"I'm happy to do it. I've been looking for an excuse to see you again."

"You didn't need an excuse ..."

Sam smiles and lifts his coffee cup to his lips. "I think we both know that I needed an excuse."

I fidget with the tea bag soaking in my cup, darkening the water. Where do I start? With the Nike box? With what Rob did? With Lainie and Gabe's engagement?

"You okay, Frankie?"

"Yeah ... yeah, I think so. I'm just trying to figure out what to say first."

"Say whatever is on your mind."

I laugh quietly. "That's the problem—too much on my mind. Moving day tomorrow and everything else that's going on."

"Hey, congrats on the house—Gabe told me you bought a place?"

"Yup. I'm a real grown-up now." Sam offers his hand for a high five. I meet it—touching his skin is electric, that night at Revelation Cove rushing back to me. I sip my tea again, scalding my tongue with the zealous gulp. "So—the Nike box."

Sam leans back against his side of the red-leather booth and folds his arms over his chest, his cheeks pinking up. "It was scary to give it to you."

"I'm just glad there were no body parts in it." The waitress brings silverware and small pitchers of syrup just as the words *body parts* fall into the air. She lifts a brow at me.

Sam waits for her to leave. "Do I want to know what that means?"

"My friend Christina is going to be in the FBI and she was worried your Nike box might be filled with trophies from your victims."

"Duh, I only keep those in Adidas boxes." He grins.

"For real, though ... The articles about my mom ... I'm really grateful for those. You know how hard it is for me to talk about her. I've been trying lately, ya know, to stop avoiding it. To deal with her death."

Sam stills across from me. "I never knew your mom, but I liked hearing your dad's stories about her. He and Gabe talked about her when you weren't around—they both knew how much it hurt you. And your dad talked about how much your mother loved you both, Frankie. He says there's a lot of her in you. You're brave, like she was."

"I'm the opposite of Lara Williamson Hawes."

The waitress reappears with our piping-hot plates. "Your lucky night," she says. "Kitchen is on warp speed."

Sam thanks her and then unfolds his napkin over his lap. He drenches his stack of buttermilk pancakes in maple syrup.

I pick up my fork and take that first bite. Pancakes at midnight with Sam—I could get ridiculously used to this.

Between bites, Sam gestures at me with his fork. "One of these days, you'll see what the rest of us see."

We eat for a few minutes, until the silence again goes from companionable to awkward. "So, the best man, hey?"

Sam nods. "I'm happy they asked me. It's about time they made it official."

"I'm allegedly in charge of the bachelorette, so if you have any ideas ..."

"Vegas?"

"She already vetoed that."

Sam laughs and tears into a strip of bacon. "Lainie's not the Vegas type." He wipes his hands on his napkin. "Did you really ask me out here just to talk about the shoebox and the wedding?"

"Partially ..."

"You still look like something's up. Are you nervous about the house and the move? What else is going on, Frankie?"

I fold my hands in my lap. "You have to promise to just listen and not freak out."

Sam's brow creases. "Whenever someone starts a conversation like that, I know that I'll probably freak out."

"Rob showed up at my apartment tonight."

He puts his fork down and leans on his elbows, the table groaning under the weight. "And?"

Tears sting my eyes, and I don't even know why—maybe because I could've been in danger? Because Rob is scary and I was alone and I need to learn how to throw a punch? "He's basically been stalking me. For years. He knew where I lived, the make and model of my car—all my little dog statuettes, the ones I thought Dad had been giving me for all these years—they're all from Rob."

The muscle in Sam's jaw ticks as his face turns an alarming crimson. Storm clouds move into his eyes.

"It gets worse." I reach into my purse and pull out the envelope with Rob's cash. "He was the one who broke into my car at the hospital and stole all the gear—well, he hired someone to do it. He brought me cash to repay us for the stolen property."

"You have to call the police. Right now. This is serious."

"I know. He begged me not to—that's why he gave me the money. But it scared me. When I realized he'd actually never been to my apartment before, even though he tried to tell me I'd invited him over years ago, and then with the little dog statues—those have been showing up for six years, Sam. In my mailbox, on my car, mailed to the studio, sometimes even taped to the studio door ..."

"There's something very wrong with that man." Sam pulls out his phone. "If you don't call the police, I will."

"Wait. Just wait a second—"

"Did you tell Gabe or your dad?"

"Dad's in Europe with Diana. I don't want to give him another heart attack," I say. "And if I tell Gabe, you know what he'll do."

"The same thing *I* want to do to that slimy little weasel."

"If I call the police, they'll take his money as evidence. Reports will be filed—he might get arrested, but he has money for lawyers. He said he could lose his job. The bottom line, though—if he goes to jail, his mother will be alone. She's had a terrible life, Sam. I don't want to take away her only support system."

"Are you kidding me?" Sam raises his voice, pulling attention from a nearby table. "Why are you still protecting him? This is just like when you guys were together and he'd say and do shitty things, but you'd defend him. *Why are you protecting him?*"

"I'm NOT. I'm thinking about his mom."

"His mother is a grown-ass woman. She can take care of herself."

"Rob said she's got PTSD and has terrible nightmares. Apparently, it was a big issue with him and Nikki—Nikki was jealous of all the care his mom requires."

"Not your problem, Francesca," Sam says. "What he did is a major felony. Like, long-prison-sentence-level crime. And the stalking —I might know a thing or two about that."

I stare at the half-eaten stack on my plate. "Maybe I shouldn't have told you."

Sam exhales and scrubs a hand over his face. "I'm glad you did. You need to be safe, Frankie. You have to tell Gabe."

"If I go to the police, that means I might have to go to court and testify and deal with Rob for months or even years on end. And then if he has the money to get away with what he's done, what's to say the stalking won't get worse, out of revenge? If I just take his money, talk to Gabe and Dad—"

"And what about when Rob finds out where the new house is? You know he will. What if he starts hiding in your bushes or showing up in your yard? Then what?"

I tell Sam about Christina, how she's coming out to the house tomorrow to help me set up a security system and lock down all my social media accounts. "I don't think Rob would ever physically harm me."

"You don't know that."

"I know that I can't live afraid of him showing up around every dark corner," I say, my own voice raised this time.

When Sam drops his cell phone onto the tabletop, I envision the little thing gasping for breath after being released from its chokehold.

"Just promise me—if he shows up again, please, *please* call the police. Call me. I'll drop whatever I'm doing. I'll finish the business Gabe and I started with him back in high school if I have to."

"I promise. If he shows up again, I'll call the police. And then you," I add.

"In that order—911, and then me. Day or night."

"Yes, sir." My insides warm. I know I'm supposed to be all tough and independent, but Sam's reaction feels almost ... romantic.

"Are you going to be okay?" he asks, his eyes locked on mine.

I nod—my throat feels too tight to talk. "It was just a little weird."

"It's a *lot* weird, Frankie."

"I know ... Thank you, for listening. And for coming out tonight. So late and everything."

"I'm glad you called. And I'm *really* glad you told me about Rob," he says. He pushes his plate aside. "I've missed you, Frankie."

Shame spikes my heart. "I'm sorry I haven't been answering your texts and stuff. I'm relieved Lisa's baby is okay."

"Me too," he says, running a hand through his curls. He looks tired in that moment. "What a nightmare."

"I suppose you won't really get updates about it—the baby, I mean ..."

"No. Which is good. It's none of my business. I just hope Lisa gets the help she needs. And the baby is safe. That's all anyone's worried about right now." Sam fidgets with an extra napkin, folding the corners in and letting them flop back open. "This month of radio silence between us, Frankie ... it's been a lot." The waitress swoops by long enough to take Sam's plate.

"I know. I'm sorry. I just had to get my head in the right place."

"I get it," he says. "And your dad's doing better? Gabe keeps me updated."

"Yeah, yeah, he's great. He and Diana seem really happy."

"I can't believe Harrison Hawes is finally settling down," Sam says, smiling. "About time."

"You know my dad ..." I drag my fork through the syrup my

pancakes didn't absorb. My heart pounds in my throat. "What about us, Sam? Where are we?" I look up at him, hoping I haven't misstepped.

"That depends on you," he says. "If you've forgiven me for not being up front about why I was at the wedding." He stops fidgeting and flattens his hands over the napkin. His green eyes are on fire.

"I wish you had told me when we were there."

"I know. But I didn't want to undermine your confidence. I know how overbearing Gabe can be, and I know his voice lives in your head, reminding you you're not doing it right, whether that's baiting a crab trap or fishing hook or taking a photograph. I grew up with him too." Sam takes my hand. "I wanted you to believe in yourself the way I believe in you."

I squeeze his fingers gently. "The letter you wrote ..."

"Too much?" Sam's complexion again rivals the deep red of the booth we're sitting in. He hates how his skin reveals his emotions; I love it.

"No. Not at all." I don't let go of him. "It was perfect."

"I meant every word."

"I'm glad you're back, Sam McKenzie. We missed you. *I* missed you."

A broad smile on his handsome face, Sam stands, leans over the table, and plants a soft kiss against my lips.

"Any more coffee or tea here?" the waitress with the worst timing ever asks. Sam grins and sits back down.

"Just the check," he says. When she slides the bill facedown onto the table, I grab it before Sam can.

"Rob's buying," I say, pulling the meal total plus the equal amount for a tip from Rob's envelope. "I should let you get home to bed. You probably have an early meeting or something."

Sam laughs under his breath, but it doesn't sound like he's amused. "I'm following you home."

"Sam—"

"I'm not coming in to take advantage of you."

Pity that.

"And it's not open for debate. I will follow you to your apartment, make sure you're safe, and then I'll go home." He crosses his heart and finishes the last of his coffee. When I stand, he steps beside me, his warm hand on the small of my back as we walk out the door.

THIRTY

BEFORE SAM'S well-behaved departure last night, he did a thorough, reassuring check of my apartment and made me pinkie-promise that I'd tell Dad as soon as he gets home from his trip. And I have to tell Gabe and Lainie and even Bryony immediately—they all need to lock themselves down too. If Rob is cyberstalking me and *clearly* isn't beyond breaking the law to get what he wants, there's no telling where he draws the line. If Rob even knows anything about drawing lines. He probably hires thugs to do that sort of thing for him.

Jane Bond, a.k.a., Christina, is due at the new house at 2:00 p.m. to help me "get off the grid," as Aunt Monica would say. She was all too happy to talk about all the stuff she could do to make me safer online, and some of it sounded expensive. As she talked, I counted Rob's money. *This should more than cover it.*

With last night's unsettling revelations, I'd buy an invisibility cloak if Harry Potter were interested in selling.

And even though it was a little uncomfortable, I'm glad I told Sam. Just in case something bad *does* happen.

But today—today is moving day. I'm moving to my new, grown-up, big-girl house!

It's not as grown up as going to a war zone and saving lives, but ...

As I repack the items from Sam's Nike box, I pause on the article about the lady from Salem who talks about how much my mother's work meant to her and her children, who must be adults by now.

Reading it again, I'd love to be able to say that this is the part where I throw caution aside, sell all my belongings, and devote myself to picking up the plow in the field where my mother left it.

But like Bryony tells me all the time—whether at my first aqua-fit class or when I have the overwhelming task of packing up eight years of my life to move: "Baby steps, Frankie."

So, I'm taking baby steps—and the first one includes sending Sam a good-morning text with a picture of the Canadian beer we drank up at Revelation Cove: **We should do that again sometime.**

My passport is in hand, he responds.

Baby steps.

THE COLLEGE KIDS I hired to pack the truck arrive at the apartment at eight on the dot and set right to work. They carry the boxes and furniture down to the truck I picked up yesterday afternoon—way faster than I expected—and then they leave to get breakfast, with the promise to meet me at the new house at eleven.

As soon as Bryony arrives, I yank her into the empty apartment and slam and lock the door. "You are not going to believe this." I didn't call her last night—I was worried that maybe Rob is somehow listening in on my phone calls.

I'm like an instant paranoia soup. Just add water and I'm ready to freak out.

I tell Bryony the whole sordid story, including how my prized statuette collection is all from that psychopath.

"We could kill him, you know. Hide the body. I watch a lot of crime shows—we could make this happen," she says.

"No murder. Not yet. But that young friend of the twins I told you about? She's meeting us at the new place to help me get hidden."

"You need to go to the DMV too. Get new license plates."

"I'm going to buy a new car. As soon as I'm settled. I'm super creeped out, Bry."

"As you should be."

I show her the envelope with Rob's money in it. "Well, at least he paid you back."

"He HIRED someone to destroy my car and steal all our stuff!" I say as she hands me the envelope back. "This money is tainted."

"What are you going to do with it?"

"Pay for security."

"You could hire your own thug and break his knees. Or a bodyguard! A hot one! Like a British crime drama—you hire a bodyguard and he's beautiful but conflicted, and then he has to save your life, but you end up saving his too, and then sex and then a fight with bad guys and then more sex—"

"All right, Shakespeare, come on. Help me walk through and make sure we're not forgetting anything."

I thought leaving this apartment, my home for most of my twenties, would be sad, that I'd wax nostalgic about all the fun nights Bryony and I have had here, the movie marathons and binge sessions and the great sushi place down the block that knows me on a first-name basis, the bad dates and lonely nights where it felt like everyone in the world was in love except me, the multiple failed attempts at begging the landlord to let me have just one wee little tiny dog.

But maybe Rob's unnerving performance last night helped. I'm not sad. I feel like I've outgrown this place. I'm ready to move on. I bought a *house*.

And when I'm settled, my next stop will be the local dog shelter. I can hardly wait.

~

SAM'S BOX sits nestled in the center between me behind the wheel and Bryony in the passenger seat; she's my navigator as we weave out of the busy city streets and toward my new house on the outskirts.

She rests a hand over the white swoosh on the box's faded orange lid. "I'm glad you called Sam last night," she says, beaming. "Definitely the right choice. And it's about time you put an end to his suffering."

"That might be exaggerating a little."

"Come on, Frankie. It's obvious he's in love with you, and you're being a jerk because he hurt your feelers. He's been suffering." I haven't shown Bryony the heartfelt letter Sam wrote—and I won't. It's too personal. But she's not wrong.

The truck bounces hard when I take a corner too close and scrape the sidewalk. "You should've hired a moving company to drive your shit too."

"I don't need anyone to drive my stuff." I'm glad for the change of topic.

"My back already hurts and I haven't even lifted a box."

"Except the doughnut box, you mean."

"Naturally," Bryony says.

"Those college boys are going to help us unload. Your back is safe. Besides, it's ridiculous to hire people to do something I'm perfectly capable of doing myself."

"You lift couches and drive five-ton trucks as a regular course of business?" She arches an eyebrow.

"If I were moving across the country, yes, I would've hired someone to drive. Moving to the outskirts of Portland, barely twenty miles from start to finish—are we so pampered we can't drive our own knickers to their new home?"

"See, that's why your dad and Gabe rely too much on you," she says. "You're too handy to have around. You gotta learn to delegate!" She hands me a glazed chocolate doughnut hole from the carton on her lap. "Take me, for example. At work, I'm supposed to file my own finished cases at the end of every day. New policies, changes to existing policies, like, people coming in to add a motorcycle or remove their boats because their ex-wife stole it, set fire to it, and let it drift down the Willamette River—"

"I saw that on the news! That was one of your customers?"

"The insured party was NOT happy when we told him his very expensive boat was not covered for angry ex-wives."

"I hate those."

"Burning boats, or angry ex-wives?"

"Both seem dodgy." I pop another doughnut hole into my mouth as we wait at a stoplight.

"Right you are. Anyway, instead of filing all my own shit away, I *delegate*. And by delegate, I mean tell the new intern kid that I will show him my boobs if he'll do the filing."

I almost miss the light turning green staring open-mouthed at my best friend. "You do not."

Bryony puckers her lips. "Don't I?"

The truck groans forward, its belly filled with my life. "I don't believe you. You'd totally get fired. You can't do stuff like that anymore."

"What's an office without a little drama?" she says. "Anyway, delegate! My filing gets done so I can do other more important things, like download my boss's Messenger chats with the women who are not his wife so I have better negotiating power when it comes time for my annual review."

"You missed your calling. You should have been a spy."

"That's me. Bryony Matthews, International Woman of Mystery."

"And blackmail."

"There's no mail like blackmail, baby." She winks. My phone buzzes in the cup holder. Bryony grabs it.

"Ohhhhh, it's from Sammy—it's a picture of you, eating ribs? Man, you're messy," she says, holding up the phone. I laugh.

"Revelation Cove. The wedding. We were feasting."

"Looks like it," she says. "I'm guessing that was the feast before the feast, hmmm?"

"Pervert."

"What? I'm glad he glazed your ribs."

"Bryony! Mind your manners."

"Sweetie, it's your manners that need minding. Mine are as bad as they come."

She closes my phone, drops it onto her lap, and then eyes forward, she claps like a sugared-out kid. Or a sugared-out thirty-something who has had too many doughnut holes. "We're almost there! We're almost there!"

The house is just outside the city limits, so technically still Portland but not really. I wanted to get a place with some space, and neighbors a little farther away, for when I get a dog or two. Or five.

I turn off the two-lane road, through the quiet suburb with widely spaced houses and plenty of room to run. Two rights and a left, and then we finally pull into the long, paved driveway. The sun is burning through the low fog hovering above the huge yard, the green grass still wet with dew. The far back of the property is lined with towering Douglas fir trees, the sides with tall, manicured cedar bushes, bordered by a recently painted fence that will keep dogs in and people out. A fat gray squirrel runs along the top, eyeing the empty bird feeder, pausing to look back at us before bounding onward to his business.

"Frankie, this house is perfect for you," Bryony coos.

It is. Three bedrooms, two stories with a turret on the top level, two bathrooms, open-plan kitchen with all new appliances, and a grass-and-paver-stone backyard with patio, barbecue, and stone firepit. It's an older house but the former owners stripped it to the bones and rebuilt everything, so the electrical, plumbing, flooring, and roof are all twenty-first-century updated. Again working her magic, Jerry's real-estate wife helped me find it, and we got a killer deal because the owners needed a quick sale due to their own divorce proceedings.

I hope my luck here is better than theirs was.

The college boys are already here, still sitting in the cab of their compact pickup. They climb out, phones in hand, their eyes glazed in that post-meal way boys get.

"Kids these days," Bryony mutters. "Oh, that one's cute. Are these lads legal?"

"Bryony, behave yourself."

She lifts her boobs under her hands, but I don't dare tell her that these boys might be outside her legal cougar age.

Doesn't matter. She flirts anyway. And by the time everything is unloaded, I think she has at least one of their numbers.

"He's twenty-five. Late-start student," Bryony says. "Stop looking so scandalized."

Once the furniture is in, I realize I don't have nearly enough of it. "You didn't think about how much bigger this place is."

"No. I did not think about how much bigger. It all happened so fast ..."

"Well, you got nothing but time to fill it up with more junk. It's a blank canvas!" Bryony says. She hustles into the kitchen, and I hear the unzip of the fabric cooler she brought along. Glasses tink against one another, followed by an unmistakable pop.

A minute later, she walks in and hands me a highball glass. "I didn't want to bring proper champagne glasses. I'd break 'em before we could drink." She lifts her hand in toast: "To Frankie's new start. Sláinte!"

While I push boxes into their respective rooms, Bryony throws together quick sandwiches, clucking about how awesome this kitchen is and how I should christen every surface, and with Sam if possible.

"You do know if I ask you to housesit, you cannot have sex in my kitchen!" I holler from the bathroom. Definitely going to need new towels. This bathroom is bigger than my kitchen at the apartment. I could sleep in that tub!

We finish eating just as a black Mercedes SUV pulls into the driveway. "Is that your FBI girl?" Bryony says. "Damn, that gig pays well."

"She's not in the FBI yet. And that car probably belongs to the twins. I can't see them driving a Dodge," I say. I take a quick look around, almost embarrassed that the place is such a mess. But I've been here a total of three hours. Of course it's a mess.

Sure enough, Christina gets out from behind the wheel, dressed in street clothes rather than her work uniform. She pops around to the rear passenger side—a broom skirt and sensible shoes descend from under the door.

"She brought Mariah! Oh, you're going to love her." I open the front door, Bryony close behind. "Welcome to my new house!" I say, hopping down the three wooden stairs. "FDR! You brought my boyfriend!" The little tattered white dog scurries over to me, a worn tennis ball in his mouth. He smartly avoids the lawn and stays on the pavement—guess he knows his wheelchair will get stuck in the grass in need of a trim. I scoop him up and cradle him against my chest as Mariah and Christina shuffle toward me.

"This is a snazzy place, Frankie," Mariah says, arching back so she can get a look at the whole house. "That turret. You should have a lot of sex in that turret."

"Oh, I definitely like you," Bryony says, stepping around me. "I am Frankie's best friend, Bryony."

Mariah shakes Bry's hand and then looks at us—first Bry, then me, then Bry again. "Young lady, what I would give to have legs that long," she says. "You should negotiate a trade, Frankie."

"I tried—she refused. Didn't want to give up her elf pants," Bryony says. "Come inside. We have champagne!"

"You have excellent taste in friends, Francesca." Mariah pats my cheek as she passes. She looks frail today.

Christina and Bryony help Mariah up the stairs. I set FDR down inside and he goes crazy wheeling about and sniffing everything while I clear off my comfiest reading chair for the aunt. Bryony breezes into the kitchen to pour two more glasses of champagne, though Christina turns it down—she's driving, and on the job—so Diet Coke it is. Another toast, as saucy as expected from Aunt Mariah, and then it's down to business.

"Tell me everything this scoundrel my great-niece did not marry did, Francesca, while Christina digs through your digital life," Mariah says. So I do.

"Rob stealing everything is bullshit because Frankie had already uploaded all the photos to their company cloud, so he stole the gear for nothing," Bryony says, offering around a box of chocolate-covered cookies.

"Well, not everything had been uploaded. He got away with some photos that Nikki definitely wanted."

"That girl is spoiled. Rotten to the core," Mariah says. "I've known it since she was little. Nicolette Marie Meyer has been terrorizing nannies since she could say her own name."

"Sounds like she and Rob would've been perfect for each other," Bryony says.

"Well, if she hadn't been knockin' boots with the best man," I say.

"There's a sock for every old slipper," Mariah adds, "even slippers that should be thrown into the fireplace."

Christina slides my laptop in front of me for another of my gazillion passwords. Her fingers then fly over the keys, and while she explains what we're going to do to lock everything down, Bryony offers Mariah a stroll into the backyard, FDR quick on their heels. I'm glad to see how easily he navigates the stairs on the back deck, in case he ever comes to visit again. Like my dad would say, that dog's got chutzpah.

The social media accounts are handled and I have a new account with a VPN provider. "Your internet searches and email and stuff will be protected from hackers when you're logged in, and you can choose a server in any one of these countries. It's especially good for banking and sensitive logins, so you should also add it to your phone, especially if you're ever using public Wi-Fi," she explains. "Never use public Wi-Fi without a VPN."

Christina then navigates to Amazon for our next order of business. "Security cameras. These are the ones I installed at the twins' place." Reasonably priced, capable of monitoring from my computer or mobile, easy to install. "And this system can connect to your furnace and stuff, so if you're out and you want to turn on the heat or AC so the house is comfortable when you get home, you can."

"Technology, man."

"It's awesome when it works," she says. I nod for her to Add to Cart. "I can come back after this stuff arrives and we can hook 'em up. I can show you how to do all that."

"I would be more than happy to pay you."

She flaps her hand at me. "You're family now."

"Then I'm buying dinner. And bring your little guy!"

Christina scans the room and laughs. "Yeah, he'd help you unpack, that's for sure." She then looks up different types of window locks and shows me which are the best ones, as well as a few personal security devices to keep in the house. "Don't get a gun. Most home-owners are shot or even killed with their own weapons in the event of a break-in. If someone's coming in, you need to get out. Stuff can be replaced. Lives, not so much."

If Amazon Prime does what it promises, I should be living in Fort Knox in no time.

"Thank you so much for this," I say. "I know it makes me seem paranoid—"

"As women, we have to put our safety first. It's still the Middle Ages in the minds of some humans. That dude bringing you the little doggie statues—it might as well be him bringing you bits of meat. He's letting you know he's still sniffing around."

I shiver. And I'm super pissed because I love those little dogs.

Christina quickly creates a shortcut on my desktop to access my VPN login, and then closes my laptop. "Hey, before Auntie comes back in, there's something you should know."

Christina sits back on the couch and turns to face me. "She's sick. Well, she's been sick for a long time, but she hates doctors, so this time, it's for real."

"I thought she looked frail."

"Monica is trying not to freak out—she didn't come with us today because she's having Mariah's bedroom moved around to make space for a hospital bed."

"It's that bad?"

"It will be. She's old. The cancer has been patient with her, but not anymore. The doctor who did manage an exam at the house, and only because he's an old friend, says she has maybe another month."

"A *month*?" I look through the spacious living room, through the kitchen nook windows into the backyard. Mariah is clamped onto Bryony's arm, walking the flagstone path that makes a giant rectangle around the grassy area in the middle.

"She'll be angry if she knows I told you—Mariah's the kind of lady who doesn't fuss about silly things like cancer," Christina says, her eyes welling with tears. "I don't know how Monica is going to manage without her."

"She's healthy?"

"Yes, because she goes to the doctor regularly so when her cancer popped up twenty years ago, they dealt with it."

"Same cancer?"

"No. Monica had breast cancer. Mariah's is in her gut. She'll be doped up here soon because the pain will be more than she can take, even though she says she's tougher than cancer. My great-grandfather had the same thing. He was Monica's husband," Christina says.

"You ... wait, so, Monica's your great-grandmother?"

Christina smiles. "She doesn't tell people because she wants me to earn my way on my own name, without having to rely on hers or my granddad's. If you haven't noticed, the twins are pretty progressive feminists."

"She seems very proud of you."

"She is. They both are. I'm really worried about Monica when her sister goes," Christina says, wiping away an escaped tear.

The sliding glass door in the kitchen opens, and FDR bolts back into the house, followed by Bryony and Mariah. "You get her all locked up and safe from creatures that go bump in the night?" Mariah asks, her grip on Bry's arm tight as they scoot back into the living room. She plops back into the overstuffed chair looking like she's just run a marathon.

"Ah-ha. Tears. So Christina's been gossiping in my absence, I see," Mariah chides. Christina sniffs and laughs quietly. "Well, there's no two ways about it, Frankie. I'm a dead woman walking. I already told your Amazonian friend here, and we chatted about my options during our little spin around your garden. Did you know you have at least five different types of tulips out there?"

I did not know that.

Bryony pulls a chair in from the kitchen and sits quietly.

"I have a proposition for you, Francesca," Mariah says, pulling an embroidered hankie from her long sleeve. "You have a house. I have cancer. I also have seven dogs. Monica cannot handle all of them on her own. It's too much canine for her liking. So—"

"Yes," I say, before she even finishes talking. "Yes. Whatever you need."

"Now Monica is quite attached to a few of them, but FDR needs a patient hand to keep his wheels working right. I was thinking maybe FDR and his two favorites, Jane Eyre, the miniature poodle mix, and Jupiter, the three-legged golden retriever. They're both girls, so FDR would be the man about town. And of course, I'll leave funds for their upkeep."

I rise and then kneel in front of Mariah, my throat aching with my efforts to not cry. "I would be absolutely honored to take care of your amazing dogs, Aunt Mariah."

She cups my cheek with her soft, veiny hand. "I knew I was meant to be at that disastrous wedding. We were meant to be friends, you and me. And now we can be friends long after I'm gone."

"Whatever you need, you call me. I'm there," I say. She dabs my cheek with her hankie—so much for keeping my composure.

She leans forward, wincing the tiniest bit. "What I need is for you to get off your knees and stop blubbering. Go get your doggie figurines that crazy man brought to you. We're going to sage them so you can keep them in your house without his icky germs stinking up the place. It's not the dogs' fault Bert is a moron."

She gestures to her giant carpet bag, and Christina obliges by bringing it closer. "When we're done with that, you're going to pour me more of that champagne and tell me how you're planning on getting that beautiful ginger snap of yours up in that turret."

SPEAKING OF GINGER SNAPS ...

Before her departure earlier, Mariah sent me a few iPhone photos her sister Monica took at Revelation Cove. While I sat outside the pulsating ballroom and drank Mariah's cosmo and pondered whether I should tear off Sam's clothes, Sam was inside dancing—with Mariah. She did say, "*I will flirt with your man until you slide back in to steal him away.*" A woman of her word. The grin on her face in the shot says it all.

To anyone else, it might look like a wild old granny out for a quiet spin on the dance floor before she had to go upstairs and take off her pressure hose and orthotic shoes. To me, it looks like a woman who has truly lived—who knows what heartbreak and happiness are—pushing two people toward one another before time runs out.

Given what happened in the hours after that photo was taken, I'd say her mission to push Sam and me together worked like a charm.

I send it to Sam.

As I fall asleep, my phone chimes with his response: ***Best night of my life***.

THIRTY-ONE

IT DOESN'T TAKE a month for the cancer to kill Mariah.

Two weeks later, Christina pulls into my driveway in the same SUV, her little boy Aidan in tow, as well as FDR, Jane Eyre, and Jupiter.

I meet her on the bottom stair and we hug while the dogs run loops around the yard, sniffing everything. She's trying not to cry—says it worries Aidan when he sees his momma upset. "She went quick. Just closed her eyes and didn't wake up. The doctor was giving her a lot of morphine. She didn't want anyone to know how much pain she was in, but the last week has been brutal."

I lead them into the house.

"Hey, you're unpacked," she says.

"Mostly. Still need decent furniture. I haven't gone looking, not with work and setting up the new studio and stuff."

"You got lots of time." She sets Aidan down against the couch and dumps out a bag of toys for him. Apparently he runs more than walks so the wide, open space is perfect for him. "I have crates and dog food and everything in the back of the car."

"I'll unload everything."

I make us coffee and we talk and I show the dogs around and introduce them to the backyard. Aidan eventually falls asleep against Jupiter on the floor, which provides a perfect photo op for me while Christina digs into my security goodies from the Amazon boxes. She sets to work while I photograph her adorable sleeping toddler and then unload the back of the SUV.

By the time she's done two hours later, Aidan and I are best friends—who doesn't love the lady with the cookies and chocolate milk?—my house is a fortress, and I its invincible overlord. I realize quickly how handy it'll be to have these dogs around when Lainie and Gabe start having babies. Built-in vacuum cleaners!

"Maybe Jane Eyre will lose some weight now that she won't have Aidan's high chair to perch under," Christina teases as she packs up his toys.

She promises they'll come back and visit—and she'll bring Monica around to visit the dogs and see the new place. When I hand Aidan two crisp hundred-dollar bills, Christina laughs. "I said you weren't allowed to pay me."

"I'm not. I'm paying him." I wink and walk them to the car, sad to see them go but glad that the house is filled with my new family.

Even if, upon returning, I discover that Jupiter has hoisted herself onto the counter and finished the vanilla wafers.

ONCE THE DOGS are finally settled for the night, I grab a bowl of my favorite ice cream, flop onto the couch, and call Sam.

"Hey, Frankie, everything okay?" he asks. There are voices in the background, and then it quiets.

"Yeah, I'm good. Am I interrupting? I should've checked what time it is in London."

"Eight hours ahead. I'm glad you called. The breakfast speaker is putting everyone to sleep."

"How's the conference?" I say.

"As exciting as you'd expect from a gathering of tech geeks," he says. "You sound off—what's wrong?"

I swallow past the lump in my throat. "Aunt Mariah died."

Sam pauses; I hear him exhale. "Shit, seriously? Ah, Frankie, I'm so sorry."

"Yeah ... it sucks. And as of this afternoon, I have three of her dogs. Christina brought them over—plus she helped me rig the house with all kinds of security gear."

"Good. I'm relieved to know you're safe out there all by yourself."

"Well, I'm not by myself anymore. I have three protectors. Plus Bryony is basically spending every third night in the room she's claimed as her own. She's even furnishing it. Did I tell you her latest obsession is bad taxidermy?"

Sam laughs. "I *think* I want to see that? Maybe?" he says, and then his tone changes. "No more shit from Rob?"

"Nope. I would've texted you."

"And you told your dad?"

"I told everyone. Gabe again threatened to do some murder, but Dad warned him to stay out of it so he doesn't miss his own wedding by being in jail," I say. My brother was nuclear-level pissed about Rob's antics, but thankfully, Diana's calming influence on my dad meant cooler heads prevailed.

"I'm glad to hear the security's in place. I worry about you ..."

"Bry will be staying tomorrow—she had a date tonight with one of those college movers. Don't worry about me. We're all good here," I say. "When are you coming home?"

"We're on day three of seven, and then we're in Edinburgh to pitch a new client for two days, so mid next week."

"I've always wanted to go to London. And Edinburgh—they have so many castles! Bryony will shit herself when she hears you're gonna be in her dream homeland. Tell me you're going to do some touristy stuff while you're there."

"If by touristy stuff, you mean drinking a lot of lukewarm beer, then yes, I'm definitely doing that." He says hello to someone walking by.

"I should let you go. Take lots of pictures for me. Oh! Go up in the London Eye!"

"No way. No heights," he says. "I should've brought you with. Lots of dogs in England. You could've photographed the Queen's corgis."

"Next time maybe."

"I'll message you some photos later. Probably of drooling nerds put to sleep by whomever is yammering on at the mic."

"Sounds scintillating ..."

"Pancakes next week?"

"Sounds like a date," I say.

"Miss you, F-Stop."

"Miss you too, Samwise."

Then he hangs up, and the flame in my heart melts the ice cream in my belly.

THIRTY-TWO

I CAN'T BELIEVE how busy we are, now that we have *parking*! Lainie and I keep giving Gabe shit about it, but honestly, our accessibility has made a huge difference in our bookings, so much so that Gabe has agreed to bring on that intern sooner rather than later, especially since the tasks Lainie used to help out with are falling by the wayside. She's occupied with the last-minute details for their imminent wedding, in a race against her mother's cancer.

Fucking cancer.

I took over one of the extra rooms at the back as a makeshift doggy daycare for my new fur children. It's not a permanent solution, but I left them home alone that first week and walked into mischief. Seems Jupiter is quite skilled at opening cupboards, and Jane Eyre, the accomplice, is excellent at pulling the packages free from said cupboards. I lost a lot of pasta and cereal and toilet paper that week.

And Lazarus is in seventh heaven to have cousins. Dad likes being able to pop in and take them for walks. They've been home for a couple weeks, and Diana has him on a strict cardiac rehab protocol, which includes walking. Lots of walking. Luckily, the new studio is near a huge park with a fenced area just for dogs. Good for Dad, great for the pups!

Today, however, I have my third of eight pet photo bookings for the week. I'm still answering phones, but when Gabe walked in with his own dry cleaning this morning, it was a small victory. Plus it's nice to be excited about work—every day that the door dinger chimes and a new fluffy face wanders in to pose for my lens is a good day.

First up: a Pomeranian named Noodles.

And her mom is none other than Adalynn Burnett. I won't allow myself to get nervous—yeah, Adalynn behaved as expected up in Canada, except for our oddly candid little chat while she steadied Rob's wounded leg, but today she'll be with her canine child and not her posse of mean girls. Plus, this is my turf now, and I'm about done being treated like the hired help.

At eleven on the nose, Adalynn strides through the door with an adorable golden marshmallow under one arm, but I'm surprised to see that she's not dressed to the nines in her usual rich-girl clothes. Her gorgeous brown hair is still swooped in luscious, round waves like a pinup girl, her lips still Betty Boop red, but there isn't a stitch of Prada or Burberry to be found.

"Hey, Adalynn ... this must be Noodles!" I reach out and the tiny dog licks my hand like I'm made of frosting. "Okay, I think this is the cutest creature I've ever seen."

"Don't let her hear you say that. She's already got an attitude," Adalynn says. She sets Noodles onto the floor, and I come around the desk so we can get properly acquainted.

"Are you ready for your close-up? Are you? Yes, you are. You are so beautiful. I just want to *eat* you," I coo. I look up from Adalynn where I'm kneeled. "Are you wearing scrubs?"

She smiles, and it reaches all the way to her eyes. A genuine smile. Whoa.

"I'm back at work."

I stand as Noodles sniffs around at our feet. "I thought you and your husband ..."

"I left him."

"Oh. Man, Adalynn, I'm so sorry—I didn't mean to pry."

She waves a hand at me. "Seriously, don't apologize. I was miserable. And as of last week, I'm back at the hospital, back with my old friends—god, I missed it so much."

I unzip the gear bag on my equipment shelf and pull out my camera, stuffing a few dog treats in my pocket so I can bribe Noodles into sitting pretty. "I thought you guys were trying to get pregnant."

She laughs, and it echoes around the cavernous main room. "It was the arrow."

"The arrow?" I gesture for her to follow me, clicking my tongue for Noodles to do the same. "These biscuits are organic. It's okay for her?" I ask. You think people are weird about their human kids, just wait until you meet a pet parent.

Adalynn nods about the dog cookie. "The arrow. In Bert's leg. He's a whiny dick, but being at the hospital with him and his mom—who's nice enough, but boy, there's some damage there—it made me realize how much I missed being in that environment."

"As in, the hospital." I turn on my strobes and reposition my umbrellas while we talk.

"Yeah, I'm a weirdo. I love hospitals. I love helping people," she says. "I just forgot. I got so wrapped up in a life I thought I wanted. But I'm not Nikki, and I'm not my mother. I'm not cut out for a society-page life."

I kneel again and play with Noodles to get her to sit where I need her to, offering another chunk of biscuit while clicking a few test shots to check lighting and camera settings.

"Adalynn, if it took an arrow to Rob's leg to make you find your happy place, then I am so glad Nikki shot him."

She laughs. "Me too. Although it would've been better if they'd just shot each other and put us all out of their misery," she says.

I can't disagree with that.

"So—tell me what you and Miss Noodles would like today, and I will do my very best to oblige."

"I trust you, Frankie. You're the expert here." She smiles like she means it, and though I brace for the typical cutting comment to follow, it doesn't come.

My eyes sting in a momentary blip of emotion—Adalynn Burnett, one of the cool, rich kids who used to look through me like a pane of glass, is behaving like a human.

There is hope for the world after all.

THIRTY-THREE

"HOW'D IT GO TODAY?" Gabe asks, his hands resting on the back of my chair. I'm scanning through the shots from the day's pet sessions, and every few images, he says "Mm-hmm" or points at the screen, which means he likes the photo. My brother is almost as critical as my dad, so I'll take all the "mm-hmms" I can get.

"I forgot how much harder it is to shoot cats than dogs," I say, clicking forward to the twin Siamese girls I had this afternoon. "These two were tough."

"Yeah, but look at those eyes," Gabe says. "These are beautiful, Frankie. Dad would be impressed."

"Dad would tell me I need more fill light and maybe to take a step back for sharper contours on their noses."

"See? You don't need Dad or me to nag you about stuff." He pushes off my chair. "I'm going to set up for tomorrow. That newborn shoot is first thing."

"Right." I double-check to make sure today's images are in the cloud and then put my computer to sleep. "I'm going to take the dogs out back for a pee and a quick walk."

"'K. I'll probably be gone by the time you're back in. Meeting Lainie at Gianotti's to finalize the catering details for the wedding."

"Good luck. Tell Sherlock Bones hi for me. And lock the front door when you go." I walk down the hall toward the doggie daycare. I open the half door and Jupiter bounds from her very posh new bed my dad bought her. "Yes, hello, I'm so sorry I took so long. Are you guys hungry?" I dole out food; FDR finishes first, as always. Jupiter is carrying her leash around in her mouth, anxious to get outside, so she'll eat when we're back. We wait for Jane Eyre to chew her last bite of kibble and then gear up.

My phone pings against my thigh. A text from Sam, a photo of the mound of junk food from that first night up at the resort when we did a vending machine raid after Rob's—*Bert's*—impromptu visit to my room. Sam's bent leg, dressed in his Mariners snack pants, is in the upper right of the shot, our booty piled on the bedspread: **We need to find a vending machine. That was fun. Also Canadian chocolate is weird.**

I think it's milk instead of semisweet?

The response bubbles bounce as he types. ***Can I leave my snack pants at your house?***

I laugh and then click a photo of the dogs sniffing around the grass. **Stand by ... dog duty.**

It's June, which is always a little dodgy in Oregon. You might get sun, you might get rain, you might get sun and then rain. We have the bluest skies here, and tonight, as the sun creeps toward the horizon, it's cloudless and tinged with purples and pinks, the air warm enough that I don't need a sweater.

We don't have time to go to the dog park so I let my beasts run around the back grassy area. Once they've peed and had a stretch and I've cleaned up poos, I whistle for them to follow me back inside. I lift FDR up the steps and he takes off down the long shiny concrete floor after his siblings, barking for them to wait up. Gabe's office is dark as I pass, but he's left lights on in the front studio.

"Gaaaaabe," I groan as I walk toward the open door.

But upon walking into the space, it's not the lights that are on.

It's a slideshow, playing on the huge white backdrop against the wall. Photos—of me and my dad, of me and Gabe, even a few of me with my mother when I was really little. My throat tightens upon seeing them.

"What the hell is this …," I say to no one. The dogs circle back from the main area and gallop into the room where I am, gathering around my legs.

The next photos are of Gabe and me, and Sam.

It's our childhood together. Like the photos in Sam's shoebox.

There are shots of Sam and Lainie and Gabe, and then more recent shots—some from Revelation Cove, including Sam covered in barbecue sauce from our rib lunch at the resort, me laughing as Acorn catches a ball in midair, Sam with Mariah and Monica, one of me looking out the window of the boat that took us from Victoria to the resort, my dad and Diana on their river cruise, even shots of me and Bryony and the dogs from my new house.

"How …?"

The door dinger chimes—someone has entered.

"We're closed!" I holler. Jupiter takes off out of the room and down the hall, but she doesn't bark. I turn to follow, but I'm stopped just outside the doorway.

"Hi," Sam says. He's clutching a paper bag with a dog-bone stamp on the front that Jupiter is *very* interested in, as well as a silver bucket that looks like something you'd use to milk a cow. I step closer —the bucket holds beer bottles tucked in ice, the delicious stuff we drank at Revelation Cove.

"Weren't you just texting me?" I smile. "I thought you had a meeting tonight. What are you doing here?" I stand on tiptoes; Sam bends and meets my lips.

"It's a photography studio, isn't it? I thought I'd share some photos." He nods toward the studio where the slideshow continues to play.

"And you brought beer?" I peek into the bucket.

"I figured we might get thirsty." He grins and it lights up the dimly lit hallway. He then turns and walks back toward the reception desk, setting the bucket down. "I'd better share these before she eats my fingers."

"Jupiter, be a nice girl." I raise my hand, and she sits, waiting for Sam to give her whatever is hiding in the bag. Once he does, Jane Eyre and FDR follow suit, being such good dogs as Sam offers them biscuits. "Those look tasty enough for humans."

"These are from that new doggie bakery next door to our office."

"Spoiled pups," I say, rubbing Jupiter's head so she won't pester Sam for another cookie. "So ..."

"So ..."

"That slideshow—you did it?" I ask.

"I did."

"For Gabe and Lainie's wedding? Because I think they'll love it. I've been the worst maid of honor—I've hardly done anything, with the move and the studio and the dogs."

Sam shakes his head. "The slideshow is for you."

"Oh." My heart flip-flops. "Thank you. It's beautiful, Sam."

"I'm glad you think so." He sets the bag of dog cookies on the counter and in three steps, he's in front of me, dipping to one knee.

Sam then takes my hands and pushes them against his lips. When he looks up at me, his green eyes seem lit from within. "Marry me, F-Stop."

Jupiter bounds over and licks his cheeks.

"Are you serious?"

"Marry me. Please. I want to move all my snack pants into your house. I want to raid all the vending machines. I want to carry you whenever you need carrying and fight whenever you need a champion. I want you to be the Rosie Cotton to my Samwise Gamgee."

I pull my hands free and cup his stubbled cheeks. "You're such a nerd."

"And you love it," he says.

"I do. I do love it." I kiss him. He tastes minty.

"I know it's fast. But we can have a long engagement. As long as you want. I just can't ..." His voice breaks. "I can't go another day without you, Frankie. I have to make up for lost time, starting right now."

He searches my face, and I can't look away. I never want to look away again.

"Soooo, what do you think? Because ..." Sam nods over his shoulder. Outside the front doors, my whole family awaits, their noses pressed against the glass.

I return my eyes to Sam's flushed, grinning face. "This isn't a joke."

"Would I kid a kidder?" He pulls out a jewelry box from the front pocket of his nice-fitting jeans, and pops it open.

I stare down at the brilliant emerald gemstone shining up at me. "I know this ring."

"It was your mom's," Sam says, standing again. "But I can't slide it on your finger until you answer my question. And if I have to give it back to your dad, well, that's gonna be weird. I think he's already engaged."

I laugh, my vision blurred through the tears.

Sam sets the ring aside and takes my face in his hands. "I've known you were The One since I was fourteen. I've already told you that," he says, his eyes glistening. "When I saw you at the gas station in Victoria with that crazy beagle, I knew it then. I knew it when I saw you playing with Acorn and when I saw you talking to the twins and when I saw you taking photos and when I saw you handling everything Nikki Meyer was throwing at you and when you were wiping groom's cake off your equipment and when you stole the last bread twist and gave me your mushrooms and as I watched you pick the green peppers out of your scrambled eggs.

"I knew it when I woke up and watched you sleep that night. I would've asked you right then and there, but I needed you to have time to know I was for real. And I needed to talk to Harrison first. But then his heart attack, and that shit with Rob—I wanted to wrap you up and keep all the bad stuff from getting to you, to carry you away from it like I did that time at the beach with your broken hand." He releases my face and instead interlaces his fingers with mine.

"I'm sorry I lied to you about helping out at the wedding and about Lisa—"

I place a finger against his lips to quiet him. "You've already apologized, Samwise."

"I feel like I've been waiting half my life for this moment." He picks up the ring box again.

"If I say yes, can we drink some of that fine Canadian beer?"

His laugh fills the space. "Duh. The only way you're getting some of that fine Canadian beer is if you say yes."

"Because if I say no, you're going to sit in the park and drink it all alone and sing your favorite Garbage tunes to the ducks."

"As one does," he says, looking from my eyes to my lips like I'm an ice-cream cone.

"Well, then, with respect to our local fauna, I will say yes. I do not want those poor ducks to have to listen to you sing."

"That is an excellent choice, F-Stop."

He pops the ring free of its box and slides it onto my finger. He then leans over to pick me up so he can kiss me in a way no parent should ever witness their child being kissed. No matter. My dad, Diana, Lainie, Gabe, Bryony—even Christina, Aidan, and Aunt Monica are outside the door, hooting and hollering like their team has just won the Super Bowl.

Kiss, we shall.

Just as Jupiter lifts her front paws onto the reception-desk counter, grabs the bag of cookies, and tears off down the hall, her sister and brother running and barking after her.

THIRTY-FOUR

ONE YEAR LATER

I TOLD Dad we didn't need Town Cars for tonight, but he insisted. "It's a big deal, F-Stop. Let me treat my kids once in a while."

Sam is out back with the dogs, making sure they've peed, et cetera, before we lock them in their crates. I stand in front of the full-length mirror and twirl a few times, making sure no detail has been overlooked.

"What do you think, Zod? Think your dad will like it?"

The huge tabby pauses his grooming, engages a purr that rivals a Harley engine, and rolls over on the bed, waiting for affection.

A month after Sam's romantic proposal at the studio, he got a call from a woman in Lake Oswego—she'd been fostering this big male stray that had been dumped on their property. At a second vet appointment for an infected paw pad, the vet found Zod's microchip —and it led him home to Sam.

And although I've been a committed dog person my whole life, I will admit that Zod has nudged his way into my heart. It took the dogs a little longer, but a few quick swipes to the snout put FDR in his place. Now the lot of them are like one of those sickeningly sweet Instagram videos.

Zod bounds off the bed when he hears the sliding glass door. One last spin in the mirror, and I prepare to make my descent. I waited on purpose for the crew to come back inside.

I want to see Sam's face when he sees me in this dress.

It was the right call. His eyes almost pop out of his skull.

"Red is definitely your color," he says, taking my hand and helping me from the last stair. He gives me a twirl and whistles. "I shall be the envy of all this evening."

"It's not about us, remember," I say, pulling him down so I can kiss his freshly shaved cheek.

"Maybe not, but when we get home, it's going to be all about me."

"You wish." I slap his butt, which looks delectable in his black tux, and step around him to grab my sequined clutch from the back of the couch. "Did you double-check the locks? Dogs are in bed? Zod has water? Security cameras are on? Stove is off?"

"Everything is locked, in bed, watered, and safe. All is well, my queen." He bows. "And the car is here. Are you ready to go give away some money?"

I open my clutch to make sure I have my cloth hankie from Aunt Mariah. Just seeing her initials smiling up at me will give me the courage to get through tonight.

"I'm ready. Let's do this."

AT THE MEETING where my father doled out the resources from his life's work, he also told Gabe and me about the money from our late mother's estate. I wasn't ready to deal with it back then.

But I am now.

Thanks to my dad's contacts in the journalism world, coupled with Lainie's knack for event planning and experience with charitable endeavors, we established the Lara Williamson Hawes Foundation, to be funded, in part, with a portion of the money my mom left to me and my dumb brother. This year at our inaugural event, to be held in the stunning Kridel Grand Ballroom of the Portland Art Museum, we will be giving our first series of awards to five young women who have worked to improve the lives of other women and children, particularly in underdeveloped or war-torn countries, with special consideration paid to those who work in the field of photo-journalism.

Two of our recipients are with Doctors Without Borders, and though not journalists by trade, their photographic documentation of their work in the field is what has earned them each a $15,000 award.

Their photos saved the lives of dozens of children in an abandoned orphanage in Syria.

So tonight, we're showing them how much we—how much my mother would—appreciate their selfless dedication to helping others.

I can't stand in a war-damaged neighborhood in Aleppo and save lives, but I can say thank you to those who have.

I think my mom would be proud of that.

But tonight's guest of honor is why I'm so anxious. *The Oregonian* articles Sam printed, in the Nike box—we were able to track down the woman in Salem who attributes her safety to my mother's bravery all those years ago. Zerya Salar will talk tonight, and I cannot wait to meet her. Even though I'm so nervous, I'm picking at my cuticles, threatening to ruin the manicure Lainie insisted she give me.

Nestled together in the back of the Town Car, Sam steadies his hand over mine, rubbing his thumb over my engagement ring.

"You're going to be picture perfect tonight, F-Stop. Don't you fret."

I kiss his cheek again and nuzzle into his side. I can't remember life before Sam. I hope I never have to live life without him.

When we pull up to the Portland Art Museum, it's a right shock at how many people and photographers are there. "Even a red carpet?" I ask. That Lainie is something else.

In addition to the awards being given tonight, our foundation is working with *The Oregonian* newspaper and Apple to provide money for camera and computer equipment and free classes for inner-city schools to encourage the next generation of photojournalists. It's important to my father that we make sure the Hawes' legacy of excellence in photojournalism doesn't die out just because "every bloody person has an iPhone and calls himself a photographer."

Good ol' Dad.

Who, by the way, looks absolutely dashing in his tux. Since his heart attack—and since he and Diana stole away for a cheesy Vegas wedding—he's shed weight and improved his cholesterol and stopped eating and drinking all the stuff that could kill him.

It feels ridiculous to walk the red carpet and wave to the flashing cameras, but when I realize a lot of those cameras are in the hands of the kids in our programs, I'm more than happy to stop for a pose.

Inside is as grand as any Hollywood premiere. I'd feel guilty about the expense incurred to put on such a fête, except it's all donated. The food—catering by Gianotti's—the flowers, even the alcohol. When word got out what my dad was up to, in honor of his late wife, his friends—including Donovan Meyer and family—opened their wallets. And now that Bryony works here at the PAM, she was able to secure the Kridel Ballroom for basically the cost of the electricity we're using.

It's pretty awesome.

We're escorted to our elegantly laid table near the front of the room, and Sam doesn't let go of my shaking hand for a single second. Bryony is already here—she stands and waves wildly when she sees us, hoisting her half-empty champagne glass.

"You look amazing," I say as we approach, letting go of Sam long enough to hug my friend.

"Of course I do," she says, doing a quick turn to show off her black sequined gown. "I have excellent taste." We shopped for our dresses together—or rather, Bryony dragged me through shop after shop as I complained loudly because shopping is super boring and dumb. We eventually ended up in a specialty boutique run by a friend of hers because we both struggle with buying off the rack—me, because I'm a Keebler Elf, and her because she's the Jolly Green Giant.

We really are the perfect yin and yang.

It doesn't take long for the festivities to get underway. My dad forewarned Gabe and me about the tribute to my mom—which is why I have Mariah's hankie and why there are boxes of Kleenex at the center of every table.

I surprise myself when I get through it relatively unscathed, but that's thanks to Sam. Seems like everything is thanks to Sam these days. He finds ways to talk about my mom, to get me to talk about my mom. Slowly that scab has peeled off, leaving new, pink skin behind. It's still sore, but it no longer bleeds when I touch it.

Next up is the speech by Zerya, and yes, I do cry through that, followed by the presentation of the awards to this year's recipients, which includes slideshows of their stunning work. I catch my dad hiccupping his emotion into his own handkerchief, Diana's hand rubbing his back now and again.

"Your mom would've loved this," he squeaks. "She really would have."

And then we're all crying, even my tough Sam.

After the last award has been accepted, we hurriedly dry our eyes as the whole family is invited up on stage. All those kid photographers who were on the red carpet earlier get to take our photos up here, and my dad gives a brief speech to say thank you to all his friends and colleagues who came together tonight to honor the memory of Lara Williamson Hawes. We're met with an uproarious standing ovation, and while, sure, it's glamorous and a little embarrassing, it's also wildly inspiring.

By the time I get back to the table, I can hardly wait to talk about what else we can do to save the world.

With the main part of the program behind us, the emcee introduces the music for the rest of the evening and invites attendees to partake of the dessert bar and the dance floor. Gabe wastes no time whooshing his bride out of her chair. Bryony doesn't need a dance partner—she'll find one on the floor.

"If not, I will delegate, now that I'm a boss around these parts," she says, winking and finishing the last of her champagne. Dad is schmoozing with his cronies, indulging in the whisky Diana usually doesn't let him drink.

"You okay?" Sam says, draping his hand across my chair as I dig at my tiramisu.

"I'm perfect," I say.

"I was hoping you'd say that." He smiles and reaches into the inside of his tux coat. "I have a surprise for you."

"Ohhh, I like your surprises."

"Then you'll like this one too."

I open the envelope—it's a photograph ... of a dog? "Are you pregnant, Sam? Is there something I need to know?"

"Look again."

I do. This dog looks familiar with her wide smile and pink bandana. "Is—is that Acorn?" I laugh. It's a shot of the golden retriever up at that resort in Canada. "It is! That's Acorn!"

He hands me another envelope. I look at him, mischief in his eyes. "Open it, Miss Hawes," he says.

Inside is another photo, this one of the room we stayed in up at the resort.

And then another envelope. "How many envelopes do you have in there? How is that pocket even big enough?" I ask.

"Just open it."

The next one is a picture of the bucket of our favorite Canadian beer.

"I think you're trying to tell me something," I say, arching a brow.

"I might be trying to tell you something." He reaches into his coat again. "Last envelope, I promise."

He hands it over. Inside is a printout. "Is this a reservation?"

"Read it."

"'Hawes, party of nine, four nights' stay.'" My heart races excit-edly. "This—this is for next week!"

"It is."

"We get to go back? To Revelation Cove?"

"And you don't have to shoot a wedding this time," he says.

"But—what about Zod and the dogs?"

"Christina is going to come stay with Aidan at the house while we're gone. She's already arranged it with Monica."

I lean over and kiss him. "You are very sneaky, Samwise McKen-zie." I kiss him again as a thought bubbles in my mind. "Okay, I will go to Canada with you and our family and I will play with Acorn and drink that fine Canadian beer. But I have a proposition of my own." I spin my engagement ring around my finger. "We still have that bottle of Domaine Serene, yes?" The wine Mariah gave me last year during the pep talk that set all these wheels in motion.

"We do. You wanted to save it for our honeymoon."

"I did," I say. "And you said *I* didn't have to shoot a wedding, but maybe Dad would."

Sam smiles. "I'm sure that could be arranged."

"Then bring the wine." I lean in and press my lips against his. "And your tux."

ACKNOWLEDGMENTS

Yay! Another Eliza Gordon book on the shelf! It was so much fun heading back up to say hello to Concierge Ryan and Hollie Porter at Revelation Cove. I hope you enjoyed the trip too. For a discussion about what the hell an *f*-stop is (and why this wasn't another specifically Hollie-and-Ryan book), check out my blog.

As per usual, I had some lovely help writing Frankie's story. Big thanks go to:

My awesome beta readers, Deb Hardy and Katrin Bartas. And added thanks to Deb for helping me throughout my rewrites, answering my all-hours messages (and meeting me in real life at the Vancouver Aquarium—hi, Adam and puppies!), even though she and her family were dealing with some hard, real-life stuff.

My friend Bonnie Jacoby who mentioned that the title *F-Stop* might be confusing to folks who aren't into photography. See? I do listen! Hence the name change to *Love Just Clicks*. I hope that makes more sense for readers.

The Eliza Gordon Welcome to the Raft Raftmates who read an early draft/advance reader copy of the book and provided super-helpful feedback. You've all been so encouraging, and I'm endlessly grateful. Special thanks to Cheryl Minns and Jen Allen for the editorial fixes.

Editor Amanda Bidnall (http://amandabidnall.com/) for her keen editorial eye. You guys—Amanda is an actual rock star. Check her out.

Yaunna Sommersby (Audience Development Coordinator at

Modern Dog and *Modern Cat* magazines!), a.k.a. the House Elf, my #1 dog fancier, bookstagram manager, proofreader-in-training, and my very favorite photojournalist. Photography is a big thing in our house—pop by Yaunna's photography feed on Instagram (@yaunnaraephotography). She's counting down the days till she can move out and fill her new place with All the Dogs.

The Creative Academy, run by Donna Barker, Eileen Cook, and Crystal Stranaghan, who helped me get my butt in the chair every morning for 7:30 a.m. writing sprints, for six straight weeks so I could finish the first draft of the book while also juggling other projects and humans. Sprints (a set amount of uninterrupted time where ALL you're allowed to do is write) are incredible. Writers, you need to try this.

The darling Melinda Anne Di Lorenzo for introducing me to Joanna Cramond, who steered me in the right direction for research on First Nations of British Columbia. All mistakes are 100 hundred percent mine, and because this is a novel, the actual geographic locale of (the fictitious) Revelation Cove, BC, is a bit nebulous. We could be in traditional lands belonging to the Coast Salish people, but the territory map from the University of British Columbia suggests the area I chose for the archery scene was more likely that of the Kwakwaka'wakw Nation. The point above all else: Respect the land. It's not ours.

The website of the Kwakiutl Band, which includes the history of the Kwakwaka'wakw People (www.kwakiutl.bc.ca).

The University of British Columbia Library for its extensive Aboriginal History Department available online, including the map that helped me determine which nation occupies the real geography (Discovery Islands) for my fictional story: http://guides.library.ubc.ca/aboriginalmaps.

Dreamscape Media for producing the audiobook.

My goofy Facebook friends who answer my weird polls, help me with random research tidbits, and keep me laughing so I can keep writing.

The real-life destinations that have inspired Revelation Cove from the beginning: the Sonora Resort (https://sonoraresort.com/) and Poet's Cove (http://poetscove.com/), both located in Beautiful British Columbia.

My favorite photographers in the whole wide world who inspired some of the tiny details in this book: Joe McNally, Annie Leibowitz, Paul Nicklen, Ansel Adams, Rachael Hale, Frans Lanting, James Nachtwey, Tim Palen, Sean Crane, and Lynsey Addario.

The readers who've found me through my young adult book (*Sleight*), under my real name. I write under two names to keep the grown-up stuff separate from the kid stuff. Can't wait for you to get hold of *Sleight*'s sequel, *The Undoing/Scheme*, in 2020. It's a hell of a ride.

And of course, my darling wee family: GareBear, House Elf, Brennie, KennyG, Nuit, and baby Rosie Cotton. Now go away. Mom has to write.

ABOUT THE AUTHOR

A native of Portland, Oregon, Eliza Gordon (a.k.a. Jennifer Sommersby) has lived up and down the West Coast of the United States. Since 2002, home has been a suburb of Vancouver, British Columbia.

When not lost in a writing project, Eliza is a copy editor, mom, wife, bibliophile, Superman freak, and the proud parent of two very spoiled tuxedo cats. Eliza writes stories to help you believe in the Happily Ever After; Jennifer Sommersby writes young adult fiction. Her debut, *Sleight*, was published in 2018 by HarperCollins Canada, Sky Pony (US), and Prószyński i S-ka (Poland). The sequel, *Scheme* (*The Undoing* in Canada), published spring 2020.

The name Eliza Gordon was chosen to honor two amazing

people, Martha Elizabeth (Porter) Young and Kenneth Gordon Young. Not a day goes by that we don't love and miss you. Your devotion to one another continues to inspire.

Follow her on social media, or go to her website at www.elizagordon.com, and sign up for her newsletter.

It's time to get jolly with Hollie.

Hollie Porter's
Hat Trick
Christmas

A Revelation Cove novella

ELIZA GORDON

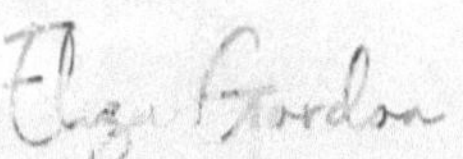

Find the Eliza Gordon books at the following retailers in e-book, print, and audio.

Did you know you can ask your local library to order in Eliza's books?

Visit elizagordon.com for links.

Amazon globally | Angus & Robertson | Apple Books | Audible | Audiobooks.com | Barnes & Noble | Biblioteca | Bold.de | Books-A-Million | Bookshop.org | Booktopia | Chapters/Indigo | Chirp | Everand | Google Play | Hoopla | Ingram | Kobo | Libby | Libro.fm | Mondadori | Overdrive | Powell's | Scribd | Thalia.de | 24 Symbols | Waterstones

SGA
BOOKS